Shattered Angel

Carrie Beckort

For by brother Steve
Thanks for teaching me the importance of respecting books

24: The Offer

I had escaped from him once before, but the knot in my stomach tells me not this time. The impossible isn't supposed to happen at all, so I should be grateful that I'd attained it once and accept that it won't happen again.

I push the thought from my mind and open my eyes. I think it's mid-day, but it's hard to tell. There are several high windows in the warehouse, but they're covered with several years of grime. At least there are enough clean spots and holes to allow some light to filter through. There's a slow drip coming from somewhere, and the sound echoes hauntingly around me. I smell something. I'm not sure exactly what it is, but it's not pleasant.

My breathing is short, disrupted by the occasional sob that involuntarily escapes. I know crying will only make my situation worse, but I can't seem to stop. My hair is sticking to my face, and I desperately want to wipe it away.

I pull instinctively at my restraints again. Eventually I stop, realizing that the only thing I'm accomplishing is further depletion of my energy. My arms had gone numb hours ago from being tied behind my back for so long. They left me alone in this small room, but occasionally I can hear their muffled voices in another part of the warehouse. I'd given up on trying to hear what they were saying about the same time I'd given up on hope. My awkward position on the cold floor is uncomfortable, but at least the coolness of the concrete gives me some relief from the suffocating heat.

Something crawls across my foot, and I'm certain it's a rat. The fact that it doesn't bother me, the fact that I'd had a rat crawl across my foot before, causes a fresh wave of tears to fall.

The door suddenly opens and I struggle to get into a sitting position, but my lack of arms prevents me from being successful. The man I've come to call Goon pulls me to my feet by my hair. I bite back the cry of pain, knowing it would only give him satisfaction. He turns me around to face the door and pushes me to my knees. There's so much hair in my face I can't see anything. I shake my head, trying to shift the tangled mess, but it doesn't help.

I hear footsteps from someone entering the room. They stop right in front of me and I tense, anticipating the horror I know I'm about to experience. Even though I can't see who it is, I know it's him. Painful memories try to surface as the scent of him invades my senses. I flinch slightly when rough hands gently wipe the hair from my face, and I look up into the eyes of the one man I hate most in the world.

I hate him so much I never gave him a name.

Giving him a name of any kind would assign him some sort of significance in my life, and that was simply unacceptable.

"It's been a long time, Angel. Your hair is too long and you've gained a little weight, but other than that you look about the same as when I last saw you." I blink and try to look away, but he holds my face firmly in place. He lowers down until our eyes are level. "Have you missed me as much as I've missed you?"

As anger wells within me, I collect all the moisture left in my mouth and spit as hard as I can into his face. He doesn't even flinch. He closes his eyes, takes a deep breath, slowly stands, and wipes away the spit with the bottom of his shirt.

His hand swings fast and connects with my face in a sharp force that knocks me down on my side. Goon laughs and pulls me back up to my knees by my hair. Now there's blood mixing with my sweat and tears. I blink my eyes in rapid succession, trying to focus and rid my vision of the bright specks of light dancing before me.

I hate seeing stars.

The man squats back down, sitting back on his haunches. He traces his finger through the blood running down my cheek and smears it across my mouth. I try to recoil but he grabs the back of my head with his other hand and holds me in place.

"After all these years apart, that's how you decide to greet me?" He shakes his head and lets out a disappointed sigh. "I was told you were being feisty. Still, I'm going to give you the offer I came in here to make. You've got twenty-four hours to reflect back on your pathetic existence. I'm sure you think you're just a victim, but really you're nothing but a whore. You were born a whore and will always be a whore. As you reflect over your life for the next twenty-four hours, I'm certain you will see that you deserve the life you have been given. When your time is up, you'll decide if you want to return to me . . . or die."

The confusion must be clear on my face because he smiles. It makes my stomach clench, and I swallow back the bitter taste of bile that bubbles at the back of my throat.

"No matter what you think, I'm not a monster. I didn't force you to come with me that first day. You willingly left your old life, and I'm not going to force you back now. However, I can't let you remain out there free. Out there for someone else to claim. No, you will either choose to come back to me or you will die. It's that simple." He pauses and his smile spreads wider. "You know, I'm feeling so generous today that I'll give you a bonus. After every hour passes, someone will bang on the door so you'll know exactly how much time you have left."

He looks at me with the eyes I've fought so hard to forget over the years. After several unbearable seconds, he moves his face to mine and slowly licks from one side of my mouth to the other. I tighten my lips as hard as I can and hate myself for the whimper that escapes. He doesn't stop when he reaches the other side of my mouth, continuing to run his tongue along my cheek to my ear. His whispered voice sends a chill down my spine.

"I've always loved the way you taste. Every part of you is so sweet, and you taste the best after you've been beaten." His hand grips my hair tighter, and his other snakes between my thighs where he squeezes just as hard. "Should I give you a reminder of how good times used to be before you betrayed me?" I can feel his breathing become more ragged. "Yeah, I think I will. And because I know how much you enjoy this, your clock starts now—and I'll take up as much of your twenty-four hours as I like."

He shoves me down hard on my face and I will my mind to go to the safe place I'd created years ago. It was the only place where I could escape the horror of my life. But this time not even my mind will save me. Maybe it's because I know my ultimate fate is only twenty-four hours away. Maybe it's because of what he'd said—not the part about me liking what he was doing. I can't express how much I hate it. How it makes me hate myself. But maybe it's because of what he'd said about me not really being a victim. Did I deserve my life, and is going back to it better than dying?

I have the next twenty-four hours to do nothing but think about it.

23: A Choice

I startle awake at the sound of three loud bangs on the door. I force my eyes open, and the reality of my situation becomes clear.

My first hour must be up.

I shift onto my side, triggering a sharp pain that stabs me from my nether regions all the way up my spine. I had been successful at blocking out the events from the last hour, but the shooting pain brings it back. I'm suddenly grateful for the absence of this pain over the last four years. I suppose I'm lucky that the man still feels possession over me, because if he didn't then I'm sure he would have let Goon have a go too. Although, the man hadn't been opposed to letting Goon watch and pleasure himself while I was being violated.

I roll back onto my stomach and try desperately to hold back the sobs. I've already wasted enough time on tears. I'm not sure how long I had been in this room before the man came in to give me his offer, but I know I only have twenty-three hours left before he returns.

My mind tries to go back to the events that happened right before his men captured me, but I push them aside. It's too painful, and it would just make me want to hope for a different outcome.

There's also no point in wasting my energy on trying to escape my fate. It would be better to do as the man says and spend my time thinking about how I got here, and whether or not I hold any responsibility. It won't change my circumstances, but maybe it will help me decide. He's given me such an incredible choice after all—a life of pure misery, or death. He says he won't force me. That he never forced me the first time.

I close my eyes and my mind wanders logically to the moment when it all started.

Something hits my wall and I push harder into the corner. Mommy told me to be quiet but the noises are scaring me. I heard them before, but this time they won't stop. She screams, and I put my face in my knees, just like she taught me, to keep my sounds quiet. Her friends don't like to see me. They get angry if they open the door and see me. I have to be quiet. I squeeze my arms around my legs and count all the numbers I know. Another loud sound makes me forget my number, and I start all over. I get to the last number I know and start again. I don't know how many times I do this before I stop.

The noises are gone. All I hear is Mommy crying. She cries a lot. I wait. She will open my door soon and let me go potty. I really have to go, but I'm not supposed to go out until she opens the door. I move forward when she stops crying. She will open the door now.

It doesn't open. I wait.

I really have to go, and it's starting to hurt. I put my ear to the door. I do this sometimes, but Mommy doesn't know. I don't hear anything, and I start to get scared.

What if she forgot about me? Maybe I could open the door this one time.

I touch my hand to the handle but remember what happened the last time I opened the door, and I hurry back to my wall. I wait. I start to cry when I feel the pee run down my legs and onto my blanket. Mommy will be mad, and I'll have to sleep on a dirty blanket. I crunch it up and put it in the corner and hug my legs.

I close my eyes and count all the numbers I know.

A bright light hits my face and makes my eyes hurt. I put my hands over my eyes and scrunch my face. I think I fell asleep. I peek out of my fingers and see Mommy. She looks mad.

"Damn it, why'd you have to go and piss yourself? You couldn't have held it for a few goddamn minutes? You're going to ruin everything, you little shit, just like you have since the day you were born. You better not have gotten anything on my clothes; I don't have money for the wash this week." She looks at me with her mean eyes. "I was going to make all that change today, but you might just mess it up once he sees you can't even hold your piss. Get out here."

I stand on my feet and follow Mommy through her room to the kitchen. I stop when I see one of her friends. Mommy never lets me see her friends. I've only seen a dickhead two times—once when I opened the door, and once when one opened my door when I cried. This one looks like the other two, but different. This one is sitting at our table, smoking and drinking Mommy's drink. Mommy walks over and takes his smoker and walks to the sink.

"Well, how much?" Her words sound funny with the smoker between her lips.

"I need to have a closer look. Come here, my sweet."

I look at Mommy, but she's not looking at me. I look back at the dickhead and there's a hand reaching for me. I step back. No one touches me. Not even Mommy unless she has to make me quiet.

Mommy takes the smoker out of her mouth. "Well, do as you're told and get over there."

I make little steps to the table. I get closer, and I can see the dickhead's eyes better. I don't like the dickhead's eyes. The eyes make my skin feel cold, so I look down at the floor. A hand touches my arm and I jump. It grabs me tighter and pulls me closer. The other hand takes my face and turns it a little.

"Look at those big, brown, doe eyes." The hand moves to my hair. "These curls are unruly, but that can be fixed easily enough. It's hard to tell since it's so dirty, but once clean it might even be a bit blonder than it appears now." My arms are lifted to the side. A hand touches my tummy while the other one pulls up my nightdress, and I remembered that I peed. It's dry now, but there's a stain. A finger tries to touch my pee-pee and I jump back. I don't know why, but I don't want that.

"Good. It looks like you can be trusted. I don't think she's been touched."

"Of course she hasn't been touched. You're the first man she's even seen up close."

Man? What's a man? Mommy said her friends were dickheads. He looks like a dickhead, but a man must be something different.

"She's a little thin, but we can fix that. What's your name, sweetheart?" The dickh—I mean man—is looking at me. I look at Mommy to see if I should talk. I'm not supposed to talk. She gives me the mean eyes, and I guess that means I should talk.

"Little Shit." The man gets mean eyes too. It makes me hate the eyes even more.

"She thinks her name is Little Shit?" I look at Mommy. She smiles and puts the smoker to her mouth. The man makes a funny sound. "I guess I shouldn't be surprised since you're trying to sell her to me. Makes me wonder why you kept her around this long."

"I knew I'd catch a better price by waiting until this age."

"How old is she?"

"She turns eight in December."

"A Christmas baby?"

"We don't do Christmas here. But yes, around then."

"You have her birth certificate?"

"Yes."

The man looks at me again. I don't like those eyes. I try to look away, but a hand holds my face. "Well, Little Shit just won't do. With a birthday near Christmas you should be Angel." I like Angel better than Little Shit. I don't know why.

"What have you taught her?"

"She knows how to count to twenty, and she can carry a basic conversation. She knows about things she has been exposed to here. No reading."

"Has she been outside the apartment?"

"No."

"Not even for a doctor's appointment?"

"She's never been sick. At least not enough to do anything about it."

The man squeezes my shoulder. "I need to talk to your mommy. Go in the other room."

I look at Mommy. She hurries from the sink and pushes me from the kitchen back to my room and shuts the door. I don't hear anything, and I don't know if I should stand or sit. Mommy's clothes are hitting me in the face so I sit. I play with my fingers while I wait. The door opens and I look up to see Mommy, but it's the man. The man is really tall. I don't see Mommy.

"Okay, my little Angel. It's time to go." I don't know what that means, so I don't move. The man drops down and I can see the eyes again. "I know you're nervous. Look, I have something for you." The man pulls a bag over and reaches inside. My eyes go wide when I see it. I don't know what it is, but I want it. I look from it to the man.

"Do you like it?" I nod my head. I look at it again, afraid it will be gone. "This doll is yours if you come with me."

Doll.

I want that doll. But my tummy feels funny.

"Where's Mommy?"

"Your mommy wants you to come with me."

"Will Mommy go too?"

"No, you won't need a mommy any more. You'll have me. I'm all you will ever need, Angel." I feel scared. I don't know why. I want that doll, but to have the doll I can't have Mommy. I chew on my lip. It hurts, but I can't stop. Tears get in my eyes and make the man look blurry.

"Don't be scared, Angel. You can have this doll, and you'll get new clothes. You'll even have your own room."

"I have a room."

"You have a closet." The man makes that sound bad. I feel the tears fall down my cheeks. The man lets out a sound and starts to put the doll in the bag. I jump up and try to grab it. The man pulls it up so I can't reach.

"Do you want the doll?"

"Yes."

"Then come with me, my little Angel."

The hand reaches for me again, and I put my hand in it. The man hands me the doll, and I hold it close. The man walks with me through Mommy's room and to the door that I'm not supposed to go near. I stop and look behind me. Mommy is at the sink. I only see her back. She doesn't look at me, and the man pulls me through the door. The man walks me through a hall and there are other doors. We get to something in the floor that goes down. I stop. The man tugs my arm and I fall. The man looks at me with mean eyes. I hate those eyes, and I want to turn and run back to Mommy, but I remember the doll. My doll.

"Right. You've never seen stairs before." The man lifts me up and

I almost scream, but the man tells me to be quiet or my doll will go away. I close my mouth and my eyes and hold my doll tight.

I keep my eyes closed until I feel something on my face. It feels like when I sit in front of Mommy's fan. I open my eyes. It's dark but I can see things around me that I only see through the window. It smells better. My tummy feels better. The man takes me to something Mommy called a car. I always pointed to things out the window asking what they were, but she never told me. Only one time she told me the things that moved were called cars.

The man opens a door and puts me in the car and tells me to lie down. I don't at first and the man reaches for my doll. I fall down real fast, and the man tells me not to move or make a sound. I curl around my doll and close my eyes. I count all the numbers I know. I feel the car move, and I forget my number. I don't like it and my tummy starts to hurt again. I squeeze my doll harder and count.

The car stops and the door opens, but I don't move. The man pulls my leg. My feet touch something that hurts and I look down. I don't know what it is. The man takes my hand again and pulls me. We go in a door and down a hall. I stop again when we get to those things in the floor. The man called them stairs. The man makes that sound again and picks me up. I still don't like it, but this time I don't try to scream. We get to another hall and the man puts me back down and pulls me. There are lots of doors and I can hear sounds, but not much. It's dark and smells funny. The man turns a corner and stops. I bump into the man and almost drop my doll. I hold it tight.

"Son, what are you doing down here?" I look past the man and my eyes go wide. Son looks a lot like the man, but shorter. Taller than me, but not taller than Mommy. Son looks at me, and I like Son's eyes. They are brown, like Mommy's.

"Dad, uh, I was just learning about this area."

"Whose idea was that?" The man sounds mad.

"Uncle said it was time."

"You take orders from me and not Uncle. Is that understood?"

"Yes, sir." Son looks at me again. "Who's this? A new girl?"

The man looks at me, and I let out a sound when the hand squeezes mine too hard.

"Son, this is Angel. Actually, you being here may be a good thing. I don't want any of your good-for-nothing cousins to manage Angel. I don't trust them, and she's too important. I think she can take our business in a whole new direction. It is time that you learned this side of the business, so I'm making you responsible for Angel. You're the only one I can truly trust around here anyway. Walk with me."

I look at Son and Son looks at me. Mommy never looked at me that way. The man didn't look at me that way. I don't know how Son is looking at me, but it makes my tummy feel better. The man pulls me down the hall and Son walks behind me. The man opens a door and pushes me inside. It's bigger than my old room. Nothing hits my head. And there's a bed just like Mommy's! It's smaller, but it's a real bed. I turn and look at the man. The room is big enough for the man to stand in too. There's no room for Son to come in, but if the man left, Son could come in.

"This is your room, Angel. Welcome home. You need to be quiet if you want to keep your doll. Get some rest and someone will check on you tomorrow." The man walks out and I see Son. Son is looking at me that way again. The door closes and I hear a click. I sit on the bed. It's hard, but not as hard as the floor in my old room.

I think about Mommy. I start to feel scared, but I remember my doll. I really want to keep my doll.

This is not so different than my room with Mommy. I had to be quiet there too. But this room is bigger and I have a bed.

I look around the room and see water on a small table. I wonder if I can drink it. There's a cookie too. Mommy doesn't give me cookies very much. I want that cookie. I look at the door and back at the cookie. I don't want to make the man mad, so I look away.

I get up and walk around my room. There is a light switch by the door. I put my hand to it and push it down. The room is so dark I can't see my doll, and I turn the light back on real fast. I walk over to the table with the cookie and water. There's something under the table, but I don't know what it is. I look at the cookie again. I want that cookie. I look back at the door and hear something that makes me jump. I run to the bed and hide under the blanket. I start to cry. I'm scared, but I want to keep my doll so I stay quiet. I don't want Mommy any more. I just want my doll. I close my eyes and count.

"Angel?" I hear my doll talking to me. I pull it tight. "Angel, wake up." I try to open my eyes, but it's bright and I pull the blanket over my head. "Angel?" I jump because it's not my doll talking. It doesn't sound like Mommy. I peek out of the blanket and see Son.

"It's okay, Angel. I'm not going to hurt you, but you need to be quiet. Will you trust me?"

I don't know what trust is. My mommy told me to trust her. I asked once what it was and she laughed. I look at Son's eyes. I like his eyes better than Mommy's. I think that means I should trust him too. I nod my head and pull the blanket down.

Son looks at me and smiles. "I like your eyes."

"I like your eyes too."

Son's smile gets bigger. "Your name is Angel?"

"That's what the man said."

"The man? You mean my father?" I don't know what a father is. "The one that brought you here tonight, he's my father. Did he tell you your name was Angel?"

"Yes."

"Did you have a name before that?"

"Little Shit."

Son makes a face. The eyes I like look like they get all wet. "Well, my dad can call you Angel, but how about I call you Ang? Would that be okay?" I nod. I don't care what Son calls me. I like Son's voice as much as I like Son's eyes. "Does your doll have a name?" I look at my doll and shake my head. Son looks down at the floor and then back at me with wet eyes. "How about we call her Abigail? Do you like that?"

"Yes." Son gets quiet and looks at the door. I don't want to be alone so I talk. Son talked to me so I think I can talk too. "Do I call you Son?" Son's face gets all scrunchy.

"No, my dad calls me son because I'm his son." I don't understand. Son's face gets all funny again. "Looks like tomorrow I'll have to spend time understanding what words you know and don't know. I'm not supposed to tell you my name, but you can't call me son. That's just weird." Son stops talking. I like it when Son talks. "How about you call me Isaac?"

"Okay." Isaac stands up and looks at my table.

"The water and cookie are for you. Are you hungry?"

"No, but I want the cookie."

"Then you should eat it, and I'll bring you another one tomorrow. If you, um, if you have to go to the bathroom you're supposed to use this bucket." Isaac kicks the thing under my table. "Just leave it after you go, and someone will empty it tomorrow."

I remember I peed on my blanket before the man took me. I look at my new blanket. I don't know how to pee in a bucket, but I don't want to make a stain on my new blanket so I nod my head.

Isaac walks to my door and turns back to look at me. "I'm sorry you're here."

"But I have a doll. Abigail. And I have a room. And a cookie." Isaac's eyes look all wet again. I don't like it when they're wet. It makes me sad. Isaac nods and leaves my room. I jump up and grab the cookie before Isaac or the man come back and tell me not to.

⁂

I gave it all up for a doll. I know now that it wouldn't have mattered. The reality was that my mother had sold me. If I wouldn't have taken the doll, the man would have found another way. He would have found something to make me willingly go with him. He wanted to give me the illusion of choice.

But even though he would have found a way to make me go, in my heart I went willingly—I had traded my life for a doll. I think what's worse is that I would do it all over again. Knowing what I do now, I'd still take the doll and resulting life over a life of squatting in my mother's closet. My mother didn't love me. She didn't want me. She was a drunk and a junkie. My choice to go willingly didn't affect her or anyone else. It's my later actions that would do that.

But in my heart I feel guilty. In my heart I traded a life of neglect for one of slavery. And I know I would do it again, because if I hadn't I never would have had Abigail and I wouldn't have met Isaac.

Isaac.

It hurts to think about him, but I like remembering the way things were between us in those early years. It helps to keep the current pain away.

I jump at the sound of someone hitting my door. I guess I'm down to twenty-two hours.

22: Life Lessons

I try again to roll to my side. The pain is still there, but I roll anyway and bite back the cry that wants to escape. It hurts, but I'm tired of having my nose pressed to the floor. My hair is back in my face, and this time it's crusted on by drying blood. For the first time, I wish I hadn't let my hair grow so long.

I jump at the feel of something brushing up against my leg. Must be that darn rat again. I kick my leg and feel it run away. It reminds me of the first time I felt a rat touch my leg.

I had been in my new home for several months. I'm not sure exactly how long, but I know it hadn't been a year because it was before my birthday. The man always made a big production of birthdays. Not because he wanted to celebrate our lives—he wanted to celebrate being another year closer to when we could start making him money. It was the symbol of a countdown.

I began my life with him in a countdown, and he's ending it with one. I'm amazed at how things come full circle in life. The thought makes me chuckle, and the absurdity of laughing in my current situation makes me laugh even harder.

"What the hell's so funny in there?" Goon bangs on the closed door, yelling from the other side. "I'm not sure why you're laughing when you might have less than a day to live. You sadistic little shit."

Did he know my name for the first seven years of my life was Little Shit, or is it just coincidence?

The question causes a fresh eruption of uncontrollable laughter. I laugh so hard, tears leak from my eyes.

The door opens and Goon's almost running at me. His foot connects with my abdomen and the laughing stops abruptly, replaced by the urge to puke.

"Shut your goddamn mouth, or I'll shut it for you!" He's standing over me, making sure I'm done. I pull myself back into control and he walks out the way he came.

It takes me several minutes to focus on anything other than the pain I'm feeling. The image of Goon standing over me, telling me to be quiet or he'll make me, fits neatly into the memory that was interrupted by my laughing fit.

Again, things come full circle. It's my indication that I'm right where fate wants me to be.

I think back on that night so long ago. Like so many others, it's burned into my memory. I remember it well, not only for the fear and pain I experienced that night, but also for the lessons I learned.

It was the first time I had encountered death.

⁂

"You're all done for today." Isaac stands and puts his books in a pile. He looks at me again. "I was thinking, since we'll finish this lesson a few days early, I could test how well you remember things. I think you have a crazy good memory, and I'd like to experiment. But it will have to be our secret."

"Like Abigail?" Isaac told me not to tell anyone, especially the man, that my doll's name is Abigail. I don't know why it matters, but I don't tell because I like to keep Isaac's secrets.

"Yes, just like Abigail." He looks at me for a few seconds and reaches out his hand like he's going to touch my hair. He never touches me, but I think I would like him to. I like Isaac. He makes me not so scared. And he brings me a cookie every day.

But he doesn't touch my hair. He pulls his hand back and picks up his books.

"Do you have to go?"

"You know I do, Ang. I'd like to stay, but I have to go when my time is up."

It makes me sad when he leaves. "But you'll be back tomorrow? And bring me a cookie?"

"Of course. And since tomorrow is Saturday, I can come early. Play a dream for me, and I'll play one for you." He waves good-bye before leaving.

I like when he tells me to play a dream for him. The first time he said that I didn't know what it was so I asked. He said I had to play a happy dream in my mind. One I think he would like, and I tell him about it when he comes back the next day. My mind always plays the same dream—Isaac stays with me and talks to me all night. Then he plays a dream for me. I like the dreams he plays. He dreams about me seeing things I've never seen before. Like the lights.

When he plays that dream, he takes me to see the lights. He said we live near a place called Reno, and at night the streets and buildings are lit up with a whole bunch of lights. I couldn't see it in my mind, so he drew me a picture. He wouldn't let me keep it, but he brings it every time he comes back so I can look at it. I want to see the lights with Isaac.

I eat the dinner Night Man left me, but save the cookie for later. I go pee in my potty bucket, put on my nightdress, and get back into bed. I play with Abigail and tell her about the dreams Isaac plays for me. They're supposed to be a secret too, but I can tell Abigail. His dreams always include her too, so I know he won't be upset if I tell her. I pretend we go see the lights. Isaac told me my birthday was soon. I'll be eight. Maybe he could take me and Abigail to see the lights for my birthday.

When I lived with Mommy I didn't even know I had a birthday. Isaac said it will be my special day, and that I'll get cake. I'd really like to have some cake. I've never had it, but Isaac said it's better than a cookie. I remember my cookie and get out of bed to get it. I take a small bite and take it with me to bed. I share it with Abigail and put the rest under my pillow for after we play.

I fly Abigail above me in the air like a bird. Just like Isaac showed me.

Suddenly I can't see Abigail or anything. Everything is black. I scream.

I hug Abigail to me to make sure she's still here. She is but I can't see her. I sit up and hear other screams and loud noises, like what I used to hear when I was with Mommy. I scream again. My eyes must be broke and I'm scared. I rub my eyes but they won't work. When I scream again, my door opens. Night Man comes in and he's holding something that lights up his face. It makes him look scary. I scream louder.

"Shut up! The damn power's out, that's all. Quit your screamin' or I'll come in there and shut you up myself." I get quiet and he leaves my room.

He said the power is out. Isaac told me power makes the lights work. I guess it's my light that doesn't work, not my eyes. I never shut my light off in my new room. Not even when I sleep. When I was with Mommy, my room was dark but I could always see. In this room I don't even see my hand when the light is off.

I'm scared. I want Isaac. I think about the dreams Isaac plays for me. I close my eyes and try to play his dreams in my mind, but I don't know how any of it looks. I only see Isaac, sitting in my room telling me about the dreams. It makes me feel better.

I hear a noise in my room. I want to scream, but Night Man told me not to or he will make me be quiet. He might take Abigail. I hug her tighter. I hear the noise again, and I hide under my covers. I try not to cry, but I do anyway. I hug Abigail and start to count all the numbers I know. Isaac taught me how to count to one hundred, so I know lots of numbers now. I hear the noise again and it makes me forget my number. I start over. I count all my numbers two times and then stop. I don't hear the noise any more. I peek out of my covers, but I still can't see.

I close my eyes and try to sleep. I play a dream where Isaac is with me when the power goes out. He talks to me and tells me about his dreams. I then play the dream where he talks to me about the lights.

I feel something brush my leg. I start to scream, but cover my mouth with my hand. I scoot up in my bed and kick my blanket. Something crawls across my foot and I scream. I scream really loud. My door opens and Night Man comes in, walking fast to my bed.

"I told you to shut it!"

Something hard hits my face, and I fall against the wall. I think he hit me. Mommy used to hit me sometimes, but this hurts more. He points his light in my face, and now my eyes hurt too. I put my hands over my face to stop the hurt. He takes the light away, and he turns to leave. I remember why I screamed.

"There's something in my room! It touched my foot and my leg!"

It's the loudest I ever talked, but I don't want him to leave. I don't want him to hit me again, but I'm scared of what's in my room. He stops and turns around.

"Scared of a little rat are we?" He laughs and I get scared again. He walks to my bed, and I hug my pillow in front of me. He doesn't hit me again. He gets down on the floor and looks under my bed. "Come here you little bugger. I've been lookin' for you. Can't have you makin' the girls scream." I hear him make funny sounds and my bed shakes. "Gotcha."

He gets back up and holds his hand out. He points his light at something in his hand. I scream again. He drops his light on my bed and grabs my neck. It hurts and it's hard to breathe. I pull at his hand, but he won't let go.

"You need to stop screamin', little girl. Otherwise, I'm gonna do to you what I'm gonna do to this rat."

His light is still shining on Rat. He squeezes his hand holding Rat. The eyes look like they're going to pop out of its head. I want to scream but I can't because Night Man's hand is still around my neck. Rat stops moving and Night Man drops it in my lap and lets go of my throat. He picks up his light and walks out.

It's dark again and I can't see Rat, but I can feel it. My throat hurts. My face hurts. I cry. I try to be quiet because I don't want to look like Rat. I try to close my eyes and play one of Isaac's dreams, but all I see is Rat with its eyes popping out.

I hug Abigail and cry until my light comes back on. Rat is still in my lap. It doesn't move. I don't want to touch it, but I don't want it on my lap. I jump out of my bed and Rat falls to the mattress. I squat in the corner by my table. I count all the numbers I know.

My door opens and I start to scream, but I stop when I remember Rat. I cover my face with my hands.

"Ang? What are you doing over there?" I'm happy when I hear Isaac's voice, but I still cry. I feel his hands on my arms.

Isaac is touching me.

I cry harder.

"Ang, please stop crying. Tell me what happened." I still have my hands over my face. It hurts where Night Man hit me. My throat hurts too. I can't stop crying so I point to my bed. When I point, he sees my face. "Oh my God, what happened to your face?" He pulls my other hand away. His eyes get all wet again.

I try to talk but it's only a whisper and it hurts. I put my hand to my throat and it makes Isaac look at that too. He says a word he never taught me and stands up. He walks the two steps to my bed and stops. He's looking at Rat. It's on my bed and it still doesn't move. I look away.

"Ang, please, I need you to tell me what happened."

"My light went out." I can only whisper so he comes back over to me.

"The power went out last night for a few hours. Did that scare you?"

"Yes. I screamed."

"What happened next?"

"Night Man came in and told me to stop or he would make me." Isaac covers his eyes with his fists. He looks at me again and his eyes look mad.

"Is that when he hit you?"

"No. He left, and it was dark, and I heard a noise. Then I felt something on my leg. I tried not to scream, but I did."

"And that's when he hit you?" I nod my head. He points to my throat. "And that?"

"Yes. He squeezed me like he squeezed Rat. He said if I screamed again I would look like Rat."

"Son of a bitch." Isaac stands and turns to Rat again. He looks around my room.

"Have you peed yet?"

"No."

"Can you try to go now? I want to use your bucket to get rid of the rat. I won't look."

He turns around so I only see his back. I've never peed with someone in my room before. If I have to go during lessons, Isaac goes out of my room. I use the bucket and slide it next to my table.

He picks up Rat and drops it in. "I'll be right back."

The door closes and I sit and wait. I hug Abigail. We're both happy Rat is gone. I wish the hurt in my face and my throat was gone too. I close my eyes, but I see Rat so I open them.

Isaac has been gone a long time and my legs are starting to hurt, but I don't want to go to my bed. I can still see where Rat was laying. I look away from the bed and see Isaac's books on my table. I look at the door and then pick one up. I turn the pages and look at the letters and the pictures. I wish I could learn to read like Isaac. Maybe he will teach me. I hear the click on my door and I put the book back real fast. Isaac walks in and then the man is in the door. The man doesn't come to see me much. I still don't like his eyes.

"Look what that son of a bitch did to her, Dad." Isaac points to me. The man comes in, and Isaac has to sit on my bed to make room. The man crouches down to look at my face and neck.

"I thought you said there was a serious problem here?"

"You don't think hitting and choking little girls is a serious problem?"

The man stands and looks at Isaac. I turn my head to look at Isaac too, but the man swings his hand and hits me hard on my face.

"Dad!" Isaac jumps off my bed, but the man pushes him back down and holds his throat like Night Man held mine.

"The only problem I see here, son, is that you seem to be getting too close to the girl. Maybe you're too young for this after all." Isaac pushes at the man's hand. He finally lets go and Isaac sits up in the bed, away from the man. "The girls need to know their place, and if they don't follow orders, then there are consequences. Same goes for you. Next time you bring me down here there had better be an actual problem." The man walks out.

Isaac is still on the bed, and it looks like he's shaking. Finally he comes back over to me. He tries to touch my face but I pull back. It hurts real bad and I'm still crying. He takes off his shirt, tears off one sleeve, and puts it back on. It looks funny, but I don't feel like laughing. He takes my water and gets the part he tore off wet.

"I just want to clean your face, is that okay? It might hurt a little, but I want to wipe off the blood." I nod and try to hold still. It does hurt. I look at his neck and see marks.

"Does mine look like that?" I point to his neck.

"I can't see what mine looks like, but I guess so." He finishes cleaning my face. "That's a little better. Here, I brought this. I'm not sure how much you're supposed to take though." He pulls a bottle out of his pocket and looks at it.

"What is it?"

"Medicine. It should make it not hurt so much." He opens the bottle and takes out a little white thing.

"Is that the same as what I have to swallow with my breakfast?" They look the same, just a different color.

"No, that's a vitamin. Medicine is different. I take two pills, but you're a lot smaller than me so maybe just half a pill." He puts the pill in his mouth and bites it. Now there are two little pills, and he gives me one. "I'll give you the other half before I leave today. Here, swallow it with water if you can." I do what he tells me and it hurts, but I don't cry.

We sit and stare at each other for a long time. I think the medicine is working because the hurt is not so bad.

"I'm sorry my dad hit you. If I would've known he was going to do that, I wouldn't have brought him here. I really thought he would fire Night Man, not hit you again."

My eyes get big. "You mean fire like in the picture you showed me?" I don't like Night Man, but I don't want him to be put on fire. It looks like it would hurt.

Isaac laughs. "No, not that kind of fire. I just mean that he wouldn't work here any more." I like the new kind of fire and would like it to happen to Night Man.

"What happened to Rat?"

"I threw it out."

"Why wasn't he moving any more?"

Isaac doesn't speak. Finally he takes a big breath. "The rat died."

"What does that mean?"

"People and animals are either alive or dead. You and me—we're alive. We breathe and eat and move and walk around. Also, we feel things—both outside and inside. Outside is like when someone touches you or you touch something. Feeling things inside is like how you were scared when the rat touched you. That's being alive. When you're dead you don't feel anything, and there's no more breathing or moving. Dead is forever. I don't know about rats, but some people believe that when you die your soul—the part of you that makes you feel and makes you who you are—goes to someplace else."

"Do you believe that?"

"I'd like to think it's possible, but I don't know. I go to church with my mom and all, but what I learn there is opposite of what I see my Dad do."

"What's church?"

He tells me all about his church. I like hearing him talk, and I like the new stories he tells me. I start to get sleepy and I can't keep my eyes open.

⌘

That day I had learned all about life and death, thanks to a rat that died because I couldn't stop screaming. Isaac had taught me more about life and death that day than he had probably realized. His intentions were to define the concept in a way that my almost eight year old mind could easily process.

He had told me that being alive was not only breathing and moving, but feeling things both inside and out. He made it sound so definitive—you're either alive or you're dead.

Even though I had Isaac, I spent the majority of my time in those days alone with Abigail. I had no other stimulants, so all I had to occupy me were my thoughts. His description of life and death consumed my thoughts until I came to the conclusion that it wasn't really one or the other.

I realized that I could be alive on the outside, but dead on the inside. I could exist without feeling.

With my mother, I had lived for seven years with no feelings except occasional pain and fear. I didn't know what it was like to be around others, so I had been spared loneliness. I suppose it was the one kind thing my mother did for me—even though I'm certain she never realized keeping me isolated actually helped me. If she had, she would have taken that away too.

Isaac showed me what it felt like to have someone care about me. It was the first seed of love that had been planted inside of me, and I knew even then that I wanted more. Being alive is better when there is someone to love, and someone who loves you back.

However, I also learned that there would be times when the feelings of being alive were so awful that I'd wish I were dead. The definitive kind of dead.

21: Making Wishes

Another hour is up. I'm so hungry I'm lightheaded, but I'm actually grateful I haven't had anything to eat or drink for a long time. I don't know how I'd be able to relieve myself with my hands bound behind my back.

Somehow I'm able to shift to a sitting position and decide quickly that it's a bad idea. I fall down on the opposite side I'd been laying on. It's a little better.

The sting of getting hit that night is still fresh in my mind. It was the first time I had taken a beating in my new home, but it hadn't been the last or the worst. Not by a long shot. Another came on my eighth birthday. It wouldn't end up being the worst beating, but it had been really bad.

<hr />

"Today's my birthday, Abigail!"

I'm excited. Isaac said I'm going to get cake today, and I can't wait to see what that tastes like. I also get a special dinner. I picked pizza and a juice box. Isaac said I'm eight. It's a school day for him so he can't come for my lessons until later. I play with Abigail until it's time for Isaac to come.

My door opens and I think it's Isaac, but it's just Cleaning Lady. It's not my day for a bath, but I guess I get an extra one since it's my birthday. She puts a box on my bed and tells me to follow her. We walk to the bathroom and I get in the tub. She scrubs me clean and then takes me back to my room.

"Put that on." She points to the box and leaves my room.

I open the box and see a pretty dress. I put it on and spin around. I show Abigail my new dress. She'd like a new dress too. I spin around again and keep spinning until my head feels dizzy. Isaac taught me how to spin and get dizzy. I like it better when he's on my bed watching me spin. Then I get to watch him spin. It's more fun with Isaac, but I still like it. I pick Abigail up and spin her. My head gets too dizzy so I sit on my bed. I like the way my dress falls in a big circle around me. My door opens, and this time it's Isaac. I jump up and spin again.

"Isaac, look! I got a new dress and it floats when I spin!" I get so dizzy I bump my table. I laugh and so does Isaac.

"Careful, Ang. You don't want to get hurt on your birthday." I stand up straight and smile. Isaac looks at my dress and he smiles too. "That's a really pretty dress. Here, I got you a present." He puts his books on my table and holds out a small box. "Happy birthday, Ang."

I sit down on my bed and take the box. I look for the lid. "How does it open?"

"You have to take off the wrapping paper first." I look at the box. I don't know what he's talking about. He knows I'm confused because he sits down next to me and reaches over, tearing a part of the box. "See, you tear this part off and then you can open the box underneath." I frown. "What's wrong?"

"The paper is so pretty. I don't want to tear it."

He laughs. "Then here, just lift off the tape. I'll help you." He helps me take off the paper, but doesn't tear it any more. I open the box and look inside. "Do you like it?"

"What is it?"

"It's a headband. Your curls are always falling in your eyes, so I thought you might like to have one. It's what all the girls in my class wear." He takes it out of the box and shows me how to put it on. It feels funny but I like the way my hair is out of my eyes. I smile.

"I like it."

He looks at me funny but doesn't talk. I think I have the headband on wrong. I go to take it off but he grabs my hand.

"Leave it. It looks good on you. You look really pretty." I've never been called pretty before. It makes me feel happy. I look down and see he's still holding my hand. I like that too.

My door opens and I see the man. Isaac quickly jumps off the bed and stands by the table. The man is holding two boxes. It smells good and I hope it's my pizza and cake. And my juice box.

"Son. I see you got here early."

"Yes, sir. I wanted to make sure Angel was ready."

The man looks at me. I still don't like his eyes. "Stand up, Angel." I stand up. The man puts the boxes on my table. There's not a lot of room with the man and Isaac in here. I want to sit on my bed, but I don't want to make the man mad. "That dress looks nice on you. Where'd you get that thing in your hair?"

I look at Isaac.

"I gave it to her."

"You gave her a present?"

"Yes, sir. But it's just a headband. I thought it would help when we study her lessons. Her hair is always in her eyes." Isaac's eyes and face look funny. I don't know how, but he looks different when he sees the man. The man is really quiet, and I look back at him. He looks mad.

"It sounds like we need to go over the rules again. But since it's a practical gift, I'll let it pass this once." The man looks at me again. It makes my tummy feel funny. I don't want him in my room. I want him to go away so I can eat my pizza and cake with Abigail and Isaac. "How's she doing on her lessons?"

"It's hard to tell. She doesn't talk much."

The man looks at Isaac with his mean eyes. "It's my understanding that you spend more time here than you're supposed to. Based on that, you should have a very good understanding of her progress. Or are you doing something else when you're here?"

"We just work on her lessons. I'm here a lot because it's quiet in her room and it's easier for me to get my other homework done. Besides, I find that the more time she spends with me, the more she talks. Her vocabulary is better, but there's still a long way to go. We're working on manners now. She has difficulty remembering things." Isaac has been giving me what he calls a memory test every day. He said I remember really well. But it's a secret, so I keep quiet. The man folds his arms across his chest.

"Sounds like a lot of work for just one girl." The man looks at me and I look down at the floor. "Although, I think she could make us some good money with her unique looks." He turns back to Isaac. "I'll allow the extra time, just make sure you stick to the assigned lessons." The man points to the boxes. "Enjoy your dinner. There's enough for both of you—you can eat with her and use it as an opportunity to work on her table manners. Happy birthday, Angel." The man leaves and closes the door.

Me and Isaac stand still, looking at the door. Finally, Isaac sits on the floor and grabs one of the boxes.

"Are you hungry?" I smile and sit down next to him. He hands me a piece of pizza then opens a juice box for me.

"What are table manners?"

He shakes his shoulders. "It's the way people are supposed to eat. You know—like chew with your mouth closed, don't talk with food in your mouth, use the right fork—that sort of stuff. I'll teach you all that soon. But this is your birthday, and pizza is meant to be eaten with your hands." I watch Isaac take a big bite of pizza then I take one too.

I finish my piece of pizza and decide I like birthdays. I wonder if Isaac has one too. "Do you have a birthday?"

"Everyone has a birthday. Mine is April 14th."

"How old will you be?"

"I'll be thirteen. So, if you're eight, how many years older am I than you?"

Isaac told the man I was learning manners, but he's really teaching me math. It's another secret. I count the numbers in my head like Isaac taught me. "Five."

"Very good." He smiles and it makes me smile.

"Will you have cake and pizza and presents for your birthday too?"

He looks down and shakes his shoulders. His brown hair falls over his eyes, so I watch his mouth. "My mom usually throws me a party, but only for family. I'm not allowed to have any friends over. My dad says that my cousins are the only friends I need."

I ask him what a party is.

"Kind of like this. We're having a party—me, you, and Abigail. My parties just include more people who are really loud and eat a lot of food. I get a lot of presents, but most of it's just a bunch of crap I don't want."

"I like my present." I touch my headband and he smiles.

"That's cool." He takes a drink of his juice box. "You remember I told you about Christmas?" I remember what he said about not talking with food in my mouth so I nod. "Well, I may not like my birthday so much, but I like Christmas. It's just me and my mom mostly. My dad opens presents with us, but then he goes out with Uncle and his other friends. Christmas is only two days away." He gets quiet. I want to ask him who Uncle is, but I have food in my mouth. He starts talking again before I swallow. "I usually stay with my mom all day, but I might be able to come see you while my dad is gone." I hope he does. I see Isaac every day and I would be sad if he couldn't come.

"Who's Uncle?"

"He's actually my dad's uncle, but everyone just calls him Uncle. I have other uncles, my dad's brothers, but Uncle is the one who helps my dad run the business. The others all just do small jobs. My mom doesn't have any family."

"What's your mom like?"

"Nice. Pretty. Quiet. I don't think she really likes what my dad does for a living, but . . . well, as she says, 'It is what it is.'"

"What does he do?"

He shakes his head. "I'll have to tell you some day, but not today. Not on your birthday."

We finish the pizza without talking. "Can I have cake now?"

"Absolutely." He opens the other box and pulls out the cake. It looks pretty and it smells good. He sets it down in front of me and I go to touch it but he stops me. "Wait, you need to make a wish first. They don't allow candles down here, but you can still make a wish."

"What's a wish?"

"A wish is something you really, really want. Some kids waste their wishes on stupid things—like a new bike or all the candy in the world—and then they get upset when they don't get it right away. But a real wish should be something special. Something that may take a long time to come true, but you wish for it anyway. Then, when it comes true, it's totally cool."

I think about what I really, really want. I can only think of one thing. I want to see the lights.

"Do you know what you want to wish for?"

"Yes, I wish that—"

"Wait! Don't tell me. You're not supposed to say your wishes out loud, or they won't come true. Just close your eyes and say your wish in your head. When you're done, open them, and we'll eat cake." I close my eyes and do what he said. I open my eyes and watch him cut me a piece of cake. I take a bite, and it really is better than a cookie. When I finish, I ask for another piece and he gives me one. When the cake is gone my belly feels full, and I lay down on my bed.

"I like birthdays."

Isaac laughs and scoots closer to my bed. "I like your birthday better than mine." He grabs his books from the table.

"Do I have to do my lessons today?"

"Not if you don't want to, but I have another present for you." He opens one of the books and takes something out. "Sit up." I do and he sits on the bed next to me. "These are for you. They're postcards that show pictures of some of the things I told you about. This one is the desert and look, there's a cactus right here. These next ones I got on a vacation we took a couple years ago. This one's a picture of Hoover Dam. Remember I told you all about the dam and how it works? And this one is Red Rock Canyon. And these—these are the lights of Reno and Las Vegas, which is a city like Reno."

I look at each of the pictures he hands me with wide eyes. He's played each of these as dreams for me, but I couldn't see them in my mind. Now I know what they look like. When he hands me the ones with the lights, I bounce on the bed.

"My wish!"

"Your wish?"

"Yes, my wish! I wished I could see the lights and now I can!"

He looks at me not talking. He puts his arm around my back and pulls me to lean on his side. "I don't think I've ever seen a wish come true so fast. You must be a really good wisher. Maybe you should make another one before your birthday is over."

I don't have to think about my wish for very long. I wish that Isaac would stay with me all night and talk to me about his dreams. And keep his arm around my back.

I look at the pictures. "Can I keep these?"

"They're yours, but it has to be another secret. We need to find a place to hide them." He gets up and looks around my room. He gets on the floor and looks under my table. "Here, hand me the postcards." I do and he tucks them under the table. "They should be safe here. Come see how I put them in so you can do it when I'm not here." I get up and look under the table. He takes them out and tells me to try. I do and they stick just like when he did it. We sit back on my bed and he puts his arm around my back again.

"Did you make another wish?"

I nod but don't tell him because I want it to come true. "Have any of your wishes ever come true?"

"Not yet. I used to wish to see the ocean. I think you would like the ocean too. I know you don't know what the ocean is, so I'll bring in a picture sometime to show you. I'll find a map too, that will help me show you how big it is. I still make that wish sometimes, but now I have a new wish." I wonder what his new wish is, but I don't ask. I want his wish to come true too. "So, what dream do you want me to play for you tonight? It's your birthday, so you get to pick."

"The lights." I close my eyes as he plays the dream, and I can see it in my head now. When he's done, he starts to play a new dream and I get sleepy. I hug Abigail and put my head on Isaac's shoulder. He pulls up the blanket and keeps talking.

I open my eyes and try to move, but I'm all squished. I turn my head and see Isaac. He's sleeping. I smile because my second wish came true. I like making wishes and wonder if I can only make them on my birthday. I poke Isaac to wake him up and ask. He opens his eyes and smiles at me. His smile is gone and he sits up quickly.

"Shit." He kicks off the blanket as the door opens. The man walks in and looks mad. He steps to Isaac and pulls him out of the bed.

"What the hell is going on here?"

"Nothing! I just fell asleep by accident."

"Did you touch her?"

"No!" The man hits Isaac in the face and I try not to scream.

"Don't lie to me, boy. Did you touch her?"

"She fell asleep on my arm. That's it, I swear. I was tired and fell asleep too. That's all." Isaac is crying and it makes me cry. The man looks at me.

"I damn well knew it. You got too close to her. Didn't I warn you about getting too close? Now we're going to have to do something about it." The man grabs my hair and pulls. I scream. I fall out of the bed, but he's holding me up by my hair.

"Dad, stop! You're hurting her!" The man hits Isaac again.

"It almost sounds like you're trying to protect her. That's crossing the line too far, and if that's the case I'll have to get rid of her."

"No! I promise! I'm not protecting her. I just don't want her to get hurt."

"She's nothing but a whore, which means she doesn't count in this world. She's my possession, and I can do with her as I please. You're going to take over the business some day, and you need to understand the difference between who counts and who doesn't. She doesn't count." The man pushes me toward Isaac. "Hit her."

"What? I'm not going to hit her—"

"I said hit her! If you don't, I will and I can guarantee you she won't walk for at least a week after. Then I'll sell her off to someone else. And believe me—the people who buy her won't wait until she comes of age to make her start earning her keep. You have a problem with a few hits to the face? You can't even imagine what would happen to her at some of those other operations. Now. HIT. HER!"

Isaac looks at me. He's still crying. He hits my face. It hurts, but not like when Night Man hit me.

"Harder."

"Dad, please. I hit her like you said."

"Not hard enough. Hit her till you see blood."

"Dad, please don't make me." The man pulls my hair hard, and I scream. He pushes me against the wall and he's going to hit me, but Isaac grabs his arm. "STOP! I'll do it. I'll do it."

Isaac is crying really hard now. The man steps away and pushes Isaac in front of me. Isaac mouths 'I'm sorry' before hitting me with his fist. It hurts more this time and I try to put my hands over my face, but the man moves forward and pulls me to him, holding my arms. Isaac hits me again. And again. I count all the numbers I know, but I forget my number each time he hits me. Finally he stops. I must be bleeding.

The man lets go and I fall to the floor. He grabs Isaac's books and pushes him out the door. I hear it click. I cover my face with my hands. It hurts real bad. I cry until I fall asleep.

My head hurts. I sit up and walk to my bed. I climb in and hug Abigail. I look down and see blood on my new dress. I cry again.

I wait for Isaac to come back. He'll tell me why he hit me. He'll bring me a cookie and give me another one of those pills to make the hurt stop.

But he doesn't come. No one comes.

A long time goes by and my face still hurts, but my tummy hurts now too. I'm hungry, but no one brings me my food. My potty bucket is almost full and it smells bad. It must be a new day. Maybe a few days have gone.

When the hurt in my face is not so bad I take off my new dress. I look at the blood again and cry and throw it in the corner. I put on my old dress. When I turn to get back in bed, I see my headband under my bed. I pick it up and throw it on my bloody dress. I sit on my bed, but then I go and get my headband and put it on.

I play with Abigail. My tummy now hurts more than my face. I can't keep my eyes open.

I hear the click on my door and I look for Isaac. It's Day Man. He puts food and water on my table, gives me a new potty bucket, and walks out with the stinky one. I eat all my food and I start to feel better. I miss Isaac. I don't know why he hit me, but I want to see him anyway.

I count thirty days since Isaac hit me. Isaac taught me how to count the days. The day starts when Day Man brings me food and a new potty bucket. He comes again with my second meal, then after that Isaac comes for my lessons. Then Night Man comes and brings me more food and another new potty bucket. That's one whole day. The only times it's different are when Isaac doesn't have school. Then he comes with my breakfast and stays most of the day. Cleaning Lady comes once a week, so Isaac taught me how to use that to make sure I'm counting right.

I couldn't count the days when no one came, so it might be more than thirty.

My door opens and I look for Day Man. I see Isaac. I sit up real fast and smile but he gives me a look that makes me stop. I want to ask him why he looks mad, but I stay quiet. He walks in my room and sets down my food and his books. I hear a sound at the door and see a man I've not seen before. He stands in the door and watches Isaac.

"I brought your breakfast. You can eat while we do your lessons." Isaac sits down on the floor and opens a book. He reads the page and then turns the book to show me the pictures. It's one he's read before, so I already know all the words. I look back at the door. The new man, Watcher, is still standing there watching Isaac. I eat my breakfast and listen to Isaac. He won't look at me. He just looks at the book or down at the floor. His eyes look different, but I still like them.

He finishes my lessons and leaves earlier than he used to. Watcher goes with him, and it's just me and Abigail again. Isaac acted different, but at least he came back.

I count thirty more days. It's the same each day. Isaac comes for my lessons, Watcher stands at the door, and then they leave.

I finish my dinner and sit on my bed, playing with Abigail. It's not as much fun as it used to be. I don't have any new dreams to play for her. I get off my bed and take Abigail to the table. I lay under it and pull out my pictures. I like looking at them. I hear my door and put the pictures back real fast. No one is supposed to come until Day Man comes back tomorrow. I sit up and see Isaac. He stands at the door looking at me before he walks over and kneels next to me.

"Ang. I'm so sorry. I didn't want to hit you, but if I didn't my dad would have, and it would have been a lot worse. And if he would have sold you off to someone else . . ." He starts to cry. He rubs his eyes then looks at the door and back at me. "I don't have long. I can't be in here. They've been watching me, but I snuck away. I had to tell you that I was sorry."

"It's okay. It doesn't hurt any more."

"No, it's not okay. But thank you for saying that." He looks back at the door again. "We have to be careful for a while. If anyone is around, I have to pretend I don't care about you. That we're not friends. But we are—it just has to be a secret." He wipes his eyes again. "We have to pretend. Sometimes it might feel real. I might have to hit you again, to make sure they don't know. But you have to always remember, it's just pretend." He holds my hand, and I nod my head.

"I'll remember. It's just pretend." He looks back at the door. I don't want him to go. "Can you play me a dream?"

"Not tonight, Ang. Not for a long time." His eyes make me sad. Something is wrong with them. "You'll have to hold on to the ones you already have. Someday we can play new ones. I have to go now." He stands up and starts to leave, but I remember something.

"I'm sorry too!"

He looks back at me. "Why are you sorry?"

"For my wish. My second wish. I wished that you could stay with me all night and play me dreams. It came true and you got hurt and had to hit me and go away. I promise I won't make any more wishes, ever."

He walks to me quickly and bends to give me a hug. He never hugged me before.

"Don't ever stop wishing, Ang. Your first two wishes came true right away—that's amazing. You're the best wisher I ever met. Your wish didn't make this happen. I should have left before my dad found me. It's not your fault. Don't stop making wishes, please." He looks at me and I nod.

But I still don't think I ever want to make another wish.

❧

I continue to think about the time of supervised visits with Isaac. They lasted almost three months. During that time, he had to hit me twice more when the man visited. There was no specific reason for it—he just wanted to make sure Isaac didn't hesitate before hitting me. He didn't, but I always knew that each hit hurt him just as much as it hurt me. Now I understand that the depth of his pain was actually much deeper than mine.

He never did tell me what happened during the month he couldn't visit me. Whatever it was, I know it was bad. Even then, with my innocence of a child, I knew something in him had shifted. I could see the haunting in his eyes. He often wouldn't hold my gaze, as if he were afraid I would catch a glimpse of the horrors he'd had to witness at the hands of his father.

The man's intention was to drive a wedge between us. In reality he only drove Isaac to take more risks. After the supervised visits were over, we went back to the way we were before. Isaac taught me my lessons and still took the risk to teach me beyond the approved material.

That's when Isaac started the long process of teaching me how to read. He was subtle about it—not even telling me at the time what he was doing. He used my memory as a way for me to teach myself. He read me the same story every day for a year until it was burned into my memory, word for word. One day he 'accidentally' dropped the book and pretended not to notice it had slid under my bed. Naturally I kept the book, and when I looked inside I realized I could match the words in my memory to the words on the pages. We never talked about it, but we both understood what the other was doing. I was learning to read and he had set it up to happen.

I think about the other risks he took during that time. I'm still not sure which would have been more severely punished—him teaching me to read or the other things he did. One of those risks was creating a better hiding space for the book and postcards by building a hidden compartment for under my table. One day he came in wearing a big sweater and it made me laugh. He told me he wore it so he could sneak in the box. He attached it under my table and showed me how I could open and close it. Isaac started bringing me other items I could keep in the box—medicine for the times when I got hit, more postcards, extra cookies, candy.

He told me about his dreams and we played with Abigail. Things lasted that way for years, and I was happy. I didn't know any different. I didn't know I should want to be free. Sure I wanted to see the things that Isaac told me about, but I didn't want for anything beyond that. I had Abigail and I had Isaac. It was more than I'd ever had before. In that time I grew closer with Isaac, both mentally and physically.

After the supervised visits had ended, Isaac started touching me more. He would wipe my hair out of my face or hold my hand during lessons. He always hugged me good-bye when he left. There were still times when Watcher would show up and make Isaac hit me, but after he left Isaac would lay with me on the bed and hug me until my tears stopped. Every time Isaac touched me was a risk. If someone walked in and saw him even touch my hair, Isaac would have been beaten and I would have been sold off to someone else.

The memories of Isaac taking so many risks for me are too much. Even after experiencing a brutal month of unspeakable punishment, he still pushed the limits for me. And I couldn't even give him the one thing he'd asked of me.

I never did make another wish.

It would take me years to understand that he just wanted me to hold on to the innocence of my youth for as long as possible. But for me, in my eight year old mind, it was too much of a risk for another wish to come true and hurt Isaac again. Or worse, lose him all together. I was okay with him taking the risks, but I couldn't bear the thought of his suffering as a result of my wishes.

I had learned that very first night that even though wishes generated happiness, they also came with consequences. When I was young, I refused to wish because I feared my power to make them come true. However, as I got older I understood it wasn't really the wishes that were the problem. It was having hope and wanting something more. That's what wishes really are anyway. While I never made another wish, I would eventually learn to hope again. I would want for more, and sometimes I actually believed I could have it. That time of hope came many years after those wishes, and it didn't last for long.

The sobs take over and I try to hold them back. The longing I feel for Isaac is intense. I have to remember the man is asking me to come back to him, not Isaac. That's no longer an option.

I can't think about it any more.

It hurts too much.

I start to count.

20: Questions

The sound of someone banging on my door wakes me. Another hour is up. Twenty more to go and I'm still no closer to knowing what my decision will be. If it were Isaac asking, I wouldn't even need twenty-four seconds to decide. But it's not.

This is the kind of situation where having the power to make wishes come true would be helpful. I might actually make one again. Instead, I try to summon the courage to pray. I've been told it's more powerful than wishing, but it requires faith. And hope. Unfortunately, my time of having either is over.

There's an itch on my leg. I try to scratch it with my other foot, but I'm too sore to flex that much. I pull at my restraints again out of frustration. I kick my legs before I finally grow still. I need to think of something positive before I go insane.

I'm still dressed.

I had actually thought about wearing jeans, but now I'm grateful that I had changed my mind and put on a dress. The man would have had to take pants off to accomplish his earlier task, and then I'd be lying here half naked. It seems odd to value modesty after the life I've led.

The man said I deserved my life. Maybe I did. I couldn't even give back to the one person who truly cared about me and fought for me every step of the way. It was my innocence Isaac tried to protect the most. Ironically, it was also the very thing that caused us to have our first fight.

I was eleven and Isaac had just turned sixteen. He said he would sneak out after his birthday party to bring me cake, but he didn't show up until several days after.

⁂

Night Man opens my door and brings in my dinner. He looks me over before setting down a new bucket and walking out with my dirty one. I'm allowed to go down to the bathroom twice a day now to use the toilet, but sometimes I can't hold it so I have to use the bucket.

Even though I'm hungry, I'm sad Night Man brought my food. It means another day has gone by without Isaac. I think maybe he couldn't get away after his party, but I don't understand why he didn't show up the next day. Or the day after. Or today. I miss him.

I eat my food and change into my nightdress. I sneak my book out, after looking over my postcards again, and sit on my bed to read to Abigail. Each week Isaac sneaks me in a new book. It's hard sometimes because I can't visualize most of the things I read about, but when Isaac comes for my lessons he tries to draw me pictures. If he can't, then sometimes the next day he shows up with a picture. I like knowing what things look like, but I don't like how it makes me want to wish to see them. I won't make any more wishes.

I hear the click in my door and quickly hide the book under my mattress. I see Isaac and start to smile, but the look on his face stops me. He stands by the closed door and looks me over. His eyes settle on my legs. I look down and see that my nightdress is pulled up and my panties are showing. I hear something that makes me jump and look back at Isaac. He punches the door, making the same sound I just heard. He walks out of my room, shutting the door hard. I'm confused and something about the visit makes me cry. I put my book back in the hidden compartment under my table and snuggle under the blanket with Abigail.

A full week has gone by and Isaac only came that once when he just looked at me and punched the door before leaving. I jump slightly when Cleaning Lady comes in with my fresh laundry. She watches me put the clothes away in my small chest and then takes me down to the bathroom. I'm happy that I get to take a shower. When my period started, I was promoted to three showers a week during non-menstrual times and every day when I'm bleeding. I don't like having my period, but I like being able to take more showers.

Cleaning Lady watches me use the toilet and shower before taking me back to my room. She opens my door but doesn't follow me in. I almost scream when I enter, but I quickly realize it's just Isaac sitting on my bed. He looks over my robe and then looks away.

"I thought tomorrow was your cleaning day."

"I started my period early."

He nods and clears his throat. "Well, you should get dressed. I'll wait outside. Tap on the door when you're done." He gets off my bed and steps past me to leave. He's a lot taller than me now. As he goes past, our bodies bump and I almost fall back on the bed. He grabs my arms and pulls me back upright. He holds me by my arms, looking down at me, for several seconds before he rushes out the door.

I stare at the closed door in confusion. I finally move my feet and get dressed in my favorite pair of sweat pants and t-shirt. Cleaning Lady said it was about time for me to start wearing a bra. I asked her what it was and she showed me hers. I hope I don't have to wear one for a long time.

I tap on the door and then sit on my bed to comb out my hair. My door slowly opens and Isaac peeks inside before coming in and sitting in the chair. He asked the man for a chair a few years ago. It makes my room smaller, but it makes Isaac happy to not have to sit on the floor all the time. He's not supposed to sit on my bed, even though he usually does.

"Let's practice answering questions today." For the last six months we've been working on ways to make me not sound so smart. He's been teaching me some of the things he learns in school and we still keep it a secret, but he said that soon it will be hard to hide how smart · I am. He decided the best way to keep people from knowing was for me to not talk, but I have to speak when the man asks me questions. I can't answer the same way I would answer Isaac, so we practice and he tells me if I sound too smart.

"Okay. Ask me a question." I put my comb down on my table and rest against the wall behind my bed. I pick up Abigail and hold her in my lap.

He asks me questions and I answer. He tells me when I don't

hesitate long enough, or when I use too many big words and we go again. After a while, he picks up one of his books but doesn't say anything. I take the opportunity to ask him questions.

"How was your birthday party?"

He looks up at me quickly and then back at the book. "I don't want to talk about it."

I know he doesn't like his birthday, but he was excited about this one. He'd said his dad had agreed to let him invite some friends from school to the party. Something must have gone wrong for him to not want to tell me about it. "Why didn't you come visit me after?"

"I was being 'educated' and couldn't get away."

"What does that mean?"

"I said I don't want to talk about it, okay?" He sounds frustrated and rubs his eyes with his hands.

"What happened that night you came to visit me, but left without saying anything? Why did you punch my door and why didn't you come back until now?"

"Ang, I said I don't want to talk about it!"

"Did he hit you again?" I don't know why I'm pushing him to give me answers. Usually if he doesn't want to tell me something, I stop asking because he will tell me anyway a few days later. I guess I can sense that this time he won't tell me unless I push.

He laughs. "I wish that was all that had happened." He gets up and stands facing the wall with his back to me.

"Why won't you tell me what happened?"

He turns to face me. He looks mad. "Because you shouldn't have to know these things! You shouldn't even be here."

"I'm sorry I asked. Don't be mad at me." Tears prick my eyes, making them sting.

He runs a hand through his hair. It's long, but not as long as mine. He pushes it back with his hand, but it falls right back in his eyes. Sometimes he lets me comb his hair while he reads, but it never stays where it's supposed to.

"I'm not mad at you, Ang. I'm mad at this whole situation. I'm mad that you came here at all." The tears now fall down my cheeks and I hug Abigail tight.

"But if I hadn't come then I wouldn't have met you. Do you not like coming to see me every day?"

"No! Shit, that's not—you don't get it do you? It's not going to be this way for much longer, Ang. Soon you have to start your new lessons. The ones that teach you how to do the stuff you're really here to do. Now that I know what all you're going to have to do some day, I don't think I can watch that happen."

"What am I really here to do?"

He turns and kicks the chest that holds my clothes. It's loud and it causes Day Man to open the door.

"I was walking by and heard a noise. What's going on in here?"

"Nothing. This damn room is too small—my chair hit the chest by accident when I reached for a book."

Day Man looks from Isaac to me. "What's she crying for?"

"She wasn't listening, so I yanked her hair to get her attention. I guess I pulled a little too hard."

Day Man smiles and nods as he closes the door. Isaac looks at the closed door for a few seconds before looking at me again. He sits back down and hangs his head.

"Why do you think you're here?"

"Because the man asked me to come."

"But why do you think he took you in? What do you think is behind all those other doors you pass each time you go down to the bathroom?"

I have wondered, but I've never allowed myself to think about it for too long. The doors are always closed.

"I don't know. I—"

"Come on, Ang! You're smart. What do you think is behind all those other doors?"

In an instant I know the answer, but I don't want to say it. Isaac is looking at me and I know he won't talk until I answer him.

"Other girls like me."

"Yes. Other girls. And how do you think they got here?"

"The same way I did." I'm crying harder now and can only manage a whisper. He sounds so angry. I don't like it. I don't like knowing there are other girls behind those doors.

"Yes, they were bought, just like you!"

"I was bought? You mean he paid my mother money to take me?" Isaac had taught me about buying and selling stuff during one of my math lessons. He said people sold things to make money or to get rid of stuff they didn't want. But he talked about things like clothes and dolls and food. Not people. My mother must have sold me like a doll because she didn't want me any more.

I look down at Abigail. I always thought I had picked my doll over my mother. Suddenly I don't understand anything, and I throw Abigail against the wall before curling into a ball on my bed. I hear Isaac say a few words he doesn't want me to say before I feel him sit behind me.

"Ang, I'm sorry. I didn't mean to make you cry. This is why I don't want you to know these things." He rubs my back and it calms me. "Can I ask you something?"

I don't want to speak so I nod my head.

"Have you been happy here so far? Not counting the times when you get hit."

"I'm happy when you're here."

"Then how about we not talk about the other stuff? Let's enjoy being happy while we can." He lies down next to me and pulls me into a hug. I turn in his arms and finish crying into his shoulder.

I'm in bed, trying to sleep. It was only yesterday that Isaac told me there were other girls like me. Even though I think I knew all along, yesterday was the first time I let myself really believe it. I wonder if they all have dolls too. I wonder if Isaac goes to see any of them. For a reason I don't want to think about, that makes me mad. I wonder if that's where he was on those days he didn't come to see me. I wonder if they call him Isaac too. A tear leaks from my eye and I wipe it away.

I put my hand on the wall beside my bed. I wonder if the girl on the other side of the wall is doing the same thing.

Does she know about me?

For the first time since I've lived here, I talk to someone other than Isaac or Abigail. I know she can't hear me, but I pretend that she can.

Isaac is sitting next to me on my bed. I'm trying to concentrate on the math he's teaching me, but my mind keeps wandering. It's been a week since we fought. He asked me to forget about it, but I can't.

Every night I think of the others. I wonder how many there are. I wonder why we're here.

"Ang, are you listening?"

I look up and see him watching me. I want to ask him about why I'm here, but I don't want him to yell at me again. I look down at my arm resting next to his and decide to ask something else.

"Are you black?"

"What? Where did that come from?"

I point to my arm and then his. "In that book you showed me, about the different people, black people have darker skin. Your skin is darker than mine."

He laughs. "No, I'm not black."

"So if you're not black, what are you?"

"I'm white, like you."

"But you're not, see?" I raise our arms up in the air. I know he's smarter than I am, so I don't understand why he's confused.

He laughs harder and I feel my face get hot. I don't know why. "Aw, Ang, I'm sorry. Don't be embarrassed."

"I'm not embarrassed." We've had lessons on emotions, but I still don't really understand all of them. I could be embarrassed, I just wouldn't exactly know.

"I think you are. Your cheeks are pink." He touches my cheek with his finger and my face feels even hotter.

"Now I'm pink?"

He laughs harder and I try to get up. He grabs my waist and pulls me back down, holding on to me so I can't move.

"I'm sorry, really, I'll stop laughing. I just forget sometimes that you don't know basic things that everyone else takes for granted. And, it's okay to be embarrassed. It even happens to me sometimes."

"Fine, you're right. I'm embarrassed. Whatever that means. Just tell me why you say you're white when we don't have the same color skin."

"You are just *very* white, and I have a tan." I lean back into him, no longer interested in getting off the bed.

"How did you get a tan?"

I feel him shrug his shoulder. "Just being out in the sun." He gets quiet. He does that when he mentions something I've never seen before. Well, I used to see the sun when I lived with my mother and she let me look out the window, but that was so long ago it's hard to remember. I do remember it being really bright. And warm.

"Would I be tan if I were out in the sun?"

He chuckles and I'm happy that he's not sad any more. "No, you're so white you'd probably burn." I turn to look at him, scared at the thought of burning. "No, no, not that kind of burn. I mean your skin would turn red and it would hurt. That's called a burn." I relax at his explanation, but still don't like the idea of being burned.

He goes quiet again, but he doesn't let go of me. I know we should move. The way we're sitting would make it hard for him to get up if someone comes in. But I don't want him to move. I decide to ask my other question.

"Isaac, why am I here?"

He shifts behind me, but he doesn't let me go. Instead, his arms get tighter around my waist.

"I thought we agreed not to talk about it."

"But I can't stop thinking about it. When you're not here to talk to me, it's all I can think about."

"I'm sorry, Ang. I'm not telling you until I have to."

I turn my head so I can see his face. He doesn't look angry this time, but he looks the way he looks when the man hits me. I would rather he be mad than look like that, so I decide never to ask again. But it doesn't stop me from asking another question.

"Do you visit the other girls too? When you're not with me?"

"No. My dad says it's important for me to get into college, so I have to spend most of my time studying. He only has me with you because he doesn't trust my cousins."

"Why doesn't he trust your cousins?"

"That falls under the category of things I'm not telling you about."

"Then will you tell me what college is?"

"Remember how I told you I was in high school? Well, college is just another type of school that comes after that. I'm supposed to major in gaming management with a minor in criminal justice. After that, I'm supposed to go to law school. I'm told it will help me make the family business more successful."

"You sound like you don't want to do it." I don't understand much of what he told me, but I do understand the tone in his voice. It's the same tone he usually has when talking about the man.

"I don't want to have anything to do with the family business."

"Then do something else."

"I can't. Just like you can't leave here to go see the lights, I can't do something else. I may be able to be in the sun and go to school and see other people, but I'm just like you in many ways."

"When do you go to college?"

"Too soon."

"Will I still be able to see you when you go?"

"I'm going to UNLV, which isn't far, but—" He doesn't finish, and I don't want him to. I understand by the way he's looking at me. Instead, he does something he's never done before. He puts his lips to the side of my head. For some reason I feel my cheeks go hot again.

⁂

I never did ask Isaac again why I was there, and he didn't tell me until he had to. Unfortunately, that ended up being sooner than he'd expected. There was a timeline he'd been counting on, but life decided to shake things up a bit.

The new lessons were supposed to start after my twelfth birthday. From the time of our fight, that would have given us eight months to happily ignore what was to come. Turns out we were only given four months. An incident had occurred that—

19: The Incident

"I thought I'd check in on you before I leave for the night."

My back is to the door, so I didn't see the man come in. I try my hardest not to flinch, but my leg muscles twitch involuntarily. I know there's nothing I can do to stop him from touching me again.

"It's been five hours. Have you made your decision early?"

I don't respond.

I hear his footsteps walk in my direction. They stop just a few inches away. I anticipate his touch as I hear him crouch down next to me. His touch always starts off gentle—a way for him to make me drop my defenses, even if it's just for a split second.

He told me once that his pleasure is heightened when he's given that small measure of response to his tenderness.

The involuntary closing of the eyes.

The slight hitch in breath.

The goose bumps that travel across the body.

He's addicted to the high of having the power to take it all away in the next second.

His hand runs over the back of my hair in a feather-like touch. I stare at the wall in front of me, fighting against the instinctive way my body wants to respond. I force my mind to imagine how it will feel when he yanks on my hair. I assume I've been able to suppress the reactions he desires, because he suddenly turns me to face him and shoves my head onto the concrete floor. His mouth is set in a hard line, and he grips my face with his hand, squeezing hard.

"I'm curious where you've been these last four years. Something has made you resilient. I had shattered you once—no one is supposed to recover from that." He pauses and taps my nose. "But you . . . you found a way."

I pull my thoughts down and block my mind. I'm afraid I'll forget that I'm still keeping secrets and say something. I'm actually surprised it took him this long to ask where I've been. His reach is extensive, and I'm not sure what irks him more—the fact that I was able to escape at all, or the fact that I had remained hidden for so long.

He lets out a frustrated sigh. "Where have you been hiding, my little Angel? You might not have much time left to live, so just tell me. I'll consider giving you a gentler ending if you cooperate."

I close my eyes in response and start to count. He shakes me and I stop counting, trying to determine his next move.

"Say something!"

"My arms are numb." It's not what I intended to say. I didn't want to say anything, but I'm glad that's what my brain decided to purge from my mouth. It must have surprised him too, because he lets go of my face and suddenly stands. My eyes are still closed, and I hear him kick something next to my head. I don't understand his reaction—I expected that I would have been his target.

"Everything all right in here, boss?"

"I thought I told you to stay out!"

"Sorry, boss. I heard something and thought I should—"

"Get out!" I hear the door close. My eyes are still closed, and I hear the man walk away from me and then back again. I take a measured breath. I'm lying on my bound hands and it's uncomfortable, but the man's reaction bothers me more. Something isn't right. He doesn't seem in control. He's always in control.

I cry out when I feel the impact of his boot in my side. I was so lost in my confusion that I forgot to anticipate. The pain is sharp and I can't catch my breath. I try to roll to my side, but he's suddenly on top of me. His hand is holding my face again, keeping me immobile. His erection is pressing into my stomach, and my panic tries to surface. I push it away, knowing that I'll need all my strength to recover from what I expect is about to happen.

"Open your eyes!" I don't do it and he hits me. I barely feel it because my side is still demanding all the attention from my pain sensors. "Open your fucking eyes and I'll release your hands!"

I open my eyes, and I hate myself for it. He's looking at me, and I've never seen his eyes more dark than they are now. The corner of his mouth twitches. He reaches down with his free hand, and for a second I actually believe he's going to untie my hands. Instead, he lifts the hem of my dress. I close my eyes and start to count as a tear escapes from the corner of my eye.

I slowly open my eyes. He's gone. I'm still lying on my hands. My side hurts. My face hurts. I hurt where he penetrated me again. But now my arms are tingling. I shift to my side, and I'm surprised when my arm flops down in front of me. He actually cut my restraints.

I'm not sure what to make of this. He told me he would, but he doesn't make deals. I assumed it had only been a ploy to get me to open my eyes. His first pleasure is that split second of involuntary reaction to his touch. His second is my surrender through eye contact.

Over the years I'd come to see a pattern—he wanted me to believe everything in my life was a result of my own actions and not his. He'd given me the illusion of choice with the doll, making me believe I had joined him of my own free will. He hit me because I broke the rules, or because Isaac did. He violated me because I wanted it—or so he said based on that moment of eye contact. It would be a long time until I understood what was happening to me.

Rape.

While he was the first to succeed, he wasn't the one who introduced me to the concept. I suppress the laugh disguised as a sob trying to surface. I've come full circle—again. Before the man came in, my mind had been returning to that unpleasant night so long ago. For the past few hours, I'd been focused on the times when I was happy with Isaac. I'd rather think about those moments, but it won't help me make my decision. That's not what I'll be going back to if I choose emotional death over physical death.

Because let's face it, life is not a part of either of my options.

*　*　*

"Hurry it up in there. I've been behind schedule all day, an' I'm ready to get my supper."

I sigh and finish rinsing out my hair before turning off the water. I'm supposed to take my showers in the morning, but Cleaning Lady didn't come for me until after Isaac had left. She's never been late before, and I wonder why today's different. I turn and see her watching me.

"Well, what are you lookin' at?" I can tell she's angry by the way her voice sounds. I know I should keep my mouth shut, so I just look away and pick up my towel. "I swear, he keeps you girls so dumb it's like herdin' a buncha goats." She pushes me out of the shower and throws me my robe.

I think about her comment as I brush my teeth. It's the first time she's mentioned other girls in front of me. Maybe she thinks I'm too dumb to understand what she said. I want to know more about the other girls, but don't think it's a good time to ask her questions. Maybe I'll ask the next time I get to shower.

I just need to remember to sound dumb when I do it.

I glance at my reflection in the small mirror, and I wonder if the other girls look like me. Cleaning Lady cuts my hair once a month so it stays at my shoulders. Sometimes she's in a hurry and cuts it when it's still wet. Then, when it dries, the curls make it scrunch up to around my chin. When she comes to get me the next time, she curses and mumbles something about how she hopes the man doesn't come down for a visit because she'd get a lickin' for having my hair too short. I'm thinking a lickin' is the same as when I have to get hit.

I like how my hair looks longer when it's wet. Right now it's touching my shoulders, and I know when it dries it will only touch my chin. Cleaning Lady blamed me for cutting it too short this last time. She said I moved too much. I know she's wrong—I remember sitting real still because Isaac said he likes my hair longer. But I didn't correct her. I've learned that the sting of her cane hurts more when I'm not wearing any clothes.

I spit out my toothpaste and turn to face Cleaning Lady. She hands me my dirty clothes and leads me out of the bathroom. As we pass by the closed doors, I try not to think about the other girls. It doesn't work and I sneak glances out of the corner of my eye as we walk.

Suddenly, a door to my left opens and someone stumbles into the hall. It's a man. Or rather a boy. He turns and I can see that he's about the same size as Isaac, but he looks a little older. He looks first at my feet, then up my legs, and finally to my face. He looks a little like Isaac, but his eyes remind me of the man's. I decide I don't like him.

"What in the blazin' hell are you doin'?" Cleaning Lady rushes past me and slaps the boy in the face. As she reaches for the door, I look inside. The image is burned into my mind before the door shuts.

A dark room.

The light from the hall falling on the bed.

An arm, limp and bruised, hanging over the side of the bed.

Eyes staring, red and wet from crying.

Blood on the sheets.

"Now, now, Ma, don't get all worked up. I'm just sampling the product. Making sure the customers are actually getting what they pay for. Ironic, isn't it, that when I'm done they *won't* get what they paid for." He laughs as he walks slowly toward me. I step back without thinking and bump into the wall. He's so close I can feel his hot breath on my forehead. The smell of it makes my stomach feel funny. My heartbeat speeds up as the image from inside the room flashes brightly in my mind.

The touch of his hand on my bare chest is unexpected, and I scream in shock. His other hand clamps down on my mouth, and he presses his body up against mine.

My chest hurts where his hand is squeezing me—my heart pounding just underneath. Maybe he's squishing my heart. I try to move, but he pushes on me harder with his body.

Suddenly he's gone and I drop to the floor, gasping for breath. I pull my robe closed and look up to see Cleaning Lady slapping the boy's face.

"You stupid, stupid, stupid! What are you doin'? Do you know what would happen to you if he found out? What would happen to me an' your father? How'd you get in that room? Answer me, boy!"

"You must have left her door unlocked after her shower." He smiles as he says this and then starts laughing again. Cleaning Lady slaps him again and he pushes her, making her stumble to the floor.

"Don't you ever hit me again, you bitch!"

"You're drunk! Your father's gonna—"

"What the hell's goin' on back here?" I turn to see Night Man coming around the corner.

"I caught him comin' out of Daisy's room." Cleaning Lady isn't able to get to her feet, so Night Man yanks her up. "He's messed around with her! How did he—"

"Hush! Get that girl back in her room!" Night Man pushes Cleaning Lady in my direction. She pulls my arm until I stand up. The boy starts in my direction again, but Night Man grabs him by the throat. I'm being pushed and turned toward my room and can't see what happens to him. Cleaning Lady quickly opens my door and pushes me inside.

My door slams shut with a click. I stand and stare at it, trying to figure out what had just happened. I lean against my door to try and hear what they're saying. I hear the rumbles of voices, but no words. I turn and sit on my bed, pulling Abigail to my chest. I hug her as the tears start to fall.

I shiver and remember I'm still in my robe. I put on my nightdress and climb under the covers. I close my eyes and try to play one of Isaac's dreams.

But all I see is the arm, the eyes, the blood.

I hear my door click and I sit up, clutching Abigail to my chest. I see Cleaning Lady and relax, but only a little. She shuts my door and drops my dirty clothes on the floor. I don't remember leaving them in the hall. She turns and stands over my bed, looking at me.

"Do you know what you saw out there?"

I'm not exactly sure what she's asking, so I keep quiet.

"Damn it, girl! This is not the time to be mute. You answer me right now—what'd you see out there?"

I don't want her to start hitting me like she did the boy so I answer, but something makes me not mention what I saw in the room. "Just the boy. The one who grabbed me."

Tears sting my eyes as her hand connects with my face.

"There was no boy, you dumb little shit. Now, I ask you again, what'd you see out there?"

Tears try to escape my eyes, but I blink them back. I want to be confused, but I'm too smart. I know what she wants me to say. But if I give her the right answer too quickly, she'll know I'm not so dumb after all. She moves her cane into her hitting hand, and I brace myself for the hit I know will come after my answer.

"There *was* a boy. He grabbed me. He hurt my chest. You saw him too."

The sting is sharp on my bare arm, and my stomach clenches in response.

"There. Was. No. Boy! Let's try this again, an' remember—if you get it wrong again, I'll bring the mister in to teach you the right answer. What'd you see?"

"Nothing?"

"That's right. You didn't see nothin'. If I hear you sayin' anything else, the mister'll make sure you don't never speak again! You understand?"

I nod my head. She looks at me a couple more seconds before she turns and walks out the door. I hug Abigail tight and try not to cry. I look at my arm and see the red mark from the cane. I don't know how I'll be able to keep this from Isaac. We keep secrets together, not between us. There are some things he won't tell me, like what happened on his birthday, but I know that's not because he wants to keep a secret from me. He said he didn't want me to have to know those things yet.

I wonder if the thing he doesn't want to tell me has something to do with why the boy was in that other room.

Daisy's room.

I wonder if the boy will come in my room sometime. If that's what I'm here for, then Isaac is right—I don't want to know. But I do want to know. I think I need to know. I want to ask Isaac, but I can't tell him what happened, or Night Man might hurt me really bad.

I close my eyes and try to sleep, but all I see is the new dream I don't want to have. I open my eyes and count the brown spots on my ceiling. I keep counting until my eyes get heavy.

"Ang? Ang, wake up."

I open my eyes and look at Isaac. The happiness I feel every time I see him is there, but it's gone when I remember I have to keep a secret from him. I don't think I can do it. I close my eyes. Maybe it won't be so hard if I don't look at him.

"Ang, what's wrong? You never sleep this late."

He's right. I always get up early on the days he doesn't have school. He brings my breakfast and stays most of the day. But today is different because of what happened last night. My nose gets tingly and I know that means my tears want to fall. I turn away so Isaac won't see.

"Ang, you're starting to make me worry. Answer me, what's wrong?" He pulls back my cover and I hear him let out a sound. "What the hell happened to your arm? Were you hit with the cane?" I stay quiet and I feel him sit on my bed. "I'm not leaving until you tell me what happened."

I think about my words. The fake words I'm supposed to say are in my mind—I can see them and hear them—but I can't make them come out of my mouth. I can't lie to Isaac, but I can't tell him the real words either.

"I took too long in the shower." They are the only true words I can tell him. Even though they're not the words to answer why Cleaning Lady hit me with the cane, they are true. I hear him sigh.

"Does it hurt?"

"A little."

"Why won't you look at me?"

"I don't feel good." That's also true. My stomach knotted all night thinking about what I saw in that room. In Daisy's room. And about not telling Isaac the truth. It's all making me feel very sick.

I feel Isaac's hand on my forehead. He keeps it there for a few seconds before playing with my hair. For a moment I forget about everything else. The tingling starts at my head and runs all the way to my toes. I asked him once how he did that. He smiled and told me it just meant that I liked the way it felt when he played with my hair.

"Do you just want to sleep?"

"Yes."

"Do you want me to leave?"

I don't answer. I should say yes because I won't be able to keep my secret. But yes would be a lie, and I still can't make my mouth tell him a lie. My mind tries to count to keep my mouth from speaking, but I don't want to count because I do that when I'm scared. I don't want to be scared with Isaac. I'm about to cry when I hear him sigh and then put his lips to my hair. He leaves them there a few seconds before standing up.

"I'll check on you a few times today. I hope you feel better tomorrow." I hear my door click and now I do cry. I cry because he left and because I know that tomorrow I won't feel any better.

What if I can never see him again because of my secret?

I close my eyes and start to count.

I listen as Isaac leaves my room for the third time today. I pretended I was asleep. It's like a lie, but I didn't have to speak any words so I was able to do it. I didn't want him to leave, but every time he comes to see me I can feel the words trying to escape my mouth.

I roll over and look at the ceiling. I think about the other girl named Daisy. I wonder if she's feeling okay. I didn't like how she looked when the boy left her room—she looked hurt. Maybe she was just sad. Or tired.

I feel a twitch in my chest where the boy squeezed me. If he touched her like he did me, then I think he must have hurt her too. I wonder why there was blood on her sheets. She might have started her period early. Sometimes I don't know mine is coming, and I bleed a little on my sheets. It makes Cleaning Lady mad when she has to change the sheets early. But Daisy's bed had a lot more blood than mine do with an early period.

I try to forget my thoughts by looking over at the food Isaac left for me. Night Man should have brought it, but Isaac said he wanted to do it so he could check on me. My stomach growls because I haven't eaten all day. I get up and sit on the floor to eat my food. When I finish, I pee in my bucket. Day Man came to take me to the bathroom for my scheduled time, but I didn't want to walk by Daisy's room again, so I told him I didn't feel good enough to go. He was mad he had to empty my bucket, but he said he didn't want to clean up puke either, so he did it without hitting me.

I cover the bucket, push it back under the table, and climb into bed with Abigail. I'm not tired because I slept a lot, but my head hurts. I try to think about a way to tell Isaac what happened, but not tell him what happened. I can't think of a way, so I start thinking about how I can tell him a lie. I know it's the only way I can keep Night Man from hurting me and still see Isaac too. I hear my door click and I jump.

Night Man comes in and walks straight to my bed. He puts his finger in my face.

"You were told to keep your mouth shut."

"I didn't—"

The sting of his hand on my face stops my words.

"Did I say you could speak? I may not be as smart as some of the others 'round here, but I'm no idiot. I know you didn't say nothin'. But you're actin' all funny, making Junior ask questions he don't need to be askin'. I'll beat the life right outta ya and tell the boss you had it comin'. So you better get back to actin' normal while keepin' your trap shut, or tomorrow'll be your last day here."

He shoves my head against the wall before leaving and locking my door behind him. I sit and stare at the door and wait for my ears to stop ringing. I put a hand to my face and then get down to find the medicine Isaac keeps in my secret drawer. I swallow a pill and climb back in bed.

I think about what Night Man said. I have to find a way to lie to Isaac, or I'll never see him again. Not because I won't let him come back, but because Night Man will make me dead.

I hear a familiar noise, but it's far away so I ignore it and go back to floating. A louder noise that sounds like my door makes me open my eyes, but I can't see. I think I must be sleeping when I feel a hand on my mouth. I try to scream, but a weight presses on my body and I can't scream because I can't breathe.

Then I smell it—the smell of his breath—and I know I'm awake. I try to move, but he's too heavy.

"Hush now. If you stop fighting, it won't be so bad."

I hear something that sounds the way it did when Isaac tore his shirt that first time the man hit me. The hand on my mouth moves, but then I feel something else. It's on my mouth and it's holding it closed. I try to scream but it doesn't work.

"Somehow I knew you'd be a fighter, so I came prepared. We don't want my dad to interrupt us, now do we? It was bad enough that my ma had to find me with the other one."

My breath comes easier as his weight lifts off me, but then I'm flipped to my stomach. He pulls my arms behind my back and ties them with something so I can't move. I try to kick my feet, but I think he's sitting on them. He's too heavy to move.

My breath becomes short and hard. I hear and feel my heart pounding in my ears. I think my head is going to pop. I squeeze my eyes shut and try to count, but he turns me back over and I forget my number as he lifts my nightdress. He pushes it up over my face and now it's really hard to breathe.

I shake my head, trying to get it off.

"I was going to keep your light off, but I realized, you've already seen me. You already know who I am, yet you didn't tell Junior about me, did you? I guess my parents can be kind of scary sometimes." I hear his laugh and feel his hand move slowly down my chest. He pinches me hard and my body jerks up on its own. He pushes me back down and then takes off my panties. "Yeah, this time I think I'll turn on the light. I want to see how you look."

I feel him get up and I see the light as it comes through my nightdress. I shake my head again, but it won't come off. I can't move my hands. I remember I can move my legs, and I roll to my side. I put my feet on the floor but he picks me up and throws me down on the bed. I'm back lying on my hands and he's holding down my legs.

"Such a beautiful sight. No wonder men pay big bucks for you innocents. Too bad—someone's not going to get all they paid for with you, because I'm going to have you first."

His hands move up my legs. Then one is gone and I feel my bed shift. I hear a noise and I try to see what he's doing. My nightdress is keeping me from being able to see everything clearly, and all I can see is a dark shape that must be him. He pushes my legs apart.

My heart beats even faster. I close my eyes as tears make my nightdress covering my face wet. I don't know what he's going to do to me, but I know I won't like it. Somehow I know it's not right.

He lays back on top of me, and I feel something hard poking my leg. My breath is fast and short and a cry comes out of my throat.

"This might hurt a bit, but not as much as what's coming in the second round." His voice is right in my ear, his hot breath is on my neck. I think I hear a sound, but I can't tell over the sound of my heartbeat and his breathing.

"What the—" It's Isaac.

The weight of the boy is gone. I still can't see very well, but I know the sounds I hear—one of them is hitting the other. I hear Isaac yelling words so I think he's the one doing the hitting. I twist and turn until I'm sitting. I use my knees to get the nightdress off my face. Finally it comes off, and I turn to see Isaac punching the boy on the floor. The boy isn't moving and he's covered in blood. I put my face on my knees so I don't have to see.

"What's goin' on—"

I don't look up when Night Man comes in. I don't want to see anything. The hitting sounds have stopped. I hear another sound and my eyes open even though I don't want them to. I see Isaac holding Night Man up against the wall.

"If you value your life, or your son's, you had better go and get my father. Right now! If you're lucky, the only thing you're going to lose is your job. My father had better be down here in ten minutes, or I'll kill you both. Starting with him!"

"But, I think he's 'cross town. No way he'd be here in ten min—"

"I don't give a damn where he is—in ten minutes I kill that piece of shit you call a son!"

Night Man looks at the boy on the floor before running out the door. Isaac quickly turns and comes to my bed. He sits down and puts his hands on my cheeks. His eyes look like the man's and I pull back. Isaac's eyes aren't supposed to look like that. I close my eyes and shake my head, not wanting to see Isaac with those eyes. I feel his thumbs rub my cheeks softly.

"Ang, look at me. It's okay. I'm not going to let anyone hurt you. Will you look at me, please?" His voice is soft, almost too soft to hear. I don't want to, but I look at him. His eyes are back the way they should be and my fear goes away. "There's my girl. I'm going to take this tape off your mouth—it might sting." He yanks at the stuff holding my mouth shut and I cry out when it's gone. He then quickly reaches behind my back, freeing my hands.

"Isaac—"

"Shh, don't talk. They'll be back soon. You shouldn't say anything, okay? When they ask you questions, just nod yes or no. Understand?"

He's looking at me, waiting for me to nod so I do.

"I'm so sorry this happened to you. If he had—" He doesn't finish. Instead he puts his lips to my forehead. He pulls me into a hug and we stay that way until we hear the sound of my door.

Isaac quickly jumps off my bed. He stands right in front of me. At first I think it's to keep the man away from me, but I remember my room is small. There's not much room with Isaac, the man, and the boy on the floor all in here at the same time.

"Does someone want to tell me what's going on in here?" The man looks at the boy on the floor, at me, and then at Isaac.

"He was trying to rape Angel."

I can see the man's jaw twitch. His hands ball into fists and I shrink back against my wall.

"Tell me exactly what happened."

"When I came in, he had her tied up and was on top of her. I pulled him off before he could do anything."

The man looks at Isaac for a long time before looking down at the boy. "Then you beat him to a bloody pulp?"

"We're not supposed to touch the girls. He broke the rules."

"I think a couple of punches would have gotten the message across, then you should have called me and my men would have taken care of the rest. Don't you think that was a little extreme?" He points down at the boy while looking at Isaac again. I see Isaac shift on his feet.

"No. I think it might not have been enough."

The man raises his eyebrows and looks from Isaac to me. Isaac shifts again and I can't see the man's face.

"Are you back to protecting your young charge?"

"You said we're not to touch any of the girls. You told me not to let anyone near Angel. That's part of my job. She wouldn't be any use to us if he had succeeded in raping her. You couldn't bid out her first time. After what I imagine he was going to do to her, it's likely she'd be too scared to do anything at all in the future. I was told I'm to make her comfortable with sex. To do that, I can't have her fear it. Look at her." Isaac shifts again and the man looks me over. I don't like his eyes looking at me so I bury my face in my knees. "She's scared to death. He violated our rules and our trust. So, no, I don't think my beating was too extreme."

The room gets quiet and all I hear is the mixture of everyone breathing. I'm afraid the man will hit Isaac. I almost open my eyes to see why everyone is so quiet.

"Why were you coming to her room so late at night?" The man's voice is low. He didn't yell, but for some reason it makes my skin chill with goose bumps.

"She wasn't feeling well today. The last time I came to check on her, she was sleeping and wouldn't wake up. I wanted to see if she was awake. I was worried we might need to call the doctor."

"And you couldn't have called down to the desk to have someone check for you?"

"I did call—twice. No one answered, so I came down myself before going to bed."

The man gets quiet again. I hear feet shift and my door click. I lift my head, thinking that they left. Isaac is still standing in front of me, but the man is at the door. He yells down the hall and turns back to look at Isaac.

"Do you know how he got in here?"

"I found those on him." I see Isaac point to something.

"Son of a bitch." The man picks up the thing Isaac pointed to as Night Man is brought to the door by someone I haven't seen before. The man turns to look at Night Man. "Show me your keys."

Night Man looks at the thing in the man's hand. His eyes get real big. "I, I—I swear I didn't give him my keys. They're here on my ring. I don't know where he got those." Night Man reaches down and shows the man something. It looks exactly like what the man is holding.

"He's your son. Explain how he got a set of keys."

"He musta lifted 'em when I wasn't 'round. Had a set made for himself."

Suddenly the man has Night Man against the wall by the throat. "How many other rooms has he visited? And how am I supposed to believe he hasn't told his buddies? Maybe even made them a set of keys as well?"

Night Man's face turns red as he pulls at the man's hand. He looks like Rat did when he squeezed it. The man shoves Night Man at the other man I don't know. "Get him out of here. You know where to take him and what to do. Take his wife too. Get someone else down here to take out this trash on the floor." Night Man disappears out the door and the man drags the boy out by his legs. He starts talking to someone I can't see. "We'll need to change all these locks. Now. And we'll need to get Doc down here to check all the girls."

I look over at the spot where the boy was. He's gone—out the door with the man—but his blood is still on my floor. I look around my room and see that my potty bucket got knocked over and my pee is moving along the floor toward the blood.

I notice for the first time that my chair and table are turned over. My heart jumps and I nudge Isaac's leg. He turns to look at me. He shakes his head and tries to turn away again, but I nudge him harder. He looks at me and I dart my eyes to my table. He looks and quickly jumps to stand the table on its legs.

We both know the beatings wouldn't be over if the man found my hidden drawer and everything in it.

The man comes back in just as Isaac finishes fixing the table. "You can leave it."

"No, it's my mess. I should clean it up. There's no one else here to do it at the moment anyway."

The dirty clothes Cleaning Lady dropped on the floor yesterday are still there. Blood and pee got on them, so Isaac uses them to clean up more of the mess.

"We'll have to get her some new clothes. Some of these don't fit her any more anyway."

"The mop and bucket are down the hall. Go get it." Isaac stops and looks at the man. I've spent a lot of time with Isaac, so I can tell his mood just by the shift in his breath. He doesn't want to leave me alone with the man. Isaac hesitates one more second before walking out of the room.

The man turns to look at me. He grabs my face with his hand. His hold is softer than I expect and I don't know how to react. He runs a finger from his other hand over my face where the tape held my mouth shut. Then he runs his hand down my hair.

"Your hair is too short."

I remember that Isaac told me not to speak, so I don't. Isaac comes back, and I can tell by his breathing that he ran. He told me he does that sometimes when he sneaks down here to see me. The man turns and then sits down on my bed.

"Well, clean it up." We both understand that the man isn't going to leave Isaac alone with me. I watch as Isaac cleans up the mess.

18: New Lessons

I hear the sound and know that another hour is up. I've regained the feeling in my arms, and I use them to help me shift into a different position. It still hurts to sit so I lean against the wall, half on my hip and half on my butt. I'm tired and my eyes fight to pull me into sleep. Although the memories are painful, I don't want to sleep. These might be the final hours of my life, and I want to remember how I got here.

I need to remember.

I know that no matter how many pieces of the past I dig back up to inspect, it won't help me make a decision. I finally let the truth float to the surface.

I've already made my decision, and I need the memories to keep me firmly on track. I've been fighting it from the moment the offer left the man's mouth, but now the truth won't hide.

The incident with the boy—who had turned out to be Isaac's cousin—had been a trigger that set Isaac off on a mission. Isaac had decided he wouldn't wait the remaining four months until my twelfth birthday to start teaching me the things he thought I needed to know.

❧❦❧

"Again."

I fall back on my bed, trying to catch my breath. I don't think I can do it again. Isaac pulls on my arm, but I don't move.

"Ang, get up. You need to do it again."

"But my arms hurt. And my hands. And my stomach and my legs . . . and every other part of me."

"That's just because you're not used to it yet. It'll get better."

"You've been saying that for—" I stop to do the math like Isaac taught me. "—three weeks. It's not better."

I feel the bed shift, and I open my eyes. Isaac's face is right above mine. His hair is getting longer and it's hanging down, almost touching my forehead. I want to reach up and touch it, but for some reason I don't. I watch his eyes trace around my face before they stop at my mouth. He blinks a few times and looks at my eyes.

"Tell me this, what hurts more—your body right now, or when someone hits you?"

"When someone hits me." I can only whisper the words.

"Did you like it when my cousin tied you up and tried to force himself on you?"

The reminder causes my throat to close so I just shake my head.

"Then get up, and let's go again."

This time I let him pull me to my feet. He turns me around so I can't see him. I make my breathing real small and listen for any sounds. My mind tries to tell me again that my arms hurt, but I concentrate hard on listening.

I hear a slight shift in his breathing, and I think he's coming from my left. I'm right, but I'm not quick enough and his arms are around me. He pulls me to the floor so that I'm on my stomach, and my heart starts to race the way it did when Isaac's cousin was on top of me. I hold my breath and concentrate on the things Isaac taught me. I twist the way he showed me, and this time I'm able to turn around in his arms. I know he's going to try to lie on top of me, so I pull my knee up just like I'm supposed to do. I hear him groan and his arms loosen. I push out from under him and jump up on my bed. He's still on the floor.

"Isaac, I did it!" He just nods while lying face down on the floor. "Isaac? Did I hurt you?" I sit on the floor next to him and pull on his shoulder.

He turns and pulls me down to the floor. He's back on top of me, and he laughs when I let out a yell.

"I guess I forgot to teach you to never go back near the person once you've escaped."

"I thought you were hurt!"

"I tricked you. Sorry, I couldn't resist. Just like I can't resist doing this." I jerk and try to pull away from his hand tickling my side. I start to laugh. He tickled me for the first time last week. Now, he does it every time he visits. He stops before my laughing gets too loud. Day Man might hear and that would be a bad thing. Isaac lies down on the floor next to me and I try to slow my breathing.

"Isaac, what's wrong with tickling? I mean, when you do it I really want you to stop. My body moves and tries to get away without my mind thinking about it, but it makes me laugh and that makes me happy. So why would my body want it to stop?"

"I don't know. I guess sometimes even good things are too much for us to handle."

We stay on the floor, looking at the ceiling, without talking. I close my eyes and concentrate on Isaac next to me.

I feel his arm close to mine. We're not touching, but I can feel him. I hear his breath—slowly going in and out like he's trying to match it with mine. My skin tingles as he pushes his fingers between mine and then closes them, holding my hand tight to his. I hold real still because I don't want him to stop holding my hand.

"You're getting good at anticipating what's coming. I could tell you knew which direction I was going to grab you, but you're still not quick enough. And you need to be stronger."

"But I got out that time."

"Yes, but it will still help you to be quicker and stronger. Are you doing the exercises I taught you when you're alone?"

"Yes."

"Good. Do you think anyone has suspected anything? You understand that no one can know about this, right?"

"I don't think anyone suspects anything. And yes, I know it's a secret."

"Okay, good. I've been looking up some stuff at the library during my free period at school. I'm trying to find out how to make you stronger without making you *look* stronger. We have to be careful with this, Ang. Make sure you stick to the exercises exactly as I taught them to you. No more, no less."

"Okay." I turn my head to look at him. He's watching me. When he squeezes my hand, I blurt out the questions I've wanted to ask since we started my new lessons. "What happened to the boy? And Night Man and Cleaning Lady?"

"They're gone."

"Did they get fired? Is that what you called it that one time?"

"Something like that."

"You won't tell me?"

"No."

"Is Daisy okay?" I remember how mad he got when I finally told him about what happened that night and what I saw in Daisy's room.

"She's gone too."

I think about all the things the man has said before. "Did he sell her to one of the other places?"

"Yes."

"Will you tell me what the boy was going to do to me? Why I have to learn all this stuff?"

"You need to learn self-defense because it's important for you to know how to protect yourself."

"But why? Protect myself from what? What was he going to do?"

"Ang—"

"Please. I can't make the pictures in my head go away. Maybe it will help if I know." I had already told him how I see Daisy and what the boy tried to do to me in my head, and that they keep me awake at night. He called them nightmares. I don't want them any more. I don't know why, but I think they will go away if I talk about it. He looks at me for a few seconds and then turns his head to look at the ceiling.

"He was going to hurt you."

"I know that much. How was he going to hurt me?"

I watch his chest grow as he pulls in a big breath. I count the seconds until he lets it out slowly. I know he doesn't want to tell me, but he doesn't tell me to stop asking so maybe he will.

"He was going to have sex with you."

"What's that?"

He tries to take his hand away. I'm afraid he's going to leave and not tell me, so I squeeze to keep his hand in mine. He stops trying to move his hand, but he shifts so that I can't really see his face.

"Sex is what two people do when they . . . I don't know. When they like each other I guess."

"But if it hurts, why would they do it?"

"It doesn't always hurt. When it's done right, it feels really good. But when someone doesn't want to do it and the other person forces it, like what my cousin was going to do to you, then it hurts. Both people need to want to do it, or else it's wrong."

"How does it work? When it's done right?"

"Ang, I'm not going to tell you that. You'll learn soon enough when your 'sex teacher' starts your lessons on your birthday in a couple months."

"But why can't you teach me?"

He laughs instead of answering my question. It's not the same kind of laugh as when he tells me a joke or is tickling me, and I'm not sure I like it.

"Fine. Then will you tell me why I have to learn sex?"

He finally turns his head and looks at me. He slowly twists his body so he's on his side, facing me. He pulls my hand to his mouth before holding it to his chest.

"Because that's why you're here."

"To do sex?" He nods. "With who?"

"With anyone who pays for it."

I don't really understand what he means, but the hairs on my arm go up and get all tingly. "But what if I don't want to? What if I don't like the person?"

He opens his mouth, but nothing comes out. He pulls his lips in and bites on them. He closes his eyes and takes a deep breath before looking at me again.

"It won't matter. You'll have to do it anyway."

"But you just said that's wrong."

"Yes, it is." I watch as a tear slides over the side of his nose. It hangs there for a second before falling to the floor.

I pick Abigail up, hug her, and then put her back down on the bed. I don't know what to do, but I don't feel like playing with her. Isaac didn't come this morning because it's my birthday. I'm twelve now, and he said because of that I have to start my sex lessons. New Cleaning Lady told me to put on my new dress after my shower. I look down at my shoes. I don't wear shoes often, but I guess at twelve I have to start wearing them. They have what New Cleaning Lady called a heel. My old shoes didn't have a heel, but she took those away and gave me these. They make my feet wobble when I walk. I don't like heels.

I hear my door click and look up to see Isaac come in.

"Happy birthday, Ang."

"Thanks."

He doesn't speak for a few seconds as his eyes move up and down my body. "You look really nice in your new dress. Can I see it spin?" I stand and start to spin, but my foot falls to the side. It hurts and I fall against my bed. Isaac grabs my arms and holds me up. I look at him and see that I'm taller in my new shoes with the heels.

I like heels.

"Not used to wearing heels yet, I see. At least they're not very high. But, I guess no more spinning until you can at least walk in them."

"They make me taller."

Isaac smiles and laughs a little. "I can see that. But you're still very short." I frown at him and he smiles again. He pulls me tight to his chest. "It's okay, I like you short. Or tall. Either way, you're perfect."

He's still hugging me, and I suddenly don't want to go down to the special room for my new lessons. I want to stay in my room with Isaac and eat pizza and cake and talk about his dreams. He steps back and looks down at me. I look at the thing hanging down from his neck.

"What's this?"

"This . . . is a tie. We have to wear suits to special occasions."

"It looks like it's choking you."

He smiles again. "Sometimes it feels like it is. Here, I wanted to give you your gift before we went down to the other room." He opens one of the buttons on his shirt and takes out a small present. I take it and open the wrapping. It's a book. I can't read the name, but I try. Isaac helps me after I mess up the third time. "*Wuthering Heights*. I had to write a paper on it for my English class. I thought you might like it."

"What's it about?"

"You'll just have to read it and see. It might be difficult for you, but I'll help you." I open to the first page. He's right—I'll need his help to read this one. That makes it more special, because I like it when Isaac reads with me.

"Thank you." I put it in my hidden drawer.

"Are you ready?"

"I guess so."

"We have to be careful, Ang. This will be the longest time we've spent together in front of other people. I won't be able to touch you. I shouldn't even speak to you very much. I might have to act mean to you. I won't seem like the same person in there, but remember—it's only pretend. Only you get to see the real me, when we're alone. But you and me—our friendship—has to be a secret, so we have to pretend to be different in front of others. Do you remember what you're supposed to call me?"

"Boss."

"Yes, that's right. You've done a good job so far to not tell anyone that you call me Isaac. But tonight's going to be different. He'll be there and I have a feeling he'll be watching us. I don't know yet who you will be working with on your new lessons, but she should be there too. Just keep to our plan and don't talk too much. Also, try to look down as much as possible. When you have to look at someone, don't look for very long. It's important that you don't appear too strong or self-confident. We talked about that, remember?"

I nod to let him know I understand. He looks at me without talking for a long time. He suddenly leans forward and puts his lips to my forehead.

"I'm happy it's your birthday, Ang. Really, I am. But I wish we could stay in yesterday forever." He whispered it and I almost didn't hear the words. They make my stomach feel funny—kind of like it's happy and sad at the same time.

He's said a few times that things will change now that I'm twelve. I'll still get to see him, but not as much as before. Maybe not every day, unless he sneaks down to see me. Tears wet my eyes, and I blink them away.

He pulls away from me and opens the door. I follow him down the hall, the same way I go to the bathroom. When we pass Daisy's old room, I sneak a glance. I feel Isaac's fingers brush mine for a second, and then he walks faster to be a step ahead of me. I want to tell him to slow down because my feet wobble more when I walk fast, but I think he wants me to be quiet. We get to the end of the hall and he turns the opposite way of the bathroom. We pass more doors and at the end of the hall he opens a big door. I follow him inside and then stop.

The man is in the room, sitting in a chair by a table that has a cake on it. I'm excited about the cake, but I can't take my eyes off the man. Or at least not off the woman that's sitting on the man's lap. Their mouths are pressed together and his hands are squeezing her butt. It looks like she has on a dress, but I can see her butt so maybe it's just a shirt. Her skin is dark brown—now I understand why Isaac laughed at me when I asked him if he was black. It looks like her long, black hair is made up from a bunch of ropes. I saw rope once before— Isaac brought in a small piece and tried to teach me how to tie a knot. I never did it right.

I hear a giggle and take my eyes off the man and the woman. There are other women standing around the room—I count five. They are wearing clothes that don't look like clothes. One puts something to her mouth and blows out smoke. A cough tries to escape, but I swallow it back.

I suddenly have a flash of a memory from when I lived with my mother. She used one of those smokers. I remember her taking one from the man the night he came to get me.

There are four other men in the room behind the women. I know one is Watcher, but I don't know who the others are. They are all wearing ties like Isaac.

"Would you look at her? She's fucking adorable." I look back at the women, but I don't know which one spoke.

The man turns his head to look at the women. "Watch your mouth, Rosie. I like my women to act like ladies, remember?"

"Right, sorry. I forget sometimes." Rosie giggles again.

The man stands and turns to look at me. "Well, well, well, my little Angel. You're certainly growing up fast. I think you've somehow grown even more in the last two months since I've seen you." He walks over and stands in front of me. He looks at me for several seconds and it makes me want to look away. I don't like his eyes. I look down and I feel him touch my hair. "I see your hair has almost grown back to the right length. I had no idea those curls would remain so pronounced." He pulls on one of the curls and lets it go.

"The new lady seems to be doing a better job of following the rules." Isaac's voice sounds different—like it always does when he talks to the man.

"That's good to hear. Well, let's get started. I have some important business to attend to." I hear his footsteps walk away and I look up. He's walking back to the chair and then sits down. He stares at me while he smokes on his smoker. "Ladies, you know what to do."

I hear more giggles as the women walk toward me. I look over at Isaac, but he's walking toward the man. I stare at his back, waiting for him to turn around. He doesn't. The ladies form a circle around me, look at me for a few seconds, and then start touching me. They play with my hair. Tilt my head from one side to the other. Look in my eyes. Lift my arms.

I try to pull away, but they keep grabbing. When I try to pull away again, the woman that was sitting on the man's lap waves her hand at the others and they suddenly stop touching me.

"Back-up, you overeager hoes. Can't you see you're scaring the poor chit?" Her voice sounds funny. I'll have to ask Isaac why she sounds different when she talks. Now that she's not sitting on the man's lap I can tell that she's really tall. Almost as tall as the man. I look down at her feet. Her shoes have really big heels—maybe that's why. I let my eyes travel up her legs. She is wearing a dress, and I can't see her butt any more.

"You may be in charge, Roxy, but that doesn't mean you know everything." I can't tell which woman spoke, so I look at the floor.

"Haven't you heard? I *do* know everything. Why do you think I'm in charge of you skanks?"

"I assumed it had something to do with you blowin' the boss." I look at the woman called Rosie, recognizing her voice. She has nice eyes and a constant smile. Her hair is red. I've never seen someone with red hair before.

"That's enough. The rest of you come sit by me until Roxy makes her choice." The women turn and sit down on the floor by the man's feet. I look at Isaac again. He's still looking at the cake and all I can see is his back.

I feel a sudden chill on my back and wonder why Roxy pulled up my dress. "Lift your arms, love." I'm confused and don't move, until she pokes my back. "I said, lift your arms."

I do as I'm told and she pulls my dress off over my head. She pokes at my belly and then squeezes my chest like the boy did. She does it softly, but it still makes me jump. She then pulls down my panties. She lifts my right leg and tries to slip them off, but they get caught in my heel and I almost fall over. She steadies me and I hear more giggles.

"Are you sure she's twelve? She looks like she's only about ten." I again recognize Rosie's voice. It sounds happy, like she's giggling the whole time she talks.

"She's twelve. She's even started her cycles. Isn't that right, son?" I hear Isaac mumble yes to the man. Roxy pulls my legs apart and I look down. She's looking at where I go pee, like the doctor does when he comes to inspect me. I wonder if she's a doctor too. She pulls my panties back up and stands to look at me. I look back at her, but only for a second because I remember what Isaac said about not staring for too long. I look at the men standing behind the man. I don't like the way they are looking at me so I look back down at the floor.

"Looks like she's developing well enough—we should be able to pass her for older once she turns sixteen. Yet she'll still look young— the unusual hair and eyes, combined with her shorter height, makes her very unique. That should bring in high interest, and you've been trying to tap into that market for a while. This one just might be your golden ticket."

I don't understand anything she said, but I stay quiet. I look up and see the man watching me.

"What do you think, son?"

"I think she'll do all right. Depends on how she takes to the training." Isaac's voice sounds different again, but I don't know what it sounds like.

"I want you to look at her, son. Or have you already seen all this?"

"No, I haven't looked at her. That's against the rules."

"Well, now I want you to look. Tell me what you think—is she our golden ticket? Do we train her for a special role? Use her to attract all the men who fantasize about little girls?" Isaac still doesn't turn around, and the man looks like he's getting angry. "What's the matter? It's not like this is your first time looking at a whore naked."

Isaac slowly turns around. He looks at me, but not at my eyes. His cheeks look pink, like when he teased me about my cheeks when I was embarrassed. I don't know why he would be embarrassed to look at me. He sees me every day. This time I just don't have clothes on, but I don't know why that would embarrass him.

"I think she might be too slow to be really good. She doesn't learn well. I'm not sure we should invest too much in her." I know Isaac is only saying this because we're playing pretend. When we're alone, he's always telling me how smart I am.

The man stands so suddenly the chair tips and almost falls over. "I'm going to credit your poor assessment to the fact that you're new to this side of the business, rather than reading too much into it. I suppose it might also be because you've only ever worked with Angel. Now that she'll be learning with one of the ladies, maybe I should assign you to another girl."

Isaac looks at the man. I can hear his breathing and I know he's trying not to be mad.

"I don't have time for another girl. I need to spend more time on my studies. I'm graduating this summer, and I want to make sure my grades are solid before I start college. I thought school was to be my top priority right now. You gave me Angel because I needed to learn this side of the business, and I have. Although, it sounds like you think I still need to understand the value of what a girl like her can offer. I can get that by sticking with Angel. It's the best way for me to learn quickly—I won't have to take the time to learn a new girl and I'll be able to focus on my classes. Besides, I'd like to see why men would pay for her scrawny ass and mute mouth."

The man smiles. I've never seen him smile before. I really don't like it. "In this line of business, a mute mouth is about the best thing a girl can have. But you make a good point. I'll keep you with Angel, and we'll see who's right. I think you'll find that most men don't really care how well the girl performs if she looks young and innocent. In fact, if we use her for the child fantasy market, then the customers would prefer that she wasn't skilled. It's more about the fantasy than the reality." The man walks over to me. He puts his finger to my chest and touches me all the way down to my bellybutton. It makes me shiver and my stomach gets tight. The man's eyes look darker and I want to pull away, but I know that would make me get hit. "I'm looking forward to seeing how you develop over the next few years. Roxy, who are you going to assign to Angel?"

"I think you're right about the whole innocent bit on this one. She'll bring in more if she stays sweet. Rosie, she's yours."

The man nods. "Excellent. Rosie, stay and get to know your new protégé."

The man walks out the door and all the others follow, except Rosie and Isaac. Rosie's by the cake, running her finger through the frosting. She walks toward Isaac, holding her finger up with all the icing. She sticks her finger by his mouth.

"Want a taste?"

Isaac takes a step back. "No, thank you."

"That's not what you said on your birthday, sugar." She smiles and sticks her finger in her own mouth. She pulls it out slowly, staring at Isaac the whole time. "Or is it that you only like eating it from a different body part?"

I wonder what she's talking about. I feel my face get hot when I think about her getting to be at his birthday party and eat cake with him. And I don't know why he would want cake or icing on any body part. When we ate cake on my birthday before, he sometimes ate it with his fingers and then licked off the icing—but those were his fingers and not hers. Maybe that's what she means.

She steps closer to Isaac and runs her hand down the front of his pants. "We could get rid of the kid and have some fun. Or, maybe you'd prefer to have her watch." She leans in and bites on Isaac's ear. He pulls away and I wonder if he's hurt. Rosie seems nice, so I don't know why she bit his ear.

"Stop. Today's Angel's birthday and she was promised pizza and cake. Angel, put your dress back on and get over here." He doesn't look at me while he talks, but I can tell by his voice that he didn't like it when Rosie bit him.

I walk over to get my dress, but Rosie gets there before me. She slides it over my head and then smoothes down my hair. "You sure are lucky to have Junior as your daddy." I look at her confused. "What, you don't know who your daddy is?"

"I don't use that term. She calls me boss."

Rosie giggles and looks at Isaac. "I guess I can understand that. You are a bit young to have anyone calling you daddy." She turns back to look at me before walking over by Isaac. She slides her hand down his chest before sitting down. "Too bad he can't touch you,

Angel. Even with a lack of experience, he sure does know how to make a girl's toes curl. Speaking of toes, you all don't mind if I take off my shoes, right?" She lifts her foot and rubs it up and down the front of his pants, like she did with her hand before. He pushes it away.

"Take off your own shoes, Rosie."

She rubs her foot up and down his leg. "I need help with the buckle."

"I said no."

"Why are you being such a prude? I know you had fun with me. Is it because she's here? Like I said, she has to learn anyway. Why not give her a live demonstration rather than making her watch the tapes?"

Isaac looks over at me. It's the first time he's looked me in the eyes since we left my room. I see something in his eyes that makes me sad, but I don't know why.

"Holy shit! You like her! Oh, this is rich. You've got the hots for your little whore in training." Rosie laughs loud, like I do when Isaac tickles me.

Her laughing stops before I realize what's happened—Isaac hit her. He grips her face with his hand and pulls her up. A chill runs down my spine. He looks like the man and I don't like it. I try to remember what he said in my room—that everything that happens in here is just pretend. But he looks so much like the man right now it's hard to remember.

"You need to shut up. I may not be the top boss yet, but I still have leverage. If I hear that lie again, I'll see to it that you won't be able to use your mouth for at least a month. You don't get exclusive access to me just because you were given the opportunity to share in my birthday celebration. It also doesn't give you the freedom to say whatever damn nonsense comes into your head. I do who I want, when I want. At the moment, it's not you. So shut up and eat your food so I can get on with my day." He pushes her back down in the chair.

Rosie rubs at her face where he hit her and then puts a slice of pizza on a plate. "Come and get your pizza, Angel."

I slowly walk over to the table and sit across from Rosie. Isaac walks to the other side of the room and leans against the wall. He stands there with his arms folded across his chest, and his head down. He doesn't look up or speak again.

I sit on my bed and pick up Abigail. I hug her to me as I hear my door click shut. I don't look, but I know Isaac followed me in and is standing by the door. My room is too small not to know he's there, but I can also hear his breathing. I know he wants to say something, so I wait until he's ready. My bed shifts as he sits next to me.

"I'm sorry you had to see me like that. I'm sorry that I hit Rosie. She didn't deserve it, but . . . I don't know, I had this feeling she was testing me. I think she was asked to see how I act around you when he's not in the room. I had to hit her. If I didn't, she would have told him that I was showing a preference toward you."

I take a deep breath and look at him. My eyes are stinging from tears and I blink, trying to make them go away.

"Did it scare you? I told you it would all be pretend. I tried to not hit her too hard."

"You looked like him." My voice is only a whisper.

Isaac closes his eyes and puts his head in his hands. He rocks back-and-forth a few times. I reach out to put my hand on his back, but he stands up fast.

"I can't become him. I can't. I have to get out of this place before it's too late, but I can't leave you."

I don't know what to say so I keep quiet. He walks the few steps to the other side of my room and then turns to look at me.

"I'll be back tomorrow. We'll continue working on your new lessons." He walks out the door. He didn't say good-bye or tell me to play him a dream.

He didn't remind me to make a wish for my birthday.

I hug Abigail to my chest and put my head on my pillow. It's the first time I don't like my birthday.

17: Understanding

The knock on the door interrupts my thoughts, even though it's not as loud as the previous warnings. Goon must be getting tired of hitting the door every hour.

I try shifting to a new position, but decide it would be best for me to stand for a while. My arms still ache from their earlier confinement. Actually, everything hurts—but standing makes me feel a little more in control of my situation. I lean against the wall, and it helps.

I attempt to work some saliva into my dry mouth. I spit the small amount that forms onto the hem of my dress and use it to wipe the blood off my face. It's crusted on and feels disgusting. I wince when I press too hard on the cut beneath my left eye. My attempts are causing more pain than progress, so I stop.

My mind tries to wander, but I force it back to my current situation. I can't afford any detours on my hike through the past.

I think back to the day after my twelfth birthday. I had spent the entire night wondering about the exchange of words between Isaac and Rosie, so when he came to visit I started asking him questions almost immediately. I had wanted him to explain what Rosie meant by everything she'd said. What he'd meant by her participating in his birthday celebration. He never did tell me. Now that I'm older, and wiser from personal experience, I can make my own conclusions.

I'm glad he never told me.

Two days after my birthday, Isaac had arrived early in the morning carrying my breakfast in his hands and a notebook and pencil under his shirt. That was the day he started teaching me how to write. We would read through *Wuthering Heights* together, and I would have to write out the words I couldn't pronounce or understand. It was a way for him to teach me both at the same time.

My mind lingers for a moment on the book that communicated so many of our thoughts and feelings over the years. My mind cycles through meaningful quotes until my eyes start to blur. I shake my head and force my thoughts back to those months after my twelfth birthday.

Isaac would sneak into my room to see me as often as he could. It wasn't every day, and in the beginning I struggled on the days I didn't see him. When he did visit, we made the most of our time together. Since he never knew when he would be able to come back, he divided our time. When he first got there, it was all about reading, writing, and self-defense. Then we would spend the remainder of his visit talking.

The majority of my time without Isaac became absorbed by my new lessons. I spent several hours with Rosie, learning sex education. I remember the first time I had to watch one of the porn videos. I was intrigued and wanted to learn more. It's why the man started the lessons so young—he wanted us to view sex as a normal, even desirable, act rather than something taboo at our age. I'll admit, he had a good system to accomplish his goals. Rosie showed me videos, brought in props, showed me pictures—she even used her own body as a map for me to explore. The only thing she didn't use was an actual man. There were strict rules about not letting men be present during the sex lessons. The girls were to remain pure for their first time.

I also spent more time around the other ladies, the same ones that were at my birthday celebration. I usually remained quiet when we had our group sessions, and they didn't seem to mind. The main point of exposing me to the group was to make me become more comfortable around other people. It was difficult for me to socialize with others after having spent most of my life in a box, interacting with only a handful of people. I never did adjust to it well.

Isaac started at UNLV that fall. He had to live on campus, but he came home every weekend and made time to see me. Sometimes he even snuck back to see me during the week, but it didn't happen often. When he was able to visit, it didn't last long. He wasn't able to sit with me for hours, talking and teaching me new things. He only had time to check my progress on the lessons he assigned to me each week.

I thought I was losing him.

Three years passed and I clung to whatever time I could have with him. Rosie was nice and she made me feel happy when I was around her, but it couldn't compare to my time with Isaac.

I was fifteen when I thought I had lost him forever.

⁓⁕⁓

"Rosie, I want to feel what it's like to have sex. Or at the very least how it feels to be kissed." I've been learning about sex for over three years. I know all the positions, I know the different types of sex, but I don't know how anything *feels*. Based on what I see in the videos Rosie makes me watch, it must feel really good.

Rosie giggles. "Oh, Angel, if only I could show you. But the number one rule is no touching, and I'm not getting my sweet cheeks marked just to get you off. Besides, don't you touch yourself like I taught you?"

I shrug my shoulder. "Sometimes. But doesn't it feel different when someone does it to you?"

"Oh, yes. It feels amazing." She has the funny look she gets when talking about sex—her pretty blue eyes looking up to the ceiling, a smile on her lips that are about as red as the hair she's twirling around a finger. She shudders, and when she looks back at me her face has changed. "Well, at least most of the time. I'm not supposed to tell you, but there are a few johns who push it too far."

"What do you do when that happens?"

"Hold still and take it—and pray the next one is into normal shit." She stops and looks off into nothing behind me. She blinks her eyes hard and looks back at me with a smile. "I'm glad you're curious, because that means I've done a good job teaching you. But I'm sorry, you'll just have to be satisfied with your hand for now. It's not like you have that much longer to wait."

I'm told I'll have my first experience right after my sixteenth birthday. That's only two months away, but my body has been feeling funny these last few months. Every time I watch the videos I get a tingling sensation and my heart rate speeds up. Rosie told me that it's a good thing because it means I'm ready to have sex, but I still have to wait. She said that johns pay a lot of money to be a girl's first. The man is very strict on his 'no touching' rule. I ask her to tell me about her first time, but she gets quiet and instead tells me about a guy she had been with just that morning.

There's a knock before I can ask any other questions. Day Man opens the door a crack, but doesn't come in. "Time's up." The door closes.

"Looks like we're done for the day, Angel. I won't be here the rest of the week. There's a special high-roller in town and I was requested personally! Even though I'm in the upper circle of girls, I've never been to one of the private parties. Usually it's the same three girls that go, but not this time. I guess being the only natural redhead of the pack can have its perks. Oh, I'm so excited!" She claps her hands and bounces on her feet. "I hear that the girls who please the men the most get special gifts—like jewelry, dresses, shoes, and furs. I've never had any complaints about my performance, so I'm certain I'll get a gift! I'll bring it and show you when I get back."

She shuffles me out the door to the waiting Day Man. His eyes flick over me before he turns and leads the way to my room. I steal glances at the other doors we pass. Except for that one night with the incident in Daisy's room, I've never seen any of the other girls. I've used the forms of logic that Isaac had taught me to see if I could come up with some sort of pattern—the order in which we are taken to the showers or to our lessons. A few times, in rare moments of bravery, I requested an emergency trip to the bathroom. I'd fake stomach cramps or something so I could see if another girl was there during that time. There never was.

One time New Night Man refused to take me. I assumed it was because there was already another girl there. I didn't sleep much that night, my mind wondering who she was.

I'm brought back to the present when we reach my door. Day Man unlocks my door, and I go in to find my lunch waiting for me. I look at it, but don't touch it. I'm not very hungry at the moment. My body is too worked up after my lessons. I lie down on my bed and hug Abigail to my chest. My thoughts instantly drift to Isaac.

I haven't seen him in six months.

I close my eyes, knowing it will make the image of him sharper in my mind. His dark brown eyes staring back at me. His dark hair, probably grown even longer, falling over his eyes. His slightly crooked tooth that shows when he smiles wide.

My stomach knots and I have to open my eyes. Even though I'm not hungry, I eat my food for a distraction. It doesn't work and Isaac pops back into my mind quickly. I wonder what he's doing. Does he like his classes? Is he taking care of another girl?

Appetite gone, I push my food aside and reach under my table. I take out my now well used copy of *Wuthering Heights*. It's the first time I've looked at it in the six months since Isaac has been gone. I run my hand over the cover and think about how many times I've read it over the years. It's not a happy story, but it captivates me anyway. The first year after Isaac gave it to me, I read it simply to understand the words. Then I started reading it to understand the story. Now I'm trying to find any hidden messages—any reason why Isaac gave me this particular book.

He's given me several books over the years, so it's not the fact that he gave it to me that's intriguing. It's the book itself that's the mystery. Each book he gave me before increased in reading difficulty, but compared to this book they were all easy. This book is set in a different time and a different place with different words. It was hard to learn and then understand.

Then there is the story. All the other books had happy stories. Some were even funny. He told me once that he liked to give me books that would make me smile when he wasn't around. That's why I believe there's a reason he gave me a book that's so different from the rest.

About a week before he stopped coming to visit, I asked him why he gave it to me—his only response was a blush and a shrug of his shoulder.

I open the book and flip through the pages. Instantly I realize that it's not the right book. I look at the front cover again, but that looks the same. I turn the pages more slowly, looking for Isaac's notes in the margins. He often wrote the meaning of words I didn't understand right on the pages. It's been one of my favorite things about the book—it was like having a piece of him with me even when he wasn't here.

When did he exchange the books? Why did he do it? Just as a sob threatens to escape, I turn to a page with new markings. Part of a sentence is underlined.

"My great miseries in this world have been Heathcliff's miseries, and I watched and felt each from the beginning . . ."

My mind and heart race as I search further, looking for more clues. I read each underlined passage I encounter, trying to understand why Isaac marked them. I read through them all once more, and one takes hold of my thoughts.

". . . the thing that irks me most is this shattered prison, after all. I'm tired, tired of being enclosed here. I'm wearying to escape into that glorious world, and to be always there . . ."

Is this what he's trying to tell me? Has he finally left this place, and me, behind?

I can't bear the thought of never seeing him again. Confused and on the verge of tears, I put the book back away and climb into bed.

"I see you still sleep with the lights on." I open my eyes and see Isaac. His eyes are just above mine, his hair falling slightly over them. I must still be dreaming so I close my eyes again and roll over. "You don't see me for six months, and you can't even wake up to say hello? Have I officially been replaced by the always eager Rosie?" There's a touch of sadness in his voice that makes me believe it's not a dream. I never dream of Isaac sad.

I open my eyes again, turn, and reach out to touch him. He closes his eyes and takes in a deep breath when my hand connects with his cheek. "Are you really here?" He nods. I sit up quickly and wrap my arms around his neck, burying my face in his chest. "Where have you been?"

His hands hesitate, but then I feel them on my back, holding me tight. "I can't stay long."

I pull back to look at him. "Why haven't you come to see me and why can't you stay?"

He pushes my hair out of my face and gently tucks it behind my ears. "A new security system has been installed. There's now a camera on the entrance that leads down to this area. I haven't yet figured out how to get past it without getting caught. There hasn't been a legitimate reason for me to come and see you, with me gone at school and Rosie teaching you now. I was able to make some excuse today because your birthday is coming up."

"How long can you stay?"

He looks at his watch. "Ten minutes, maybe fifteen."

He settles against the wall and pulls me back to his chest. There are so many things I want to talk about with him, but wanting to know when and why he replaced my copy of *Wuthering Heights* is at the top of my list. Trying to figure out why he marked the passages has consumed me since I discovered them two weeks ago. In that short amount of time, I've been able to memorize each underlined word, but I still don't know what they mean. I know what they mean in the story, but I want to know the importance of those words to Isaac.

"I noticed you gave me a new book."

He stiffens and pulls in a sharp breath. "Yeah, I thought the other one was getting difficult to read with all the notes written in the margins."

"I noticed that you underlined certain passages in the new copy."

His shoulder shrugs behind me. "Just some quotes I connected with for one reason or another."

"Will you tell me what they mean to you—why you marked them?"

He's quiet and I can hear his breathing become strained. "Some day, but not today."

I want to push the point, but I can tell he doesn't want to talk about it. Wanting to enjoy the few minutes we have together, I let it go and change topics. "Tell me about your classes."

I feel him instantly relax. As he talks, his hand moves up and down my back. It never stops, except when he occasionally plays with my hair. I try to concentrate on his words, but the tingling sensation is back. It has all my attention and I start to wonder how it would feel if he put his hands in other places.

"Ang?" I blink and look up at him. "Did you hear me?"

"Sorry. My mind got distracted."

"What were you thinking about?"

He never talks to me about my sex lessons. I know he has to ask Rosie how I'm doing because she tells me that he does, but he never asks me. This is the only reason I hesitate to tell him. I don't think he wants to talk about it. But I don't understand why, and it's Isaac and I tell him everything. I shift so I'm sitting up and facing him.

"I want to know what it feels like to be kissed."

He opens his mouth to respond, but no words come out. He runs his hand through his hair and shifts on the bed. He clears his throat and looks away. "Why are you thinking about that?"

"I've been thinking about it a lot lately. I also want to know what it feels like to have sex, but I know I have to wait until my birthday for that. But I was hoping I could at least feel a kiss. Rosie won't do it, so I thought maybe you would."

He jumps off my bed. "No."

"Why not?"

"Ang, we're not discussing this."

"No one would have to know, unless the doctor would be able to tell when he comes to inspect me." I put my fingers to my lips, wondering if something would be different after a kiss.

"No he wouldn't be able to know if you've been kissed or not."

"Then why won't you kiss me?"

He grabs his hair with his hands the way he does when he's frustrated. "Because it's against the rules! You're not to experience anything with someone until it's your scheduled first time."

"Since when have you been against breaking the rules? How many secrets do we have?" I'm suddenly angry and I don't know why. I've never felt this way before.

"This is different!"

"Why? How can a hidden box full of secrets that break the rules be okay, but not a kiss that can never be seen?"

"Damn it, Ang, don't do this to me! Don't I already risk enough for you? I can't risk this! It's too big. The consequences are too high."

"Why? It's just a kiss!"

I watch as his shoulders drop. His eyes are filled with sadness that makes me want to cry. "If you really believe that, then he's already turned you into one of his mindless whores." He walks out of my room without another word.

I have no idea what just happened. Or why he's upset, or why I'm upset. I turn into my pillow and cry as I hug Abigail.

I hear the click of my door and I look, hoping it's Isaac. Instead I see Day Man with my breakfast. It's been six days since Isaac left, and I can't stop the tears from falling.

"You crying again? What's wrong with you? Are you having your lady cramps?" I don't answer. I just turn over in my bed and face my wall. "I called your boss and let him know how you've been carrying on. He told me I could take care of it if you got too out of control. Just told me not to mark your face since your time is coming up. Boy, I've never heard Junior sound so pissed before." Day Man laughs as he closes my door. My tears fall faster, but I keep them quiet. I never would have thought Isaac would tell anyone to hit me.

Rosie should have been back yesterday, but she didn't show either. Day Man just said she wasn't coming and he didn't know when she would. My room is no longer a comfort—the silence is painful, the walls are cold, the space is confining. This is how it feels to be alone, and I don't like it.

I try to think of something, but I have nothing to occupy my mind. Even the items hidden in my drawer don't satisfy me. They all remind me of Isaac. I try talking to Abigail, but I've come to realize her flaw as a friend.

She can't talk back.

I hear the click of my door but don't bother to open my eyes. It's either Day Man or New Cleaning Lady. I don't particularly care to see either one of them, so I pretend to be sleeping. I didn't eat the breakfast Day Man brought in earlier, and he won't be happy about the wasted food. I concentrate on keeping my breathing steady. I hear the sound my chair makes when Isaac drags it across the floor to sit down. My pulse quickens, but I don't dare look. It may not be Isaac and I couldn't handle the disappointment.

"Come on, Ang. I know you're not sleeping."

I'm so happy to hear his voice that my nose tingles and tears push against my closed lids. I turn my head and open my eyes. The first thing I notice is that he's cut his hair. It's short and sticking up in all directions. The second thing I notice is that he's holding a book.

I choose to acknowledge my first observation. "You cut your hair."

"I was told it was time I started looking like a man since I graduated college."

I sit up. "You graduated college? That means you're done, right?"

"Yes. I tried telling you this the last time I was here, but you had other things on your mind and weren't paying attention."

I feel my face heat up at his reminder of what I asked the last time I saw him. "But I thought you had another semester to go."

"As you know, I've had some extra time these last few months, so I took additional classes and finished early."

"What does that mean? Will you be spending more time here?"

"For a while. Then I'll need to go to graduate school. I'm not sure yet where I'm going for that. I have a few options."

I sit back against my wall and study his face. I can't tell if he's still mad, and I can't stand the thought of him being angry with me any longer. "I'm sorry I asked you to kiss me."

He closes his eyes and sighs. When he opens them, I see tears that he refuses to let fall. "Do you know why I was so upset?"

"Because I was asking you to break a rule. And not just any rule, but *the* rule. I know if we got caught we would both get punished."

He leans forward, elbows resting on his knees, and hangs his head. "That's not why I was upset."

Tears sting my eyes and I press my palms against them. If he wasn't upset because I asked him to break a rule, then it must have been because he didn't want to kiss me. A sob tries to push its way up my throat, but I swallow it down. I don't know why it hurts so much to know he doesn't want to kiss me.

"And it's not because I didn't want to kiss you."

My breathing stops. It's as if he could hear what was in my mind. I try to hold my other thoughts so he won't hear them too. I look up at him.

"Ang, I shouldn't have said what I did. I'm sorry. I didn't mean any of it, but you hurt my feelings when you said it was just a kiss. I got angry, and I took it out on you."

"Why would that make you angry?"

"Because for me, it wouldn't be just a kiss. It would be every wish I've ever made coming true in that one moment. And it hurt to know that it didn't mean the same for you."

He becomes quiet, but I don't speak. I try to process his words, but my mind can't put them together in the logical order. Afraid I'll say the wrong thing, I wait for him to speak again.

He's looking at me, his eyes sad and tired. "The way you were talking that day—you sounded so much like Rosie. It was just as I had feared. You changed with your new lessons, becoming who he wants you to be. I tried to keep it from happening, but I failed. I couldn't bear the thought of you being like Rosie and all the other girls, so I left. I gave up. This past week I tried to tell myself that I didn't care about you. I tried to convince myself that I could let you be just another one of his whores, and I'd move on with my life. When I got the call today about you crying, I responded the way I was expected to respond, and I tried to believe that I meant it. But it didn't work. I care about you too much."

He gets up and sits on the bed next to me. He looks in my eyes and then down to my lips. His thumb rubs softly over my bottom lip, making it twitch and my stomach flip.

"I want to kiss you, Ang. Very much. I can't stand the thought of someone else getting to do it in a couple of months. But I can't. If I did, he would know. Not because you would look different, but because he would see it in my eyes when I look at you. He'd see it in my anger when I have to let someone else touch you. And he would know. If I kissed you, I'd no longer be able to hide my biggest secret of all, and you'd be gone. Sold or traded to another organization. I can't let that happen." By the end he's whispering and my heart is beating so hard I can barely hear him.

He stands and turns toward the door. "I'll try to visit again before your birthday. Rosie should be back with you tomorrow. Just try to still be my Ang the next time I see you, and not another Rosie." Before he leaves, he drops the book he's holding on my bed. The click of my door takes him away from me once again. I look down at the book he left.

Wuthering Heights.

I didn't hear him get in my hidden drawer, so it must be yet another copy. I quickly pick up the book and search the pages. I pause when I see an underlined passage. It's one that wasn't marked before.

". . . he's more myself than I am. Whatever our souls are made of, his and mine are the same . . ."

I process the words and then search for more. I read each new quote, lingering over the last one I find.

"If he loved with all the powers of his puny being, he couldn't love as much in eighty years as I could in a day."

In the silence of my room I think about his words, or rather the words in the book. I know now why he gave it to me. He wanted me to understand love. A love so deep you would risk everything, because without it you would not exist.

He's trying to tell me that he loves me.

But could I be in love with Isaac? I've barely existed in the six months I didn't see him. And he's right—I have been acting more and more like Rosie. It was easier to be like her than be the version of me that existed without him. It hurt not to see him or talk to him, so I focused on the things she taught me. I replaced his stories of lights, and school, and wishes with those of sex, and gifts, and more sex.

I close my eyes and concentrate on how I feel when I'm with Isaac or when I think about him.

It doesn't take me long to figure out the truth, and my body is overcome with a lightness I've never before experienced.

Now that I understand, I'm not sure I'll be able to look at Isaac the same way. I'm not sure if I can listen to Rosie say how she wishes 'my daddy' would let her do to him all the things she teaches me.

I've forced him to let me in on his biggest secret and now we're in danger of being discovered.

The first thing I notice when I walk into the room is Rosie sitting in front of the television, eyes focused on the blank screen, with the smoke from her cigarette floating around her. This is the only clue I need that something is wrong. She's always doing something while she waits for me—dancing to music, playing with the props, looking through the stack of videos. When I come in she doesn't always stop what she's doing, but she immediately starts talking. Today she acts as if she doesn't even know I'm here. Not wanting to startle her, I call from across the room.

"Hi, Rosie. I'm glad you're back."

She's quiet for a few seconds before she pats the open space on the couch next to her. "Come sit. We have some catching up to do."

I do as I'm told, but sit facing her and not the television. I expect she'll want to tell me all about the special party before we watch any videos. "How was the party? Did you get a gift?"

She's not looking at me and her hair is hanging down so I can't see her face. "I got a few gifts." It's not said with the level of excitement I expected. She takes a long drag on her cigarette and blows the smoke out slowly. "Stop with your questions. We have work to do." She presses play on the remote. I'm confused by the way she's acting. Maybe she's been sick and still doesn't feel good.

An image comes on the screen and I notice it's a video she hasn't shown me before. A man appears and leads a woman to a bed where he ties her hands and feet to the four corner posts. Next he blindfolds her and checks the tension of the ropes. Something in me instantly turns as I'm reminded of when Isaac's cousin tied me up. The growing knot in my stomach makes me want to turn away, but I can't. There's a larger part of me that wants to see what he's going to do to her. It starts with one man and the knot in my stomach starts to go away as they perform an act I've now seen many times.

But then another man comes in. In just a few minutes there are more men and they are doing many things to her at the same time. She doesn't look like she's enjoying it. She looks like she's in pain and just wants it all to be over. My stomach clenches and I think it's possible I might throw up. I stand and turn to walk away.

Rosie pauses the video. "Sit down, Angel." The tone of her voice surprises me.

"I don't want to watch that—"

"Sit down, or I'll call someone in here to beat you until you do."

"Why? I thought you were supposed to teach me what to do. It's not like—"

Rosie stands suddenly and steps in front of me. She's in her heels and it makes her a lot taller than me. For the first time since I arrived I can see her face. Her lip is cut and her left eye is bruised. I can tell she used make-up to hide it, but I can still see it. There are marks around her neck—marks that I recognize from when the man held Isaac by his throat. She puts her cigarette to her mouth and I see a red mark that circles her wrist. A chill runs down my spine as understanding sets in.

"I *am* teaching you. I wish someone had shown me this particular video before the 'special party' I was invited to. It wouldn't have changed what happened, but at least I would have been prepared. So sit down."

She rewinds the video and pushes me back down on the couch before she presses play. Instead of sitting next to me, she goes to sit at the table. Now that I understand things clearly, I study her more closely. I see the way her hand shakes as she puts the cigarette to her mouth. How she sits slightly on her hip, as if it hurts to sit down the right way. How her body shudders each time the woman on the video cries out. I realize that this is the first time I've seen the real Rosie. The giggling, smiling, dancing Rosie is a fake—a pretend person to help her accept her life. The way Isaac pretends to be someone different when we're not alone. The way I was pretending to be like Rosie so it wouldn't hurt so much to not be with Isaac.

I see it all now. I see why Isaac was trying to protect me from these things. Why he wouldn't tell me what I would be forced to do. Why he won't talk to me about my lessons with Rosie. Why he was upset when I told him it was just a kiss. Why he said I was turning into a mindless whore.

I also see what Isaac won't risk. Why the consequences are too high. It's not about not kissing me because he won't break the 'no touching' rule. I'm told that's *the* rule—the most important one. But that's not right.

The most important rule is that there can be no love.

Love is never mentioned in my lessons. It's never spoken of in the videos. I don't see it between Isaac and the man. In fact, I've noticed that Isaac never refers to him as his father any more. He's become as nameless to his own son as he is to me. I don't see love between the other women when we have our gatherings. I don't see love anywhere.

Except when I look at Isaac.

Isaac was right—it wasn't just a kiss I was asking him to give me. It was everything.

* * *

Isaac was able to make up reasons to visit me a few more times before my birthday. Although with the new security cameras, he was never able to sneak down for extended visits. My new understanding of the situation had made our time together different. I was desperate to remember every detail of those moments together. I watched him differently, noticing that he watched *me* differently. He held me closer, tighter, longer. Many times we didn't talk at all. We just sat on my bed, wrapped in each other's arms.

Before this new understanding, Rosie had me counting down the days until my birthday with excitement and anticipation. I couldn't wait to finally explore this new world I was learning so much about. After, I counted down with dread. I didn't want anyone but Isaac to touch me.

Because I knew.

I knew that as soon as someone else did, he'd never look at me the same way again.

16: Sweet 16

I'm starting to resent the warning at each hour. Not because it reminds me that I'm sixty minutes closer to the end, but because it interrupts the flow of my thoughts. The memories are getting more painful, and each time it's harder to start thinking about them again. It would be so easy to just go to sleep right now. To let my mind play all the dreams Isaac gave to me one last time, before it goes blank forever.

But my life has never taken the easy path, so there's no point in starting now.

I walk a few steps around the room they have me locked in, and then stop to look up at the windows. They're too high to reach. Even if I were the average height of most women, I wouldn't be able to reach them. I look around and take note of what's in the room. It's getting dark and soon I won't be able to see very well. Mostly it's broken crates and skids. I move a pile of boxes around and find a bucket. I want to laugh at the irony of it all. Instead, I use the bucket to relieve myself as I've done so many times in the past. When I'm finished, I push it aside and look under another pile of boxes. I find two more buckets. I take one over and place it upside-down under the windows. I stand on it and reach up.

Still too short.

I go over and inspect the crates. They are rotted and broken—not useful in gaining leverage to reach the windows. I break off a piece of wood from one of the skids. I might be able to use it to fight my way out the next time someone opens the door. I foolishly let my mind strategize for a few minutes before I realize how stupid the idea is. There's no way the man will risk letting me escape a second time. He wouldn't leave me here with Goon as the only guard. There's bound to be others, and they'll have guns. My small plank of rotted wood would get me nothing but a severe beating.

Because they wouldn't kill me. No, the man won't allow that to happen. I've been given a choice, and he will only let them kill me if I choose death once my time is up.

I toss the piece of wood off to the side in frustration. I want to slam it against the wall over and over again until my hand splinters from the effort. While that would release some of my anger, it would only cause Goon to come in and use it on me in return. I'd like to make it through the rest of my life without another beating. There are only a few hours left, so surely I can accomplish that much.

I push the bucket up against the wall and sit down. I miscalculate my position and land on the hard edge of the bucket. Pain shoots up my spine and I bite back a cry. When the pain reduces to a dull ache, I look down at my hands. I try to rub out the blood with my dress, but it remains. I feel the urge to cry, and I long to have Abigail and hold her to my chest. The need is almost crushing, and I force myself to think of something else before I lose my mind.

I had been thinking about the time I realized that I loved Isaac and he loved me. I take my mind back to that moment. I linger on it for a while before going a short time forward to a few days before my sixteenth birthday. I knew for a long time that things would change once I turned sixteen. Isaac and I had tried to accept it, but neither of us could have anticipated what would actually happen.

⁂

I hear the click of my door and look up to see Isaac. He's wearing a large Christmas sweater and I smile. Whenever he wears a sweater or sweatshirt, he has something for me.

"What's under the sweater?"

I expect him to smile, but he doesn't. "Nothing yet. I wore it so I could remove the items from your drawer." I watch as he bends under my table and starts tucking items under his sweater. I want to tell him to stop, but I'm too confused to say anything. I finally force words out of my mouth when he takes out my copies of *Wuthering Heights*.

"Stop! Why are you taking my things?"

He looks at one of the books in his hands and opens it to one of the marked pages. I watch his eyes read a few lines before he closes it. He stands and tucks it under his sweater. "I'm sorry, Ang. I have to take them. You're getting a new room after your birthday, and if they find these items then something very bad will happen to both of us."

My lip starts to shake. "But . . . but they're all I have. Besides Abigail, they're all I have when you're not here."

He closes his eyes and lets out a sigh. "I know. I don't want to take them, but I don't know when they're going to move you. They'll clean out your room, getting it ready for the next girl. I have to take them. I'll be back for the drawer later. I can't take it all at once without someone noticing." He steps over and gently wipes the tears from my face. His eyes flick over to Abigail on the bed next to me.

I grab her and curl her to my chest. "No. You can't take her."

"I don't have to take Abigail. He knows you have her so it's not a problem."

I can hear it in his voice. There's something he's not telling me. "What? Tell me, Isaac."

"There's a good chance he will take Abigail away from you when you get a new room. You'll be expected to act like an adult, and that means no more dolls."

My heart feels like it might burst. The tears are so thick I can't see clearly past the blur. "No, no, no. He can't take her. She's all I have."

Isaac kneels in front of me and wipes my tears again. "You have me, Ang. You'll always have me."

"No, you can't come every day. And when you do come, you don't stay long. We don't get to talk like we used to. You haven't played me a dream in years. Now you've taken the things in my drawer. Abigail is all I have."

"Don't you see? That's what he wants. He makes you stay in this hole for years, with little more than what you need to stay alive. You're an investment to him, so he keeps you healthy—but he restricts your food. He keeps you from seeing any of the other girls to limit the number of people you can form an attachment to. After your birthday, he's going to take away everything that reminds you of this place and give you so much more. As soon as you start working, he'll give you gifts, you'll attend parties with the other girls, you'll eat more food than you can imagine. He wants you to experience a dramatic change where the luxuries in your life improve by leaps and bounds, simply because he wanted it to happen. He'll try to make you believe he had nothing to do with this part of your life. Why do you think he never comes down here, except for the celebrations or if there's a major issue? He doesn't want you to associate him with this place. He wants to make you depend on only him for your happiness. Even if she's just a doll, she's a threat to your dependence on him."

"What about you? You would remind me of this place—does that mean he's going to take you away from me too?"

"He's going to try. That's the way things are done around here. But I won't let him, Ang. I don't know yet how I'm going to do it, but I'll figure something out. I'm his son—and his expected successor— so I have some latitude. I'll figure it out."

I look at Abigail. "Can you take her? Hide her for me so he can't take her?"

"I wish I could, but he knows you have her. It would be suspicious if she suddenly went missing. We don't want to give him any reason to check into us. But I promise that I'll find her after he takes her away. The dolls have to go somewhere. I'll find Abigail and keep her safe for you." He pauses and looks at his watch. "I have to go. I'm sorry, Ang." He kisses the top of my head and walks out the door.

I adjust my dress again. Something's poking my back and I want to scream. It's not the kind of dress I usually wear. It's the kind of dress Rosie wears. It shows a lot of my skin, and New Cleaning Lady said I can't wear a bra with it. Although, I'm not sure why I need to wear a bra at all. Nothing seems different when I put one on. I look down and pull on the two sides of my dress, hoping to cover up some of my chest. It doesn't work. I rub my lips together. New Cleaning Lady put make-up on my face and it feels funny.

I look over at Abigail. I want to hug her, but I'm trying to let go of her. I'm hoping that if I start the separation now, then it won't hurt so much when she's taken away.

I hear the click of my door and see Isaac come in. He's wearing a suit and tie again, and it makes my heart skip a beat. I stand, knowing it's time to go.

Isaac looks over my new dress. "Wow, Ang. You look . . . different. It's not exactly the dress I'd want you to wear, but you look really pretty."

"Why do we have to wear dresses like this?"

His cheeks go a little pink. "It's what men like to see." We become quiet, knowing we have to go, but not wanting to leave. Isaac reaches into his pocket and takes out a small box. "Happy birthday, Ang."

I open the box. It's beautiful. "They're wings."

"Every angel needs a pair of wings. How else are you going to fly far away from this place?"

I run my finger over the small pair of wings. They're shiny and smooth. "Where am I going to put them?"

"I've been thinking about that. It's actually a charm, for a bracelet, but obviously you can't wear it like that. So, I also got you these." He holds out another box. I open it and find several headbands inside. "This gift was approved—it's your special birthday and I'm allowed to give you a gift—so it's okay for others to know you have them. I'm just supposed to tell you that they came from him and not me. Anyway, I've cut a small hole in the fabric on each headband." He takes out one of the headbands and shows me the hole on the inside. He then takes the charm from me and slips it inside. He shows me how to get it out before he puts it back in.

I put the headband on and can feel the charm, but it doesn't hurt. I take the headband back off, knowing I can't wear one to the party. I tried to put on the one I already have, but New Cleaning Lady told me I couldn't wear it today. Not with this dress. I place the new headband in the box with the others and set it on my table. "Thank you."

"I wish I could give you more." He looks at me and blinks his eyes fast a few times. "There's so much I want to say to you, Ang, but I won't because that would feel like saying good-bye. So I won't say anything, and then I'll have to find a way to see you again."

I feel the tears coming, so I close my eyes and take a deep breath. I can't cry right now. This party is supposed to be bigger, with more people. They will all be looking at me and I can't cry.

Isaac takes my hand and gives it a squeeze before letting go. "Ready to go play pretend?" I nod and he leads the way down to the room where I meet with Rosie every day. We walk slower than usual, and I know it's because neither of us want to go where we're headed.

I glance at the other doors as we pass. My room is near the end of the hall, and over the years I've continued to try not to think about the other girls. But I wonder. I wonder about their age, how they got here, if they know why they're here. I know from Rosie that all the girls in training have a boss, or in her terms a daddy. Once we turn sixteen, only the man will manage us with Roxy in charge when he's not around. Going forward, Isaac is only supposed to see me on certain special occasions. Isaac has always been able to find a way to see me, except for the six months I didn't see him earlier this year. I have to believe he'll still find a way. There's simply no other option. I'm not sure I can survive this place and what I'll have to do without him.

My palms feel sweaty and I wipe them on my dress. I'm worried that I'll say or do something that will make people see the new secret that Isaac and I have.

We reach the door and Isaac hesitates a second before opening it and stepping inside. There are so many people, I don't know where to look. My eyes finally find Rosie and I relax slightly. She's smiling at me, but not in her usual happy way. The marks on her face and neck are gone, but not the sad look in her eyes. She walks over to me.

"Happy birthday, Angel! Welcome to the family. Look at you in that dress and your make-up! Junior here is going to have a hard time keeping dogs off you tonight." She giggles. If I hadn't spent the last few years alone with her for several hours a day, I would have never known she wasn't truly excited. But I can hear the difference. Something in her changed after the 'special party' she attended. "Come along, let's get you introduced." She takes a drag of her cigarette before grabbing my hand and pulling me behind her.

I'm lost in a sea of faces and names. Some I know, like Roxy and the other girls from our group sessions, but there are more girls— some not much older than me. And there are many men. I recognize two from my twelfth birthday party. Some of the men are older, like the man, and some are a similar age to Isaac. All of them look at me in a way that reminds me of the man. I don't like any of them. I want to find Isaac and stay by his side, but I know I can't.

I look around the room and realize that the man isn't here. He was at all my other birthdays, so I assumed he'd be at this one. I haven't seen him since my last party when I turned fifteen.

I finally get the nerve to look for Isaac while Rosie is talking to someone, and I see him talking to Roxy. He looks confused.

I turn at the sound of the door suddenly slamming open. The room goes completely quiet as the man enters, followed by Watcher. They walk fast in my direction, and my pulse quickens with each step closer. When they're almost to me, I realize with relief that the man's not looking at me.

I hear Rosie scream. Something wet hits my arm and face. I look at my arm and see drops of blood. My dress is red so I can't tell, but I assume there is blood on it too.

Suddenly people are moving. Some are moving away from Rosie and the man, and some are moving toward them. Someone pulls on my arm and without looking I know that it's Isaac. I let him pull me away.

I look to find Rosie, but the man is blocking her from my view.

"Did you really think your plan would work? You stupid whore. Don't you realize what kind of control I have?" The man turns around, dragging Rosie by the hair with him. Blood is running down her face. A lot of it. "Let this be a lesson to all you girls. I own you. You don't even get to take a shit unless I say it's okay. Rosie here thought she could run off with one of her regulars. Probably thought he'd marry her pathetic ass. It's too bad he's not in a position to take her anywhere now." He shifts and gives Rosie a punch to the face. She falls to the floor with a loud thud and doesn't move. "Get her out of here and finish taking care of her." Two men drag Rosie out the door.

The room is quiet. I feel my legs start to shake. I feel my throat tighten.

I want to know where they're taking Rosie and what's going to happen to her. I close my eyes and start to count, needing to gain control over my emotions. Isaac pulled me behind some people, so I don't think the man can see me. I'm too short, even wearing heels, but if I don't get control over my emotions he'll be able to hear me. I'm starting to breathe easier, and I focus back on the man's voice.

"Is there anyone else here interested in choosing a new life? If you speak up now, your punishment won't be as bad as when I find out later. Because I will find out. I have eyes and ears everywhere. There's no limit to my reach, I can promise you that. You belong to me, and as long as you respect that you'll be treated well. When you disrespect me, the way Rosie did, you will be punished. It's that simple. Now I ask again, is there anyone else who's making plans for a new life?"

I suddenly realize that I want a new life. I don't want to be hit, or live in a room without a window. I don't want my only friend to be a doll who can't talk back. I don't want to wonder about the girls behind the other doors. I don't want to have to do the things I saw in the videos.

I want to be able to be with Isaac all the time. I want to go and see the lights whenever I want. I want Isaac to be able to go to school for whatever he wants. I want to see the ocean with Isaac. I want to read books.

But I don't speak up. Isaac told me that everything we do in front of other people has to be pretend, and I trust him to know what's best. So I pretend that this is the life I want. I look around and no one else speaks up either.

"Good. Now, where's the birthday girl?"

I know I should move. The man might hit me like he did Rosie if he has to ask again, but I can't make my feet move. A shove on my back sends me forward, tripping on my heels. There are some soft giggles around me. The man looks at me and I see his jaw tighten.

"Son, Roxy!" I stand completely still. The man sounds as angry as he did when he was talking to Rosie. I hear Roxy step up to my left, heels clicking the tile, and Isaac to my right. The man looks from one to the other and then points at me. "Why in the *fuck* does she still look like she's twelve?"

Roxy tugs on my dress. "I had hoped the dress would age her up a bit."

"Well it didn't work, did it? Son, what do you have to say?"

"She looks about the same as she did last year, except the dress."

"Great fucking observation. Glad to see my hard earned money went to good use at that university of yours."

"I'm not sure I get the issue. I thought the entire strategy for Angel was to make her appear young and innocent. I was under the impression that's what was going to bring in the big money—men paying for the illusion of being with a child." I can hear the edge in Isaac's voice when he talks about men paying for me.

"Yes, they will pay a mountain of cash for the experience. But she looks like goddamn jail bait! That stupid dress just makes it worse. Take it off her. Now!"

Isaac doesn't move, but Roxy steps up to me and starts taking off my dress. I glance at Isaac out of the corner of my eye. He's staring straight ahead. He looks mad. Really, really mad. I hear someone whisper behind me as I step out of my dress, but I can't hear what they say or who said it. The man walks up to me and looks me over with his eyes. He reaches out a hand and pinches my chest so hard I have to bite my lip to keep from crying out.

"Why doesn't she have any tits? Has she been eating her food?"

I don't look at Isaac to see if he's still mad, but I know he is because I can hear it in his voice. "Yes."

"Then what in the hell is wrong with her?" He lifts my arm and turns it over. His eyes get narrow as he picks up my other arm and does the same. He looks at Roxy. "Who's here that just got out of the hole?"

Roxy turns and looks at the people behind us. "Kitty, get up here." The girl named Kitty steps forward.

The man points at Kitty and then at the space behind him. "Take her dress off and put them side-by-side over there."

Roxy helps Kitty out of her dress and pushes us both to where the man pointed. I don't need to look closely at Kitty to see how we're different. It was obvious even when our clothes were on.

The man walks back and forth in front of us a few seconds before turning back to Roxy. "Kitty's coming out was about six months ago, in June, right?"

"Yes, that's correct."

The man stares at us for a few more seconds and then walks over to Isaac. "Kitty here is sixteen, but looks about twenty. Same goes for most of the girls here. Angel was supposed to be our ticket to the guys that like to get off on little girls. She needs to give the illusion of a child, but not make people believe that she actually is one. You know the legal age for prostitution here is eighteen. We have a very thin line with her—she needs to look young enough to attract those with a child fetish, while looking old enough to pass her fake identification. I don't need the attention that comes with pushing children. She—" The man pauses and points at me. "—will bring me unwanted attention. Some jackass with a conscience will report that he may have been tricked into paying for sex with a child. The officials would come to investigate, and I don't need a spotlight on that side of the business. It could risk the rest of the deals we have in place. Get the issue now?"

"Yes, sir."

The man turns and steps to Roxy. He grabs her by the throat and she makes a coughing sound. She raises her arms, but then drops them by her side. The man puts his face close to hers. "You said she was going to be my goddamn golden ticket. I've already started to promote for her coming out. I can't have her working when she looks like a goddamn child. Find me another girl, who looks young but will pass the age test, to put in her place. You've got six months to get Angel looking close to legal. I don't care how you do it—fatten her up, cut her hair differently—just figure it out. If it doesn't work, then you'd better pray she's worth something to another operation. Otherwise, I've wasted a lot of money on nothing. And you know how I feel about wasting money." He lets go of Roxy and turns to walk toward me. He looks at me for a few seconds before touching my hair. I pull in a breath. I had expected him to hit me, so his soft touch is unexpected. His eyes narrow slightly. "It's a shame really. I do think you could make men become obsessed with you. That's good for business. But this—" He pauses as he waves his hand in front of me. "—this is trouble." He turns and walks out the door, Watcher following close behind.

Kitty and I are still standing naked in front of the group. The whispers get louder as the men look from me to Kitty. "I don't care what the old man says—I'd take the sweet little angel over the pussy cat any day." I don't see which man says this, but all the men laugh in response.

Except Isaac.

Isaac walks over, picks up the dresses, and tosses them to Kitty and me. "Get dressed. The party's over."

"Aw, come on, Junior. We ain't breaking any rules. Looking's allowed, so long as we don't touch. Can't you give us a few more minutes, you know, to help prolong the memory until we can fantasize about it later?"

Isaac walks fast to the man who's speaking and gets right in his face. Isaac is taller than the other man, even though I can tell he's younger. The room becomes quiet as Isaac grabs him by the tie. "Are you challenging me?" The guy can't talk, so he just shakes his head. Isaac lets go and turns to the others in the room. "I said the party's over! Everyone out, except Roxy and Angel."

Next to me, Kitty struggles to put her dress back on. Realizing I'm still holding my dress, I step into it and pull it up over my shoulders. By the time I'm dressed, everyone has shuffled out the door, leaving me alone with Isaac and Roxy.

Isaac looks at me for a second before turning to Roxy. "What's your plan to get Angel to pass the age test in six months?"

Roxy, rubbing at her neck, shakes her head. "I don't know yet."

"Well we obviously can't count on Rosie to teach her any more. Based on what you told me at the start of the party, I think you knew what was going to happen here today."

"I told you what I knew. Your father was upset yesterday and wanted to see Rosie's list of appointments. I didn't know he'd come in and take her out. I also didn't know he'd refuse Angel. I really thought the dress would age her up enough."

"I want you to come up with a plan for Angel, and bring it to me tomorrow. There's a lot at stake, so you better get it right." He pauses and looks at me again before looking back to Roxy. "Just don't cut her hair. I think that will make it worse. You can try to straighten it, but don't cut it short."

Roxy pauses and looks from Isaac to me and back to Isaac. "You're awfully concerned about her future."

"Of course I'm concerned! She's my first charge and I'm not interested in failing. I may be his son, but that doesn't mean I get a free pass. I have to prove myself just like everyone else. And so far, it's not looking good. I want a plan in front of me tomorrow."

"Fine. Oh, and there's the issue of her room. A new girl is arriving soon. We don't usually move a girl out of the hole until she's working."

"Move Angel out anyway. Maybe the change of environment will help her mature somehow."

"The boss won't like it, but maybe if we just give her a new room without the other perks he'll approve. I'll ring you tomorrow with a plan. Now, I'm off to see if I can calm the old boy down." Roxy walks out of the room without looking at me.

Isaac flicks his eyes in my direction. "Let's go." I take one glace at the untouched cake on the table before following him out the door. We walk in silence down to my room. He holds my door open and whispers in my ear as I pass. "I'll be back later."

My door closes with a click, and I'm left wondering what just happened. I try tȯ process, but my mind won't focus. I step out of my heels and throw them at the door. It feels so good I pick them up and throw them again. As I start to take off my dress, I hear the click of my door. New Night Man sticks his head in.

"What's all the racket?"

"I tripped and fell while taking off my shoes." I rub my head for added effect. New Night Man eyes me for a few seconds before stepping back and closing my door. I get the dress off and put on my sweatpants and T-shirt. I then put on the new headband with the charm hidden inside. I lie on the bed and hug Abigail to my chest.

My thoughts go first to Rosie. I want to know what happened to her. I was so surprised by what the man said and did that it had taken me a while to follow the conversation.

Rosie tried to leave and the man found out. Now she's gone. And the man did something to the person that was going to help her.

My tears fall and I don't try to stop them. Rosie had been nice to me. She tried to help me by showing me that video. I know it was against the rules, but she did it anyway. That was when I had decided I didn't want to have sex with men, but I had found a way to accept it. As long as Isaac didn't leave me, I could do it. Now I have to wait at least six months. The thought makes me happy.

The mixture of being sad about Rosie and happy about getting six more months before my coming out is confusing. I'd never felt happy and sad at the same time before.

I close my eyes, but the image of Rosie hitting the floor jumps out at me. I push my thoughts in another direction and I see Kitty. The man said she just came out of the hole six months ago. I remember that Isaac said something about keeping me down in this hole. Kitty must have been one of the girls behind the other doors.

It's the first time I've seen another girl my age. Her hair is darker than mine and straight, but it's cut to the same length. That's the only similarity we share. She's taller than me and she has tits—she actually needs to wear a bra. The man made it sound like there was something wrong with me. But when the doctor comes to inspect me, he always says everything is fine.

I rub at the make-up on my face. It still feels funny and I want to take it off. Rosie had always said she couldn't wait to see what I looked like with make-up on.

Rosie.

I close my eyes and try not to cry. I picture the wings that Isaac gave me. I imagine them to be big and I can put them on my back, just like one of the birds in the pictures he's shown me. I try to imagine what it would be like to fly. Just when I start to feel like I'm falling asleep, I hear my door open. I look up and see Isaac.

"Did I wake you?"

I sit up and move over to give him room to sit down. "No."

"I brought you some cake." I smile as he holds the cake out for me. We sit without talking while I eat. I'm not hungry, and the things that happened at the party have made me sad, but the cake is still good.

I set the plate on the floor when I'm done. "Thank you."

He nods his head. "Did he hurt you? When he pinched your chest?"

I rub at the spot where the man pinched me. "A little."

He closes his eyes and takes a deep breath. "I'm so sorry. I was so mad he made you take off your dress and stand in front of everyone. Then when he pinched you—" He rubs at his eyes with the palms of his hands. "I thought I was going to kill him, Ang. I could feel the anger trying to push me forward. All I wanted to do was bash his head into the ground. But I wouldn't have gotten far with all his men around him."

"Why do you care if they saw me with my dress off?" I'm scared to ask, afraid that it's something he expects me to know. The way he expected me to know that asking him for a kiss was asking for something so much more.

"I guess you wouldn't really understand that. You've been forced to take your clothes off for anyone who asked from the day you got here. The parts of your body that are usually covered by clothes are considered your private areas. You should get to decide who sees them. When a man looks at a naked woman, he thinks about sex. I don't want anyone to think of you in that way." He pauses and looks at me. I must look embarrassed because he puts his arm around me and smiles a little. "I guess it's not such a big deal if it's only in front of the other women or the doctor. They probably aren't thinking about your body in a personal way."

"Why did he do it then?"

"I don't know why he does anything he does. I suppose it was to prove that he has power over you. That he can make anyone do anything he says. To show the others that you're nothing more to him than an object. It's not right, and I hate him for it. And for everything else he does."

"If it's not right, how can he do it? You told me once that there were police—that they were in charge of making people follow the rules."

He takes in a deep breath and pulls me to his chest. "That's too big a question to answer right now. We don't really have time, and I don't want to talk about any more of this on your birthday. I can't stay much longer, so how about I play you a dream?"

It's been so long since he played me a dream. I smile and lean against his chest. "Yes, I'd like that very much. Can you play me a new one?"

He doesn't speak for a few seconds. "How about I make up a story this time? It'll be about a girl with big, beautiful silver wings, and she flies all over the world."

"Yes, play me that dream." I close my eyes and listen to his dream about the brave girl with beautiful silver wings.

15: Falling Stars

I'm so caught up in the dream of the little girl with beautiful silver wings that I'm startled when Goon bangs on my door, indicating another hour has passed. I look around at the darkened room, and I'm grateful for the soft glow filtering in from an outside light. I never did become accustomed to being in a dark room.

Thinking of a little girl with wings, flying away, takes me back to the weeks following my sixteenth birthday.

It's one of my best memories, yet at the same time one of my worst.

⁂

There are three hundred and fourteen concrete blocks that make up my room, not counting the partial ones that surround my door. Eighty-six of them have cracks. That's approximately twenty-seven percent. I have eight large tiles in my ceiling and seven small. I've often tried to count the brown spots on my ceiling, but they run together in many places and I'm not able to get an accurate number. I am able to count the small holes in the ceiling tiles—fifteen. I know these things because I've counted them many times. I have nothing else to do but count the objects in my room now that Isaac took my things away.

And now that Rosie is gone too, I've been alone in my room most of the time. Before my lessons with Rosie, I always felt comfortable in my room. Now it just feels too small and boring.

It's been one week since the party. Roxy visited me the day after my birthday, but hasn't been back since. Isaac hasn't come to see me either.

I look down at my plate and what remains of my dinner. The amount of food in each of my meals increased after my party, and I'm not used to eating so much. I'm so full I fear I might explode. Or throw up. I don't think I can't eat another bite, but if I don't I know I'll get hit. I learned that the first, and only, time I didn't finish the food brought to me. I take a deep breath and shovel the rest of the food into my mouth, hoping the pause I took to count up my room somehow created new space in my stomach. I have to force it down, but luckily it doesn't come back up. I put the plate on my table and lean back against the wall behind my bed.

I look over at Abigail on the bed next to me. I pick her up and run my fingers through her hair. I try to put it in a braid, the way that Rosie once taught me on her own hair. I'm not very good but I have nothing else to do, so I keep working at it. The day is over, but I'm not yet tired enough to go to sleep. I'm halfway through my twelfth attempt at the braid when I hear my door open. I smile automatically when I see Isaac.

"I brought you a cookie." He smiles and holds up a chocolate chip cookie as he sits down on the chair in front of me.

I cover my stomach with my hands. "No, please, no more food."

"I thought cookies were your second favorite food, behind cake?"

"They are, but I can't eat any more. Really. I think my stomach might break open if I do. That or I'll throw it up, and then I'll get a beating from New Night Man."

"Is he still hitting you?" He shifts forward in his seat. I look at the cookie in his hand—he's crushed it.

"Just once, when I didn't eat all my food. He told me I couldn't waste any of it. He also said that I'd get a beating if I threw it up."

"Son of a bitch." He stands and walks the few steps around my room before throwing the crushed cookie on my empty plate. He sits down on the bed next to me and takes my face in his hands. "Where did he hit you? Here?" He rubs his thumb softly over my right cheek.

"Yes."

"Did he do anything else, other than hit you?"

"No."

He closes his eyes for a second. When he opens them, I see that I've made him sad again. I know he doesn't like it when I get hit. I don't like to tell him, but I won't lie to him either.

"I'm sorry he hit you again, Ang. We were doing good for a while. That's what makes what I'm about to ask you to do even harder. I didn't know Roxy told him to make you eat, or I would have tried to come up with a better plan."

"Plan for what?"

"You can't eat your food tomorrow. None of it."

My body instantly tenses. New Night Man hit me for leaving four bites on my dinner plate. I don't even want to think about what will happen to me if I don't eat anything.

"Why can't I eat tomorrow?"

"Tomorrow is New Year's Eve. Do you remember what that is?" I nod. He's told me before about how a new year starts and everyone celebrates the old year on the last day. It sounds strange to me, but Isaac said people like to have reasons to celebrate. "Well, every New Year's Eve there's a big party around here. This year is different because they're celebrating an anniversary for the business. Everyone's attending, which means there won't be a lot of security— only one guard will be in this area. In addition to all that, a new security system is being installed. They won't take any chances of something going wrong and you girls getting out, so they're going to put something in the food to make you go to sleep. It's just for the day and the doctor said it was safe, but I still don't like it."

I'm confused by what he's said, but I trust him. "How am I supposed to not eat my food? New Night Man will hit me until I do."

"I was thinking you could put it in your bucket. You would then need to actually use your bucket a few times, to cover it up."

"What if I don't have to go?"

He pulls at the side of his hair and sighs. "I don't know. I suppose I'll come by in the morning and use the bucket myself if you can't go."

"But won't they figure it out when they check on me and I'm not asleep?"

"You'll have to pretend to be asleep. In the morning, after breakfast, you should just act really tired. When they come with your lunch, you should pretend to already be asleep. That way, we'd only have to hide the breakfast food." He stands up and walks the few steps around my room. "You're smaller than the other girls so I could say that the medicine affected you quicker, and that they should just leave you alone. I'll tell them that we'll check on you once more, later in the day."

My stomach cramps, and I know it's because of Isaac's plan and not all the food I had to eat for dinner. "Are you sure this will work? Won't we get in a lot of trouble if we're caught?"

He sits back down on my bed. "Yes, we would be in more trouble than ever before. That's why it's important for you to do everything you can to pretend to be asleep. You can't react to anything—not even if they hit you. Do you think you can do that?"

I think about how many times I've been hit already. I've learned to do just about anything to keep it from happening. "Yes, I can do it."

"Good." He lets out a breath and his shoulders drop slightly. "I'll be back in the morning with your breakfast. Then I'll come back tomorrow night when it's safe."

"But how are you going to explain coming down here if I'm supposed to be asleep?"

He smiles. "I've got another plan, but it's a surprise."

I'm waiting for Isaac to show up with my breakfast that I'm not supposed to eat. I didn't sleep much last night. My mind would not stop thinking about what Isaac asked me to do today. My stomach rumbles the way it does when I'm hungry—I don't think it likes the idea of not eating at all today. I hear the click of my door and take a deep breath. I see Isaac walk in and he darts his eyes quickly to the door and back to me. He does this to let me know he's not alone. I look back at the door and see New Cleaning Lady.

"Good morning, Angel. We're doing things a bit differently today. We need to take you down to the bathroom before you eat your breakfast." Isaac steps to the side after he finishes talking to make room for me to get off my bed.

"I don't have to go." It's a lie, but I know I have to go in my bucket later to cover the food.

"Well that's tough shit, now isn't it? Get up and go. We're on a tight schedule today." I look at Isaac a few seconds before standing. I can see in his eyes that the plan hasn't changed. Somehow I need to pretend to use the toilet, or save some for the bucket to cover my food.

"I don't know why you need to be down here, Junior You're more involved in your whore than any of the other managers."

"Yeah, well, I've got a lot riding on her. If she screws this up for me, then I'll be out of a job as well as a future. And probably a family too since my father would likely disown me for blowing what might be his biggest potential."

New Cleaning Lady laughs. "I don't envy you, that's for sure. Come along, Angel."

I follow the small, round woman out the door and down the hall. She's taller than me, but shorter than old Cleaning Lady. And larger. She hasn't always been as large as she is now, but over the years she's grown in width the way I've grown in height. Well, maybe more since I haven't grown all that much taller. She has a funny walk that makes her whole body move from side to side with each step. And she makes funny noises when she bends over. I once made the mistake of asking her why she had hair between her nose and upper lip. The beating she gave me kept me from asking again.

We enter the bathroom and I sit on the toilet. New Cleaning Lady is watching me, and I'm trying to figure out how I can go just a little and save the rest for my bucket. It's hard to stop once I start, but I find a way to hold some back. I must have made a face because New Cleaning Lady is looking at me funny.

"What's wrong with you?"

"Nothing."

"Well get done. I've got a lot to do today."

I stand and then wash my hands before following New Cleaning Lady back to my room. Isaac is outside my door, talking to Day Man. New Cleaning Lady walks away and I go in my room. Isaac follows behind me, carrying my breakfast. He hands me the bowl and raises his eyebrows. I give a little nod, hoping that he saw but not Day Man.

"Enjoy your breakfast, Angel." Isaac turns to leave, but Day Man doesn't move.

"Need to make sure she eats it." Day Man crosses his arms over his chest and nods in my direction.

Isaac hesitates and then turns to look at me. I can see by his eyes that he didn't expect Day Man to insist on watching me eat my breakfast. We didn't talk about this in our plan and I'm not sure what to do. My stomach cramps and I get an idea.

"Can I eat it later? I don't feel so good right now."

"No you can't. Eat. Now." Day Man takes a step into the room, but has to stop since Isaac is taking up most of my extra space.

I look down at my food, and my hands start to shake. I put some of the oatmeal on my spoon and raise it to my mouth. I decide to try one more time and lower the spoon back to the bowl.

"I can't. I think I'll throw up." Day Man hates throw up.

"What the hell is wrong with you? You seem fine to me."

"I think I'm getting my period." Day Man also hates periods.

Day Man mumbles out a few curse words. "I don't remember it being your time of the month. You're on the pill, so it's supposed to be regulated." I just shrug my shoulders.

Isaac looks from me to Day Man. "Can't they come early sometimes, or late, even on the pill?"

"How the hell should I know? I'm not a goddamn woman—or a doctor. However, I think my old lady is on the rag twenty-four-seven, so I suppose it's possible."

"Just leave it with her, and check back in a couple hours to make sure she ate it."

Day Man throws his hands in the air. "I don't have time for this shit! You know what all I have to get done today. I can't keep coming back to make sure she's eaten all her food."

"Well it won't do any good if she throws it up either." Isaac turns back to face me. He leans in and grabs my face with his hand. It makes my jaw hurt. "I'll be back soon. Your food had better be gone. If I come back to find you didn't eat, or that you threw it up, I'll give you a lesson to make sure you don't ever think about disobeying me again. You saw how pathetic you looked standing next to Kitty at your party. I don't care if you have the stomach flu—you will eat all your food and keep it down. Understand?"

He's so convincing that it takes me a few seconds to remember he's just pretending, but it sounds and feels real. I look in his eyes—they are Isaac's eyes, not the man's. It's all that I need to convince me it's not real. Even though I know he's pretending, I can't stop the tears from falling. I can't find my words so I just nod my head.

Isaac pulls away and turns to the door. "I'll check on her later so you can do what you need to do. Let's go."

Day Man looks at me one more time and smiles as he places his hand on Isaac's shoulder. "You sure can be one scary son of a bitch when you want to be, Junior. Kind of reminds me of your old man." I hear Day Man laughing as Isaac shuts the door.

I look down at my bowl for a few seconds before wiping the tears from my face. He was just pretending. He had to say those things so Day Man wouldn't be suspicious. He doesn't think I look pathetic.

I'd heard the word pathetic a few times before when working with Rosie. I asked Isaac what it meant and he tried to explain, but I still didn't understand it very well—except that it was something I didn't want to be.

I wipe my face and eyes again before getting up and dumping my oatmeal into my bucket. I then relieve myself of everything I held back at the bathroom. When I'm convinced my uneaten breakfast is well hidden, I cover the bucket and slide it back behind my table. I then crawl in bed and wait.

I hear my door click and I quickly roll over and close my eyes. My heart beats faster, and I try to keep my breath even. Although, I don't really know what my breathing is like when I'm sleeping. I hope I have it right. I hear feet shuffle into my room. I feel someone's breath on my neck, and my body starts to tense. I steady my thoughts, and suddenly I know it's Isaac by the smell of his soap. I relax, but I keep pretending to be asleep since I don't know if he's alone.

"It's okay, Ang. I'm alone, but don't move in case someone else comes in. I just wanted to make sure you were able to cover your food in the bucket." He moves away and I hear him shift my bucket. A couple seconds pass and I feel him lean over me again. "Good job, Ang. I can't see your breakfast. I have to go, but I'll check on you again later. Just keep doing what you're doing. Oh, and I'm sorry about what I said before. Always remember, it's only real when we're alone—the rest is just pretend."

He runs his hand over my hair before stepping away. I wait until I hear the door close behind him before rolling over. I stare at my ceiling, wondering what I can do to pass the time. Normally I'd get up and do my exercises before practicing my writing on the wall with my finger. Most of the time, I write out the dreams that Isaac has played for me in the past. I love to write the words, even though I can only see them in my mind.

I don't think I should do any of that today since I don't know exactly when Day Man will come back to check on me. It would be hard to pretend to be sleeping if I were sitting on my floor. I roll over and face the wall, deciding I can write my words while lying down. It's hard to do because I'm on my right side and that's the arm I write with. It's awkward to use my left hand, but it's fun so I keep doing it. I'm writing out the dream where Isaac takes me and Abigail to the Grand Canyon when I hear my door unlock. I drop my arm and close my eyes. I hear footsteps and this time I know right away it's not Isaac. I feel a shove on my back.

"Wake up. It's time for your lunch." I hear Day Man set my plate down on the table. At first I don't move, but then remember that Isaac said at this point I should just act really tired, not asleep.

I roll over and make my eyes open slowly. I look at Day Man and then close my eyes again.

"I said wake up. Time to eat."

I open my eyes again. "Not hungry. I'm tired." I close my eyes and hope that my voice sounded sleepy enough.

"Shit." His hands are on my shoulders and he shakes me hard. I bite on the inside of my lip to keep from reacting. "Wake up." I keep my eyes closed and I hear him walk to the door and open it. "Hey, get down here for a minute!" I can faintly hear someone respond from down the hall. "I don't care, get down here now!" I listen to the sound of Day Man's steps as he walks back over to my bed. I hold still as he uses his fingers to pry open one of my eyes.

"What's all the fuss about?" It's New Cleaning Lady.

"She's knocked out. It was supposed to happen slowly with each meal." I realize that I've done something wrong. I can't change it now, so I keep pretending that I'm asleep.

"You sure she's asleep?"

"She responded to me once, but then I can't get her to do it again. Watch." He lifts me up by the hair and there's a sting on my cheek as his hand connects with my face. My eyes instantly water, but I'm able to keep from moving or making a sound. He lets go of my hair and I fall back on the bed.

"Jesus. Did we kill her?" New Cleaning Lady's voice is a loud whsiper.

I feel Day Man's hand on my throat. I prepare for him to choke me like he's done before, but he just puts pressure on it with his fingers. "No, she has a pulse."

"Thank the Lord. What do we do?"

"I'll call Junior. He can check her out."

"Why in the hell would you do that? He'd have our necks if we messed up the dosage and damaged her. Worse yet, he'd tell the boss and we'd get a new address in the middle of the desert."

"He won't tell the boss. Junior'll lose his hide if something goes wrong with her, so he won't say a word." Their conversation disappears as my door closes.

I let out a breath and start to move my hand to my cheek. I stop, worried that they will come back and see that I've moved. I lay there, pretending to be asleep for no one. I count in my head to pass the time. Eventually my door opens and I stop counting. I hear footsteps and feel a hand on my neck, then my forehead. I know it's Isaac and relief replaces the knot growing in my stomach. However, it starts to come back when I worry that he'll be upset because I did it wrong.

"Angel, can you hear me?" I don't move. He shakes me softly, and still I don't move. His hands pull away and I hear the shuffle of his feet. "She's fine, just sleeping."

"But the Doc said it would take affect slowly throughout the day. The others are still awake, just a bit fuzzy—if you know what I mean." Day Man still sounds worried.

"I don't know. She's smaller than the others, so maybe it affected her faster." There's a pause in the conversation.

"What if she wakes up too early? The whole plan was to keep them asleep until late tomorrow morning—after we verify all the new systems are working properly."

"I'll talk to Mickey. He can check on her later tonight. Leave her food here, and if she wakes up he can make her eat." Mickey must be what they call New Night Man.

"Yeah, all right." They leave my room and my door locks once again. I count until the numbers make me confused before moving—just to be sure no one is coming back.

"Ang, it's me. It's okay, you can wake up now." I slowly open my eyes and see Isaac standing over me. "Hurry, we don't have a lot of time." He removes my blanket and pulls my legs over the side of the bed. He puts shoes on my feet as I sit up.

"What are you doing?"

"No time for questions. You trust me, right?"

"Of course."

"Then, just keep quiet until I tell you it's safe to talk." He finishes tying the laces on my other shoe and pulls me out of the bed. He unties a black sweatshirt from around his waist and pulls it over my head. It hangs down almost to my knees and the sleeves cover my hands. "You've got your sweatpants on—that's good. Let's go." He pulls the hood over my head and then takes my hand. He opens my door and peeks out into the hall.

He leads me out of the room and down the hall. He turns left down a hall I've passed many times over the years, but have never been down. We pass several doors. Isaac slows down as we get near one that's open. I hear music coming from inside the room. Isaac walks close enough to the door to look in, pauses a second, and then pulls me forward. I look inside as I pass and see New Night Man sitting in a chair with his head on a table. It looks like he's asleep. My heart starts to beat faster and all I can think about is following Isaac. He leads me up a set of stairs and out a door.

The first thing I notice is the darkness.

The second is the smell.

The third is the cold air on my face.

I realize we're outside. I stop moving and try to look around, but it's too dark to see. I feel the sting of the cold air in my nose and in my throat.

Isaac tugs on my hand. "Come on! We need to keep moving." His voice is barely more than a whisper. He drags me around a wall and then stops by a car. He opens the back of it. "I'm sorry about this, but you have to get in the trunk. We can't let anyone see you." I hesitate for a second but then climb in and he shuts the door.

It's completely dark and my heart starts to pound so hard it hurts. I hug my knees to my chest and squeeze my eyes shut. I start counting in my head, but before I get too far the top opens again.

"Ang, I'm sorry. I almost forgot—here's the flashlight. I know you hate the dark. It won't be long, I promise." He quickly shuts me in again and I turn on the flashlight he handed me. I still don't like it in the trunk, but it's better now that I can see. The car starts to move, and I wonder where he's taking me.

This is only the second time I've been in a car. It's only the second time I've ever been outside. My stomach feels funny, and I know I'm excited. I don't know where he's taking me, but I don't care. I'd go anywhere with him. I feel the vibrations slow as the car comes to a stop. I hear some muffled voices outside for a few seconds before the car starts moving again. I don't know how much time passes before we stop again. This time the trunk opens and I see Isaac. He holds his hand out to me and helps me out of the trunk.

"Are you all right? Was it too rough back there?"

He's whispering so I whisper back. "I'm fine. It was bouncy, but not bad. Considering it's only the second time I've been in a car, and the last time was about eight years ago, I don't have much to compare to."

The wind blows lightly on my face and I close my eyes, taking a deep breath. It's cold and it stings, but it smells and feels amazing.

Isaac moves me slightly to the side, and I open my eyes to see him pull out a coat. "I know it's cold, but we got lucky that there's no snow and the ground isn't muddy. Here, put this on. It's probably too big, but it's better than being cold." I slip on the coat and it is too big, but not as big as the sweatshirt I have on. Isaac pulls out a bag and puts the strap on his shoulder before closing the trunk and turning back to me. He takes my hand in his, locking our fingers together. "Come on, I want to show you something." As we walk I think about the feel of the wind on my face. We walk for a while before he stops and turns to me. "Okay, now close your eyes."

"Why, it's dark and I can't see much anyway."

"Just trust me. Please?"

He's smiling and looks really happy, which makes me smile in return. I close my eyes and let him lead me. I stumble on something and feel his arm wrap around my waist. He hugs me to his side as we continue to walk. When we stop, he moves me so that he's standing behind me. He wraps his arms around my waist again and pulls me to his chest. I suddenly feel his breath next to my ear and I forget to breathe for a second.

"Okay, open your eyes."

I do as he says and open my eyes. The view before me is so amazing that I can't help the gasp that escapes. It's just like the postcard I've looked at hundreds of times, but even better. Lights dance and sparkle in an amazing array of colors.

"It's the lights." I turn my head to look at Isaac. He's looking at me and it makes my heart beat even harder than seeing the lights. He's smiling—and it's the best smile I've ever seen. He looks so happy it almost makes me cry. I'm not sure why. I don't understand the feelings moving inside of me and I look away before the tears fall. I don't want him to think I'm sad.

Isaac lets go of me, and I turn to see him pull a blanket out of the bag. He puts it down on the ground and sits on it. He holds his hand out to me and helps me sit in front of him. He adjusts our position so that my back is resting against his chest, wrapping his arms around me once again. I relax against him, enjoying the view in front of me and the wind on my face.

"Oh, I almost forgot. I figured you might be hungry so I brought you a couple slices of pizza." He removes a box from the bag and hands it to me. After I take it he settles his arm back around my waist.

After I finish eating, I decide to ask him questions. "Where are we?"

"On some private land that my family owns. It's the only place where we could view the show without anyone else around. I talked to my mom and told her I had a date. She agreed to cover for me— saying I wasn't feeling well. It was the only way I could get away from the party without him being suspicious."

I turn my head and try to look at him. "What show?"

"You'll see in—" He pauses and looks at his watch. "—about twenty minutes."

"Did you tell your mom it was me you were bringing?"

"Not exactly. It's safer for her if she doesn't know anything—in case we get caught. But I think she suspects."

"How did you get me out?"

"Everyone is so paranoid about what's going to happen tonight with the security system being installed. It's stupid really, but he's not taking any chances. I don't understand all of it, but they decided to do a clean break of the old system. That required them to take all the systems off line while the new one is being installed. Maybe he's afraid that the tech would be able to learn all his dirty secrets if the system was still up during the switch. Anyway, that took the cameras down, so I was able to sneak you out without being seen. That only left the guard to get past—so I put some of the stuff Doc prescribed to put you girls to sleep in his food. I might have used too much." He laughs and I smile at the image of New Night Man sleeping with his head on the table.

"In the car it sounded like you stopped once to talk to someone."

"Oh, yeah, that. There are some guards working the gates tonight since the systems are off line. That's why you had to be in the trunk."

"What's going to happen if we get caught?"

I feel him tense behind me. "That's not something we're going to talk about. It's not going to happen. I've been planning this for a long time. I've thought through all the things that can go wrong and have planned for them. When tomorrow comes around, no one will ever know you've been gone."

"Why do we need to go back?" I'm surprised by my own question, but now that I've asked I hold my breath waiting for his answer.

"Because I'm not ready for us to leave permanently. He'd find us."

I picture the map Isaac used in some of my lessons a couple years ago. In my mind I see where we are in Nevada and all the other states around it. I also remember the world map we studied for a few months. "Isn't the United States really big? That's what you told me when you taught me the maps. And there are other countries. How could he find us?" I sit up and turn to look at him. I've never thought about leaving before. Not like this—not in a way that actually seemed possible.

"Believe me, I've thought about this a lot. I wish we could hop back in the car and just start driving. But he would find us. Do you remember what he said the night of your party? About how his reach has no bounds? He wasn't joking. His business has given him connections in every state and practically every country."

"But aren't there police we could go to? You've said before that what he does is wrong."

"He has the police in his pocket, or at least the important ones. He works with them as an informant—he gives them information on other criminals that are larger scale than he is. He leads them to the big busts, and as a reward they look the other way when it comes to his business. Much of what he does is legal in this state. The police know about the small scale illegal activities and practically encourage it. He's good for business in this town. However they don't know everything that goes on. At least I don't think they do."

"I thought you said there are police in every state."

"Cops who support this kind of business are connected. That makes nowhere safe. You also have to factor in his clients. The casinos bring the rich guys in, but he keeps them hooker-happy and narcotic-numb. They love him because he gives them what they want, and he keeps it quiet. Most clients are powerful business men with a lot of money and connections. The result is that there is no town—large or small—in this country where he doesn't have someone he could pay off to find us."

"What about another country?"

"We would need papers—passports, birth certificates, driver's licenses—some form of identification to fly to another country. There are other ways to get out of the country, but those channels are connected to the business my father is in, and he would find us."

Tears sting my eyes. I hadn't thought about actually leaving until this moment, but now I know it will never be a reality. I'll have to have sex with men. I'll have to be separated from Isaac.

Isaac gently places his hand on my cheek, and I look back in his eyes. "Don't cry. I wanted tonight to be special. I'll find a way. I just need time to find a safe place to go and a way to get a job without identification. Maybe even a way to get new identities—that's where we would pretend to be other people and even have papers that say we are them. I just need more time, but I promise I'll find a way."

He pulls me to his chest and I hug him tight as I wait for the tears to stop.

I jump when I hear a sudden, loud noise and see a bright flash of light. Isaac's arms tighten around me. "It's okay, Ang. Look." I follow his pointing finger and look up in the air. "It's the fireworks show I wanted you to see."

It's loud, and bright, and scary, and wonderful all at the same time. I jump with each new pop of light and Isaac covers my ears, making it better. I hold my breath after the last one fizzles away, hoping for more. None come, but I still don't move. Isaac takes his hands away from my ears.

"I'm sorry I didn't think about the noise. I didn't realize they'd be so loud from this far away. I should have brought you some earplugs."

"No, it was perfect. They were so beautiful. They were like . . ." I can't think of a comparison.

"Like thousands of falling stars." I look up at the stars in the sky.

"Yes, like falling stars. If only I could have caught one." I turn and look at him at the same time he looks down at me. Our faces are so close that I can feel his breath on my lips. My heart skips a few beats and I'm not able to move. I hear the change in his breathing. I feel his heart beat faster.

I feel his lips press soft against mine.

It's over before I can even blink my eyes. Even if I could move, I don't because I want him to do it again. I watch his eyes searching mine, and I see something happen. I don't know what exactly it is, but somehow there's something different in the way he looks at me.

His lips are back on mine and my eyes close automatically. A shiver runs down my spine when his hands gently slide into place on either side of my face. His tongue brushes my lips and I open my mouth. I start to think about all the things I learned in my lessons with Rosie, but then I let them go. I let my mind go blank, forgetting about everything I'm supposed to do, and I just let my body respond naturally to Isaac's kiss.

When he pulls away he puts his forehead to mine. My eyes are still closed, and I'm thinking about the kiss that I can still feel even though it's gone.

"I'm so sorry, Ang. I shouldn't have kissed you."

"It's okay." I'm only able to manage a whisper.

"No, it's not. Everything's going to change now. I'm not sure I'm going to be able to hide my feelings any more. It was hard enough before, but now—" He hugs me so tight to his chest that I feel like I might break. Even though it's crushing, it's comforting because I know that if I do break he would be strong enough to hold my pieces together.

"I don't want to go back."

"I don't either, Ang. I promise I'll figure something out. I have to. I can't stand the thought of someone else touching you, or of you going through any more pain because of him. I'll find a way."

We stay wrapped in each other's arms, not speaking and not moving, for several minutes. I allow myself to believe that this is my life. That I'm free to love Isaac and stay in his arms forever. A beeping noise behind me brings me back to reality. Isaac lifts his arm and pushes a button on his watch.

"It's time to go. We have to get back before the others leave the party. One of them might decide to check the hole, and if they find the guard sleeping they'll start checking rooms." He helps me up and puts the blanket back in the bag. As we walk back to the car, he holds me to his side. We reach the car and he opens the trunk. I start to get in but he stops me. "Take off the coat, and after you get in take off the shoes too. We won't have a lot of time when we get back. I'll carry you back to your room."

I take off the coat and he puts it in the bag with the blanket. He kisses me one more time before picking me up and putting me in the trunk. He hands me the flashlight before closing me in. I take off the shoes and hug my knees to my chest. The whole ride back I think of nothing but the kiss. I'm so lost in my thoughts that I'm startled when the trunk opens and Isaac reaches in to pick me up.

"Turn off the light." I do as he asks and drop the flashlight in the trunk before wrapping my arms around his neck. He's able to close the trunk without much of a sound and then starts walking quickly. I bury my face in his neck, not wanting to see what happens.

I know when we are inside—not because of the sudden light or the sound of the door, but because of the change in smell. My stomach churns, and I have to swallow back a lump that rises in my throat.

I hear the music from New Night Man's room and feel Isaac stop. Within seconds we're moving again at a fast pace. I hear the familiar sound of my door and then Isaac sets me down on my bed. He immediately takes off the sweatshirt and starts looking at my legs. He must know I'm confused because he looks at me and smiles.

"I just want to make sure there's no mud or grass on your legs. That would be hard to explain when you're taken down for your shower." I must be clean because he tucks me in under my blanket. "Remember to act tired tomorrow. You don't have to pretend to sleep too late since they think you fell asleep after breakfast." He brushes the hair out of my face and looks at me for a few seconds before placing a kiss on my forehead. "I want to kiss you again, but not in here. Never in here."

He starts to pull away, but I grab his neck. "Thank you. This was the best day of my life."

He pulls my hand to his mouth and presses a kiss to my wrist. "I'd do anything for you."

He's out the door before I can respond.

I roll over and think about my evening with Isaac. It had been the best day of my life—seeing the lights and the fireworks, being able to smell and feel the outside air, kissing Isaac . . . it was more than I ever thought I could have.

But it's also the worst day. Because despite what Isaac has promised, I no longer believe that I will have any life other than this.

14: Big Mistake

This time I welcome the hour warning. I need the break, even if it's just for a few seconds. I stand up from my seated position on the bucket and walk around. After a few laps around the small room, I stand on the bucket again. I find a small part of the window that's not covered with grime and look out. It's dark and I can make out a few stars. The sight of those tiny white dots causes my stomach to clench, and I climb down from the bucket. I sink to the floor and rest my head against the wall, eyes shut tight.

I hate seeing stars.

I take a series of deep breaths, forcing my body to relax. I feel the tension start to melt away, and I open my eyes again. I kick the bucket and watch it roll across the floor.

No more looking out the window until the sun is back up.

But, unfortunately, that little glimpse of the stars has taken me right back to where my mind left off. My memories are following their own natural course, and it seems there is no escaping them. I know what's next and I don't want to think about it.

But I know I have to.

Getting lost in this last memory has made me start to second guess my choice. It has made me wonder if there is another way—if it's possible to agree to go back, only to escape once again.

That's why I need to think about what happened after that night on the hill in Isaac's arms, underneath our version of falling stars. I need to remember that going back is not an option. My life there was only bearable because of Isaac.

We were never caught for our night out, and I think it made Isaac feel as if luck was on our side. As a result, he took a chance that ended in the most painful experience of my life.

⁓•⁑⁑⁑•⁓

"Let's go, wake up. It's moving day for you." Someone gently shakes my shoulders. The voice is soft, almost a whisper, and I don't recognize it. I open my eyes and see a man I've only seen once before, at my sixteenth birthday party. He's about as tall as Isaac, but really skinny. I think he might even be skinnier than me. He has gray hair and several wrinkles around his eyes and mouth. His eyes are brown and don't match with his voice. Looking only at his eyes I would assume he was like the man, but his voice makes him seem kind. "I'm going to give you time to get dressed." Again, it's almost a whisper, and I can tell that he's not trying to be quiet—it's just the way he talks. I rub my eyes and sit up as he walks out of the room. It takes me a few seconds to fully understand what's happening.

I'm moving out of the hole.

I don't know what to expect from my new room. Isaac would never tell me because he wasn't sure where they would put me. Rosie used to talk about sharing a room with two other girls. I'm not sure if I'd want to have a room to myself or not. I'm so used to living alone that I'm not sure I'd like sharing a room with other girls, but it might be nice to have someone to talk to who can talk back.

The thought makes me look at Abigail. I wonder if they will take her away from me today. Not wanting to think about it, I quickly get dressed. I'm not sure what to wear, so I put on one of the dresses I used to wear for my lessons with Rosie. It's still comfortable but a little nicer than the sweatpants I like to wear when I'm alone. I move toward the door to let Whispers know I'm ready, but I stop when I remember my headband with the charm hidden inside. I go to my table and take it out of the box and put it on. I knock twice on the door and step away. Whispers opens the door immediately and looks me up and down.

"You can leave your things, and someone else will come for them. The boss and Roxy have determined which items you can keep, and those will be brought to your new room. Turn around please." I'm momentarily frozen in surprise of how he's talking to me. Isaac is the only person who has ever asked me to do something, rather than tell me. I do as I'm asked and feel something slide over my eyes, blocking out my vision. I tense, remembering what happened the night with Isaac's cousin. "Relax, I'm just covering your eyes so you can't see where we're going. I'll help you walk." He takes my arm and guides me out the door.

I'm able to imagine where we're going only because of my trip with Isaac to see the lights. Whispers guides me gently up the stairs and even though I know the door to the outside is next, I still stop the moment the wind hits my face. The air is not as cold, and there is no sting, but it feels and smells just as wonderful as it did a few nights ago. I also feel something warm and I instinctively turn my face upward. I can tell the light is bright even though I can't see anything. My mind suddenly produces a memory of me sitting in the sunrays of my mother's bedroom window.

It has been so long since I felt the sun and it makes my eyes water with the threat of tears. I'm starting to get used to this new feeling of wanting to cry, even though I'm happy. I cycle through the emotions I learned in my lessons with Isaac until I find the one that I think I'm experiencing.

Overwhelmed.

Yes, that's what I think I'm feeling. I'm so happy to be outside, in the air and the sun, that it's almost too much. I never understood that emotion when Isaac tried to explain, but now I do.

"Are you ready to keep moving? I understand it's been a while since you've been outside." I'm still unsure about Whispers. He's too calm and too nice to fit into this place. His eyes suddenly flash to the front of my mind.

Yes, he fits here.

He may be calm and polite at the moment, but I don't doubt for a second that he would beat me until I'm almost dead if I broke a rule. I nod my head in response to his question and we start moving.

When we stop again I hear the door of a car open, and he helps me get in without hitting my head. The car starts to move, and I rest my head on the back of the seat. The movement of the car reminds me of my night with Isaac. Really, everything seems to remind me of that night, but being in the car makes it more vivid. At one point I lift my head and wonder where he's taking me. My concept of time has been altered since we left, so I'm not sure how long Whispers has been driving.

I finally feel the car come to a stop, and seconds later my door opens. Whispers puts his hand on my arm, guiding me out of the car and into another building. The first thing I notice is that the smell is not as bad as it was in the hole. It's different than outside, but not bad. The other thing that's different is what I hear. Several smaller sounds mix together into one. At first it's distracting, but the consistency of it turns it into something that's comforting. Hearing it makes me realize just how alone I was in my old room.

I'm led through a series of doors—I count seven, but I may have missed one in the beginning when I was distracted by the sounds. Whispers removes whatever it is covering my eyes. I'm surprised to see how big my new room is compared to my old one. It has the same furniture—a bed, a table, and a chair—but they are all larger as well. I turn and see two doors in the wall to the right. I look back at Whispers.

"Go ahead, you can check it out."

I walk over to the door on the right and open it. I'm instantly hit with a memory. The image of a little girl, sitting in the corner of her mother's closet, is so vivid I'm tempted to push the clothes aside to see if she's really there.

I close the door without even looking at the clothes and turn to the second door. It's a bathroom. It's not large, but it has a toilet, a sink, and a shower. I turn and look back out into my new room. I see a patch of light on the floor and I look up. There's a window in the ceiling. I walk over and stand in the light, looking up at the blue sky.

"I know it's a lot to take in, Angel. Your life now will be very different." I turn to look at Whispers. I feel the urge to move closer to him, so I don't miss any of his soft words. He guides me to sit on the bed and he pulls the chair over to sit across from me. "You were in the hole for your protection. Many people like to take advantage of young children, so that's the safest place you could have been. Now you're an adult and expected to join the family. You will be given things you'd never be able to obtain on your own. You will be protected and cared for as long as you follow the rules. The rules up here are the same as they were before. You do as you're told. It's that simple. Do you have any questions?"

I have lots of questions. I'm tempted to ask, but when I look into his eyes I'm reminded that he's not someone I can trust. I decide a simple question would be okay. "Will I share this room with any other girls?"

"Not this room. We know the transition can be difficult. You haven't spent much time around other people, so we want to ease you into this phase of your life. Remember—we want to take care of you. We want to give you everything you need. You will stay in this room by yourself until it's determined that you're ready to join the others. At that point, you will move to a room that you will share with at least one of the other girls."

He stands and I blink my eyes a few times. The way he speaks makes my head feel strange—almost as if I were sleeping.

"Will I have the same boss?" It's a risky question, but I hope that I've worded it in a way that isn't suspicious.

"Roxy will attend to your needs, or assign one of the girls to do it." I notice that he doesn't exactly answer my question. He turns to the door but pauses before leaving. "This door will be locked from the outside. Again, this is for your protection. Your food will be brought to you, and Roxy will ensure you have everything else you might need. I'll check in on you again in a few days."

He leaves and I hear the click of the lock. The room may be different, but some things will never change.

I look around my room, unsure of what to do. Suddenly missing everything that was once familiar to me, I lay down on the bed. Wanting Abigail, I hug my pillow to my chest. I turn my head and look up at the ceiling. I can see out the window, and I calm myself by watching the clouds drift by.

Three months have passed since I moved into my new room. In that time, Isaac has only been to see me once, and that was with Roxy.

I look at my reflection in the small mirror above my sink. I think this attempt might be the worst yet. Once a week, Roxy comes by to try something new with my hair, make-up, and clothes. She takes a picture of me and then disappears until she comes back to do it all over again.

I turn on the water and start washing off the make-up. When I'm done, I take off the dress that's too tight and put on my sweatpants and T-shirt. I slip the headband with the charm hidden inside on my head before sitting down to eat my dinner. My portions are still too much, but I force myself to eat it all. When I finish, I set the empty tray by the door, turn off my light, and go to lie on my bed.

I have nothing to do.

Aside from the once a week visits from Roxy, the only other person I see is Kiki who comes twice a week. She's basically Rosie and New Cleaning Lady all rolled into one person. She makes sure I haven't forgotten the things Rosie taught me, and then she shaves me and trims my hair. Kiki is not nice and I don't like her much. She often hits me for no reason and calls me words I've never heard before. Even though I don't know what the words mean, I know by the way she says them that they're not meant to be nice. And she looks a little funny. Her breasts are really big—so big that most of the time her dress can't cover them all the way. Her lips are big and she wears a lot of make-up. The only thing I like about the way she looks is her long blonde hair. It's very shiny.

I look up at the window in my ceiling. With the only light in my room coming from my nightlight, the stars are easy to see. They're really bright tonight, and it reminds me of my night out with Isaac. I'm searching for my favorite constellation when I hear my door open. I sit up and see Isaac. He's alone and I start to get excited, until I see the look on his face. He looks scared. Really scared.

And there are tears in his eyes.

He comes straight to my bed and drops on his knees in front of me. He takes my hands and presses them to his face.

"I'm so sorry, Ang. I've messed up. I'm so sorry." He makes a sound and I realize he's crying.

I try to raise his face so I can see his eyes, but he won't look at me. "Isaac, please tell me what's wrong."

"I thought it would work. I was sure it was the answer to all our problems. But it went wrong. Terribly wrong, and now I don't know what he'll do."

"Isaac—"

He stands and paces around my room, pulling at his hair. "Maybe we still have time to get out of here." He stops pacing and looks up at my window. "I wonder if that will open." He pulls over the chair and stands on it. He's tall enough to reach the window and he pushes up. It doesn't move. "Damn it!" He jumps down and kicks at the chair.

"Isaac!" It's the loudest I've ever talked to him and it makes him stop to look at me. "What happened?"

"You're still not looking old enough. We only have two months left, and it's not working. I've looked at all the pictures Roxy has taken and none of them work. You still look too young. I started to worry because I was afraid he'd trade or sell you to another organization. If he does that, I—" He stops and drops into the chair he kicked. "I can't let that happen. I've been trying to find another way, and then I remembered that I still haven't selected my girl. I thought that would solve all our problems."

"What does that mean?"

"Most of the men in the family get to have a girl that will . . . service them whenever they want. She will still have sex with paying customers, but she has to be available whenever her 'owner' demands. Since I'm his son, he told me I could select any girl I wanted, within a certain range of experience, and she would belong only to me. I'd be the only one she could be with unless I said otherwise. I haven't selected yet."

My heart pounds in my chest so hard I can feel and hear each beat in my ears. "Me?"

"Yeah. I thought it was perfect. I was so excited. I told him that I'd made my choice. That I wanted you because you weren't going to pass the age test. I tried to make it sound like I was doing him a favor. I wanted him to think I only wanted you so we wouldn't waste our investment in you. I even told him that giving you to me was the best option—he wouldn't have to take a hit in a trade and it would also keep me from taking another girl out of the rotation. It would basically be a wash. But he saw through it."

"What?" The tears fall down my face, and I know I'm close to losing control.

"My feelings. He saw through it all and knew I asked for you because I wanted you. Because I love you."

I shake my head, not wanting to hear what he's said. It's the first time he's specifically told me that he loves me and I should feel happy, but all I can feel is pain. It was supposed to be the one thing that we didn't say even to each other. Our feelings were supposed to stay hidden in the words on the pages of *Wuthering Heights*—it was the only way to keep anyone from knowing. But then I had to go and let him kiss me on the hill above the lights of the city and under the fireworks that looked like falling stars. Love cannot exist in this place. It's not allowed.

"I'm so sorry, Ang."

"What's he going to do?"

"I don't know. He'll probably trade you to another—"

The door bangs open and we both jump. The man walks in, followed by Watcher. He looks from Isaac to me and back again.

"Well, now isn't this just cute. Did you come to tell your girlfriend the good news?" The man walks over to me and grabs me by my hair. I let out a cry of pain.

"Stop! Please, she had nothing to do with this. Punish me, not her." Isaac jumps to his feet in the direction of the man, but Watcher grabs him by the arms.

"Oh, you'll be punished. Have no doubt about that. But the real question is what I'm going to do with your little whore." The man pulls me from the bed, still holding strong to my hair. It feels like it's going to be ripped from my head when I stumble to the floor. I lift my hands on instinct and he twists one behind my back. I let out another cry as my shoulder moves in a way it's not supposed to.

"Stop! I'll do anything you say, just please leave her alone."

The man lets go of my hair and grabs Isaac by the throat. "You know, I think your idea of keeping Angel as a personal sex slave is actually brilliant. There's no reason to waste her or let anyone else profit from her unique looks. Since I can't afford the risk of her working and making people suspicious about my business, I think I'll use her for my own personal pleasure."

"No, no, no. You can't—"

"I can and I will. See, that's the problem with love. It only gets in the way and causes pain. Because you were foolish enough to fall in love with her, I now know your weakness. I know how to hurt you the most." The man shoves me back down on the bed and grabs

Isaac with both hands. "You are my son. This is your legacy and I will not let you throw it away! I'm going to hurt you until you break, and then you'll see why love cannot exist in this world. If you had been able to be the man you were supposed to be, you would have never felt the pain you are about to experience." The man shoves Isaac back down in the chair and turns to Watcher. "Hold him. Make sure neither one of them tries to stop this."

Watcher takes out a knife and holds it to Isaac's throat. Everything in me becomes heavy, yet I try to move. I don't know what I intend to do, but I can't let him hurt Isaac. The man catches me before I'm off the bed and slams me back down onto the mattress. He grabs my face with his hand and turns it to look at Watcher—he has a gun pointed at my head. Isaac told me about guns and what they can do.

"Please, don't do this!" Isaac's cry is muffled by his sobs and the press of Watcher's knife. I watch a small drop of blood crawl away from the knife and down Isaac's throat.

"You will watch this, son. Every second. If you look away even once, he'll shoot." I feel the man's touch, soft on my hair. The softness is unexpected and I don't know how to respond. "Angel, look at me." I hold Isaac's gaze, not wanting to turn away. "Look at me, and I might let him go." Isaac's eyes are pleading with me not to look away, but I have to. I want him to be safe. I look at the man and he smiles. "Yes, that's it. Now you belong to me."

He slaps me hard across the face. Before I can react, he's on top of me. Everything is happening so fast. It's not what I expect based on the hours I spent watching videos during my training. It reminds me of the last video Rosie showed me. My chest tightens and I try to move my legs, but he's pinned me down so I can't move.

I feel his tongue on my neck.

I hear the rip of my clothes.

I hear Isaac's constant pleas for him to stop.

And then I feel nothing but pain. It tears through me, causing a scream I didn't know I was capable of creating. I try to push him off me, but he's too strong.

I hear Isaac scream and suddenly I remember the self-defense moves he taught me. I fight the pain to concentrate on the man's movements. There's a rhythm that I quickly pick up on. I wait until he's pulled back and I move. I'm able to roll to the side and the man falls off me in surprise. I'm almost off the bed when he pulls me back.

The man lies on top of me, his breath on my face. "I must admit, that was actually kind of impressive. But it was also very stupid." He turns my head so I'm facing Isaac. Watcher drags the knife across Isaac's cheek, leaving a trail of blood. "See what that little stunt cost you? Don't do it again." He holds my head in place and slams into me again. I close my eyes in pain, feeling the tears drop over and over to my pillow.

I don't know how long I lay there, forced to take him, before I make the mistake of looking at Isaac. The pain I see in his eyes hurts more than anything the man is doing to me. I try to force myself to look at him, feeling that I shouldn't be allowed to look away if he can't. But even though his eyes are on me, he's not looking at me. I know he no longer sees me the way he used to. The love I used to see is replaced by only pain, and I can't look. I shift my eyes and look out the window in my ceiling.

I see the stars.

I count them until it's finally over.

13: Black Hole

I'm crying. I must be louder than I realize because the door opens and Goon comes in. "What the hell is wrong with you now?"

I'm curled into a ball, held up only by the wall. I want to scream at him. I want to point out that his question is ridiculous. How could he not know what's wrong? I'm locked up in some warehouse with less than twenty-four hours to live. I've been imprisoned, beaten, and raped for the majority of my life.

But I don't say anything. It's not who I am. I'm not a fighter—I'm a survivor, and I learned a long time ago that the way to survive my life was to keep my mouth shut.

"I said, what's wrong?" Goon pulls on my hair to look at my face.

"Nothing." I take in a deep breath and force my sobs to settle.

He looks at me a few seconds before letting go of my hair. "Just make sure your 'nothing' is not so loud next time." He walks out the door, and once again I'm left alone with my thoughts.

I feel the black hole trying to pull me back in.

My mind wants to paint vivid pictures for me—images of the man doing whatever he wanted with me. He made me do everything I learned in the training videos, in addition to things I hadn't. Some of our encounters even included things I saw in the video Rosie showed me, with the exception of other men participating. He never allowed anyone else to touch me.

But worse than all of that—he made Isaac watch over and over again. At first I counted how many times he had to watch—because that's what I do—but I stopped when it became too painful. The man made Isaac watch until he was convinced that Isaac no longer loved me, but instead despised the very sight of me.

When he had achieved his goal, he sent Isaac away. At least that's what the man told me, and I had no choice but to believe him. I certainly didn't want to believe the alternative.

I feel the gravitational pull of the black hole and it's hard to resist. I fight against it, knowing that if I fall in I'll be lost forever. I close my eyes and start to count. I shift through the numbers quickly, not counting anything but the passing of time. When I finally feel the pull begin to release, I slow my pace. The numbers start to blur and my mind goes blank.

"Come outside with me. The stars are bright tonight."

He's in a shadow and I can't see his face, but I know his voice. While the words spoken start a rapid firing of spasms within me, the sound of his voice tells me that I'm safe.

"But I don't like the stars."

"Why?"

"You know why. When I see the stars, I see him. I feel him."

"It will be fine. You trust me, don't you?"

I do. I trust him without question. I reach for his extended hand, and he locks his fingers with mine. He leads me out the door, into the darkness. I keep my eyes down, still not wanting to see the stars. My heart beats hard in my chest, but I don't feel pain.

"Look up. It's amazing."

I slowly tilt my head up, eyes closed. I take a deep breath and open my eyes.

Pain instantly stabs through my abdomen. I feel the sting on my face and hear the ringing in my ears. I feel the hot breath fast on my forehead. My knees start to shake and I sink to the ground. I'm pulled up by my hand.

I look at him in confusion. "You were supposed to keep me safe."

I'm yanked forward, and I crash hard into his chest. He puts his face close to mine. "The only thing I'm going to do is shatter you."

I was wrong. It's not Isaac at all. It's the man. I scream.

I sit forward, gasping for breath. The door bangs open.

"Shut up! Screaming's not going to get you out of here!" I look toward the unfamiliar voice. He must be Goon's night relief.

I open my mouth to respond, even though I'm not sure what I'm about to say. Before I can utter a sound, Goon Two's hand closes around my throat. Instinctively my hands grab onto his.

He brings his face close to mine. "You make a sound like that again, and I'll rip out your tongue." He shoves me back against the wall and removes his hand. He checks his watch as he walks away. "It's five minutes early, but consider this your hour warning."

12: On the Edge

The door slams shut and I rub the back of my head. Goon Two must have shoved me harder than I realized because my head is pounding. I take a steadying breath and try to remember what just happened.

I had a bad dream and must have screamed out loud.

I've had terrifying dreams so many times over the years that I should be able to know they're not real. But that's the power of a sleeping mind—it can transform any memory or imagination into something more vivid than reality.

I'm frustrated that I wasted time by falling asleep, but I do feel more refreshed. The last memory was too much. I've kept that moment, and the two years that followed, locked away in a black hole that I've fought against every hour of every day.

Isaac had once given me a series of lessons on space, and I found a connection with the concept of black holes. It was as if I were living my life walking on the edge of an event horizon. One step in the wrong direction and I'd fall in—leaving me with no escape.

It was hardest to fight in those years I spent as the man's personal sex slave. I often felt there was no hope for a different life, and twice I had almost surrendered to the black hole. However, each time I was given a reason to believe I could defy the odds.

⊙⟡⟡⊙

I'm staring at the television, but my mind is somewhere else. The man hasn't come to see me for a couple days. While this would seem like a good thing, I've learned that it's not good at all. A prolonged absence always makes his following visits longer and more abusive.

I touch the side of my face. In the mirror this morning I saw that the latest bruises had faded, but the lump is still there. At first he didn't hit me every time. Now the question isn't if he will hit me or not—it's how hard he'll hit me and if I'll have enough time between visits for the marks to heal.

I try to focus back on the television. The man gave it to me about the same time he sent Isaac away. I know he's using it as a way to show me he will take care of me. That he will give me things I've never had before. But I hate it. The only reason I turn it on is because I have nothing else to do. Besides, all I can watch on it is porn. They are similar to the videos Rosie used to show me, but I no longer watch them to learn, or to fantasize about how wonderful it would feel when I had my own chance to have sex. After a year of being under the man's control, I don't want to have anything to do with sex.

But my body won't listen.

Sometimes I have a physical reaction to the things the man does to me or makes me do. Even though I hate it, and it hurts physically and mentally, my body craves touch. Since he's the only one touching me, my body responds in ways that aren't acceptable.

So I still watch porn, hoping to find a way to crush my physical desires. I watch the interaction between the man and the woman on the screen until I feel a tingling sensation. Then I pull my mind in, forcing it to go blank.

An image of the man appears and he's on top of me. I can feel the pain as if he were really in the room. I turn away from the television and curl into a ball. I want Abigail, but I haven't seen her since I left the hole. For a while I still talked to her, pretending that she could hear me. I hug my pillow to my chest and feel the tears roll off my cheeks.

I miss Isaac. The pain of missing him is actually much stronger than what the man does to my body. I don't know where he is or if I will ever see him again. I no longer wait for him to show up in the middle of the night. I don't pretend that he comes to sneak me out again to sit on the hill under the fireworks of falling stars.

This is all that there is for me.

I wonder if it would be better if I were no longer alive. If there was some way I could make myself dead. Isaac never really told me how someone becomes dead, except for when he explained how guns work. He told me they were used to kill people. But I don't have a gun. Since I can't make myself dead, I've been trying to make my mind dead—to stop feeling. But I haven't been able to do it, so I don't think it's possible.

I jump when I hear the door open and I brace myself for what's about to happen. I pull in a sharp breath and look at the door.

It's not the man.

It's Whispers.

I haven't seen him since a few days after I arrived in my new room. He looks from me to the television and then walks over to turn it off. He sits down in the chair across from me. I wipe my eyes and sit up on the bed. He stares at me a few seconds before pulling something out of his coat pocket and placing it on the table. He then takes out a cigarette and lights it up. I count four puffs of smoke before he starts to talk.

"Did you know that I told my nephew he should get rid of you?" He takes another long drag of the cigarette. "No, of course you wouldn't. It was a few days after you arrived. You were sleeping when I came to meet you. You looked so peaceful in your sleep, and I couldn't make myself wake you. I just watched. It was obvious he named you accurately—you were like a little angel, floating on a pillow of white clouds."

Of course his voice is barely above a whisper, and it's hard for me to hear over the pounding of my heart. I sit forward, drawn in by his words. The glow of the sun on the smoke from his cigarette gives him a strange look. It's almost as if he wasn't really there at all. I move closer still, almost to the edge of my bed.

"Naturally he didn't listen. I never did like the direction he took the business. I don't believe in using children, but I think he truly believes that he's saved each and every one of you. He only picks girls that come from a crack whore mother with no future ahead of them. It's likely they would end up dead at an early age, or working the streets if they happened to survive. Since he said he wouldn't put the girls to work until they were of age—which is close to the legal limit in our line of work—I kept my mouth shut. It's not my business after all. But I am the elder in the family, so he respects my opinion—even if he doesn't follow through on my suggestions—and so he asks my opinion of each new girl brought in. I never had an issue with any of them. Until you."

He finishes his cigarette and sits forward. The cloud of smoke is still around him, but now I can see his eyes. I don't like them and I look at his mouth instead. I read the words as he speaks them.

"From the moment I laid eyes on you I knew you would be trouble. I'm not sure how, but somehow I could feel that you would change things. I wasn't sure if it was for good or bad—only that there would be change. That part of the business was still too new and I didn't think it was worth the risk, so I told him you should be sold to another organization. But he disagreed, thinking that you would offer us good fortune with your unique looks. He hoped you would bring in a new set of clients that we hadn't yet been able to attract. I thought he was being reckless, but he was determined to have his way. Besides, I knew it would be a few years until you'd be put to work. It would give me time to change his mind if needed."

He pauses, a smile on his lips. He places his hand on the thing he put on the table, spinning it in a circle with his fingers.

"Then the day came when you turned sixteen, and the most amazing thing happened. I assume you remember your sixteenth birthday party, so I don't need to remind you."

He stares at me, waiting for a response. I nod and look back at the item slowly spinning in circles on the table. He stops playing with it and folds his hands in front of him. He starts speaking again when my eyes find his.

"The day I delivered you from the hole was a happy one for me. One look at you and it was obvious you'd never look old enough to be of use to our business. I knew my nephew was in denial, and that's why he planned to keep you around for another six months, but I was satisfied that I was proven right and you'd be gone. But then . . ." He pauses again and this time closes his eyes. He shakes his head a few times before continuing.

"But then he had to go and claim you for his own. I understood the reason why he claimed you at first. You and my great-nephew needed to be punished. What I don't understand is why he still keeps you around. We have plenty of girls that can hold his interest and satisfy his desires, so it must be something more. Some intangible connection that I'm sure even he doesn't understand. You are no longer a danger to the business, but you are a danger to my nephew. I can't even describe what he's like when he talks about you."

He picks up the thing on the table, stands, and walks over to the bed. He crouches down to my eye level and holds my face in place with his free hand. A chill runs down my spine as I'm forced to look into his eyes. He holds the thing in his hand up so I can see it.

"I came in here to kill you. The contents of this syringe will make your heart stop beating within just a few seconds. He'd never risk having an autopsy done on your dead body, so he'd be left to assume your heart just gave out."

He lets go of my face and pulls something off the syringe. Now one end of it is pointy. He places that end to my neck and I feel a little prick on my skin.

"It would be so easy. You'd be gone and my nephew would return to normal, concentrating on taking the business to new levels."

I hold my breath. I think about the words I used in my mind before Whispers came in my room. Did I accidentally wish to be dead? It's been a long time since I thought about the power of my wishes. I've been very careful not to wish for anything—ever. But I was thinking about being dead, and now Whispers is here to make it happen.

Whispers pulls the syringe away from my neck and puts the cap back on. "As much as it pains me, I'm not going to kill you. Sitting here, looking at you, I realize that's not the right answer. My nephew deserves his fate if he can be destroyed by nothing more than a wisp of a girl. If he can't conquer you, there's no way he'll be able to withstand any other challenge thrown his way."

He stands and looks down on me. I watch him put the syringe back in his coat pocket, and for a moment I think about trying to take it from him. He steps away before I can decide.

"My prediction of you was correct—you've changed things. As of right now, it's not for the better. I can see now that you were sent here to reduce my nephew to ashes. However, a new question emerges with that knowledge. Will he arise, like a phoenix reborn, or will he, along with the rest of us, be swept into the winds of hell?" He turns and leaves without another word.

My breath catches and something stirs inside me. I'm not sure what it is, but I feel as if I might actually have a chance at something else. Moments ago I wanted to find a way to become dead, then that desire was answered in the form of Whispers. But he didn't do it. He had a strange way of saying it, but if I understand his words correctly then he thinks there is a chance I can defeat the man. Somehow the words transform me.

They give me hope once again.

I breathe easier as the man lifts off me. He walks slowly across the room, his unbuckled belt making a noise with each step. I want to move, but he left me tied to the bed. He does this sometimes. He likes to sit and look at me. Sometimes he decides he'll have another round before he removes the restraints.

I watch as he bends over the white powder sitting in neat little rows on a tray on the table. He sniffs in one line, then another. He straightens and takes a deep breath before looking back at me. I watch as he slowly walks to the chair and sits down.

"I usually let the girls take a hit every once in a while, but you're still being punished. It's too bad because that's some really good shit. Maybe you'll have worked off your debt in a couple more years, and then I'll let you have a taste." His eyes travel the length of my body. He shifts in the chair then stands, and my stomach rolls. It's going to be a round two kind of night.

Before he can finish making his way over to me, there's a knock on the door. The pattern lets us know it's Roxy, and he lets her in.

"Sorry to interrupt your sport, but it's time to go." She glances at me for only a second before walking over to the table. "Looks like you saved me some?"

"Go ahead." The man walks over to the bed and stands over my head, stroking my hair. "I want you to change my plans for tonight. I don't think I'm done here yet, and I won't be for a while."

I hear the sound of Roxy taking down the last two lines. "No can do, love. It's the big fish from Japan—he leaves town tomorrow. You can't miss this opportunity."

He doesn't respond for a few seconds. Finally, he sighs before withdrawing his hand. "I guess this will just have to wait until tomorrow." He buttons his pants and fastens his belt as he turns away. He steps to the door and looks back at Roxy. "Let's go."

She darts her eyes to me again. "You can't leave her like that."

He's in front of her in three long strides and grabs her by the back of the head. "Did you just challenge me?"

"No, I—I just, I mean she'll lose feeling in her arms. I didn't think you'd want to screw a girl with no arms. That's all."

He tugs at her hair before letting go. "Then cut her loose, and let's go."

Roxy quickly walks to the bed and unties the knots restraining my arms to the bed. At first I think I imagine the quick squeeze of my hand before she walks away, but when her eyes lock with mine for a brief moment I know it's real. They are out the door before I can roll to a sitting position.

On the way to the shower, I rub at one arm and then the next. I turn the water on the hottest setting I can tolerate and climb into the tub. I sit under the water, trying to wash off the still lingering feel of the man's touch. I watch the last of the blood go down the drain, and then I start scrubbing. It hurts, and some of the cuts bleed again, but I don't stop.

My stomach clenches and I start to cry. I try not to, but I'm at that point of surrender once again. It's been another year. I still haven't seen Isaac. I don't even know if he's alive.

I look at the shower wall and run my hand up and down the tile. I wonder if I could hit my head hard enough, or enough times, to make it all stop. I think it might work because once the man hit my head against the wall so hard it knocked me out. When I woke up, the doctor was there. My eyes were still closed so they didn't know I was awake. I heard the doctor tell the man that he could have killed me, so it must be possible. I just don't know if I can do it myself, or if I need someone else to do it for me. I'm about to try when someone pulls the shower curtain to the side.

I look up and see a woman I've never seen before. She has light brown hair to her shoulders. I think she must be one of Roxy's girls, but she doesn't dress like them. She's wearing pants and a shirt that covers up her breasts and her arms. My stomach rolls with uncertainty, until I look at her eyes.

I'd know those eyes anywhere.

"You're going to scrub yourself raw. I suppose I can understand why, but I'd say you're clean enough." She drops the curtain and I hear her walk out.

I hesitate a moment and then turn off the water. I quickly dry off with the towel and put on my T-shirt and sweatpants. I walk slowly into my room and find her sitting in the chair, staring at the bed—or more specifically at the restraints. I sit on the bed facing her.

I watch her eyes move from the mark on my left eye, to the one on my chin, to the next one, and keep going until she's seen them all. Her eyes stay on the last one for a few seconds before moving back to meet my gaze. Once again, I see Isaac's eyes reflected through hers. It makes my heart hammer in my chest. I miss him so much.

"I'm not supposed to be in here, but my husband will be busy with an important meeting all night. He took most of his men with him, so I figured this might be my only opportunity."

I'm right—she's Isaac's mom. I relax, feeling instantly safe. Isaac trusts her, so I do as well.

"You don't speak much, do you?" I shake my head. "My son said as much."

"I talk to him." My eyes well up with tears, and I blink rapidly. I don't want to cry in front of her, but I don't think I can stop them from falling.

"I know. Of course, he never told me exactly who the girl was that had claimed his heart, but over time I had surmised it was you." She pauses and lets out a small laugh. "I never thought I'd be in this position. I never imagined I'd have the opportunity to meet the woman who somehow claimed both my son and my husband."

I pull my knees to my chest, wrapping my arms around them tight. Somehow her words had caused a sting—as if she had slapped me across the face.

Her smile drops and she sighs. "I didn't mean that the way it probably sounded." She pauses and looks away. "I'm sorry, I didn't exactly have a plan coming in here. My son asked me to give you something if I ever found a way to do it without getting caught, so here I am."

Isaac. She's here for Isaac. He has something for me. "Is he okay?"

"If you're asking me if my son is alive, then the answer is yes. But he's not okay, not without you."

Isaac is alive. Relief washes over me and the sobs hit hard. When I regain control of my emotions, she hands me something.

Wuthering Heights.

My tears start fresh, but I wipe them away. I open the book, searching.

"He's marked the pages for you—the ones with the corners bent back."

I look up, startled. For a brief moment I'm angry that she's seen the messages he's marked. It's supposed to be a secret that only we share. However, the anger fades as I read the first passage.

". . . you know that I could as soon forget you as my existence!"

I wipe my eyes again and turn to the next marked page.

"Because misery, and degradation, and death, and nothing that God or satan could inflict would have parted us . . ."

There is one more marked page.

"I cannot live without my life! I cannot live without my soul!"

I hug the book to my chest. He hasn't forgotten about me. The quotes he's marked make me want to believe that he also still loves me—but how could he after all that's happened? I look back up at Isaac's mom to find her watching me closely.

"Those are some powerful words of love my son wanted you to hear."

I bury my face in my knees, not wanting her to see my pain. "He can't possibly still love me."

"I know what my husband did to the two of you. He may have shattered you both, but he didn't take the love away."

I want to believe her. I want to believe in the words that Isaac marked in the book. But I can't. I had seen Isaac's eyes each time the man forced him to watch. The love was gone, replaced with pain and emptiness.

"Look at me, child." It takes me a few seconds, but I finally look back at her through my tears. "I've learned something about being shattered, and I'll tell you the secret. The pieces are still there. They may be scattered and out of order, but they're still there. It will take time, but you can pick them up and put them back together. They will never fit the same way again and there will be cracks and small holes, but they will go back together. You just have to be strong enough to hold them until the glue sets."

I remember the night on the hill with Isaac. In his arms I had felt that he was strong enough to hold all my pieces together. Now his mom is here, putting my own thoughts into her words. I want to believe her, but I don't know how.

Isaac's mom sighs as she looks down at her hands. "When I first met my husband, I didn't know that he was a high end pimp. He talked to me about other plans, big plans that I wanted to be a part of. I was young and he charmed me right off my feet. I married him only three months after we met. We had a very romantic honeymoon, and then he brought me here. I had always thought I was an intelligent woman, but I must have been wrong because it took me two years to figure out how he earned his money. I confronted him and he beat me so hard I ended up in the hospital. He had never laid a finger on me before that night. It seems that somehow he had been able to compartmentalize everything—being one person with me and another in his business. But I had crossed the line and merged his worlds. I finally saw who he really was, and I was terrified. I resolved to leave once I was out of the hospital, but that's when I found out I was pregnant. My husband made it clear I would never be leaving him."

She pauses and shifts in the chair, uncrossing and then crossing her legs in the other direction.

"I still thought about leaving, until I saw what he did to one of his girls that tried to leave. If he reacted that way with a woman he considered nothing more than a doormat, I didn't want to find out what he'd do to me or my son. So I stayed. Over the years I found happiness in—" She stops and gives me a half smile. "I almost forgot, you don't use real names. Will you tell me what you call my son? That might make this story a little easier to tell."

I wipe the remaining tears from my eyes and bite on the inside of my lip. This is Isaac's mom and I know that he trusts her, but if he didn't tell her the name he gave me then it must be for a good reason. I shake my head and her smile widens.

"Very well. I'm actually happy you said no—I've been hoping you'd risk as much for him as he has for you. Anyway, my son gave me happiness and my life became bearable." She pauses and looks down at her hands again. "Did he ever tell you he had a little sister?"

What? Isaac has a sister? Why didn't he ever tell me?

"I can tell by the look on your face that the answer is no. I'm not surprised. She died when he was nine—she was seven. She had cancer—I'd rather not go into the details if you don't mind." She wipes a tear away from her cheek before continuing. "My son took it hard, but my husband took it harder. He felt he should have been able to save her. He may run a prostitution business, but our little girl was his princess. He was a monster before her death, but after . . ." She shakes her head and looks away. One deep breath and she starts again.

"About two years after she died, my husband went to a crack house to find one of his girls that tried to leave. While there, he found a child. She was around seven and her mother was passed out on drugs. When he found her, she was about to stick one of her mother's needles in her arm. My husband believed that he had been led there to save the child, so he brought her home. At that point he didn't know what he would do with her. She was a child which made her okay to save, but she was also the product of a crack whore which made her insignificant by default. That's when he got the idea to train her as a prostitute—claiming she would have ended up as one if he had never found her, and at least this way he could make her a really good one. I didn't like it, but what could I do? I hate to admit it, but there was some truth to his words. If her mother's needle hadn't killed her, she likely would have ended up as a child sex slave. It happens all the time. I knew that here she would at least have a roof over her head, food in her belly, and clothes on her back. When he declared that no one could touch her, and that she wouldn't work until she was near the legal age, I chose to look the other way. At least until he wanted my son to get involved in learning the business." She gets up and walks around the room. "This room is depressing."

"It's better than the hole."

She looks at me, clearly surprised that I responded. "Yes, I suppose that's one way of looking at it. Do you remember anything of your life before coming here?"

"Not much. I know my mother kept me in her closet. And that she was a prostitute."

She nods and sits back down in the chair. "As I was saying, I didn't like the idea of my son getting involved. Since the day he was born, I have done everything in my power to keep him from turning into my husband's clone. I was evaluating my options, trying to figure out if I should try to run away with him, when something amazing happened. One day, practically overnight, my son started smiling more, and so I started watching more closely. I watched as he snuck things under his shirt before coming to see you—books, postcards, drawings. I saw how he looked when he talked about you. I also watched when he wasn't talking—it was clear that even in those moments he was thinking about you. And I saw how he pulled himself farther and farther away from his father. I'd decided you were probably the best thing that could have happened in his life. Unfortunately, I had forgotten how dangerous love could be. I knew the risk he was taking and I wanted to stop him, but I also knew that would be impossible."

Her words slowly cut away at my uncertainty. I look down at the book once again. Isaac, and his mom, took a great risk to tell me that he hasn't forgotten about me. He wouldn't do that if he didn't still care. The only question that remains in my heart is how much—he may still care about me, but does his love run as deep as it did before the man shattered us?

Isaac's mom stands, catching my attention. She holds out her hand. "I wish I could leave the book with you, but I think you know what will happen if my husband finds it."

I don't want to let it go, but I know she's right. I reluctantly hand it back, and she moves toward the door.

She stops before leaving and turns back to face me. "I don't know exactly why my husband has become so obsessed with you. I'm sorry—truly sorry. I wish there were something I could do to make it stop."

I can hear the pain in her voice, and I believe her. She's just as much under the man's control as I am. I give her a small nod to let her know I accept her words.

She nods in return. "One last thing—I've been tempted over the years to ask my son to give you up. I wanted to tell him that nothing good could come from loving you and holding on so tight. Look at how much pain you are both in right now, simply because you love each other. I wanted to convince him that he'd live a happier life without you in it." She looks down at the book in her hands, then back up at me with tears in her eyes. "Now, having read the underlined words in this book, I understand that I was wrong. I'm grateful to you for giving him a chance to know how it feels to love someone, and be loved in return."

She leaves and I fall back on my bed, clutching my pillow to my chest. Isaac is alive. Even if I can never see him again, I'm relieved to know that he's out there, somewhere.

And that he still cares about me.

I let the sobs take over until I fall asleep.

11: Flying Away

The bang on the door is louder than it has been for the past few hours, and it makes me jump. I try to figure out the time based on the warnings. I don't know exactly what time the man gave me the offer and started my clock, but I figure it must be sometime after midnight.

It is now the day of my death—because as I've said before, life is not a part of either of my options.

I look up at the window and wonder again if there's any chance for another outcome. If there is a way I can somehow escape. I look at the bucket I kicked just a couple hours ago. I get up and put it under the window—this time on the opposite side, where the grime is thick and the stars are blocked. I walk over to the other buckets I saw earlier in the evening and grab one that I didn't use as a toilet. I take it over and stack it on top of the first bucket. I carefully climb up and reach for the window.

My fingers touch the glass and I push, but it doesn't budge. I push harder and only succeed in nearly kicking the buckets out from under my feet. I contemplate trying to break it, but even if I could, it would make too much noise and Goon Two would be in before I had a chance to pull myself up and out. I don't even know if I currently have the arm strength to pull myself up.

My whole body aches and I don't know if I can take another beating without surrendering to the black hole I've been fighting. It's been four years since my body has been abused this way, and I'm out of practice. I may not have a choice about dying today—either physically or emotionally—but at least I have control over my state of mind when it happens. I choose to not be in a coma of pain, so I once again climb off the tower of buckets.

For the first time I walk over to the door, putting my ear against the metal to listen. I can't hear anything. I know the door is locked so I don't even try the knob. A lock clicking into place is a sound I've known my whole life, and I've heard it every time someone has come and gone from this room.

I cycle through other options of escape. The only way past the guards would be to steal a gun and shoot my way past. I instantly know there is a problem with this plan, because I don't remember seeing a gun on Goon Two. It's possible that he has one hidden, but I wouldn't be able to find it before the others came in and stopped me.

Thinking about the possibility of escape takes me back to the night I finally broke free from the man. I sink to the floor and let the memory take control.

***

I can still feel the sting of his touch and hot breath on my skin. I desperately want to scrub myself clean in the shower, but I can't because he's in there. He doesn't usually take a shower after he has his way with me, but this is one of the rare occasions when he does. Just as he's done many times before, he's left me tied up. At least this time my wrists are tied to my ankles rather than the bed. I'm cold and this position allows me to hug my knees to my chest—it's a little better than being stretched out.

The water turns off and I wait. He walks into my room, holding a towel in one hand and his clothes in the other. He puts them both on the chair and reaches for the clothes he hung in the closet.

"As much as I want to stay and continue our fun, I have to go. Did you know that today is my birthday?" He pauses as he puts on his shirt. "No, I don't suppose you would know. Anyway, some of my best clients are in town and we're having a big party." He pulls up his pants and walks over to the bed. He strokes my hair and then tugs it until I look up at him. "I would take you, but it's the kind of party where we share—everything—and you belong only to me." He slides his hand down my arm and stops at the restraints. "It's going to be a long night, but I think I'll leave you tied up. It'll keep me turned on, thinking of you here waiting for me like this. And as a bonus, when I show up tomorrow you'll be ready to go."

Tears start to form and I squeeze my eyes shut. "What if I have to go to the bathroom?"

He must have crouched down to my level because his breath is hot on my face. "If you piss or shit this bed, I will give you a beating like you've never had before—so you'd better hold it."

I feel his tongue as he licks the tears from my cheek.

I hear his laughter as he walks out the door.

I allow myself to cry for a few seconds before trying to pull one of my hands free of the restraints. I have enough room to move my hands out about an inch—it's hard to know for sure. It's been so long since Isaac taught me measurements.

Isaac.

I miss him. His mom had said he was alive, but that was a year ago. I think. It's been harder to accurately keep time since the man claimed me. I don't have regular visitors, and the man no longer recognizes my birthday. I don't have much to use as my time anchors, other than my monthly cycle which isn't that reliable.

I pull harder at my restraints. They cut into my skin and I start to cry again. I look into my bathroom, and for a moment I pretend that I'm sitting under the hot water. The image in my mind is so real my skin starts to tingle. I close my eyes and concentrate on the feel of the water and the smell of the soap.

My stomach rumbles and interrupts my imaginary shower. It's been a long day and I haven't eaten. The man came not long after the sun first came through my window, and now it's long past dark. He took breaks that were just long enough for him to recover before going again. If he couldn't find a way to go again, he'd use something else or beat me until he could. This is only the second time he's used me for most of the day.

My stomach rumbles again. I open my eyes and look at the table where the man left what remains of his lunch. There are some scraps left.

I'm looking at the small bits of food, wondering if there is a way I can get to them, when my eyes shift and see the knife. I've never used a knife, but I know what they can do—cut things. I look down at the things holding my wrists to my ankles. He stopped using rope a while ago. I'm not sure what he uses now, but when he takes them off me he has to cut them. I look at the knife again and then down at the floor. I might be able to make it over to the table if I can roll off the bed.

But what will the man do to me when he comes back and finds me out of my restraints?

I decide that I don't care any more.

My tears have stopped and I no longer feel any of the pain from my day with the man. The need to get to that knife is all that exists. I look down at the floor again. Without thinking about it further, I push off the bed with as much force as I can manage.

I hit the floor hard on my back and suddenly I can't breathe. I'm gasping, the pain gripping my chest.

I'm not sure how long I lie there, desperately trying to pull in air. My chest finally starts to ease, and I'm able to manage small breaths. I remain still, concentrating on each breath. When the pain is down to a small throb, I start to roll toward the table. I reach the table leg and have to rest. My breathing is still not back to normal, and the effort it took to roll has made me dizzy.

I count to fifty, hoping it's enough time to make my body relax. I then roll and push and try several ways to bump the table, trying to knock the knife down to the floor. It doesn't work and I'm almost out of breath again, so I stop to think. When I regain control of my breathing, I start rocking back and forth on my back until I'm in a sitting position. Once again, I'm worn out from the effort so I rest.

A few minutes later my chest still hurts and I'm still a little dizzy, but I start bumping the table with my head and shoulder. It's not working, so I work myself into a position that allows me to rock into it with my knee. Finally, the table starts to move. It's not much, but it's enough to keep me trying. I'm not sure how many attempts it takes, but something finally rattles to the floor. I scoot around, looking for the knife. When I find it, I realize it's the fork. A sob breaks through and I rest my head on my knees. I take a few deep breaths and start again. This time it's loud as the plate and knife crash to the floor together. I freeze, worried that someone heard it. When I'm convinced it's safe, I scoot my way over to the knife. It takes a few attempts, but I'm finally able to pick it up.

I'm not sure what to do, but I've watched the man use one many times. Isaac also used to use one to cut my cakes. I rotate it around in my hand until I'm able to get the part that cuts under my restraint. I flex my wrist to move the knife back and forth.

I cut and cut and cut.

I don't know how long I've been cutting, but my hand and wrist have started to hurt. I can't see the restraint where I've been trying to cut so I pull to see if I've cut enough.

I'm only able to move my arm the same amount as before. My shoulders drop and I rest my head on my knees again. I want to cry. I want to scream. Instead, I start moving my wrist again.

I cut and cut and cut and then test again—still nothing more than before.

Now I do cry, but I keep trying. It has to work. Maybe I have it the wrong way. I don't think so, but I'll cut fifty more times and if it still isn't working then I'll turn it around so the other side of the knife is on the restraints.

I'm at thirty-nine when I hear the click of my lock. I look at my bed in a panic. There's no way for me to get there in time. Even if I could, there would be no way for me to get back on the bed. I start to shake as I imagine the beating that I'm about to receive. I bury my head into my knees and hug myself into a tight ball.

The footsteps approach me fast. The hands that touch my hair are soft. I'm confused. The man touches me this way when he wants me to submit, but I can tell it's not him. I hold my breath as an image comes to mind.

"My God, Ang. What has he done to you?"

It can't be him.

I'm shaking so hard now that I roll to the side. His hands hold me up. I'm crying so hard I can't speak. I want to open my eyes, but if I do I'm afraid his voice and touch will go away. He gently pulls my face up from my knees, but I keep my eyes closed.

"It's okay now, Ang. I'm going to get you out of here. Can you please look at me?"

I take a deep breath and open my eyes.

It's him. My Isaac is here.

"You're really here?"

There are tears in his eyes, but he gives me a small smile. "Yeah,

I'm really here. But I'm not staying, and this time neither are you." His hands are on my wrist—the opposite of the one I was trying to free. "Shit, I need something to cut these." He looks around the room.

"I have a knife in my other hand. I was trying to cut free."

His smile gets a little wider. "That's my girl." He takes the knife out of my hand and his smile disappears. "Ang, baby, this is a butter knife. It will never work."

I hang my head, the urge to laugh surprising me. I don't know what a butter knife is or why it would never work—all I know is that it wasn't working and now I know why.

"I don't want to leave you, but I have to find something to cut these. I can't carry you out like this. I need you on your feet. It's our best chance. I'll be right back, then I'll help you get dressed, and we'll make a run for it."

"I need a shower."

"Ang, we don't have time. You can take one on the road."

"Please." I know he doesn't understand. I also know that we would be taking a risk. But I have to wash the feel of the man off my skin. He holds my gaze and I think he does understand. He puts one arm under my legs and the other around my back. He squeezes me to his chest and carries me to the shower. He puts me down, facing the door, and turns on the water. It's too cold. "Hotter."

"Ang, you'll burn if—"

"It needs to be hotter." I look up at him. He hesitates but turns up the hot water. It stings at first, but within seconds I'm breathing easier. Isaac turns toward the door. "In here."

He stops and looks back at me. "I'm just going out to find something to cut those ties."

"Yes, in here. He always comes in here to get whatever it is he uses to cut me free. That cabinet is locked." I nod my head in the direction of the cabinet over the toilet.

He quickly moves to the cabinet. He feels around the door before trying to shake it from the wall. I know that won't work—I've tried it myself a few times. He looks at it a few more seconds and then pulls a gun out from under his shirt. Seeing it reminds me of the times Watcher pointed a gun at my head while the man made Isaac watch. A shiver runs down my spine, and I attempt to clear the memory by focusing on Isaac. He starts hitting the door with the gun's handle, and after a few hits it pops open.

He starts pulling out items from the cabinet—they're all things the man uses on me when he comes to visit. Seeing Isaac touch them makes me want to cry.

"Sick son of a bitch. I swear to God, I'll kill him if I see him tonight." The sound of his voice reminds me of the night his cousin tried to attack me. It was the only other time I've heard his voice sound this way. He kneels next to me, puts the gun on the floor next to the tub, and reaches in to cut my restraints. He cuts it from my right wrist first, and then from my right ankle. I immediately pull my arm up and stretch out my leg. I have a cramp, but it's better than being tied up. I'm watching him clip the restraint on my left wrist when he suddenly yells out and falls on top of me.

"Who are you? No one's supposed to touch the boss' girl!" Isaac is pulled off me. He's wet from falling into the shower and he's holding the back of his head. I look at the man behind him. It's the guard that the man has check on me sometimes. He shoves Isaac up against the counter. A scream works its way to the back of my mouth, but I hold it back. If I could move, I'd try to help him.

I look down at my arms and remember that I can move. I also remember Isaac's gun. I pick it up and point it at the guard the way Watcher used to do to me. I don't know what to do, but I have to help Isaac. I put my finger in the circle in front of the handle. There's a lever and I push on it. Nothing happens. The guard now has Isaac by the throat and slams his head into the mirror. It falls and shatters on the counter.

Isaac screams out again. I see blood dripping onto the broken glass. I climb out of the tub, but my legs are weak from being tied up for so long and I fall to the floor.

The guard looks down at me. "What's this little bitch think she's going to do?" His foot connects with my face and my head hits the tub. I try to get up, but I can't move. I look for Isaac. Everything is blurry and I can't hear anything.

I feel the gun being tugged from my hand as everything goes black.

I open my eyes and instantly close them again. My head hurts and it feels like I'm moving. I roll to my side and nearly fall over the edge of my bed.

"Ang? Oh thank God you're awake. I thought I was going to have to take you to a hospital." At first I think Isaac's voice is part of a strange dream.

Then I remember.

I sit up too fast and my head spins. I lean to the side and my face rests against something cold. I open my eyes. I'm not in my bed, I'm in a car. I look down—I don't have any clothes on and I'm wrapped in a blanket. My hair's a little damp and I run my hand over the back of my head. I feel a bump and my hair is crusted in that area.

"What happened?"

Isaac looks back at me for a second. "What do you remember?"

"The guard coming in. He had you against the wall. I saw blood. I tried to use the gun, but it wouldn't work, and then I tried to hit him, but he kicked me. Then I woke up here."

"The gun's safety was on, but that was probably a good thing since you've never used one before. He didn't know you had a gun. The way you fell out of the tub somehow hid it. I was able to get to it and, well, he won't be coming after us."

"Is he dead?"

"I don't know. I didn't waste time sticking around to find out."

"Are you okay? I saw blood when he pushed you against the mirror."

"I'm fine—just a scrape. Well, maybe a little more than a scrape, but it stopped bleeding and I don't think I need stitches."

I pull the blanket tight around my neck and look around me. "How did you get me out?"

"After I shot the guard, I picked you up, grabbed the blanket and some clothes, and carried you out. Everyone else was at the party, so we were able to make it out without another incident. I had already disabled the security cameras for that side of the ranch before I came in. They shouldn't know we're gone for hours—unless the guy I shot was supposed to report in. We'll just have to take some extra precautions. I planned for a few contingencies, and this was one of them." He pauses and looks back at me again. "I'm sorry I didn't dress you, I didn't want to risk taking the extra time given we were interrupted. Your clothes are there on the seat."

I lock eyes with him through the little mirror in the front window. It's dark, but there's enough light to see him.

It hits me hard how much I have missed looking at his eyes. How much I've missed hearing his voice.

Trying to keep control of my emotions, I shift on the seat and find my clothes. I pull the shirt over my head and when I pick up the pants something falls to the floor. I bend over to pick it up. My headband. I look back to Isaac.

"You remembered my headband."

"I saw it with your clothes. Luckily it was the one with the charm inside."

"Thank you." I put it on. My head hurts, but I don't care. I need to feel the charm. I pull on my pants. "Can I sit up there?" I point to the empty seat next to him.

"Yeah, it should be okay for you to come up here now." I climb over and then reach back for the blanket. "Are you cold?" He reaches for something in front of him and hot air blows in my face. I close my eyes and take in a deep breath. "Better?"

"Yes, thank you."

He reaches over with one hand and gently touches my hair. "Are you in pain?"

"My head and wrists hurt a little, but not more than what I'm used to."

Isaac hits his hand on the circle he's holding on to. "I'm so sorry I didn't come for you sooner. I had to make sure my plan was solid enough that he couldn't find us."

I look out the window. It's dark out, but occasionally there's a light and I can see trees. I haven't seen a tree since the night on the hill with Isaac. I look up, but the sky is dark. No stars. I relax into my seat.

"What's the plan?"

"I'll fill you in, but first I thought you might want to eat. It's been sitting awhile, but it's good cold too."

He hands me a box and I open it. Pizza. Even though it's my favorite and I haven't had it for years, I'm not sure I can eat given everything that's happened. However, my stomach demands food so I pull out a piece. I look at him before I take a bite. "We're really not going back?"

"No, we're not going back."

"What happens if he finds us?"

He doesn't respond for a few seconds. He reaches over and I think he's going to grab my hand, but he pulls back. "I pray we never find out."

I turn my head to look out the window. "What about the others?"

My question is met with silence, and I think maybe he didn't hear me. I look back over at him and I can see that he did. He glances at me before finally responding.

"I couldn't save everyone, Ang. I picked you, and keeping you safe is all I'm able to focus on for a while."

That's the real reason I don't think I can pull off escaping again—the last time I was only able to do it because of Isaac. Had he not shown up when he did, I would have been sitting on the floor trying to cut through my ties with a butter knife until the man returned. Then I probably would have been beaten until I was almost dead, and wishing that I were.

I rest my head against the door.

I want to fall back into the memory of Isaac. I fight it, knowing the road only leads to more pain. Even though I don't want to, I know I need to think about those times on the run with Isaac. I shouldn't make a decision without looking at all the angles. Isaac taught me that. His plan—

The bang on the door makes me jump.

10: On the Run

I think about moving across the room, but I'm so tired and I'm afraid I'd miss the hour warnings if I do.

I only have ten hours left.

I spent the first half of my time thinking about my life with the man. Even though I've already made up my mind, I also need to think about my life after Isaac helped me escape. It's the only way to be certain of my decision.

Isaac had a good plan. He had spent his two years away putting everything into motion.

The first part of the plan was the escape. Although Isaac shot a guard, we went out undetected. Isaac was confident no one had seen us leave. This was a critical part of the plan. Even though the man would suspect it was Isaac that had rescued me, it would take him a while to verify it because Isaac was supposed to be out of the country at the time.

The second part of the plan was to be on the road for a while. Isaac thought it was the best way to keep the man from discovering our trail.

❧

"Ang, wake up." I open my eyes and quickly close them. The light is so bright it makes my eyes hurt.

"Too bright."

"Right, the sun. Sorry, I forget that you haven't been in the sun for a while. Really, I guess you've never actually been in the sun. The window in your room gave you some light, but it wasn't much—"

He stops abruptly and I look at him. He has the look he gets when he mentions something I've never experienced before. "It's okay. It feels good, it's just bright." I put my hands over my eyes.

"Here, put my sunglasses on." I take the glasses and put them on. Much better. He readjusts my headband as he looks over my face. His thumb brushes over the cut on my lip. "I'm so sorry I didn't come sooner."

"You already said that."

"I'll never be able to say it enough." His eyes tear up and he blinks a few times before reaching in the back seat. "Put on this sweatshirt and pull up the hood. I was able to get us a room in the back of the hotel so we can use the back door, but I still don't want to take a chance of someone seeing the way you look. We can't afford to make anyone suspicious."

I look out the window. There's a large building in front of us that I assume is the hotel he's talking about. He's told me about hotels before, when he played me dreams about his vacations. There are a few other buildings nearby that also look like hotels.

Everything is so bright. And beautiful. The sky looks the way it has many times through my small window—blue with a few clouds floating by. Although, somehow it looks much different when I can see it along with everything else—the green of the trees, the white of the buildings, and the lighter green of the hotel's rooftop all make it more beautiful. Even more wonderful is the movement I see. The leaves on the trees move with the wind and a bird flies across the sky.

"Ang? Is everything okay?"

I blink a few times and look back at Isaac. "Yes, I've just never seen any of this up close before. I remember a little from when I lived with my mother. If she was having a happy day, then she would let me look out her window for a few minutes. I don't remember all the details of the view, but I remember feeling like it wasn't real. That it was something I'd never be able to be a part of. But this . . . it feels different."

"It's going to take you some time to adjust. I'll help you."

I smile, even though I don't know if I believe him. I'm not sure if

I'll ever adjust to this world—even if it is better than the one I just escaped from. I figure there's only one way to find out, so I put on the sweatshirt and pull up the hood. It's one of his and it's too big. "Okay, I'm ready."

He opens the door and steps out of the car. I turn to my door to do the same but realize I don't know how to open it. I think about what I just watched Isaac do, and I reach for the lever. I pull and the door pops open. I feel an unexpected surge of happiness. Isaac grabs a bag from the back of the car as I step out.

"Ow!" I look down, trying to figure out what I stepped on. Isaac is quickly by my side.

"Shit, I didn't think to grab shoes. Let me see." I lift my foot as he crouches down. "It was just a rock. Luckily it wasn't glass." He stands and takes my hand. "I'll go out today and get you shoes and more clothes. Just keep your head down, and watch where you step. That's best anyway, so others won't see your face."

I don't want to look down—I want to look at everything around me. I'm not sure why he doesn't want anyone else to see my face. Maybe it's because we might be recognized and they'll tell the man. Isaac said he knows people everywhere.

Or maybe it's because of my cuts and bruises.

I feel my face flush as I look down to the ground. I'm not used to feeling embarrassed and it makes me want to cry.

Isaac leads me to the building and through the door. We turn immediately and go up some stairs. By the time we stop at a door, I'm tired and breathing funny. Isaac releases my hand to open the door. I take off the sunglasses and look around. It's so big.

"Why don't you rest on the couch while I go down to the lobby and get some food? Will you be okay here by yourself?"

I nod and he squeezes my shoulder before leaving the room. I think about sitting the couch, but instead I walk over to the window. Our room is up high and I can see the tops of the cars down below. I have a sudden memory of looking out my mother's window.

"What's that?"

Mommy walks over. She looks at me and I think I'll get hit. I'm not allowed to ask questions. But she doesn't hit me. She looks out the window.

"It's called a car. People drive in them to go places."

"Do we have a car?"

Mommy laughs. "No, we don't have a car, you stupid little shit. I can barely afford to eat with you sucking all the money and life out of me." She puts her smoker to her mouth.

I look out the window. I see something that moves like a car, but bigger. "What's that?"

"No more questions, back to your room. A friend is coming over soon." Mommy shuts the window and walks away. I think about peeking one more time, but I know it will make Mommy mad. I crawl to my room and hug my blanket. I'm counting the cars I still see in my head as Mommy closes the door.

The sound of a door opening makes me jump, and I turn to see Isaac. The smell of food makes my stomach growl. I start to sit in one of the chairs at the table, but Isaac points to the couch.

"Let's sit there, it's more comfortable. I wasn't sure what you felt like eating, so I brought a variety of things." He hands me a plate and sits next to me.

I look at the food. I don't know what any of it is. I've only ever had oatmeal for breakfast. "What is all this?"

Isaac hangs his head. "Damn it. Sorry. I guess I wasn't such a good teacher after all. I was so concerned with teaching you how to read and write and do math that I never considered teaching you some very basic things. I'll have to add new lessons to our plan. Anyway, here you have your basic variety of quick breakfast foods—bagel, muffin, yogurt, cinnamon roll." He points to each item as he names them. "If you don't like any of it, I can go down and get something else. They have cereal and hard boiled eggs too. I could also make you some toast. I know you're used to oatmeal, and they have that downstairs too, but all this is better. I promise."

I decide to start with the muffin, like Isaac. It's good, but it makes my mouth dry. "Do you have anything to drink?"

"I couldn't carry drinks up with the plates, but I've got water in my bag." He walks over to where he left his bag and brings it back to the couch with him. He reaches in and pulls out a bottle of water. "Here, I also have an apple if you want."

The apple is something I recognize, and I take it. I've never had a whole apple—the ones I ate in the hole were always cut up into slices. I take a bite. It tastes good but it hurts my teeth a little, so I put it down on the table for now. I look over at Isaac and see him watching me. The silence feels uncomfortable between us, and I don't like it.

I ask a question, hoping we can talk the way we used to. "You mentioned a plan, when do I get to know what it is?"

He scratches the side of his head. "Well, since I've been driving all night, I'm going to rest after we finish eating. Then I'll tell you all about my plan."

I'm not all that tired, having slept in the car, but it would be good for him to sleep. I watch him eat. His tired eyes are concentrating on his food. I can see the scar from when Watcher cut him with the knife. My mind flashes back to that first night when the man made him watch. Tears hit my eyes and my body goes warm. For distraction, I put my plate down and take off the sweatshirt.

"Ang, can I ask you a question?"

"You've always asked me anything."

"I know, but—" He looks down at his food again. "I guess things have changed after what he did to us."

The tears I was trying to hold back break free. I wipe them away quickly, before Isaac looks back up at me and notices. I knew he would never look at me the same. He may have rescued me, but it doesn't mean that he still loves me. Despite what his mom said.

"You can still ask me anything, and I'll tell you the truth."

He nods, still looking down at his food. "It's just . . . you're so thin. Did he starve you along with everything else he did to you?"

I didn't know what he was going to ask, but for some reason his question surprises me. I don't want to answer, but I told him that I'd tell him the truth.

"Right after he stopped making you watch, he left me alone for a few days. I didn't get any food, but I had water from my sink. Then when he started coming again, I was given food but not as much as when I was in the hole. It was my decision to stop eating. I would eat a little less each day and put the rest down the toilet. I thought maybe I could make it all stop if I didn't eat."

His head snaps up and his eyes lock with mine. "Wait, what? You tried to kill yourself—by not eating?"

I shrug my shoulders. "Sort of, I guess, I don't know." I sigh and close my eyes, trying to concentrate on my words. "You taught me once about how food is needed to keep the body alive. So while I didn't specifically think about dying, I guess it was the reason behind my actions. I didn't know where you were, or if I'd ever see you again. Being with you was the only thing that helped me survive that place. I didn't know how else to make it stop." I wipe the tears from my face just before Isaac pulls me to his chest. He holds me while I cry. I can't tell, but I think he's crying too.

I'm still soaking in the bath when Isaac comes back from the store. I hear him move around the bedroom before there's a knock on the door.

"Ang? Everything all right in there?"

"Yes. I'm almost done."

"No rush. I put your new clothes on the bed. I'll be in the sitting room. Just take all the time you want."

I soak for a few more minutes and then drain the water. I haven't taken a bath since I was in the hole, and it feels good. In my new room, the man had taken out the drain stopper so I couldn't take a bath. I tried to block it once with a towel, but it didn't work well and I had been caught—the beating I received in response ensured that I never tried it again.

I climb out of the tub and dry off with a towel. The mirror above the sink is large, and I can see the upper half of my body. Isaac is right—I do look thin. My collar bones stick out. I can see the ridges of my ribs. My pelvic bones stick out farther than my stomach. I have bruises, some new some old, all over my body and arms. My wrists still have red circles around them from the restraints.

They remind me of Rosie.

I look up at my face. One eye is black and swollen from where the guard kicked me. My lip is cut. My hair, which is still cut to my shoulders, doesn't look as thick as it used to.

No wonder Isaac didn't want anyone to see me. I don't know how I compare to everyone else, but I know I look different than Roxy and the other girls. I turn away from the mirror and go in search of my clothes. On the bed is a package of underwear, a package of socks, a bra, three T-shirts, and three pair of pants. The pants look similar to the sweatpants I normally wear, but these are not as thick. I get dressed and go out to the sitting area. Isaac is sitting on the couch, looking at a map spread out on the small table. He looks up when I walk in.

"Do the clothes fit well enough?"

"Yes, thank you."

"I had to guess on the size. Even though I checked the clothes you wore in the car, I realized they're too big on you. That's why I opted for workout type clothes. They won't look too big, and they'll still fit awhile as you gain weight. I can buy more if you like them."

"They should work fine." I've always worn the same things over and over again, so I don't know why I would need more than three sets of clothes.

"Great. I also bought you some toiletries. They're in the bag on the table."

"Toiletries?" I walk over to the bag to have a look.

"You know—toothbrush, toothpaste, razor, deodorant—all the girly stuff you need to use in the bathroom. I also bought you a brush, comb, and . . . feminine products." I start taking items out of the bag and smile. I look at Isaac and he smiles back. It takes me a few seconds to move my eyes from his scar to his smile. I hope he didn't notice. His smile drops a bit before he talks again. "What?"

"I just think it's kind of funny that you didn't think about shoes, but you did think about tampons."

His smile disappears completely and I think I've said something to upset him. He stands up and takes something out of his pocket and hands it to me. It's a list of items on a piece of paper.

"My mom gave that to me. I found it in my bag. I didn't know what you'd need, but she did. I guess neither of us expected you'd be . . . in the situation you were in when I got to you, so shoes weren't on the list."

I look at the list and think about what his mom must have been thinking as she wrote it. "She came to see me once."

"I know. She told me." He turns away and goes back to the couch.

I want to talk more about her visit, and the sister he never told me about, but I can tell that he doesn't. Instead I go back to pulling items out of the bag. I hold up the razor.

"I've never shaved myself before." My comment is met with silence, making me glance up. Isaac looks confused. "Cleaning Lady, or New Cleaning Lady, always shaved me. When I moved out of the hole, Roxy sent Kiki to do it."

"Huh. I never knew that. I suppose it makes sense." It's my turn to be confused. Isaac points to the razor. "The razors are sharp. I suppose he was afraid the girls could use them to cut themselves—as a way to make it all stop, to use your terminology."

"You can kill yourself with a razor?"

"Yes, if you use it in the right place. You will bleed out until you die." He pauses and looks at me. "Am I going to have to keep the razors away from you?"

"No, you already made it stop. But I might need you to teach me how to shave."

His cheeks get red, and he makes a little cough as he looks back at the map. "Come over here and I'll tell you the plan." He shifts so that the open space is on his right.

The opposite side of his scar.

I sit down next to him and lean over the map. It's like the one we studied during my lessons, however I notice that it's actually a book. I flip through the pages and see a map for every state. Isaac lets me look for a few seconds before turning back to the map that shows all the states together and points to a spot.

"I don't know if you remember, but this is where we started—in Reno, Nevada." He slides his finger to the left and down. "This is where we are now. Just outside of Los Angeles, California. We will eventually end up here." He slides his finger far to the right. I don't remember which state that is, so I lean over to read it. Indiana.

"Why there?"

"It's where I've been able to set up our alternate identities. We already have a presence there, so it will be harder for him to find us. We won't go there straight away—we'll spend time on the road, trying to make sure he can't follow our trail. The objective is to confuse the hell out of him."

"What do you mean we already have presence there?"

"I've been able to secure us new identities." He reaches in his bag and pulls out a folder. He opens it and hands me a small card. It has my picture on it, but it doesn't look like me. The hair is different and I'm wearing glasses. The name says Angela Miller.

"Is this me?"

"It is now."

"How did you make me look like that?"

"Remember all those times when Roxy would change your look, trying to make you look older, and then she took your picture? Well, I made copies of the pictures. The person who I purchased the new identities from was able to edit the pictures and make you look different. Now we just have to change your actual appearance to match that photo."

"How do we do that?"

He reaches in his bag again. I'm wondering exactly how much stuff he has in that bag—it doesn't look very big. He puts a few boxes on the table. "It's simple, really. Hair dye and scissors. And fake glasses." He hands me the glasses, and I put them on.

"Why did you pick this look?"

"Roxy never tried dying your hair, and I think a dark brown will look nice on you. I had always thought about cutting your hair when we escaped, so that's why I wouldn't let Roxy cut it. The glasses will help hide your unique eyes. It's still you, but different. That's important—we want to be able to act as normal as possible in our new identities, and that will be easier to do it if we don't change too much."

"That's why you picked my name. Angela is close to Angel."

"Yes, and I can still call you Ang without anyone thinking it's weird."

"Are you still going to be Isaac?" I hope so. I can't imagine calling him anything else.

He hands me another card. It has his picture on it. I think. The name says Isaac Miller. "Is that you?"

He laughs. "Yeah—your hair is going darker and mine is going lighter. And I have to grow a beard."

"Are we changing our hair tonight?"

"No, first we're going to spend a few days here looking the way we do now. Then we're going to change our looks slightly and spend time in another city. We'll repeat that process until you're comfortable around other people, and we're confident that no one is on our trail.

At that point, we'll make ourselves look like Isaac and Angela Miller and move to the next phase of our plan, which is in Indiana."

"Won't he be able to trace us by our names?"

"He could if he knew them. There's a chance he will discover the person who gave me our new papers, so that's why we have these additional fake identities. We'll use all of them while on the road, except the Millers." He hands me a stack of cards. They all have our pictures, with slight changes—hair color, length, glasses, no glasses. Each also has a different name.

"How did you find someone to make these? That night, when you took me to see the lights, you said it was hard to get new identities."

He opens his mouth to respond, but nothing comes out. He closes his eyes for a moment, finding his voice. "My mom. Years ago she had found someone who helps women in her situation escape. She was going to take me away, but then he brought you in. She knew, even all those years ago, that I'd never be able to leave you behind." He paused again to clear his throat. "Anyway, my mom told me how to connect with this guy. He gave me the new identities and tips on how to successfully disappear."

I can see and hear his pain every time he mentions his mom. It must have been hard for him to leave her behind. "Why didn't she come with us?"

"She thought it would be too difficult for the three of us to remain undiscovered. I also think she wanted to stay behind so she could throw my father off our trail somehow." He pinches the bridge of his nose. "I'm sorry, I can't talk about her right now."

I look back down at the cards in my hand. "All the cards have different names, but in each set my last name is the same as yours."

"That's because as of now we are married. Actually, we've been married for two years."

Married. I've read about marriage in some of the books Isaac has given me over the years. I've never thought of myself as someone who would be married.

"But it's not real, it's all pretend. Right?"

"I don't know. Legally it's not real, but given our circumstances we can't legally get married because of the risk involved. I don't intend to ever marry anyone else, so I suppose it's as real of a marriage as two people like us could ever have."

Even though I don't fully understand what it means to be a wife, the thought of being one with Isaac makes me very happy. "You'll have to teach me how to be a wife."

"Don't worry. I have no idea of how to be a husband. It's not like I've had an adequate role model in my life." He pulls something else out of the bag.

"How big is that bag?"

He smiles wide enough for me to see his crooked tooth. I've missed that tooth. "Not very big, but I'm an efficient packer." He holds up a small box and opens it. "If we're going to be married, I intend to do it right. That means you need a wedding ring. The diamond's not as big as I would have liked to give you, but I hope it's okay. Here, give me your left hand." He takes out the ring and slides it on the finger next to my pinky, and then kisses it. I raise my hand and look at the ring. It sparkles in the light.

"It's beautiful. Why would it need to be bigger?"

"Some people believe the size of the diamond symbolizes how much a man loves the woman he's marrying. Based on that philosophy, this diamond is way too small."

My heart stops beating. I'm afraid to move or say anything. If I do, I might find out that he's started pretending and that he doesn't really love me any more.

"Ang, why do you look like you're about to cry?"

"It's nothing—"

"Don't do that. We've been through too much to hold anything back from each other. Tell me what upset you."

"I just, I—" I close my eyes and take a deep breath. "After he made you watch, I was convinced there was no way you could ever love me again. You were gone and I thought I'd lost you forever. Then your mom came with the book . . . and those words you underlined . . . I thought maybe . . . maybe it was possible. Now that we're together, I can feel it. I can feel that he's still between us. I just don't know how—"

"Ang, look at me. Please." He waits until my eyes lock with his. "I'm not going to lie, it's hard for me to get the image of you and him out of my head. I'm not sure if it will ever go away, but that doesn't mean I don't still love you."

"But how can you? You saw what he did to me! You told me

before that you wouldn't want to be with me if I became one of his mindless whores." I'm not just crying now, I'm sobbing. Isaac reaches out to touch me but I pull away. He moves closer and puts his hands on either side of my face.

"You are not a whore! You were raped, repeatedly, in the worst kind of way. We can't let that stay between us, because then he still wins even if we're outside of his reach."

"But he made you watch!"

"Yes, and it was the most painful thing I've ever been though in my life. But eventually I'll be able to look past him and see only you again. I have to believe it will happen, because I do love you. I always have and I always will."

"I love you too."

"Then that's all we need."

I want to believe him, but while *Wuthering Heights* taught me about love, it also taught me that love is not always enough.

We're heading north, on our way to the second city, but Isaac says he's taking me somewhere first. He won't tell me where, only that it's a surprise. It's early, the sun lighting the sky just enough to hide the stars. Isaac knows how the stars affect me.

I think about the day he first realized. It was early in our stay at the first hotel, when he was standing at the window. He called me over, and I went—not thinking. He wanted me to see the lights of the city in the distance. They were nice, but nothing like the lights of Reno he took me to see. I made the mistake of looking up, and there were enough stars visible to put me into what Isaac called an anxiety attack. I had to tell him why I reacted the way I did, and he kept the curtains closed at night from then on.

I glance at a car that passes by, going the other way. I notice it's a police car, and I instinctively drop a little lower in my seat. It's been two months since we escaped, and so far there hasn't been any sign of the man or his men. Part of that is because we've spent the majority of our days in the hotel, allowing time for my bumps and bruises to heal. However, each time we go out I can't help but wonder if someone is following us.

I glance up at the back of Isaac's head. He's let his hair grow longer for this leg of the trip. His photo matches the one for Kevin Brown. I'm Michelle. My hair is the same, but I have to blow-dry it straight and I'm wearing the glasses. A knot forms in my throat as I think about the awkwardness that exists between us. We're still not yet back to the way we were before the man broke us. It's slowly getting better, but we have a long way to go.

The need to talk to him the way we did in the past is accompanied by the need to touch him. But that's even more difficult for me than talking. Every time he touches me, I flinch. I don't want to, but my body doesn't seem to hear my heart.

I think of those times, long ago, when I desperately wanted him to stay with me at night. To lie in bed with me and talk about dreams while I snuggled close to his chest. Now we're alone with the opportunity to hold each other every night, yet neither of us is ready. We fall asleep, looking at each other from our respective beds, both wanting to join the other but not having the strength to overcome the past. A few nights, when I had a bad dream, he climbed in my bed and held me until I fell asleep. When I woke up, he was back in his own bed.

I force my thoughts back to the present. I break the silence, not comfortable with the hold it has over us. "Since you won't tell me where we're going, will you at least tell me why I have to sit in the back seat?"

"Because for the direction we are headed, this side of the car has the best view. I didn't want my big head getting in your way, so the back seat is best. We're almost there."

"Where did you get this car, and what was wrong with the other one?"

"We will change vehicles every leg of the trip—it's just another way of trying to make sure he can't find us. I've already placed a vehicle in the long term parking lot at airports near each city where we will stay. I'll park our current car, go into the airport, find a bathroom to change my clothes and appearance, and then leave in the new one."

"How do you have a car at each location?"

"You forget that I've been planning this for a long time. Prior to coming to get you, I flew around the country planting the cars and using the fake I.D. associated with it. I needed there to be records of us in each of the locations prior to the escape. It will make it harder for him to find us. Even if he somehow found the person who gave me the new identities, he wouldn't know which ones we're actually using since they all existed before the date of our escape."

"Doesn't this all cost money? You told me once that was one of the reasons why you had to wait—to have enough money so we could survive. How did you get the money?"

"As you know, I was supposed to go to graduate school. However, for the past two years I've taken the money intended for my extended education and used it to fund our escape. Some of his goons were sent to check in on me from time to time, so I also had to establish a presence at the university I'm supposed to be attending. Luckily the guys he sent weren't very smart, so they were easy to trick." His eyes meet mine in the mirror. "You look surprised."

"I am. Your education was your top priority. I never expected you to give it up."

"Ang, haven't you figured out by now that getting you out of that place has always been my only priority?"

I look down, unable to hide the emotions that I'm feeling. "How did you do all this on your own?"

"When I was a kid, I met someone who I learned I could trust completely. He helped me. You'll meet him when we get to Indiana. He's keeping our new permanent identities—Isaac and Angela Miller—active there while we're gone."

"How?"

"It's hard to explain and I'll tell you the whole story when you meet him, but basically he's living there under the same name." He pauses and then taps on his window. "Look out your window."

I do as he asks and have to hold my breath. It's amazing. "Is that the ocean?"

"Yep."

"Can we get closer?"

"This will be our view for most of the drive, but yes, we're going to stop. The beach I want to take you to is about an hour up the road."

My eyes remain on the ocean view the entire time. I immediately jump out when Isaac finally parks the car, too excited to wait another second. Isaac laughs as he takes my hand and leads me to a dirt trail.

At the end of the trail is a long set of stairs. I'm so excited I'm almost running, but Isaac keeps me from going too fast. There are other people around and I remember that we're trying to not get noticed.

By the time we reach the bottom of the stairs, I'm in sensory overload and don't know what to focus on first—the smell of the ocean, the sound of the waves, the birds flying above, or the feel of the wind and sun. Isaac walks me to the edge of the water and we stand, both silently experiencing everything around us.

I finally take my eyes away and look at Isaac. He's looking at the ocean and there are tears in his eyes. "You finally got your wish."

"It's even more amazing than I imagined." He looks at me and squeezes my hand. "Now the two things I've wished for the most have come true—I'm at the ocean, and I'm with you." He suddenly smiles and drops down to his knees, taking off my shoes.

"What are you doing?"

"We can't come here and not feel the ocean on our toes." Once my shoes are off, he rolls up my pants and then repeats the process on his own shoes and pants. We walk toward the water and I laugh when I feel the waves rush over my feet, making them sink into the sand. We walk for a while down the length of the beach and stop near some large rocks, watching as the water rushes through them. As I look at the rocks, I'm overcome with an overwhelming urge to cry.

Isaac's arm wraps around my waist as he pulls me close. "What are you thinking about?"

"I just can't believe we're here. Together."

"We'll always be together." He kisses the top of my head and I let the tears fall.

It's the first time he's kissed me since the man discovered our secret.

After everything we've been through I know that we are broken—shattered really—but I hope that together we can be strong and keep fighting to move forward.

9: Blending In

The bang on the door wakes me.

I'd been dreaming about the ocean. It was just like one of the dreams Isaac used to play for me—we were on the beach, playing in the sand, Abigail at our feet. My chest tightens and tears sting my eyes. I miss them both so much. I miss the life we could have had. I try to fight it, but the will of my mind is too strong. I have to go back to that dream, just for a little while.

I slowly open my eyes, the dream still lingering on my mind. The ache still has a hold over my heart, and I try to let go. I don't know how long I slept, but I need to find a way to stay awake.

And a way to stay focused.

That morning on the ocean was one of the best days of my life, and it's hard to leave it behind. But it's time to move on. My time is running out.

I think over the eleven months when Isaac and I were on the road. We would stay in each new city for at least two months, sometimes more. Sometimes we stayed in a hotel, and other times we lived in small apartments or houses. During that time Isaac taught me basic life skills I should know, such as how to shave and use a microwave. He also took the time to teach me some things that weren't so basic—or at least not to me—such as driving a car and firing a gun. It was strange to suddenly be exposed to so many things I'd only ever read about or saw in pictures, and I was completely unprepared for almost everything I encountered.

Isaac was also determined to show me as much as possible during that time. He took me to many of the places he had shown me in postcards or in books. Some were simple in their beauty—such as the changing of leaves in the fall and the way it feels to be hit with a snowball. Some were overwhelming in their magnitude—such as the Grand Canyon and the Rocky Mountains. However all, whether small or large, were moments that continued to pull me further away from my internal black hole and closer to Isaac.

Months passed and the more I learned, the more confused I became. I wasn't used to the outside world, and while I was happy to be out of the man's control, there were certain aspects of my old life that I clung to. With so many changes surrounding us—our environment, our names, our looks—I needed the comforts of a few familiar things. We remained mostly inside, just the two of us—Isaac the teacher and me the student. During the times when I was alone, reading became my ultimate comfort.

We each celebrated a birthday during that time on the road, deciding it was best to use the birthdays of Isaac and Angela Miller. We sat on the floor, eating pizza and cake and drinking juice boxes. It was a perfect blend of old and new.

After about ten months, I was able to go with Isaac to a few public places, such as restaurants and stores, if they weren't too crowded. I hadn't worked my way up to going on my own, but Isaac said we couldn't stay on the run any longer. He had said that we needed to start the next phase of our plan to lower the risk of being caught.

Isaac's theory was that if you hide, someone will eventually find you. But if you remain in the open and blend in with your surroundings, you'll become invisible.

That was our goal. Unfortunately, it turned out that blending in was a lot harder than hiding. At least it was for me.

⌘

I pull the maps out of Isaac's bag. I had been following along by the road signs, but I lost our location when I fell asleep. "Where are we now?"

"Indiana."

"I know that much. That's why I'm looking at the Indiana map." I wave the book of maps at him. "What I don't know is *where* in Indiana."

"Look for a town called Lafayette."

I find Lafayette on the map. "No, not where we are going, but where we are now."

"We're in Lafayette right now."

My heart rate increases. "We're already in Lafayette?" I look out the window and try to memorize our surroundings.

"Yep. We're almost there. We should go over our story one more time."

I close the book, no longer needing a map since the one we have doesn't show the streets within the city of Lafayette. I'll have to pay attention and memorize. In every city there are certain things that are the same, but there are also differences. Isaac taught me that it's the best way to blend in—knowing all the unique characteristics of the place we're supposed to call home.

"Ang?"

"What? Sorry, I was trying to pay attention to my surroundings."

"It's okay, that's a good thing to do, but we'll have time for that. I've spent a lot of time here already and I'll take you out, show you around. I want to go through our story one more time before we get to the house."

I take a deep breath. "I'm Angela and you're Isaac. Last name Miller. We've been married almost three years now. You're working as a paid research assistant and spend most of your time collecting samples at farms and analyzing the data at home. I haven't been able to live with you because I've been at home in Illinois, helping take care of my mother who was sick. That's why you sometimes disappear, so you can spend time with me. My mother passed away, and now I'm coming to live with you. I don't have a job, but I'm considering taking classes for an undergraduate degree—subject undecided."

"Good. And how did we meet?"

"Are people really going to ask me that?"

"Unfortunately, yes. In general, people are curious. They will ask a lot of questions that might surprise you."

"What if I'm asked a question we haven't talked about?"

"If the question is only about you personally, such as your favorite food, then you can answer however you want. If it's about us or our life together, then I'll answer. If you're alone and something comes up, then just find a way to avoid answering using one of the techniques we practiced. We can then come up with an answer together in case it comes up again."

I nod and look out the window, however a knot forms in my stomach. So far we haven't had to answer any questions because we didn't go out much. On the few occasions we went out to eat no one asked us anything. I look back over at Isaac to see if he's nervous too. He looks normal and I'm not sure if that makes me feel better or worse. It's strange to see him in a beard. I run a hand over the back of my neck. I'm not used to such short hair.

"Ang?"

"Sorry, what did you say?"

Isaac glances at me and then focuses back on the road. "Are you nervous?"

I figure there's no point in lying to him. "Yes."

"It's going to be okay. I promise." He reaches over and takes my hand in his. "Now, how did we meet?"

"In high school, but we didn't start dating until after we graduated."

"How did I propose to you and what was our wedding like?"

We had debated for a while on what the story would be of how he proposed. We had two memories so far that we clung to—the night on the hill under the fireworks, and the morning on the beach. The night on the hill was the first time we acted on our feelings, but it was also during a time when we were still under the man's control. Because that memory is tainted by our sorrow of having to return, we considered using the time we went to the ocean. We were both free in that moment, experiencing something for the first time together. It was magical and perfect. However, the area in Illinois where we are supposed to be from doesn't have a beach.

"You took me out to see fireworks and then asked me to marry you. We had a simple wedding in my backyard because my mom was sick."

He glances at me again as he squeezes my hand. "It's going to work. We'll be okay."

"And what if it doesn't work?"

"Then we'll use our contingency plan."

"You keep saying that, but we never talk about a contingency plan. How am I supposed to know what it is if you won't talk about it?"

"It's better that you don't know."

Frustration rolls through me, and I'm happy because at least it's better than the nervousness I've been feeling.

"Isaac, I—"

"We're here." He turns onto a driveway in front of a small white house. It's in the middle of a street full of houses that look basically the same. We're blending in, right down to the house we live in. He pulls the car into the garage, next to another car. He turns to me after he shuts off the engine. "Are you ready?"

"Do I have a choice?"

His only response is a smile. My eyes leave his smile and travel along his bearded cheek. The scar is no longer visible. It's the thing I like most about his new look—I'm no longer reminded of that night with the man when I look at him. I wish I could do something that would make it the same for him.

I take a deep breath and open the car door. I walk around to Isaac's side and look at the other car. It's exactly the same as the one we just drove in.

"Is that my car?" I don't like driving and I hope he doesn't expect me to do it often.

He hesitates and pulls at his hair. "Not exactly."

I look at him and can tell he's not telling me something. "Who's car is it, and why is it exactly the same as the one we just drove?"

"Let's go in. It's time I tell you the rest of the story."

He takes my hand and leads me inside. We enter a small laundry room that connects to a kitchen. Isaac sets our bag down on the table and continues walking. We enter a living room that's not much bigger than the kitchen. The first thing I notice is that there isn't much to the room. There's a couch, two large chairs, and two small tables, but that's it. There are no pictures on the walls, no television, no books—nothing.

Isaac's hand tightens around mine. "I know the house is small, but it's what would be expected of a young married couple. You just went through the laundry and kitchen. This is the living room. Upstairs there are two bedrooms and two bathrooms. That's it."

I'm about to ask to see the bedrooms when I hear something upstairs. I jump and Isaac puts his arm around me.

"It's all right. That's just our roommate."

"Our what?"

"Roommate. The person who will be living with us."

"We're living with someone else?" I can hear the panic in my voice, so I know Isaac can too.

"Remember I told you a friend of mine was helping us? Well, he'll be living here too."

"Why?" I'm not yet used to living with Isaac. I don't know how I'll be able to live with someone I don't even know. Isaac says he trusts this guy, and I'm grateful he's helped us escape, but I think living with him is an unnecessary risk. Isaac looks past my shoulder.

"Turn around." His voice is soft, and it calms me slightly.

I turn around as requested, and the panic returns. I can't be seeing what I'm seeing. I look back at Isaac and then again at the man that just entered the living room. "Why does he look exactly like you?"

Isaac walks over to the other Isaac. "Ang, I'd like you to meet the real Isaac Miller."

My head starts pounding and my vision blurs. It's too much. I turn and walk out of the room, through the kitchen and laundry, and out to the garage. I climb in the back of the car—the one we arrived in—and curl into a ball. I count until my mind is clear.

"Ang?" Isaac slides in next to me and puts his hand on my hip.

"Are you my Isaac or the copy of Isaac I never knew existed?"

He sighs and pulls his hand away. "I've made myself to look like him, but I hope you can still tell the difference."

I sit up, turning to lean on the car door so I can face him. "So is there a copy of me that's going to live here too?"

"No."

"I need to understand what's going on, Isaac."

"Can't we go inside? I'll tell you everything."

I shake my head. "No, I'm not going back in there until I know what's going on. You may trust this guy, but I don't know him. He looks just like you!"

"Actually, I look just like him."

I hit my legs with my hands. "What does that even mean?"

"It means that Isaac Miller, the one inside the house, has existed for twenty-three years. He's always been Isaac Miller and that's how he naturally looks. You know I had to change things like my hair color to look like this. I chose this look for my new identity because this is how he looks."

"Why?"

"One of the best ways to disappear is to become someone who already exists."

"How did you meet this 'real' Isaac Miller?"

He lets out a deep sigh and looks up toward the ceiling of the car before responding. "Remember that first day I met you, over ten years ago?"

"Of course. It was the day the man took me. Or bought me, however you want to look at it."

"You asked me what you should call me. I couldn't give you my real name, so I gave you the name Isaac. I know you knew it wasn't my real name, but did you ever wonder why I chose the name Isaac?"

"No, I've never thought about it. Although I know it's not your real name, you've always been Isaac to me."

"I met Isaac when I was ten. I know my mom told you about my sister. About a year after she died, my mom and I were allowed to go on a short vacation without my father. One of my uncles was sent to keep an eye on us, but he was too busy getting drunk to pay attention to us. It was our trip to Lake Tahoe, you remember me telling you about that, right?"

I nod. It was one of the dreams he played for me many times. However, he never mentioned another boy named Isaac.

"One afternoon I was sitting on the beach, and this boy sat down next to me. He didn't speak, and that was all right by me. The next morning, the same thing happened. We gradually started talking to each other and became friends. When the end of the week rolled around and it was time for us to leave, my mom decided that she would help me write to Isaac without my father knowing. I'd write to him and he'd write back. My mom always burned his letters right after I'd read them. She memorized his address so there was no evidence that he even existed."

"What did you write about?"

"At first, it was basic ten year old boy stuff—sports, television shows, music—that sort of thing. It evolved over time into more personal topics. It was getting bad for me and my mom at home. My mom would be beaten for something as simple as breathing the wrong way. I was exposed to things no kid should ever have to see, or even know about. Isaac was my escape. I'd write to him that I was afraid or upset, but I never told him why. I guess I was afraid he'd stop writing to me if he knew." He pauses and looks at me. "I eventually told him about you. Not your specific situation—just that I was in love with someone who I wasn't supposed to be with. When I was sent away after—" He doesn't finish the thought, closing his eyes instead. I don't need him to finish—I know he's talking about what the man did to us. He shakes his head and opens his eyes. "I wrote to Isaac that I had to find a way to run away and take you with me. He started helping me develop the plan. It was his idea for me to become him."

"Is he the one that made all the identifications and paperwork for us?"

"No, that was someone different. Isaac just gave me permission to use his identity. By doing it this way, Isaac Miller existed well before we escaped, and will continue to exist even if we move on. By living with him, I'm able to become him. When people see me, they think I'm Isaac."

My head is spinning. I have so many questions I'm having difficulty deciding where to start, so I decide to just ask the first thing that comes to mind. "What does he know about me?"

"Only that I'm in love with you, and that I would do anything to keep you safe."

"Why is he doing this? Does he understand the risk of getting involved?"

"He knows the risk. To be honest, I don't fully understand why he's helping us. I asked him once, about six months before I came for you. He only said that he understands what it's like to be living the wrong life. He also felt it was his purpose in life to help us, and that's why our paths crossed so many years ago. And why we look so much alike."

"You do look very similar."

He finally smiles. "Yes, but not exactly alike. It's enough to pass as the same person at a glance. The beard helps to hide our facial differences."

"So how does this work? Do we just hide out in his house? As you said, you're not exactly the same so how do you get away with it?"

"We do everything the same, but on opposite days. We work the same job at the research facility. As I've told you before, most of our work is in the field where no one else is around. We make sure the same person goes to the same farm every time. When Isaac Miller is expected to be in the lab, Isaac goes in. He's the 'public face' for our job. We're very careful to not be in the same place at the same time, except here at home. We share banking and credit card accounts. Essentially, we are the same person."

"And this works? This is what you've been doing the two years you were away?"

"Yes, most of the time I've been here with Isaac, testing out the plan. At first we were worried that people we interacted with on a regular basis, such as our neighbors, would notice, but no one has. I think sometimes people may wonder why we look slightly different from one day to the next, but the idea that we might actually be two different people doesn't enter their minds. We don't socialize with many people, so there aren't many who know us well enough to suspect something strange is going on."

I cover my face with my hands. It's all just too much. A thought strikes me and I snap my head up. "Am I supposed to pretend to be his wife too?"

"No. You are my wife. You are the one thing we will not share." The force of his voice convinces me and my shoulders relax.

"Why didn't you tell me any of this before we got here?"

"I didn't know how. I know it was a shock for you to see him without warning, but do you really think it would have been any better if I'd said, 'Hey, by the way, I modeled myself after this guy I've been friends with for years. We look exactly the same.' It's one of those things you have to see to understand. Besides, I thought you had enough to worry about, trying to adjust to being outside of that place. You didn't need to worry about eventually living with someone you didn't know."

I understand his point, and I forgive him. "Well, I can't call him Isaac. It will just confuse me."

He smiles. "I think he'll be okay with us calling him Zac." He rubs my cheek with his thumb. "Are you sure you're okay with all of this?"

"Do I have a choice?"

"Of course you do. I think this is the best way for us to go undetected, but if you're not happy then what's the point? If you hate it, or are uncomfortable for any reason, I'll figure out a new plan."

He's already given up so much for me. I know he'd do anything I asked of him. That's why there's only one answer to his question.

"I'll be fine. It will take time for me to adjust, but I'll be okay."

"Does that mean you're ready to go in and try again?"

I pull in a deep breath and hold it before pushing it out quickly. "Yes."

I follow Isaac out of the car and back into the house. The other Isaac, or Zac, is sitting on the couch and stands when we walk in.

"Hi, Angela. It's nice to meet you. I'm Isaac, but I guess you already knew that." I'm trying to figure out if he really sounds like Isaac, or if it just seems that way because they look the same.

I don't respond to his greeting, but I nod in acknowledgement.

Isaac looks from Zac to me and back again. "She doesn't talk much, and I think she's still in shock over seeing you."

"I told you to tell her before you got here."

"Yeah, well, I didn't agree. Regardless, here we are. Oh, and we just decided in the car that we're going to call you Zac. Two Isaacs would be confusing for Ang."

"Uh, sure, no problem."

I watch them talk to each other and my head starts to pound. I think I've had enough for the moment, and I turn to Isaac. *My* Isaac. "Can you show me to our room?"

Isaac nods, takes my hand, and leads me up the stairs. "Our room is the one in the back. Isa—Zac let us have the larger room with the connecting bathroom." He opens the door to the bedroom and lets me walk in first. The instant my eyes fall on the room, I stumble back. I bump into Isaac and he puts a hand on my shoulder to steady me. "What's wrong?"

"I—it reminds me of my old room." The furnishings are almost identical, except the bed is bigger. I don't even need to look to know where the two doors at the end of the room lead—to a bathroom and a closet. There's even a window in the ceiling. The only difference is the large window on the wall between the bed and the bathroom door.

I try to back-up but Isaac gently turns me around. "Ang, it's okay. You're not there any more. We can change this room any way you like."

"I can't go in there." I push him to the side and move into the hall, sinking to the floor. I hug my knees and rock as the numbers float by in my mind. Isaac lifts me and we're moving. I pull back and try to get out of his arms. "No! I can't go in there!"

"I'm not taking you in there." I look around and see that we're in the other bedroom. He lays me down on the bed. "I'm sorry. I don't know how I didn't realize it looked just like your old room. I'll fix it. I'll change it, somehow, and it will all be okay. Until then, we'll sleep in Zac's room."

My head hurts, and my heart is pounding in my chest. Images of the man coming at me, doing things to me, fly through my mind. They feel so real it makes my skin itch. I'm finding it hard to breathe.

"Ang! Ang, come back to me! He's not here."

I hear Isaac talking. I try to focus on his words, but the man pushes them aside. I recoil from the kick to my stomach. I try to move, but I can't. I'm locked in place. A scream tries to escape, but I fight it because I know it will only make everything much worse.

I hear words again. They are soft on my ear. I try to focus on them.

It's Isaac. He's playing me a dream. We're at the ocean. He's holding my hand as we run down the beach, chasing the waves. I'm holding Abigail tight to my chest. I can breathe again and I can hear his words. I can feel his arms wrapped around me and I know they belong to him and not the man. I use all my strength to concentrate on his voice, his smell, his breath, his touch. I anchor to him and let him pull me back. He knows and he kisses first my cheek and then my temple.

"I'm so sorry, Ang. I'll fix it. We'll switch rooms with Zac. You won't ever have to go in there again."

I open my eyes and look at him. His cheeks are wet with tears. His eyes are full of pain. I nod and let him pull me tighter to his chest. I look past his shoulder and see Zac standing at the open door.

I'm sitting in the room I share with Isaac, listening for the sound of his car pulling into the garage. We've been living here for three months, and I'm still not comfortable. I only go downstairs when Zac is gone or asleep. I haven't decided if I can trust him.

He did switch rooms with us without asking questions, and he's never mentioned the incident he witnessed on that first day, so I suppose I should at least try to get to know him. It's just difficult to get past the strangeness of it all. Whenever I look at him, I want to talk to him the way I do with Isaac. But he's not Isaac. It's too confusing, so I just stay in my room.

I finally hear the sound of the garage door, and I put my book on the side table. I know Isaac will be up in a few minutes, after he's checked in with Zac.

Time ticks by, and still no Isaac. My palms get sweaty, and I wipe them on the bed sheets. He should have been up here by now, and I worry that something has gone wrong with our plan. I walk to the door and open it a crack. I hear him downstairs talking to Zac. I relax, realizing he's fine. He just needed to talk with Zac for longer than usual. I close the door and sit back down on the bed.

Several more minutes pass, and Isaac still doesn't come in the room. I get up and walk to the door again, opening it a crack and putting my ear in the space. I hear talking. And laughing.

Maybe he thinks I'm sleeping and doesn't want to come in and wake me?

No, he knows I wait for him to come home. He always comes up to see me as soon as he returns from work. He also likes to shower and change after spending a full day out in the fields.

I close the door again and pace across the room, trying to figure out why he hasn't come up yet. On the days he doesn't work from home, I sit here with nothing to do but read. I look forward to when he gets home and tells me about his day. He's promised to take me to one of the larger farms some day. I love hearing him talk about the farms and can't wait to see one for myself.

I turn and look back at the door. Frustrated, I sit back down on the bed and pick up my book. Several more minutes pass, yet I haven't read a single word. I slam the book shut and toss it on the bed before getting up to walk back to the door. I open it and smell something delicious.

Dinner. They're down there eating dinner. Even more frustrated, I shut the door harder than I intended. I fling myself on the bed and allow the tears to fall.

Maybe he's bored of me already. Maybe he resents having me here. He did spend two years here, alone with Zac, before he helped me escape. Maybe Zac doesn't want me here, and he's trying to take Isaac away from me. I knew I couldn't trust him.

I lay on the bed, crying and thinking about all the reasons why Isaac wouldn't want me here, until I hear footsteps on the stairs. It's getting dark, and my stomach rumbles. I keep my back to the door, not wanting Isaac to see how upset I am. I wait for the sound of the opening door, but instead I hear the shower start on the other side of the wall. I sit up and stare at the door, my mouth hanging open.

He's taking a shower!

My hurt and confusion rolls into anger in a quick breath. Isaac has never ignored me for this long. I sit on the bed, staring at the door. The shower goes off, and I wait. I hear the bathroom door open after a few minutes, followed by the sound of his footsteps coming down the hall.

I pull in a breath as I hear him approach the door.

But the sound of his footsteps keep going, beyond the door, and back down the stairs.

The hurt is back, slamming into my chest with a force strong enough to make me struggle to pull in air. I pick up my book and fling it at the door before burying my face into my pillow, sobbing until my head aches.

I drift in and out of sleep.

When I finally open my eyes fully, it's dark—the room illuminated only by the nightlight I have to leave on at all times. I'm still hurt and angry, but more than that I'm hungry. Reluctantly, I get up and walk to the door. I open it and look down the hall. I see a light on downstairs, but I don't hear anything. I look in the direction of Zac's room and see that the door is closed. However, the door has always been closed since my breakdown, so I don't really know if he's in there or not. I didn't hear him walk past, but I know that I fell asleep for a while. He might have gone to bed, and I just didn't hear him. I hope so. I don't know how I'm going to face Isaac in my current state, let alone Zac too. I take a deep breath and head down the stairs before I can change my mind. I enter the living room and see Isaac sitting on the couch, reading a book.

And wearing nothing but a towel.

In all the time I've known him, I've never seen him in anything less than shorts and a T-shirt. He's seen me naked more times than I'd like to remember. Before the incident with the man, I had never felt embarrassed about being naked in front of anyone. I never knew I should be. Now, I think that if Isaac sees me naked he will be reminded even more of those moments he had to watch, or of how I looked when he came to find me the day we escaped.

My eyes travel across Isaac's torso. He doesn't have the same muscle definition as most of the men in the porn videos I had to watch, but the site of him mostly naked awakens a part of me I had hoped I'd left behind in Reno. I feel my face flush and I look away. Zac is sitting in one of the chairs, also reading a book. Thankfully, he is fully dressed.

They look up at me, almost in unison. Their synchronized movement, combined with their matching looks, sends a shiver down my spine.

"Well, it's about damn time! I was afraid I was going to have to sleep on the couch." The sound of Isaac's voice instantly reminds me that I'm angry and hurt. I glare at him for a few seconds before turning and walking into the kitchen.

"Ang?" Isaac calls after me, but I don't turn around. I open the refrigerator and see a plate covered in foil. I take it out, peel back the foil, and see what was supposed to be my dinner. I practically toss it into the microwave and hit the required buttons. When it's done, I take it out and turn to leave. Isaac is standing in the entryway, blocking my path.

"Excuse me, I'd like to go and finally eat my dinner."

"You can eat in here, at the table."

My entire body goes still from the inside out—my only movement is from my beating heart and breathing lungs.

He can't make me do this. Why is he making me do this?

"No, I'm going to eat in my room."

He moves toward me, his towel almost falling to the floor. He grabs it and lets out a whispered curse. He steps back and looks toward the stairs, and then back at me. "Zac, do you mind going up and getting me some clean clothes?"

Zac hesitates for a few seconds before responding. "Sure." I hear him move quickly in the direction of the stairs.

"Why are you doing this? Why didn't you come up to see me when you got home?"

"Because I won't let you just sit in that room any longer! You never leave the bedroom and it has to stop."

"I do leave the room!"

"To go to the bathroom! When Zac's not home, you come down stairs once in a while to get a drink or something to eat, but that's it. The rest of the time you're in that room, reading a book or studying the maps. It's got to stop."

"Why?" The stillness is now gone, replaced by a shake so strong I almost drop my plate. I set it on the table before it crashes to the floor.

"Because I didn't risk everything to release you from one prison just to put you in another! I want you to live life, Ang. Right now, you're not living. You're hiding out in a room. The only difference between your life now and what it was before is that you're not being abused. Other than that, nothing has changed!"

I hang my head and press my hands to my ears, wanting his words to stop. "No, no, no. You're wrong. I am living. I can read when I want. I can talk when I want. I can sleep without fear of when the man's next visit will be. I can see you every day. That's all the life I need. Don't you understand that?"

His free hand is on my shoulder, pulling me to his chest. My cheek rests against the heat of his bare skin. I pull in a deep breath and the smell of him calms me. I move my arms and wrap them around his waist, pulling myself closer. We've hugged this way many times, but somehow it feels different when he's wearing nothing but a towel.

I can feel every shape and contour of his body.

I feel my face flush again and I start to pull way. He stops me and I look up. His face drops, putting his lips just inches from mine. His eyes flutter shut for a second, and then he pulls back. He slides the hand holding me to him around to my cheek, leaving a trail of goose bumps, and locks his eyes with mine.

"That may be all you think you deserve, but you're wrong. You deserve to experience everything life has to offer, and you can't do that while sitting in a bedroom. We will never be able to put the past behind us if we resist living in the present. I won't let you hide out any more. I love you too much for that. Please, just try. For me."

That pushes me over. He's risked everything for me, and now he's asking this one thing from me in return. I have to give him that. "What do I do?"

I feel him relax, but he doesn't let go. "You can start by coming out of the bedroom—even when Zac is home. If you're going to live a long life outside of that hell, then you need to get used to being around other people. You need to start with Zac. Talk to him, get to know him better."

I start to argue why it's so hard for me to be around Zac, but I stop. I already promised to try. And he's right—I have to start with Zac since we're living with him. So instead of opening my mouth, I nod my head. He places his lips to my forehead and steps back.

"Thank you. Now, I'm going to go into the other room to put on my clothes. Then, I'm going to sit back down on the couch with my book. You are going to sit in here with Zac while you eat dinner. Okay?"

Again, I nod. He gives me an encouraging smile before he turns and leaves the room. I hear him whispering with Zac in the other room as I sit down at the table. I push my food around my plate and refuse to look up when Zac enters. Out of the corner of my eye I see Zac pause in the entryway, but then he sits down across from me. He watches me eat, and neither of us attempts to break the silence. Even though I'm hungry, I'm too anxious to eat much. It takes me thirty minutes to eat half the food on my plate. At that point, I know I've reached my limit and push away from the table. I put my plate in the sink, turn to leave the room, and then stop, deciding I should say something.

"I'm going to try because Isaac asked me to. But I want to make it clear—you are not my Isaac, no matter how much you look like him. I'll never trust you as much as I do him."

As I pass through the living room, I see Isaac rise to follow me. I don't wait and hurry up the stairs. I crawl into bed and bury myself under the covers. I hear Isaac enter the room and feel the bed shift when he climbs in next to me. He pulls me close, wrapping an arm around my waist, and kisses the back of my head.

A memory of the man grabbing me flashes through my mind. I squeeze my eyes shut and focus on the smell of Isaac. It works, and I'm back in the present.

We've slept in the same bed together since the day we arrived at this house, but he's never touched me. We sleep with our backs to each other, keeping a safe distance between us. The feel of his arm wrapped around me stirs my feelings once again. I want to move away, yet at the same time I want to move closer.

"I'm proud of you, Ang." His whispered voice tickles my ear and chills my spine. I grab onto his hand and squeeze it tight to my chest. I hold on with all the strength that I have, knowing that I need him to keep me anchored in the light.

8: Instinct

I'm suddenly hit with the pressure of the door.

"What's going on in there? Why won't this door open?" There's another shove and the door slams harder into my back. I scramble to my feet and move out of the way. I turn as Goon Two enters the room. He looks around, as if he's searching for something I might have used to block the door. Finally his eyes settle on me. "It's not going to do you any good to fight. The only way to end this is to tell the boss that you're ready to come back. In fact, the boss just called and wanted me to see if you've made your decision early."

He pauses, no doubt waiting for a response. I don't give him the satisfaction of even grunting out an objection. He shifts his stance, inclining his head to one side and narrowing his eyes at me.

"Why spend the next eight hours in here if you don't have to? Unless, of course, you're just a dumb shit who thinks death is the best option." He pauses again and smiles when I don't respond. It's not a pleasant look. "I should warn you—I'm the one that gets to do the job, and I don't play nice. It won't be quick and it will be painful. So what do you say? You ready to go back?"

I turn my back to him and walk across the room. My toe nudges something and I look down. I've stopped in front of the piece of wood I had tossed aside earlier.

In my mind I see a flash of hair, irresistible to my touch.

Eyes, filled with love, that pull me in.

Laughter so complete it makes me want to cry.

These images create an unfamiliar urge to fight that rushes through me. I try to suppress it, knowing it won't work. Besides, I had my opportunity to choose that life and I let it go.

Goon Two walks closer to me. I didn't hear the door close behind him, and that reignites the urge to fight. I remain still, waiting as he walks closer. He stops. I'm not looking at him, so I don't know how far back he is, but based on the sound of his breathing I'd guess about two feet. Still too far away.

"Not going to give me an answer? Should I give you a preview of what will happen if you don't agree to go back with the boss?"

Another step closer. I look down at the board without moving my head. Without thinking about it further, I let instinct take over and I drop to the floor, clutching my stomach as I let out a loud groan.

As expected, Goon Two moves toward me. He bends down. I pick up the board and turn, swinging it as hard as I can. I connect with his jaw and he falls back. I stand and swing again, this time connecting with his groin. He falls to the floor with a loud cry.

I drop the board and run for the door. I'm out of the room, but I'm not sure which direction to go. The only lights are in the office across the hall. The rest of the warehouse is dark, but I can see enough to make out stacks of wooden crates everywhere. On instinct I move to the right and run between rows of crates stacked three layers high. Every few feet there are aisles that cut perpendicular, either to the right or left or both. Because of the darkness, I can't see them until I'm right on top of them. It doesn't matter though because I decide to keep running straight—hoping the door is at the end.

I hear movement up ahead to my right, and I make a sharp left turn down one of the aisles. I try to scan the crates as I pass, looking for anything that might help me. I don't see anything. There's another break in the crates, and just as I turn right I hear shouts coming from the direction of the room I just escaped. The aisle turns to the left and . . . ends. I'm surrounded by stacked crates.

There is nowhere else to go except back the way I came. I know that's not an option because Goon Two and his other pack of goons will be back there. I look up. It's too high to climb, and I worry they'd be able to see me. The only other option is to hide, at least long enough to form a plan. I hurry to a small space between two stacks on the right side of the aisle, and I'm able to inch my way in sideways. I scoot back as far as I can, keeping my head positioned so that I'm facing the opening, and do my best to not even breathe. It's a tight fit, so it shouldn't be much of an issue.

The sounds of Goon Two and his men running through the maze of crates gets louder, and I start to panic. A sob pushes its way up, and I bite my lip. I pull in a breath and hold it for three seconds. I let it out slowly and keep my eyes glued to the opening before me. There is another stack of crates to my back, so I know there's only one way they can get to me. It's dark and I can't see anything, so I try to guess their position based on the sounds I hear.

"You stupid bitch! Do you really think you can escape? You're just going to make things more difficult for yourself." Goon Two's voice is distant, but the level of his anger is easy to hear.

Light flashes down the aisle in front of the crate where I'm hiding. I try to inch back even farther, but there's no room. As the light gets closer and the footsteps get louder, I hold my breath. I want to close my eyes, afraid of what will happen if he finds me, but my eyes are glued to the open space—now becoming more visible with the growing light. The footsteps slow and a shadowy figure steps into view. It's a guard I haven't seen before. I watch as he looks around the space. Panic surges through me as I realize he might be able to see me with his flashlight. I shift so that my knees are positioned outward, parallel to the crate, and sink lower to the floor. I'm at the lowest level I can reach when the beam of his flashlight blinds me.

I freeze. Seconds pass that feel like hours. Drops of sweat form on my forehead. I keep my breathing as shallow and quiet as possible.

The light moves on and the footsteps recede.

I stay immobile in my uncomfortable squatting position for as long as possible. My brain tries to count, but I have to remain focused. I listen, trying to locate the men. Time passes and my legs start to burn. I slowly rise back to a standing position, using the crate as leverage. Suddenly the confined space makes me feel as if I'm being crushed. I want to move, but I wait. I have to think of a plan.

I can't hide here forever, but I don't know how to get out of the warehouse. And I don't know how many men are out there. I close my eyes and imagine what I saw while running between the crates. Nothing. There is nothing that can help me. I open my eyes and shift my head to look up.

My only choice is to climb.

Maybe then I'll be high enough to see the exit and the location of Goon Two and his men.

Without thinking through it any further, I slowly inch my way forward. I stop just as I reach the opening to pause and listen. The voices of the men sound far off, so I move completely out of my hiding space.

I turn to look at the crates in front of me. They each have three boards that run horizontal, and there's a small gap between the stacked crates. I try to grip the first horizontal board with the toe of my shoe, but my foot slips. There's not a lot of room, so I turn my foot sideways. This works better and I reach up. I grip the top of the crate in the open space, pushing and pulling to get my other foot on the second board. It's awkward, my strength is low, and my legs are still weak from squatting for so long, but I'm able to get a foothold on the second board. Taking a deep breath, I push and pull as hard as I can to repeat the process. I'm almost on the third board when my foot gets caught in my long dress and I crash to the floor.

Pain shoots up my spine and I roll to my side, biting on my lip to keep from crying out. I don't wait for my vision to clear before I'm back up on my feet, trying again. This time I make it to the top of the first crate, but I'm pulled down before I can go any farther. He flings me to the floor and my head hits the concrete with a sickening thud.

"You stupid bitch!"

I see the butt of his gun coming at me—

Pain. Darkness. That's all there is. I let myself go.

I wake up enough to realize I can't open my left eye, and that there's a horrendous pain surrounding my right ankle. Bile rises to the back of my throat and I roll to my side. Nothing comes out, and the painful dry heaves send a series of spasms through my body. When they stop, I drift away once again.

7: Surrender

I open my eye and flinch at the sight of Goon Two standing over me. There's a large cut on the side of his face. I cough and try to roll to my side, but my body doesn't seem to be working. The searing pain from before is gone, but there's still a sharp ache.

"Doc said you should regain all of your movement soon. If it was up to me, you'd be on your way to a slow and painful death by now. But for some reason the boss has a soft spot for you. Only thing I can assume is that you're a really good fuck." He pauses to look me over. "I could have a go, and the boss would never know. Find out for myself what all the fuss is about. I suppose it's your lucky day that you're not my type." He pauses again, this time to let out a loud laugh. "Sorry, it's just kind of funny—thinking of today as your lucky day. I mean, based on your little attempt at getting away I assume you're going to choose to die today. I don't see why you would have risked it if you're going back with the boss. Am I right? I am, aren't I?"

I look at his smiling face for a few seconds before closing my eyes. Or eye. "You seem rather happy."

"She speaks! Ha! And here I was starting to buy into the rumors that you were just a stupid mute. To your point, I *am* happy. I get to kill someone today! And that someone is *you!*" He pokes my injured eye with his finger, and I wince in pain. He laughs again. "I always love a good kill, but since you smashed my face and balls with that plank of wood I think this might end up being my all time favorite. I suppose it's good that I still have seven hours left to plan out every detail. This will be my most masterful kill yet. You're looking forward to it too, aren't you? I mean you must be. It was going to be so much more . . . *boring* before you pulled your little escape attempt. You had to know that you wouldn't be able to get out, so the only conclusion is that you want me to torture you. I heard some stories of what the boss used to do to you. I think you came to like it. You get off on being tortured, don't you?"

I turn my head away from him. "Why don't you just go ahead and kill me?"

"Oh, I would love to. But boss man said you get the full twenty-four hours. He wants to be here for the main event. I think he has something very special planned. He did let me smash your ankle though. That should keep you from thinking about attempting any more Houdini acts. Had to call Doc down here though to get you to stop screaming—just enough meds to take the edge off, but not to kill the pain. Am I right?"

I scream out in pain when his foot slams down on my ankle. He laughs as he stands up straight.

"You have seven more hours, then you're all mine. Unless, of course, you decide to come to your senses." He leaves the room, the lock clicking into place behind him.

My head is floating, but I concentrate on the pain in my ankle. I can't fall asleep again.

Did I really think I could escape? What the hell was I thinking?

I wasn't thinking—I surrendered to instinct and paid the price. Instinct may be automatic, but it's not always the best choice. Thinking is better. Looking at the situation from all angles and assessing the risks. That's what survival is all about. Sure, let instinct offer suggestions, but think it through before acting.

I know this. Isaac taught me this long ago. But I had a moment of weakness, and now I will suffer a fate far worse than if I had followed my original plan to play the good, obedient hostage.

This wasn't the first time I surrendered to instinct and feelings. I paid a hefty price the last time too.

⁂

I stare at his eyes for a few more seconds. Of course they're brown, but I'm trying my best to see if they're a different *shade* of brown. There is no difference in the color, so I move to the shape of his eyes. I see that they are slightly rounder, and my shoulders relax. There's also a small—miniscule even—freckle at the very corner of his right eye. Feeling better, I move to his lips. It's no use, the beard is too distracting.

"Can I move now? This is starting to become awkward."

I shift my eyes and hold his gaze. "You think this is awkward?"

"Ah, yeah."

"Well, I have to live with two people who look exactly the same, even though they shouldn't. *That's* awkward. So the least you can do is sit still and let me examine your face. You both seem intent on making me spend time with you, so I need to find differences. Otherwise I'll have a constant headache. Now, please turn your face to the left."

"To the left?"

"Yes, I want to see your ears. That beard covers everything except your eyes, so I have to get creative."

Zac sighs and turns his head as requested. "Wouldn't it be better if Isaac were in here with us? You know, so you can have an accurate comparison of our features."

"Isaac's features are etched into my memory—every detail—so he doesn't need to be sitting here." I halt, realizing the meaning behind what I just said, and I feel my cheeks start to burn.

Zac must be watching me out of the corner of his eye because he notices. "No need to get embarrassed. You should be able to picture every aspect of his face. I'm sure he can do the same about you. The two of you are married after all, right?"

We've been living with Zac for six months. I've had a few conversations with him, but this is only the third time I've been in a room alone with him. I was under the impression from Isaac that Zac knew our story was fabricated, so his question throws me off.

"You know about our marriage."

He turns his head to look at me and starts speaking before I can protest his movement. "If you're referring to the legal state of your marriage, then yes, of course I know. I helped set up the plan. However, the way I see it is that in your hearts you are legitimately married. I can tell by the way you look at each other, how you talk to each other, the way either one of you would do anything to protect the other—that's a real marriage, Angela."

I'm starting to get used to him calling me by my fake name, but there's still a disconnection and it takes me a second to remember that I'm Angela. "Well, I guess I wouldn't know anything about a real marriage, so I'll have to take your word for it."

"Good, because I happen to be an expert on the subject."

I can't help but smile. "Oh really? Last I knew you weren't married."

He shifts in his seat and rests his elbows on the table. "No, I'm not married, but my parents have been married for thirty-five years—and happily at that. I've seen the sacrifices they've made for each other. That's how you can spot true love—by the sacrifices made rather than the words spoken. In my opinion, true love unites people more than any legal document can."

I look down at my hands. If that's true, then Isaac really does love me. He's only said the words 'I love you' three times. I hate that I've counted, but I can't help it. Isaac brings me several books each week from the library, and many of those stories are about love. Based on what I've read, three times is not a lot considering the number of years we've known each other. In some of those books, the people in love say it every five seconds. In terms of Zac's definition—sacrifices made—Isaac has said it every day since we first met.

I wonder how many times I've said it. I've only said the exact words once. *Once.* But what about indirectly? What sacrifices have I made? I can only think of one—agreeing to live with Zac. Oh, I guess it's two now, because I've also agreed to come out of the bedroom. Isaac has given up his education, his future stability, his mom—basically everything—all for me. He spent years working on a plan to help me escape. He's living a double life to keep me safe. He risked his life to get me out. Even when I was in the hole he made sacrifices, breaking rules and risking punishment to teach me things or spend time with me. What have I done in return?

"Angela, what's going through your mind? Why are you crying?"

I wipe at my tears and focus back on Zac. I'm starting to trust that he's a good person who honestly wants to help us, but it's still too early for me to open up to him. "I think I'm done for the day."

I push back from the table and hurry up the stairs before he can respond. I crawl in bed and wrap myself in the blankets, letting the tears fall.

I must have fallen asleep because the room is darker when I hear Isaac come in. He climbs in bed behind me but doesn't touch me. After several seconds, I feel him remove the headband from my head and reach over to put in on the nightstand. I now wear the angel wing charm on a chain that Isaac gave me for Christmas, but I still like to wear the headband.

"You haven't been straightening your hair. I suppose it's okay since you don't leave the house, but you should probably get used to doing it. It's grown longer too, so we'll need to cut and dye it again soon. You should also start wearing the glasses."

The sobs hit me hard and fast. I'm crying with such force the bed shakes. I feel Isaac's hands on my shoulders, trying to turn me around.

"Ang, baby, talk to me. What's wrong?"

"No. P-please. I-I don't want to t-talk about it."

He stops trying to turn me around, but he doesn't leave. "Well, I'm not leaving until you tell me. No more secrets between us, remember?" He rests his hand near my hip, rubbing the small of my back with his thumb. That one touch strips away all my defenses. I start talking, choked sobs making my words jumble together.

"I'm not doing enough. You've done everything. Given up everything. All for me."

"Ang—"

"I can't even keep up my new appearance! Why can't I even do that much for you? You've had to see and do unspeakable things, all because of me. You risked your life to save me. I've done nothing but complain about having to look at two of you."

"Ang—"

"What if you wake up tomorrow and decide you're tired of living half of a life with a girl who can't even leave the house? Who can't stop flinching when you touch her? You should have a real wife, one who you can take out, and—"

"Ang!" Somehow Isaac is in front of me, holding my face in his hands. "Where is all this coming from? You're the only one I want."

"Why?"

"What do you mean, why?"

"Exactly what it sounds like." I sit up now, pushed by some bizarre urge to question Isaac's feelings. "Why do you want to be with me? Is it because of your sister? Do you view me as some sort of replacement, as someone you can save when you couldn't save her?"

Isaac jumps up, stepping away from me. "Where the hell did you get that idea?" His voice is loud and filled with shock and anger.

"I just don't understand why you would risk so much for me. What have I ever done for you to make you want to give it all up? What about me is worth loving?"

He folds his arms across his chest and glares at me. He opens his mouth to speak, but closes it again. A full ten seconds pass before he speaks. "You're actually being serious?"

"Yes."

"So are you saying you only love me because of the risks I've taken for you?"

Shock hits me hard in the chest. "No, that's not—"

"No? Because that's what I hear you saying. That the reason you love someone is because of the things they do for you."

"That's not what I'm saying! Or at least it's not what I meant."

"Tell me why you're asking me these questions."

"Zac said that love was measured by sacrifices made, not words spoken. It got me thinking about all you've done for me. You've made more sacrifices for me than I can count, and I'm just wondering why."

He rolls his eyes and then tugs at his hair. "So I guess this is all my fault. I'm the one who wanted you to spend time with him, and now he's filling your head with all sorts of stupid ideas."

I'm about to defend my conversation with Zac when I realize he hasn't answered my questions. "Regardless of why I asked, why won't you answer?"

"Because I'm not very good at these conversations. You know what it was like for me at home. We didn't talk about feelings. Why do you think I underlined all those words in that book? After all these years, do you still not understand why I did that?"

"The words you marked told me how you felt, but not why you felt that way!"

He locks his gaze with mine and then his shoulders drop. He waves his hands at me, asking me to move over on the bed. I scoot back, resting my back against the headboard, and he sits down facing me. "If I understand correctly, you want to know if I view you as some sort of replacement for my sister, and why I love you. Does that sum it up appropriately?"

"Yes, I think so."

He runs his hand over his face. "First of all, I want to make it very clear that I do not view you as a replacement for my sister. She died, and it messed up my family more than it already was." He pauses to consider his words. "I'll admit that the first time I saw you, I was reminded of my sister. You were about the same age as she was when she died. That compelled me to go see you that first night. But that's where the comparison ended. I have never, *ever*, viewed you as some sort of . . . of a do-over in the 'save the sister' category. Are you clear on that now?"

I nod. Even though I feel relief at what he says, I can't find my voice.

"Good, now I don't want to hear any more about it. The reason I've risked so much for you, and will continue to do so, is because I love you. It's that simple. You have to understand that's the way it works. I don't love you because of risks taken, I take the risks because of the way I feel. Clear on that?"

I try to nod again, but I'm still not convinced that's the way it works.

He takes a deep breath and lets it out slowly. "I don't know exactly when I fell in love with you. When we were young, you were simply my best friend. It wasn't because of anything you said or did—I just really enjoyed being around you. You made me laugh and smile. You asked crazy questions, and I liked how your brain worked. Over time I realized that you were the first person I wanted to tell if something good happened, and the first person I wanted to talk to when something bad happened. I was happy to just be near you. I could be the real me with you, and I didn't have that with anyone else. You're smart, funny, kind, pretty. Your laugh . . . your laugh just makes my heart beat faster. Your smile makes your whole face light up. Your eyes are full of wonder and mischief and appreciation for everything you see. You're so tiny, yet so strong. So *incredibly* strong."

He pauses to wipe the tears he's fighting to hold back. I don't bother wiping mine away, knowing they will keep falling as long as he keeps talking.

"I may not know exactly when I fell in love with you, but I do know when I first realized that I was in love with you. It was when I found my cousin attacking you. The pain that cut through me when I walked in your room and saw him on top of you—" He squeezes the bridge of his nose and clears his throat. "I had suspected that I had feelings for you before then—when I first had to read *Wuthering Heights*. So much in that book resonated with me, and you were always first in my mind as I read the words. But I still wouldn't let love be an option for why I felt the way I did. I had been raised to believe love was forbidden, and I allowed that rule to cloud my feelings. When I saw my cousin trying to hurt you, I could no longer deny how I felt. Do you understand now? I love you because I don't have a choice—I just do."

I understand now. I know what he means because I feel it too. I don't know when I started loving him, but it feels as if I always have. It's more about the way I feel when I'm with him than any specific thing about him. But I'm aware that an imbalance still exists between us.

"Ang, baby, please talk to me. I can see there is something bothering you. Do you still not understand how I can love you?"

"No, I understand now. Everything you said, it's how I feel about you too. It's just that you've given up so much for me. I don't even come close. If Zac is right, and love is measured by sacrifices made and not words, how can I ever tell you how much I love you?"

He moves closer to me and takes my hands in his. "It's funny, because I see it the other way around. From my perspective, you've given me much more than I ever could in return."

I search his face for any sign of teasing. There is none. "What have I given you? I can't leave the house or even keep up the appearance I'm supposed to have as Angela. And I can't let you touch me—at least not the way a husband is supposed to touch his wife. What have I given you that can possibly compare to all the risks and sacrifices you've made?"

"Your trust. You trust me completely and without question. I know that doesn't come easy for you. You've never had any reason in your life to trust anyone, yet you have trusted me from the first moment we met. That's more than any risk I've ever taken."

Tears sting my eyes and my lip trembles. "You really mean it? You're not just saying that to make me feel better?"

"I really mean it." He lets go of my hands and gently cups my face as he moves closer.

I flinch. He sees it and hesitates before moving his lips to my forehead. I see the flash of pain in his eyes and it makes me cry harder. I let him hold me until I fall asleep.

I open my eyes and see Isaac watching me. We're sharing the same pillow, and our noses are almost touching. I can feel his breath, soft on my lips. I want to reach my hand up and run it along his beard, but I don't. I think back over our conversation before I fell asleep. A question has been plaguing me but I haven't asked because I know he doesn't want to talk about it. I ask anyway, hoping it will distract my thoughts from the other direction they want to take.

"What was your sister's name?"

He closes his eyes. I can see him thinking—his forehead creases as his eyebrows pinch together, his jaw tightens. He doesn't want to tell me, but I know that he will. He opens his eyes and locks his gaze with mine.

"Haven't you guessed by now?" His voice is just above a whisper.

I have guessed, and his response has confirmed that I'm right. "Abigail?"

He nods, and his eyes are full of pain. "When I suggested you give your doll a name, I didn't intend on offering you my sister's name. It just sort of slipped out. After I realized what I said, I wanted to change it, but you latched on to it and I didn't want to upset you. Later I realized that it helped. On all the dreams I played for you, when I included Abigail with us, it was like having her there. It provided me a measure of healing that I needed."

Talking of Abigail makes my heart ache. "You said you'd try to find her. My doll."

"I know. I really thought I would be able to. One day when you were down in the bathroom, I had put a small mark on her—right inside her hairline in the back. It was a small A and I—for Ang and

Isaac. My mom is responsible for cleaning up the dolls and getting them ready for the next girl. I'm not sure why she does it—I know that she doesn't approve of the business. Maybe the dolls were her idea to begin with." He pauses, and I know he's thinking of his mom. They were close, and it's hard for him to have left her behind. "Anyway, I searched the dolls, but Abigail wasn't there. I'm sorry that I didn't find her."

I think about how it felt to hold her to my chest. "I know it's silly, that she's just a doll, but outside of you she was the only friend I had. I miss her."

"I know."

I can see that he does understand. He must miss her too. I see now that she was the replacement for his sister, not me. "Why don't you want to talk about your sister?"

"What's the point? She died and it sucked and there's nothing that will bring her back." His eyes shift down to my mouth. He lifts his hand and runs his finger lightly over my top lip. My eyes shutter closed involuntarily as a shiver runs down my spine. "And because I feel guilty."

The unexpectedness of his comment snaps my eyes back open. "What do you have to feel guilty about?"

He doesn't respond. Seconds tick by and I debate on if I should ask him again. I don't, knowing that if he doesn't answer it's because it's too painful. But he does respond, in almost a whisper.

"There's a part of me that's happy she died. Because if she hadn't, I never would have met you."

He doesn't hesitate. He leans forward and gently places his lips to mine. He pulls back and searches my face. I know he's looking for a reason to stop. He's making sure I'm okay. I'm breathing heavy, but I am okay, and I want him to kiss me again. He sees this in my face and immediately captures my mouth with his. It's just as I had remembered, from that first kiss on the hill after the fireworks.

He grasps my head—fingers in my hair, palm hot on my neck. His other hand maneuvers behind me—under my shirt and up my back. I allow my hands the same freedom and thread my fingers though his hair. He lifts slightly, pulling at my shirt. He breaks away to lift it over my head. I instantly cross my arms over my chest.

"Please. Let me see you. I need to see you. Just you." I know what he's asking and as hard as it is, I lower my arms. His eyes travel the length of me, pausing where the charm he gave me hangs at the end of its chain, and then back up to my face. "Are you sure about this? We can stop."

I want to do this—to be with him completely—I just don't know if I can. I'm scared. I'm excited. I'm confused. Taking a deep breath I nod, my eyes never leaving his. He takes off his shirt and lowers himself over me.

I instantly flinch. My chest tightens. My skin burns. He pulls back. Tears escape from my eyes. "I'm sorry. Please, I want to."

He tries again and this time doesn't stop when my body reacts negatively. I close my eyes as I start to shake. I'm in pain. Pain from the memories, from the inability to react the way I want to in this moment, from the torment I know Isaac must be feeling at seeing me struggle.

"Ang, baby, open your eyes. It's me. It's only me. Look at me." I open my eyes. He waits for my body to relax before slowly tracing a delicate line from my neck to my hip. His eyes never leave mine.

I push my pain down. I anchor to Isaac, knowing that the only way to get past the pain is to push through it. I surrender to him completely.

Isaac is sleeping and I'm in the shower. I tried not to, but my skin needed relief.

I'm silently crying, not wanting Isaac to know that I'm in here. Although, deep down I know it's impossible to not hear the shower from our room.

I didn't want to take a shower. I had always hoped that being with Isaac would make the feel of the man's touch that still lingers on my skin disappear—replaced with the warm glow of how it feels to be loved.

Isaac was gentle and slow. I felt loved every step of the way and was able to remain grounded in our love. It was after it was over that the darkness seeped back in.

Scrubbed raw and emotionally drained, I turn off the water. I dry off, dress, and return to our room. I quietly climb back in bed, facing

Isaac. His eyes are closed, and the nightlight in the room casts a glow over his face. The tracks from his fresh tears glisten on his cheeks.

I knew I had hurt Isaac. We had both hoped that we could erase our past by simply immersing ourselves in each other. We were too young and naive to understand that we had to suffer the effects of pushing through the pain in order to emerge on the other side.

Despite the emotional pain, we continued down the path of intimacy. We connected and did our best to drive out the memories that held us captive. We became more obsessed with each other than we already were. We anchored to each other.

Over time, I slowly lost myself in the process. There wasn't much of me to begin with, but at least there had been something. Once I had surrendered myself to Isaac, I was no longer an individual. I had allowed myself to be defined by his love.

I retreated back to staying in our room when Isaac wasn't home. I suffered internal torment and teetered on the edge of my event horizon, fighting against the black hole that raged within. I'd accepted it—as long as I could remain connected to Isaac.

It was about six months later when Isaac realized the true extent of my suffering. Given everything he'd done for me, I shouldn't have been surprised that he felt compelled to save me yet again. We had been living in the house with Zac for just over a year when he decided it was time for me to break free completely.

I think about the ways he tried to help me find myself again. I remember resisting when he first wanted me to go for walks with him around the block. But he was adamant, and in the end—

6: Sacrifice

I'm really starting to resent the hour reminder. I realize that this was probably the man's intention all along.

I'm still lying on my back. It's uncomfortable and I want to change my position, but everything hurts too much to move. I open my undamaged eye and, not liking the view, close it again after only a few seconds. My circumstances are even more depressing when I can only see half of it.

What was I thinking about? My mind is tired and it keeps trying to cling to memories I'm not yet ready to face. However, I rationalize that I'll be dead soon, so why not? I let my mind linger for a while.

I imagine the eyes that draw me in completely.

I concentrate on the smile that makes my heart ache.

I shiver from hugs I long to feel one more time.

A sob threatens, and I push the thoughts aside again. I'll get there soon enough, in the natural course of the mental trek through my life. In fact, it won't be long at all.

I go back. Back to the house in Lafayette we shared with Zac.

Zac.

I haven't given him enough thought. Sure he didn't surface in my life until a few years ago, but my mind hasn't even tried to fight against me by bringing him to the forefront sooner. I wonder why.

Guilt? Longing? Resentment? Jealousy?

Or maybe I've simply allowed myself to finally merge Zac into Isaac after all. Maybe all my memories of Isaac have satisfied my need to consider Zac as well, because I've finally allowed them to become one person.

I forcefully shove the thought aside. Regardless of what my subconscious or my mind has done, my heart refuses to fuse the two together. I go back to Isaac, where my feelings are deeply rooted.

I was thinking of how Isaac helped me find myself again. Despite the desire to go there, to experience the happiness of his gestures—both large and small—I don't want to think about it. Those happy moments intertwine with the devastation of my world shattering for a second time.

I lay with my mind still. Immobile in every sense of the word. Dread pushes down on me, suffocating me.

But I have to go there. I have to remember how it felt. Remember how it felt to have my world shatter all over again.

✶

"You're like a kid in a candy store." Isaac laughs as he turns the car down a dirt path.

"I don't know what a kid is like in a candy store, but I know I'm very excited." We've been living in Zac's house for just over a year, and Isaac has been promising me for almost as long to bring me out to one of the farms where he works. To say that I'm excited is an understatement. I look out the window again, hoping to get a look at the expanse of the farm. Right now all I see are corn stalks that practically tower over the car.

Just past the corn fields, Isaac pulls the car over to the side and climbs out. He opens the trunk and removes a large case as I exit my side. I look around at the fields and farm buildings in the distance. I'm so consumed by what I see that I jump slightly when Isaac steps up next to me. We walk in silence for a few minutes through one of the fields. He leads me to a section of the crop that is somewhat separate from the rest and sets his case down.

"What's growing here?"

"Soybeans. They'll start harvesting soon."

He's tried several times in the past to explain why he collects the samples throughout the various stages of the farming cycles. I don't completely understand it, but I know it has something to do with the organic products his company produces and how it impacts the growth of the crops. Zac does testing at the corporate lab, but they also have to do field tests. There's where Isaac helps. While I don't exactly understand what they are doing, I'm intrigued by how farms work in general. Cultivating the land, growing and harvesting food, nurturing animals—from what Isaac has shared with me I know it's a lifestyle that requires extreme dedication and determination.

And love.

Love for land and animals. Love for the basic cycle of life. Love for the work they do day in and day out.

With the absence of love I've had in my life, it's no wonder I'm intrigued by farming.

I slowly turn in a circle, looking out over the acres of land. In the far distance I can see some sort of farm equipment moving through the fields. It's everything I had imagined it would be. The sharpness of the smells, the feel of the wind, the quiet sounds of nature, the vibrancy of the crops and trees—it creates a sense of calm that roots deep within my core.

The only thing missing are the animals. Isaac said it would be too risky to take me to see them since there would likely be more people around that part of the farm. However, he did get permission from the farmer to take me to one of the open fields for a picnic dinner.

I follow Isaac around the fields and he even lets me collect a few of the samples. When we're done, he leads me back to the car to drive over to another part of the farm. We get out of the car and he opens the trunk again, this time taking out a cooler and a blanket. I take the blanket, and he takes my hand. Up ahead I see a large tree—the only one in the field. On first look it seems out of place, however it doesn't take me long to realize it's right where it belongs.

We reach the tree and Isaac sets down the cooler to take the blanket from my hands. He spreads it on the ground and motions for me to sit. He hands me a sandwich and sets out containers of fruit and chips.

"I'm sorry that it's nothing special—I've never been much of a cook."

"You're better than me."

He shifts on the blanket so he's sitting next to me. He takes a bite of his sandwich and talks around the food in his mouth. "Oh, I don't know about that. You're starting to get the hang of it. That meatloaf you made the other day was pretty good."

"It was burnt."

"Only on the edges." I glance at him and can't help but smile at his attempt to hide his laughter. I know it was terrible, but the fact that he's trying to convince me otherwise makes me happy.

I take another bite of my sandwich and look out over the fields. It seems they never end. "You mentioned this was the largest farm you come to for samples, but are the others similar to this one?"

When he puts his sandwich down, I know I'm in for a long explanation. He proceeds to tell me about the other farms, pointing out the similarities and differences. He's encouraged by my occasional questions and continues the conversation by telling me about the farms that Zac visits. He finishes and looks out over the field.

"Speaking of Zac, he mentioned that for the past six months or so you've been staying in our room again when I'm not home."

I shift my eyes away. I don't want to answer because I know he won't like my response, but I can tell by his tone that this is not a conversation I can avoid. I sigh and pluck one of the small flowers growing next to the blanket. I spin it slowly between my thumb and forefinger, watching the white petals flutter slightly with the movement. I pull in a deep breath before responding. "I don't like spending time with Zac."

Isaac sits up straighter and turns toward me. "Has he done something?"

I snap my head up, surprised by the question. I can tell by the tone of his voice and the rigidity of his spine that he suspects something terrible. "No, not what you're thinking."

He relaxes, but only slightly. "Then what?"

I shrug and look back down at the flower. I start pulling at the petals, letting them drop to my lap one by one. He reaches out and grabs my hand, trying to help me focus. I drop the flower and shift slightly on the blanket.

"Isaac, I did try. Really, I did, but it still bothers me that he looks so much like you. The more time I spend with him, the more I find myself wanting to talk to him the way I talk with you. I feel like he should know things about me, and when he doesn't I get frustrated. However, when he does know certain things, like my favorite flavor of ice cream, I get uncomfortable. I only want you to know all the little details about me."

He pulls me close and slips his arm around my shoulders. "Ang, it's okay. I want him to know those things. If something should happen to me, then—"

I pull away. "Don't say that."

He turns to face me more fully. "We have to be realistic. Something could happen, and if it does, then he's the one who will take care of you."

"No."

"What do you mean, 'no'?"

"We're together, remember? That means if something happens to you, then it happens to me too. I don't go with Zac. I go with you."

"This is non-negotiable, Ang. If I sense trouble, Zac takes you and protects you."

"And who will protect you?" My voice is shaking. My body must be shaking too because Isaac cups my face and places a soft but lingering kiss on my lips.

"I will. Just knowing that you are out here, waiting for me, that's all I need to keep going and find my way back to you." He pulls me close and I rest my head on his chest.

"How do I keep a boundary between me and Zac if I spend more time with him? How am I supposed to look at him and not think of you?"

"If you would take the time to get to know him, you would realize that we are two very different people. We may look similar, but that's where it ends. You'll find a way to keep us separate." I open my mouth to respond, but he cuts me off. "And before you say it, yes you do have a choice. But before you decide, I want you to look around. Really look at what you see. This is where life happens, Ang. Out here in the world. Not in that small bedroom we share. I don't know how you'll ever be able to fully live—with or without me—if you can't even spend time with Zac."

I know he's right. Ever since the moment we became intimate I've let myself push Zac away along with the rest of the world. I still refuse to think about the possibility of something happening to Isaac, but he's right in that this is better. Being out here has made me realize that I do want more out of my life with Isaac. If Zac is the first step to getting there, then I'll try again.

"Okay."

He gives me a squeeze. "That's my girl. As a reward, I'll give you an extra special present for your birthday next month. Or at least for Angela's birthday."

I twist my head and look up at his downturned face. "What is it?"

"You'll just have to wait and see." He smiles and plants a kiss on the tip of my nose.

I wipe the sweat away from my forehead and look over at Zac. He's reading, as usual, and acting as if it were the middle of winter rather than summer. "Aren't you hot?"

He looks up at me, momentarily confused. "No. I guess I'm used to it. Would you like me to turn on the air?"

"No. I'll be fine. It just seems hotter this summer than last summer."

He sets his book down on the table and stands to join me at the open window. There is no breeze and the air outside is almost as stifling as it is inside, but I'm waiting for Isaac to return. It's getting dark and the constant sound of the cicadas is almost deafening, but I don't move from the window.

Zac crosses his arms over his chest. "It is hotter this summer. Although, last summer was cooler than usual. Really, I can turn on the air if you're too hot."

I stare at his profile for a moment. I'm starting to see the differences between him and Isaac. It helps. "Since we're talking about it, why don't you use the air conditioner?"

He shrugs his shoulders. "It's hard to explain. I just like living without most modern conveniences." He pauses and lets out a short laugh. "It drove Isaac nuts the first summer we lived together."

"Why do you turn on the heat in the winter then?"

"I wouldn't, but Isaac told me that if pipes burst from freezing over then he'd make me sleep out in the snow. He was convincing enough that I agreed to heat in the winter, but no air in the summer." He turns his head to look at me. "However, I do mean it—I can turn on the air if you get too uncomfortable during the day. Promise me you'll let me know?"

I nod and look back out the window. "Okay." We remain in silence for a few seconds before Zac speaks again.

"He should be home soon."

"You said that two hours ago." I know he knows what I'm thinking. He might be thinking the same thing. Isaac should have been home by now, and I'm worried that something has gone wrong.

"I'm sure he's fine. He probably just got caught in traffic. Sometimes the trip to Indianapolis can take longer than expected."

"I still don't understand why you don't use the local post office if a PO Box number can't be traced to an address."

"We don't use the PO Box address for much since all our bills are paperless, but we needed some sort of mailing address. Isaac wanted to add another layer of precaution, and Indianapolis is a large city. If his father is somehow able to track us to that mailing address, Isaac thinks we'll have a better chance of losing him from Indy. It would give us more time to run." He glances at me and he must see the worry on my face. "Really, I'm sure he's fine. We don't have to go to the Indy post office often, so the chance of someone catching him there is very slim."

"He's been there a few times these last couple of months. It's because of my birthday, isn't it?" I look at him again, and he smiles.

"He wanted to get you something special for your birthday. Regardless of how old Angela is, you will be twenty-one this year. That deserves a special gift."

I blow out a big breath and cross my own arms. "I don't need anything, except him home safe. He shouldn't have taken the risk."

"Why don't we go sit down? You waiting here at the window won't bring him home any faster. Besides, you look tired. It might help pass the time if—"

Isaac's car appears and turns onto the driveway. I instantly relax and hurry to the door that leads to the garage. I open the door and it's all I can do to keep from running to the car. Isaac gets out and walks toward me, a box tucked under one arm. As soon as he reaches me, I launch myself at him and hold on tight.

"Whoa, what's this about?" He tries to peel me off, but I refuse to let go. He chuckles and tightens his arm around my waist, lifting me slightly in the air. He carries me back in the house and sets the box he's holding down on the table before wrapping his other arm around me. "Ang, baby, what's wrong?"

"You're late. I was worried." My voice is muffled against his chest.

I feel him sigh. "Zac?"

"What? I tried to keep her mind occupied, but she's surprisingly stubborn. Besides, you *are* late."

Isaac tries to move me again, but I refuse. He moves his hands to my sides and lifts me up. I wrap my legs around his waist as he carries me into the living room. He puts me down on the couch and sits next to me. I'm instantly back in his arms.

"Are you crying?" I feel him shift his head, trying to look at my buried face.

I am crying, but I don't answer because I don't want him to know, which is silly because he obviously knows that I am. He rubs my back and I fall asleep.

I open my eyes and realize I'm in bed. In addition to the standard nightlight, the side lamp is on next to Isaac. He's sitting up, reading. I shift and he looks down at me.

"Well hello, sleepyhead."

I blink a few times to rid my vision of the lingering sleep. "Did you carry me up here?"

"Yep. It's a good thing you're so tiny." He closes his book and sets it on the table, then lays down facing me. "You've been sleeping for a few hours. Are you feeling okay?" He puts his hand to my forehead.

I lift up and look at the clock over his shoulder. It's just after midnight. I lie back down and look in his eyes. "I'm fine. I guess I was just tired. You were gone a long time, and I was worried. It must have worn me out."

"I'm sorry it took so long. There was construction on the interstate and it backed up traffic for several miles."

"Why are you still awake?"

"I couldn't sleep. I guess I'm just anxious about the package I picked up today."

I shift my eyes and look at the box sitting on the desk near the end of the bed. "Is it for my birthday?"

"Nope." I narrow my eyes at him, confused. He laughs in response and runs his thumb across my brow. "It's for Angela's birthday."

"That's good, because her birthday is today—it is after midnight."

He twists his body and looks at the clock behind him. "It seems you are correct." He turns back to face me. "Happy birthday, *Angela*."

"Since we're both up, and it is officially Angela's birthday, do I get to open it now?"

"Actually, that's a great idea. I didn't want to give it to you in front of Zac, so this is perfect."

"Why can't you give it to me in front of Zac?"

He laughs, gives me a kiss, and then climbs out of bed. "Don't worry, it's nothing embarrassing. Zac actually knows what it is." He hesitates and looks back at me. I can tell he's debating on telling me something. I sit up and prepare for whatever it is he has to say. He leans on the desk, one hand on the brown cardboard box. "There was a risk in getting this present. I talked it over with Zac first, and we went over all the possible outcomes. We agreed that the risk was minimal, so I went ahead and did it."

My heart pounds hard in my chest. "What did you do?"

He slides the box off the desk and walks back over to the bed. He sits down facing me, placing the box between us. "Open it and find out."

I stare at the box for a few seconds before reaching out with shaking hands. I suddenly feel as if something isn't right. It's probably just my nerves because of what Isaac said about a risk in getting the present, but I can't shake the feeling that something is very wrong. I pull at the packing tape until it finally gives and tears free. I open the box and peer inside. Small white puffy things fly out and stick to my hands and arms.

Isaac laughs as he pulls one from my arm. "I've always loved packing peanuts, but they get everywhere."

I wipe at my arms, but they don't fall away. Instead of trying again, I push my hands into the box until they touch something soft. The feel of the fabric makes my eyes instantly sting with tears. I slowly grasp it with my shaking hands, wanting to take my time in case I'm wrong and it's not what I think it is. I close my eyes at the familiar feel and try to smile, but my heart is still pounding out a warning I don't understand.

"Do you need help getting it out?"

I open my eyes and look at Isaac. I shake my head and lift, holding my breath. I pull in a sharp breath—it's her. He's found my Abigail.

The moment is over before it even began. This doll looks like my Abigail, but it's not her. My heart sinks as the tears start to fall. I try to find a smile, not wanting to disappoint Isaac. The effort and risk he took to get me a doll to replace my Abigail was significant, and I don't want to hurt his feelings. I look up and he's smiling, eyes darting between me and the doll.

"I told you I'd find her, Ang. It was difficult, but we got her. Abigail is back with us." He picks the packing peanuts off the doll as he speaks.

My mind stills with confusion. He thinks this is Abigail. I look down at her again to make sure. On the surface, they are identical. Same hair, same eyes, same dress. But this is not Abigail. I'm certain of it. There was a faint smudge on Abigail's right cheek. A small stain on the bottom hem of her dress in the back. I look at the two small teeth showing in her mouth. Some of the white paint had worn off on the bottom of Abigail's left tooth. I loved that most about her—it reminded me of Isaac's crooked tooth. This doll has two fully white teeth. I open my mouth to point all this out, but he starts speaking before I get the chance.

"When you were taken out of the hole and assigned to the new room, I had looked all over for Abigail. I asked my mom to help, but we couldn't find her. I knew how much you still missed having her, so after talking it over with Zac I sent a letter to my mom. It's one of the reasons we set up the PO Box. My mom and I had agreed that I would write to her once I felt it was safe. She's good at hiding things from my father, and she felt it would be safe for me to write after enough time had passed. I knew she would want to hear from me, so I wrote her and asked again about Abigail. She finally admitted that she had kept Abigail and didn't tell me. She knew that I had planned to run off with you, and she said that she wanted it as a memento. When I told her how much it meant to you, and to me, she finally agreed to send it."

"It's not her."

Isaac's head snaps up and he looks at me with confusion. "What do you mean?"

"This doll is not Abigail."

"Sure it is." He reaches for the doll and takes it out of my hands. He turns it over as he talks. "I told my mom all about the mark I left on the back of her head, just inside the hairline. Our initials—remember? I told you I did that so I could be sure to find the right one after they took her away from you." He lifts her hair and parts it near the bottom. "See, right here. This is Abigail."

I look and sure enough, two small black letters. I+A. But I know this is not Abigail.

"I'm telling you, this is not her. I don't know how those letters got there, but it's not Abigail." I point out my observations to prove my point.

He looks closer at her cheek and tooth, brow furrowed. "My mom cleans them up before they're given to a new girl. In her letters she said that she worked on Abigail. She had said she couldn't fix everything, but she must have found a way to fix her face to look like new." I can hear the uncertainty starting to creep into his voice.

"Isaac, it is not her. I can *feel* it. It's just like you and Zac—you look so much alike, but you are not the same. Now that I'm looking, I can see the differences because you are a part of me and Zac is not. It's the same with Abigail. When you weren't around, she was the only friend I had! I *know* her. Maybe your mom added those letters to make you think this was Abigail."

He forcefully shakes his head. "No. No, she wouldn't do that. She knew how important this was to me. She wouldn't do that."

"How do you know? You said that she had kept Abigail and didn't tell you about it when you asked before. Maybe she didn't want to give her up and—"

"No, you don't understand." Isaac grabs at his hair and swings his legs off the bed. He stands and paces the room a couple times. He stops and points at the doll now lying untouched on the bed. "When I first asked her to help me find Abigail, she suggested that I just give you any doll as a replacement. I told her that wouldn't work—it was either the real Abigail or no doll at all. In my letters, I reiterated that point. I told her why she was important to you and to me. That's when she felt bad for keeping the truth from me and explained why it was important to her. We wrote back and forth a few times, each trying to convince the other. Finally she agreed. She wouldn't deceive me, and if she would then she would have done it after the first letter."

He paces a few more times and then starts rummaging through one of his drawers. He pulls out some papers and spreads them across the table.

"Are those the letters from your mom?"

"Yes. Something's not right here. I need to figure out what."

I get off the bed and peer over his shoulder. He's flipping the pages too fast for me to read anything so I pick up the ones he's flipped to the side. It feels strange reading the letters. Even though he's standing right next to me, it feels like I'm reading something meant to be private between him and his mom.

I scan the letters anyway. I don't notice anything in the first or the second. When I reach the bottom of the third, and final letter, a chill overtakes my body. Somehow Isaac senses the sudden change in me.

"Ang? What is it?" He takes the letter from my hands and reads through it again. "Ang! What did you see in here?"

"The last paragraph."

He reads it out loud, and I shudder again.

I should have said this sooner, but I regret having helped you get away. Angel is no good for you. She will bring you nothing but pain. I'm asking now, let her go. This love you think you feel isn't real. I'll hold on to the doll until I hear back from you, hoping that you make the right decision.

He stops reading and looks at me. "What is it about that paragraph? I'll admit, I thought it was strange. When I told her about my plan to run away with you, she not only helped but gave me her blessing. I figured she just wrote that because she was afraid for us. I responded back that I would never leave you and that I wanted her to send the doll, and she did. Tell me what you're thinking."

"It was something she said when she came to see me. She told me that she had thought about telling you to leave me before, but after you asked her to bring me the book she realized she was wrong. She even thanked me for loving you. Why would she write this, years later? Could she have forgotten her conversation with me? Or changed her mind?"

I watch as his face pales considerably. "No, she wouldn't forget.

She's very meticulous about her choice of words. She has to be in order to avoid getting hit every day by my father's angry hands."

"Then why did she write this?"

"It has to be a warning." He looks back over to the doll. "You're one hundred percent sure that's not Abigail?"

I nod without hesitation. He strides to the bed and flips the doll over. He pulls off the dress, lifts the arms, and separates the hair. I walk over and watch as his hands surround the soft body. He squeezes it a few times and then suddenly hurries toward the door. I follow him down the stairs and into the kitchen. He takes out a sharp knife and cuts into the body of the doll. He pulls at the stuffing inside and then freezes. He pulls out a clump of stuffing and separates it until all he's holding is a small black object.

"Damn it! I'm so stupid! ZAC!" He runs back up the stairs. By the time I make it up behind him, Zac has come out of his room and is walking toward ours. I get in the room before he does and see Isaac frantically pulling stuff out of drawers.

"Isaac, what's wrong? What was that thing you found in the doll?" He doesn't even look at me. He rushes to the closet and grabs two bags, stuffing in the items he just pulled from the drawers. "Isaac! What is going on?"

"We have to leave. Too much time has passed. They could be here any minute. Get—"

"Isaac! Stop and tell me what was in the doll!" I'm frantic now and my legs are shaking.

He stops packing long enough to respond. "It's a GPS sensor."

Behind me I hear Zac turn and rush back to his room. I search my brain for what that means, because it's clear that it's not good. I remember some of the cars we had while on the road had GPS and Isaac used it to map where we were going.

Suddenly I realize the problem and a chill runs over me. "He knows where we are."

"That damn package has been sitting in this one location for several hours. They have to know where we are. He must not have any friends on the local police force in this town, otherwise we would have had a visit by now. That gives us a bit more time, but his men have to be on the way. Damn it! How could I have been so stupid? I should have seen this possibility. She never would have given him the address, or let him read the letters. He must have—" He shoves the dresser rather than finish his sentence.

I don't need him to finish to know what he's thinking. The man must have tortured his mom to get the information.

He hands me a bag before putting on pants, a shirt, and a hat. Having fallen asleep on the couch the night before, I'm already dressed except for shoes. I slip on the nearest pair as he picks up the other bag and takes my hand, leading me out the door. We meet up with Zac in the living room. I'm surprised at the speed with which he was able to get dressed and packed.

Isaac walks to Zac and grips his shoulder. "Remember what we discussed? What you promised?"

Zac nods and they give each other a quick hug. Zac grabs the bags and heads toward the garage. Isaac turns to me. I can see it in his face. The tears push at my eyes. My heart pounds in my chest.

"No. Please don't—"

"Ang, we have to. You have to go with Zac. He knows the plan."

"Why can't we all go together?"

"We can't risk it. If they're not already watching the house, then they'll be here soon. Our best chance is to separate." I instinctively look toward the window, closed off to the outside world with thick curtains. "Ang, listen to me. I'll leave first, alone, and try to draw away anyone who might be watching. They don't know Zac exists. If someone's watching, they will follow me assuming you're with me or that I'm on my way to you. You go with Zac. He knows the plan."

"But—"

"There's no time, Ang. We have to go. I love you. Always remember that. And please promise me that you will keep living, no matter what happens."

He kisses me and it feels like it will be the last time. I try to cling to him, but he pulls away and leads me to the car. He gives me one more kiss before gently placing me in the back seat and asking me to get down on the floor. I hear him tell Zac to wait ten minutes before leaving, and then he shuts the car door.

I look up and out of the side window. Isaac pauses one more time, looking back down at me, before climbing into the driver's side of the other car.

I close my eyes and count.

5: Lost and Found

Only five hours left. I've become slightly numb to the pain in my eye and ankle. My life was good training for this—teaching me how to become numb to physical pain.

I find enough strength to shift my position slightly and then return to my memories.

I was lost when we separated from Isaac. The pain was equal to that of what the man had done to us years ago. Not knowing if Isaac was dead or alive, captured or free—it was too much to bear. I crumbled, leaving Zac with the unfortunate task of keeping me together.

I think about our time on the run. We drove for almost two days straight, stopping only at gas stations when absolutely necessary. I slept most of the time, sitting on the floor of the back seat with my knees locked to my chest.

I was lost. Desperate to be found once again and pulled free to safety. I was eventually found, but not in the way I had expected or hoped.

"Ang, are you awake?"

I hear him call my name, but the voice isn't right. He's not here, he's gone. How can he be talking to me?

"Ang, wake up."

His hand gently shakes my shoulder. I finally let my eyes open, and my heart slams into my chest. I start to reach out for him, but in that same instant I realize it's not Isaac. It's only Zac. The tears come fast and I close my eyes again.

"Ang?"

"Don't call me that."

"What? I can't hear you."

I force my eyes to open again and make my voice louder. "I said, don't call me that."

He looks confused. "Call you what?"

"Ang. Only Isaac calls me that. You don't get to."

He sighs and takes his hand away from my shoulder, resting it on the back of the front seat of the car. He's still in the driver's seat, turned to face me in the back. "Sorry. *Angela*, I need you to wake up. It would look suspicious if I carried you inside."

I sit up to look out the car window. We changed cars sometime in the middle of the night, and this car has more room in the back for me to lie down almost completely on the floor. "Where are we?"

"A motel. I need some sleep, otherwise we won't survive simply because I'll run us off the road."

"Wouldn't it be safer to go in at night, when it wouldn't be so easy for someone to see us?"

He hesitates and scratches the back of his head. "It would, but it's my understanding that you . . . freak out when you see stars. I think that would be worse than going in during the day."

I stare at him. I don't like that he knows about my aversion to stars. It makes me wonder if he knows why I hate them. I start to shake, and I bury my face in my knees. I hear Zac let out another long sigh.

"Well, I'm going in. I suppose you can stay here if you want, but I thought you would enjoy sleeping in a bed and taking a hot shower. Room 113 if you decide to join me. Just don't wait too long—I plan to be asleep in a few minutes and I might not hear you knocking." He grabs a plastic bag from the passenger seat, opens the car door, and gets out without waiting for my response. I jump when I hear him slam the trunk shut a few seconds later. I look up and watch him walk slowly to our room.

I don't want to move. It would pull me from the cocoon of denial

I've created over the past couple days. Leaving the car to go to the bathroom had been enough of a challenge.

But the thought of a hot shower draws me in.

I put on my sweatshirt and look out the windows once more. I pull the hood up over my head and get out of the car. I walk quickly to the room, convinced someone will appear out of nowhere and grab me. I knock on the door, and a few seconds pass with no answer. I start to panic and look at the room number again. 113. Yes, that's what he said. I knock again, a bit louder. Still no answer. I hear a car approaching down the street, and my heart pounds faster. I bang on the door a third time. I'm about to turn and run back to the car when the door finally swings open. I stumble in and quickly shut the door.

"What's wrong?" Zac must see the panic in my face. He puts his hands on my shoulders, looks me over, and then steps to the window. He pulls the curtain slightly to the side and looks out. "Did you see someone?"

"You wouldn't answer. I heard a car. I—"

"It's all right. No one is out there. The car must have just been passing by." He leaves the window and walks back over to me. He places his hand on my lower back and guides me to the bed. I sit down and he crouches before me. "It's okay. We should be safe here."

"You wouldn't answer the door!"

"Ang—*ela*, it was only a few seconds. I was in the bathroom. Are you sure you're all right? You look pale. I know you haven't been able to sleep well in the car, and I also know you haven't eaten much since we left. I have some food—"

I stand up quickly before he finishes. "I'm fine. I'm not hungry." I head toward the bathroom, but he stops me with a tug on my arm.

"You need to eat. I promised Isaac I'd take care of you."

I yank my arm from his hand. "I don't need you to take care of me. And I don't need to eat. I need Isaac. So if you want to help me, tell me the plan. He said something about meeting up."

I watch as his shoulders fall. I know I'm not being fair to him. I know he's just doing what Isaac asked him to do. But I can't eat. Not just because I don't want to, but because I would just throw it up. I don't want to tell Zac that I've thrown up at every stop we've made over the past two days.

"I'll tell you the plan, but first I need sleep. I really wish you would eat. There's a variety of snack items in that bag. Eat whatever you want." He points to the plastic bag sitting on top of the small television. He turns to the bed, pauses, and looks back at me. "They didn't have a room with two beds. I can sleep on the floor if you want."

I look at the tiredness in his eyes, and I'm not sure how he's still awake. In that moment I feel something shift inside me. He didn't have to give up his house, his job, and his life to go on the run with us. He could have let me and Isaac go on our own.

Yet here he is. Trying to protect me, and I've never done anything nice for him.

"You need the sleep more than I do. Take the bed." I turn and head for the bathroom.

"Angela?" I stop and turn to face him again. "I don't mind if you sleep on the other side of the bed. I promise I won't touch you or anything. I'll probably be too knocked out to even notice you're there."

I don't have words, so I simply nod my head before going into the bathroom and shutting the door. I'm not sure how things are going to turn out going forward, but I know for certain I will never share a bed with Zac.

I turn the water on to the hottest temperature I can stand. I'd prefer a bath, but there is no tub—just a narrow shower stall. Frustrated, I undress and step into the stream of hot water. It stings at first, but then my skin takes on the familiar numbness. I lower my head, letting the water run over my hair. The shower pressure is poor, and my frustration grows. I quickly wash my hair and body and then sit down on the tiled floor that looks as if it hasn't been cleaned in a long time. I rest my head on my knees as the water runs over me.

I close my hand tightly around the charm dangling in front of me. I feel the little wings dig into the ring that Isaac gave me and it helps to center my thoughts.

I think about Isaac. I wonder if he's okay. I think about what the man might do if he caught him. The sobs start deep and painful, and I don't try to stop them. My stomach churns, and I launch myself out of the shower. I make it to the toilet just in time. My body shudders violently, trying to force out food that doesn't exist. When it passes, I remain on the bathroom floor. I don't bother getting up to turn off the water. I let my eyes close.

There's a loud banging sound and I lift my head, confused. I shiver and look down at my naked body. I look around the small space and suddenly I remember where I am.

"Angela? Open the door or I'll break it down!"

I put my hand to my head. It's pounding about as loud as Zac just hit the door. "Give me a minute."

I stand up and my vision blurs. I grab the sink for support until the darkness clears. I blink a few times and then find my clothes. I didn't think to bring in a fresh set, so I put on what I've been wearing the last two days. I turn off the shower and reach for the door. I'm about to open it when I remember. I stop and turn back to the toilet. I push down the handle and then run the water in the sink to rinse out my mouth. Taking a deep breath, I open the door. Zac is standing on the other side, not looking happy.

"What happened in there?"

My body stills. I had hoped he was asleep and couldn't hear me getting sick. "What are you talking about?"

"You walked in there when I went to bed—over ten hours ago! So either you decided to take a second shower in the middle of the night, or something happened. Did you pass out?"

I try to go past him but he blocks the way. I look up at him, my anger matching his. "I was tired. I sat down and fell asleep in the shower." It was almost the truth.

He looks at me for a few seconds, eyes traveling from my head to my toes and back again. He reaches out and gives the side of my hair a little flip. "Your hair's awfully dry for someone who spent ten hours in a shower."

I push past him and walk into the room. I locate my bag and start rummaging through the contents. Before I can find what I'm looking for, the bag is snatched out of my reach. I turn, stunned, and watch as Zac puts it in the bathroom, closes the door, and leans against it.

"What are you doing? I'd like to change my clothes!"

"Not until you eat something."

I open my mouth to protest, but no sound comes out. Instead, tears push their way quickly down my cheeks. Zac pinches the bridge of his nose and sighs before walking toward me.

"I'm sorry. Please don't cry. I just want you to eat something."

"I'm not hungry." I'm grateful that I'm finally able to find my voice, even though it's no more than a whisper.

"I don't believe you." ·

I drop my head and walk past him to the bathroom. I go in and shut the door behind me. I sink to the floor with my back against the door and remain there until my tears finally run dry. Once I regain control of my emotions, I change into a fresh set of clothes. I sit on the closed toilet and debate if I should go back out there with Zac or stay in the bathroom. I know if I go out there then Zac will make me eat. However, I really want to know the plan for meeting up with Isaac. I take a deep breath and stand to open the door. When I step out, I see Zac sitting in the chair by the window. He's turned on the small reading lamp and it casts a strange shadow over his features, making it difficult for me to see the differences between him and Isaac. I shake my head, looking away, and walk to the bag that's still sitting on top of the television. I rummage through the contents, hoping to find something I can keep down. I settle on a granola bar and water before moving to sit on the bed. I take small bites, hoping the slow pace will be gentle on my stomach. I glance over at Zac and find him watching me.

"Thank you for eating."

I shrug my shoulder. "The way you were acting, I figured if I didn't you would shove something down my throat anyway."

He lets out a long sigh. "I'd never force you to do anything. I hope you know that. I'm sorry if I came off as a bit . . . tough, but I made a promise to Isaac. I know that there are things in your past that I don't understand, and that's why Isaac handled you with kid gloves. But, as you've pointed out many times, I'm not Isaac. My approach may be somewhat less delicate, but it doesn't mean that I don't care. Are we still friends?"

I study him the way he's been studying me. I suddenly realize that he's right, and I'm happy for the added difference between him and Isaac. It will help me keep them separated.

"We can still be friends, but only if you tell me the plan to meet up with Isaac." I take another small bite, hoping that Zac doesn't notice the difficulty I'm having with each swallow.

He shifts in the chair, leaning forward to rest his elbows on his knees. "Isaac and I talked at length about what we would do if we were ever separated. Ultimately, we decided that the best plan was to wait three weeks and then meet up at a large public place on the following Wednesday."

He pauses and waits for my reaction. My head is spinning, but I try to focus. Unfortunately, my mind has locked on to only one detail. "Three weeks?"

"I thought you might take issue with that, but yes—three weeks. We felt it would give us time to lose anyone who might be following."

"What are we supposed to do over those three weeks?"

"We drive around. Something like what you and Isaac did right after you escaped, but with fewer days at each stop."

I feel panic trying to set in at the thought of spending three weeks on the road with Zac. Three weeks of not knowing what happened to Isaac. I push it aside and focus on my growing questions.

"Where are we meeting?"

"Navy Pier. It's in Chicago."

I don't remember Isaac ever telling me about Navy Pier. "What's that?"

"It's a place on Lake Michigan. It's a tourist spot, so there should be other people around."

My mind continues to race, but I don't know what to think of the idea since I don't know anything about the location. "Isn't it all too risky? Didn't you set up emergency phones? Why can't we just call him?"

Zac shakes his head. "Things are complicated now that they found our house with that GPS chip in the doll. We didn't have a lot of time to sweep the house—it's possible they know that someone else was living there with you and Isaac. Even though it's a burner phone, Isaac's father has strong connections. It's too much of a risk to communicate over the phone."

I look down at my partially eaten granola bar in frustration. My stomach is still churning, but my confusion is proving to be a good distraction. I'm frustrated that Isaac didn't tell me the plan a long time ago. It would have given me time to learn about everything Zac is telling me. I don't know enough about phones to understand the complications.

"Okay, fine. How does it work when we get to Navy Pier?"

He doesn't respond and I look at him again. He shifts in the chair and hangs his head. "You're not going to like this, but there is no 'we' in the plan. Only I'm supposed to go."

He's right. I don't like it. "You can't expect me to stay a—"

"It's nonnegotiable, Angela. It was Isaac's one stipulation. You don't go. That way, if something goes wrong, you go back on the run."

"How? I don't know how to run on my own! How would I pay for anything?"

"There's a package of money, along with instructions on what to do, that I'll leave with you before I go. You'll be fine."

I rub the sting out of my eyes. I don't like the plan. Not at all. However, I know that I won't be able to change his mind. "Just tell me what happens when *you* get to Navy Pier."

"There's this cruise that runs daily from the pier. I get to the pier early and sit with my book while I watch. If I notice anything suspicious, I leave. Otherwise, I get on the cruise. I'm to remain on the observation deck until ten minutes before the cruise undocks. If Isaac shows up—mission accomplished. We come back here to get you and determine where to go next."

"And if he's not there?"

"Then we do it all over again six months later."

"Six months! But—"

He holds his hand up to silence me. "If he's not there, then something went wrong or someone is still following him. We have to put a good amount of time between the meets. It's the only way to be safe."

"And what are we supposed to do for six months? It costs money to stay on the road. How are we going to pay for gas and hotels if you're not working?"

"I have enough cash to get us through a few weeks after the first meet. If he's not there and we have to wait the additional six months, then we go into my contingency plan."

"What's that?"

"Something I'll tell you about if we need to put it in place."

I'm too frustrated to remain sitting. I get up, but the room's too small to pace so I simply walk to the bathroom door and back again. I turn and cross my arms over my chest. "Why do you insist on keeping the information from me? I'm affected by all this too, you know. I want to know what we're going to do for six months if Isaac is not there."

"I'm sorry you feel left out, but I'm still not going to tell you. For reasons you probably wouldn't agree with, Isaac and I decided that we would only tell you the plans as they occur. I'm not changing my mind, so there's no point in arguing about it. If it makes you feel any better, Isaac doesn't even know the contingency plan."

I turn for the bathroom without a response. I slam the door shut, switch on the fan, and then turn to the toilet to empty my stomach of the granola bar and water. I wipe the tears from my eyes and then lay on the floor, resting my cheek on the cool tile.

It's going to be a long three weeks.

I lift my arm to pull back the curtain. I'm tired and it seems to take more effort each time I look. The sunlight stings my eyes and I blink several times. When my vision stabilizes, I glance around the parking lot. I should be used to it, but I'm still amazed at the similarities of the various motels. If Zac hadn't told me we were in a new town, I would have assumed we only drove in circles to end up back at the same motel every time. We're back in Indiana, however this time we're somewhere closer to Chicago.

I drop my arm and look at the clock again. I'm tired and it takes me some time to calculate that I still have eight hours until Zac said he'd be back. It's hard to wait. I want to know if Isaac was at the meeting place. I glance at the thick envelope sitting on the table in front of me. I've been trying to ignore it, but it's hard. Zac told me to only open it if he didn't return within forty-eight hours.

I shift the curtain to look again, and then let it fall back into place. I'm anxious, but I can barely keep my eyes open. Zac almost didn't go. He's worried about me, and I can't blame him. I'm worried too. I'm as thin as I was back when Isaac came to rescue me. I can't keep any food down, and staying in these small hotel rooms has prevented me from keeping my secret from Zac. One night was so bad he almost risked it all to take me to the emergency room. He found some crackers that I'm able to keep down for longer periods of time, and it's the only reason he agreed to still go to meet Isaac.

However, from the moment Zac left I've been too nervous to eat. I tried to drink water this morning, but it came right back up.

I rest my head on the back of the chair and close my eyes.

"Angela?"

Someone's shaking me, and it makes my stomach roll. I try to open my eyes, but my head is spinning. I roll to my side and feel my body shudder with the familiar spasms.

"Angela? Can you open your eyes?"

I try to respond, but my body slips back into darkness.

I feel something cold and wet on my forehead. I want to open my eyes, but my head is spinning. I can't tell if I'm moving or if it's just my head. I try to sit up but arms hold me tighter. I realize that I am moving. Someone is carrying me. I force my eyes open a crack. I can only see his bearded chin and nose. I try to look for something, anything, to tell me if it's him. It's too blurry and my stomach rolls. I hear a sound and realize it came from me.

"It's okay. I'm going to get you some help."

I think he's putting me in the car. I can't focus.

I wake up confused to a steady beeping sound. The first thing I notice is that I feel much better. I open my eyes and look around the unfamiliar room. I rest my eyes on the person sitting next to the bed, reading. It takes me a few seconds to realize that it's Zac, not Isaac. I try to shift my position on the bed, but there's something attached to my arm and fingers.

Zac looks up when he notices my movement and is at my side immediately. Now that he's looking at me, I can see that he's shaved the part of his beard just above his lip. I also notice that his clothing is different. He's usually in jeans, but now he's wearing a plain blue shirt and dark pants. There are black straps that connect to his pants and go up around his shoulders. I want to ask why he looks so different, but he starts talking before I get a chance.

"Oh, thank God you're awake. How are you feeling?" He puts his hand to my forehead, and I try to shake it off but my arms are weak. I try to respond, but my mouth is too dry to speak. I swallow a few times, but there's little improvement. Zac reaches over to a nearby table for a cup. "Here." He lifts a spoon to my lips and I allow the small pieces of ice to coat my mouth. After a few more spoonfuls, I decide to try again.

"Better." It's just a whisper, but at least it's a start.

"You scared me. I thought I'd lost you."

I close my eyes for a second and then open them again to study his face. I see a mixture of pain and relief. "Where are we?"

"A hospital."

I start at his response and try to sit up. "We can't—"

Zac gently pushes me back down on the bed. "It's okay. We're safe here." He sees my confusion and takes my hand in his. "First I took you to my family, to see if they could help. However you were too dehydrated. I had to bring you to the hospital. I'll explain later, but you have to trust me—no one will be able to find us here."

I want to believe him, but I'm too confused. I look around the room once again, hoping I missed him the first time. "Isaac?"

I can see the answer in Zac's eyes before he even opens his mouth. "He wasn't there. I'm sorry."

I close my eyes. I let the tears fall as my mind fights against the painful thoughts of what could have happened to him. I hear Zac say something about needing to call in the doctor, but I don't pay attention. I can't keep doing this. I can't make it another six months without Isaac. I wish Zac wouldn't have brought me to the hospital. Then it could have all been over. I can't live without Isaac.

I start counting. I hear faint sounds around the room, but I remain focused on the numbers. At least until a voice is close to my ear, and I have no choice but to listen.

"Mrs. Miller?" I keep my eyes closed to the unfamiliar voice. Pulling on long ago skills, I remain completely still in feigned sleep. I feel the unknown person move away. "How long was she awake?"

"Just a couple minutes. Maybe less."

"Was she lucid?"

"She was confused about where she was, but she seemed normal other than that."

There's a few seconds of silence. I've determined that the new person must be the doctor. His voice is soft, reminding me of Whispers. The comparison should make me nervous, but for some strange reason it makes me feel calm. I concentrate hard, not wanting to miss anything he says.

"Her vitals are good. I think she's past the danger. I'd like to keep her here one more night, and if everything is still fine tomorrow then you can take her home. You just need to make sure she stays hydrated. Here's a prescription for the nausea if it continues."

"How long should it last?"

"Some women experience it for the full pregnancy. Since this is your first child, it's hard to say."

Pregnancy.

Child.

I try to wrap my brain around what I've just heard, but I can't. I can't be pregnant. I can't have a child without Isaac.

Isaac.

I'm carrying Isaac's child. A part of him is growing within me. Seconds ago I was ready to give up. Now, I have no choice but to fight.

4: Living a Lie

I hear the hour warning, but I don't let it distract me. I'm finally where my mind has fought to take me since I was captured, and I refuse to let go.

❦

We're riding in a van, and someone I don't know is driving. I have so many questions, but Zac told me I had to wait until we got home. I'm not sure what home he's talking about since I'm certain we're not going back to the house in Lafayette. I don't know where we are, but looking out the window I see pretty much the same landscape I've seen since we drove away from Isaac.

I'm feeling better after my stay in the hospital, but I'm still tired. I lean my head back to rest my eyes. The cap covering my hair makes it too uncomfortable, so I lift my head again. I reach up to shift the cap and am about to take it off completely when out of the corner of my eye I see Zac watching me. I glance at him and he slightly shakes his head no. I drop my hands to my lap in frustration.

Why I have to wear a cap and a plain blue dress is first on my list when I get a chance to ask him questions. I don't like wearing dresses. Even if this one covers me from neck to wrist to ankle, it still reminds me of the times I had to dress up for the man. I want my sweatpants back.

I place my hands over my stomach and my thoughts instantly go to the child growing within. A child that is as much a part of Isaac as he or she is of me.

He or she. Boy or girl. I have a strong desire to want to know—a *need* to know. My mind instinctively refers to the baby as a 'he', but I don't know if it's my instinct telling me the baby is a boy, or if it's because it helps me feel as if Isaac is still with me. I decide it doesn't matter and allow myself to think of the baby as a boy.

Will he look like Isaac, with scraggly dark hair, or will he have my wild curls? I hope he has Isaac's smile.

I feel a nudge and I jump a little. I had been so consumed by my thoughts I had forgotten where I was for a moment. I look at Zac and he's studying me, worry on his face.

"Are you feeling all right?" His eyes glance down to my hands, still folded protectively over my stomach.

"Yes. Just thinking about the baby."

He nods and looks away. I glance out the window on my side of the van. What I see on the road next to us takes me by complete surprise. I snap my head in Zac's direction and open my mouth to ask. He pins me with a look that tells me to shut my mouth again. Frustrated, I turn back to the window. We have passed by the horse that was pulling a black box and I lean forward to try and get another glance. I can't see it any more, but it turns out I didn't need to because the van slows as we approach another. This one has a flat box behind the horse. There are three children sitting in the back, dangling their feet over the edge. They wave at us as we drive past. I assume the two adults sitting at the front of the box are the parents of the children.

I also notice that they are all dressed the same, and it matches the way Zac and I are dressed. My mind tries to put all the pieces together, but it comes up blank. After a few minutes, the van turns off the main road down a dirt path toward a small white house.

As the van pulls to a stop, Zac leans over to whisper in my ear. "Just play along. I'll explain everything later."

He gives my hand a brief squeeze and I stiffen at the contact. In all the time we've lived together he's never done that. I watch as he thanks the driver and then opens the van door. He steps out and then turns back to me, extending his hand. I look from his hand to his eyes. The way he's looking at me tells me that this is part of what he meant by playing along. I take his hand and let him help me out of the van. I start to pull my hand away, but he tugs me closer before I'm successful. He wraps his arm around my waist and walks me toward the house. I don't understand why he's acting this way and it makes me uncomfortable.

"Oh, Angela dear, you look so much better!"

I jump at the unexpected sound of a woman's voice. I look up and see several people standing on the porch of the house. I had been so consumed by Zac's odd behavior that I failed to notice we weren't alone. I don't know who this woman is or why she would know my name—or at least my fake name. I look to Zac for answers. Thankfully he takes the hint.

"She's doing much better now."

Another woman, who is much older than the first one who spoke, says something I don't understand at all. Apparently Zac understands her just fine because he responds without hesitation.

"Angela would love to formally meet the family too, but she's a bit worn out. I think we should let her rest first. How about at dinner this evening?"

The older woman doesn't look pleased at Zac's response, but she gives a short nod of approval.

"Let me help you get settled." It's the first woman again, and she steps in our direction, meeting us at the bottom of the porch steps. She takes my arm and gives a gentle tug. When I don't move, she smiles up at Zac. "It's okay to let her go now. I'll show her to her room, and you can join her later. I believe you owe some answers to the family."

Zac's arm falls away, and I reluctantly let her lead me up the porch steps. She's not much taller than me, but I can tell she's stronger. I steal glances at her as we move toward the door. Most of her hair is under her cap, but what I can see tells me it's a dark brown. Her eyes are the same dark shade, but they seem to have a certain sparkle.

We enter through the kitchen, and I try to look around. It's not easy because the woman leads me quickly to the living room and then up a flight of stairs. She takes me to a room at the end of the hallway and shuts the door. I narrow my eyes as I look around the mostly bare room. There's a bed against the left side wall, and a tall piece of furniture against the opposite wall. On another wall there is a small table between the two windows with a bowl and pitcher.

The woman touches my shoulder and I jump, turning around to face her. She's smiling at me, eyes still sparkling.

"I know you're confused at the moment. Isaac will explain everything later. In the meantime, I'm Mary—Isaac's cousin."

Her words shock me at first, then I remember that she's talking about Zac. I had almost forgotten that his real name is Isaac. I must not have hidden my reaction because Mary narrows her eyes and tilts her head slightly as she looks at me. I do my best to transform my face into a small smile.

"Nice to meet you."

Mary smiles back. "You must not remember, being unconscious, but we already met. I helped you when Isaac first arrived."

Listening to her talk provides an unexpected comfort. Her words are slow, as if she needs to give consideration to each before she speaks them. I try to think of what to say, but I'm afraid I'll say something that will ruin whatever plan Zac has in mind. I realize it doesn't matter because Mary keeps talking.

"You must rest, given you're with child. I live on the other side of the farm so I'll help here until you can manage on your own. I've been blessed with several children that can help take care of things at my own home, so don't you worry one bit about taking up my time." She walks over to the tall piece of furniture and opens one of the doors. "I've made you up some dresses. Please let me know if any adjustments are needed. I left them a bit loose for your growing belly." She closes the cabinet door and walks over to me. She inspects the cap on my head and then turns me around, playing with the base of the cap. "You need to make sure your hair is tucked in good. The short hair will cause attention you might not want."

The comment causes my skin to prickle. Did Zac tell her that we are hiding? I think about asking, but before I can decide there's a knock on the door and it swings opens. I turn to see Zac, holding his hat in his hands and looking very unsure about something.

Mary steps away and walks toward the door. She speaks to Zac with those words that I don't understand. He nods and she turns to look at me.

"I'm glad you're feeling better, Angela. Remember to get some rest. I'll see you at dinner."

Zac steps into the room, allowing Mary to leave. He looks at me hesitantly before closing the door.

"I suppose you want some answers."

I scratch the side of my head where a hairpin pokes my scalp. It must have shifted when Mary played with my cap. I try to fix it, but instead I simply remove it altogether. I toss the cap and pins on the bed and cross my arms over my chest. "Yes, I want answers. I'd like to start with where we are."

"We're at my grandparent's farmhouse. Well, I suppose technically it's my house."

"What do you mean it's your house? I thought the house in Lafayette was yours."

"That was just a place Isaac and I rented." He lets out a long sigh and closes his eyes. He opens them and walks over to hang his hat on a hook by the cabinet. "It's a complicated story. You might want to sit down."

I hesitate, tempted to stand out of frustration. But I'm still tired and sitting sounds too good to resist. I move to the bed and sit down, resting my back up against the pillows. I take off the boots Zac gave me at the hospital and then tuck my feet under me.

"All right, I'm listening."

He sighs again and leans against the wall, crossing his arms over his chest. "My dad's family is Amish. I'll spare you the details because they aren't important, but he fell in love with my mom who was an English woman. My—"

"Wait, slow down. What do you mean by Amish and English?"

"The short answer is that Amish people live a very plain life without modern conveniences and are guided by a strict set of religious beliefs. English is how the Amish refer to anyone who is not Amish."

"The people here—Mary and the others outside—are they all Amish too?"

"Yes. We are in my family's Amish community where my father grew up. Being Amish, my father couldn't marry my mom unless she joined the church, or he left. My mom agreed to join the church, and somehow she survived the trial period. After they were both baptized into the church, they married and lived in this house. About two years later my mom couldn't take it any more. She never would explain to me what happened, why she was fine with the life in those early years but then suddenly wasn't."

He pauses, looking down at the floor in contemplation. I have questions, but he keeps talking before I have a chance to speak.

"Anyway, my dad chose my mom over his family and religion, and so they left the church. As a result, he was cut off completely from his family. He wrote to my grandparents after I was born, asking if they would at least consider accepting me into their life since I didn't have a choice in being born English. They agreed to be a part of my life so long as when I turned thirteen I would spend my summers here, learning the Amish lifestyle. During those summers, I found that the plain way of living and the Amish's religious beliefs fit my preferences. When I turned sixteen, I told my parents I wanted to move in with my grandparents and officially become Amish. Long story short, we all struck a deal that I would wait until I was eighteen. Six months before I was to move here, my dad became sick. I mean really sick. We weren't sure if he was going to pull through. Thankfully he did, but he wasn't the same so I stayed to help. I resumed my plans to move here after my dad fully recovered, however that's when I received a letter from Isaac. I think you know what kept me away after that."

I stare at him, my mind trying to process. I don't know anything about the Amish. I have so many questions, but I don't know enough to even know what to ask. I decide to stick to things I can understand.

"How can this be your house if you've never lived here, other than summers with your grandparents?"

"My grandparents signed it over to me on my eighteenth birthday, in anticipation of my joining the community and eventually the church. I don't know—maybe it was their way of trying to make sure I carried through on my promise. I was to live here with them until I married, then they would move in with my aunt and uncle. When my plans changed, they weren't happy but they understood. They told me the deal was still good for when I was ready."

"So we are going to be living here with your grandparents?"

"No, as far as they know I'm married. They've moved in with my aunt and uncle, just as was planned."

My heart rate speeds up at his comment. He drops his gaze, clearly uncomfortable with my stare. "You told them we were married?"

He looks back up at me, and I notice a quick flash of anger in his eyes. "I show up with an unconscious woman, carrying the same last name as me, who turns out to be pregnant—what did you expect me to tell them? It's not my preference to lie, but if they knew we weren't married they wouldn't let us stay together in the same house. I can't protect you if we're separated by several acres of farmland."

"How could they have refused to let us stay here together if it's your house?"

"It may be my house, but the Amish values are very strong. We would be completely unwelcomed, and unsupported, if the community knew we were living together but not married. Even as friends—it's just not done."

I don't understand this concept of making decisions based on community acceptance, but I let it go for the moment. "What did you expect your grandparents to do for me? Are they doctors?"

"No, but Mary is a midwife. She's not a doctor, but I thought maybe she could help. I panicked and it seemed like the only option at the time. The hotel we were staying at isn't far from here."

Midwife. I remember reading about that in a couple of the books that Isaac had given me. "I assume Mary also thinks we're married?"

"She actually knows the truth. She's more . . . open-minded than most of the people here. She spent a few summers with some English family that hasn't been shunned, and I think it somehow made her more tolerant of non-Amish beliefs. She was actually the one to suggest that I tell everyone we were married."

All the blood rushes from my head and the room wobbles. I slump to the side and Zac rushes to my side. I press on my temples and try to remain focused.

"Ang, what's wrong? Is it the baby?"

My vision starts to clear and the ringing in my head stops. Zac's hands move from my shoulders to my face, and I swat them away. "I'm fine. And I said don't call me that."

The bed shifts as he sits down, facing me. "Angela, I don't—"

Having recovered, my anger prevents me from letting him finish his statement. "How could you tell her about my past?"

"What? No, I didn't tell her about your past. I don't even know about your past, other than it was really bad. It's probably good that I don't know, because then I might want to kill the bastard just as much as Isaac does." He pauses and shakes his head hard. He mumbles something under his breath that I can't hear. He looks back up at me after a few seconds, continuing in a calmer tone. "I just told her that you were married to my friend who died, and that I promised to take care of you."

I'm hit with another jolt. "You told her that Isaac is dead? But you said he didn't show. How do you know—"

"Angela, calm down. I don't know if he's dead or not. I told you the truth—he didn't show when we were supposed to meet. That's all I know. I just thought Mary would ask fewer questions if she thought you were a widow. None of this was part of the plan that Isaac and I put together. I'll admit that coming here was my contingency plan if Isaac didn't show the next time. I thought I could introduce you as a cousin on my mom's side of the family. If my grandparents thought we were related, then they would allow us to live in the same house together. I didn't expect you to be pregnant, and it threw a wrench in my plan. Apparently I don't lie well under pressure. I did what I thought was right to get you help and keep you hidden. You may not like it, but here we are just the same."

"If you were trying to keep me hidden, how did I end up at the hospital? I thought we had to stay away because we could be tracked through hospital records."

"As I told you at the hospital, you were too dehydrated for Mary to do anything. If I hadn't taken you to the hospital, you could have died. The nearby hospital is accustomed to the Amish, and they know how much the Amish value their privacy. No one would ever think to report a married Amish woman admitted for dehydration. Besides, I told them your name was Sarah—Sarah Miller is a very common name in our community. There are several Isaac and Sarah Millers here, so we can't easily be tracked."

I hit my thighs in frustration. "So now my name is Sarah?"

He shakes his head and gives me a slight smile. "Only at the hospital. I told my family your name was Angela."

It's all too much. Although I have more questions, I can't take any more surprises. I pull at the fabric of my dress. "Do I have to dress like this all the time?"

"Yes."

It doesn't seem an important thing, but it makes me want to cry just the same. "Why did you shave your beard like that?"

He runs a hand along his jaw. "Married Amish men wear beards, but not mustaches. At some point I'll explain further, but you look a bit overwhelmed at the moment."

The tears start to fall. Zac reaches out a hand, but I swat it away. "I am overwhelmed and if you don't mind I'd like to be left alone to rest." I roll over on my side, facing away from him. It takes him a few seconds, but he finally stands and leaves the room.

Once again, I've managed to find myself in a situation where I'm living a life that's not my own. Living on the road, running from town to town, isn't easy but at least I'd be me most of the time. Here, I'll have to always be Angela. And Zac's wife. And maybe Sarah if I have to go back to the hospital.

At least I only have to live this life until I can meet up with Isaac again. Six more months. He'll be there next time. He has to be. I can't believe anything else.

⚬⚬⚬

It's hard to think about that time with Zac, living in the Amish community. I never did embrace it, and as a result they never embraced me. Well, that and the fact that I had been presented as Zac's wife to begin with. His family had hopes for him, and it didn't include a silent, moody, English wife.

Mary was the only one who embraced me. Maybe it was because she knew part of the truth.

I wonder now if things would have been different if I had at least tried. If I would have made an attempt to accept the Amish beliefs and lifestyle.

Would I be here if I had? Or would it have eventually come to this anyway?

The man said that I had deserved my life. If that's true, then it's logical to assume I would have ended up in this exact situation eventually. I have to believe it's for the best that it happened now, before I became too attached.

Yes, I was dangerously close to already being too attached. I can feel it now—my heart physically aches from the pain of separation.

Yet, even though I knew it would hurt, I still left. That's how I know I hadn't yet allowed myself to give my heart over completely.

I open my eyes to find I still only have one working eye. I feel around the injured eye that's swollen shut and pull back my hand at the sudden jolt of pain.

After a few seconds of deep breathing, I find a way to get myself into a sitting position. I scoot on my butt until my back connects with the wall. Leaning my head back, I close my one good eye again.

I think another hour must be almost up. My internal clock has somehow adjusted to this twisted game.

I'm right, and when the bang on the door sounds, I'm expecting it.

3: A New Life Begins

I take my mind back to the farm. I place myself six months after we arrived—just before the scheduled time to meet up with Isaac.

⁂

I slap the dough down on the counter in frustration. I want to wipe my sweating forehead, but my hands are covered in sticky dough that won't come off. Instead, I punch the dough. Then again and again. I hear a soft chuckle behind me and I turn, hands on hips. Mary is trying to cover her smile, but she's not successful.

"Sorry, that's just a new way of kneading dough that I've never tried before."

"Well, maybe you should." I look at my hands and grab the towel from the counter. "I'll never get this."

Mary stifles another chuckle and walks over. "Jah, you will. You just need more flour."

I throw the towel back on the counter in frustration. "No, I won't! Nor will I ever learn Deitsch, or how to sew baby clothes, or milk the cows, or . . . do the laundry!" I pull at the spot on my sleeve with the ever-present stain to emphasize my point. Mary laughs again and I cross my arms, glaring at her. "I'm glad to know that you find my torment so hilarious."

She wipes at her eyes with the back of her wrists. "Nee, I don't take delight in your discomfort. It's only that it's the first time I've heard you string more than four words together at once. I'd say that baby has you all out of sorts."

I place my hands over my large belly at her comment. "It's not the baby. It's the dough. And the Deitsch, and the—"

Mary raises a hand to stop me before turning back to the offending food product. "I don't need to hear the list again. It is the baby. Did you forget that I'm the expert?"

I sit down in a chair, huffing out a sigh of defeat. Mary's right—these aren't the things that are really upsetting me. But neither is the baby. It's the anticipation of meeting up with Isaac. We're supposed to leave in two days, but Zac hasn't told me the plans yet.

My stomach tightens and I pull in a sharp breath. Mary's trained ear hears, and she turns back to me. "Are the pains getting worse?"

"No, I'm fine." She eyes me with suspicion before turning back to the dough. The fact that I can't keep from lying is probably the number one reason I'd never be able to officially become Amish.

The thought takes me back to a conversation Zac had with his family over dinner a few nights ago. Although, I think argument would be a more accurate way to describe it. Since his grandparents will only speak Deitsch, I couldn't understand a word of it and had to ask Zac to explain after everyone left. All he would say is that his family felt it was time for us to begin the preparations for joining the church. His response was that it was too much to put on me before the baby was born.

Suddenly the kitchen feels too hot. I stand and walk toward the door, but I stop as I hear Mary call out to me.

"Put on your coat. It looks nice out, but it's still rather cold."

I let out a sigh, but turn to grab my coat off the nearby hook. I slip it on as I walk out the door. I'm not used to so many people telling me what to do. I'm not used to so many people—period. I walk briskly to the spot I've claimed as my own under the large tree behind the house.

It reminds me of the afternoon I spent with Isaac out on the farm.

I ease myself to a comfortable sitting position, resting against the tree. It's a decent spring day, but the ground is wet and cold. I won't be able to stay out for long, but the fresh air is just what I need. I look out over the fields, currently absent of any workers. I had been so intrigued by farm life when I was with Isaac. If he had told me he was bringing me to live here, I would have been very happy. But at the moment all I want to do is leave.

Maybe Isaac can come back here with us. Although, I'm not sure how Zac would explain that to his family. No, Isaac and I will have to leave, saying our final good-byes to Zac. He'll have difficulty enough explaining why his 'wife' will no longer be around. I wonder if it would be inconsiderate to ask if we could stay until the baby is born. Mary would be able to safely deliver the baby, taking out the risk of going back to the hospital. It's only one more month after all.

Regardless of when we leave, I'll tell Isaac I want to find a place like this. We could buy our own farm, just a small one, and live a quiet life. I do like that part of my fake Amish life. I like the slow pace and simple living. It would make it easier to stay hidden.

But Isaac says we can't hide. We need to integrate.

I wonder if he still feels that way, since the man found us in our previous well integrated life. Maybe now he'll be willing to give hiding a try. If he will, then I'll do my best at learning how to make bread from scratch. And milk cows, if we have any. I'm better at feeding the chickens. We should definitely have chickens. Although, just for eggs.

"You look deep in thought."

I jump and look over my shoulder at the sound of Zac's voice. I eye him suspiciously. "You've been avoiding me."

He crouches down next to me and pulls at a piece of grass. "Not true. I've just been busy."

"Ever since I asked you about the plan to meet up with Isaac, you stay out until dinner knowing I can't ask you questions in front of your family. Then you go help your uncle in the barn, and you don't come back in the house until I'm in bed."

He pulls at another piece of grass, never looking at me. He stands and turns away. "I just wanted to say hi and make sure you were feeling all right. I need to get back to work."

I struggle to my feet as he takes a few steps. "Zac!"

He stops but doesn't turn to face me. "We'll talk tonight."

He walks away and all I can do is hope he's telling the truth.

My feet are aching and I should probably sit. Instead, I pace the room again. Zac has been outside telling his grandparents good-bye for at least ten minutes. He's probably just trying to avoid talking to me about the plan to meet up with Isaac. I don't know why he's refused to talk about it, but I intend to find out tonight.

I stop suddenly and grip my abdomen with my hands. The baby just kicked something that I'm sure is a vital organ. The pain disappears about as fast as it occurred.

I turn at the sound of the door opening and watch as Zac takes his time with his coat and boots. I feel another stabbing pain and decide to sit. I don't want to give Zac any reason to delay this conversation again. Unfortunately, I don't recover before he enters the room.

"Is everything all right?" He grips my elbow and shoulder as he helps lower me to the couch.

"Fine. He's just kicking things he has no business kicking."

"Maybe you should go up to rest—"

"No. You don't get to avoid this conversation again. We're supposed to leave to meet with Isaac in two days. I want to know the plan. Are you going with me, or am I going alone?"

He closes his eyes for a moment as his shoulders drop. He lets out a deep sigh before turning and sitting in the chair across from me. He looks at me for a few seconds before speaking.

"You're not going."

All the air seems to have escaped from my lungs, and it takes significant effort to pull any back in. "What do you mean, we're not going?"

"I said *you're* not going. I haven't decided yet if I will go."

I'm so shocked and angry I can't form a single word. Although I shouldn't be surprised. I realize deep down that I knew he wouldn't let me go and that's the reason he's been avoiding me.

"Angela, you can't be surprised by this. You could go into labor at any moment. I can't let you go on this trip."

"I have a month left!"

"Not necessarily. I know you've been having pains. Mary said it could be any day."

"She also said it could be another month!"

"It's not a risk I'm willing to take. Have you thought about what would happen if you went into labor while gone? Mary can't come with us. You'd have to go to a hospital, and then there would be a record—of you and the baby! It's not worth the risk."

I haven't thought about what would happen if I went into labor. I've only been able to focus on seeing Isaac again. Tears sting my eyes and don't fight them off. "You don't get it, Zac. There is no option here. I have to go. If there is even the slightest possibility that Isaac will be there, then I have to go."

"Even if it's a risk to your health, or the baby's?"

"Yes."

There's no mistaking the shock in his face. What I'm not sure of is the accompanying emotion—it could either be disappointment or disgust. "Just like that, without even thinking it through, you're willing to risk everything? He may not even be there, and you may get caught in the process. But you don't care do you? All that matters to you, all that's ever mattered to you, is Isaac?"

"Yes." I can only manage a whisper, but even I can hear the conviction in my voice.

Zac sits back, frustrated. "I think it's time you tell me exactly what happened to you at the hands of his father. I'll never force you to tell me, but maybe it will help me understand this connection you and Isaac share. A connection that has you both risking life and limb for each other."

"Why do you need to know my past to understand? You've risked your life too, just by being involved. Isaac said you understood that much at least. I don't question your loyalty to Isaac, and now to me, so why do you question mine?"

He sits forward so suddenly I think for a moment he's going to jump across the room at me. He remains in his seat, but just on the edge. "It's not your loyalty that I question—it's your twisted definition of the word! You think that risking your life, and possibly your child's, just to see if he's there is being loyal. He didn't risk everything for you to simply throw your life away! Now that you're pregnant, your child should come first. All your decisions should be based on how you protect the life you two created. That should be your definition of loyalty to Isaac—protecting his child! From my perspective, you're confusing the idea of loyalty with obsession. You can't live without Isaac. That much has become very clear to me in the past few months. I thought maybe if I understood your past I'd understand that connection."

The intensity of his glare is too much, and I look down at my hands. In the few seconds it took him to utter those words, I realized he was right. Protecting my child should be my first priority. Yet I can't live without Isaac. He's not just a part of my soul, but the light that keeps it alive within me.

I take a quick glance at Zac. He's watching me, waiting for some sort of response. "If I tell you, will you promise to go? You've convinced me that I should stay here, but you can go."

He doesn't respond for a few seconds. Finally, he nods his head. "Yes, I'll go if you tell me."

And so I do. I tell him everything from the moment my mother opened her closet door to the moment that Isaac rescued me. Some parts are more difficult to tell, yet I tell them anyway. The only change I notice in Zac while I talk is the continued hardening of his jaw and his grip on the arm of the chair.

I feel ashamed and depleted of all my energy. I can no longer look at Zac, afraid of how he must now see me. Yet at the same time I feel a lightness I don't understand. The silence between us becomes unbearable. I'm sure he's questioning why he let himself get involved in our situation. After all that I just told him, he probably can't wait to go find Isaac and get me out of his house and away from his family. Wiping the tears from my face, I stand.

"So now you know all about my past. Hopefully you can see why Isaac is so important to me. Why I have no choice but to be with him if I can."

I turn away and walk toward the stairs. Before I reach the bottom step, his hand is on my arm, turning me around. He pulls me to his chest and wraps his arms around me. He holds me so tight I almost can't breathe. To my surprise, instead of pulling away, I push myself closer. His lips touch the top of my head. Not a kiss, but one just the same.

And for just a moment, I allow myself to imagine that the arms holding me belong to someone else.

We stay connected until another pain to my abdomen causes me to shudder. He gives me one more squeeze and then leads me upstairs where he tucks me into bed. He checks to make sure my lamp has enough oil to last through the night before he leaves for his own room. I close my eyes and drift into a dream where Isaac is waiting for me.

"No, you will not come today. It's not time. You have to wait until your Daddy gets here." I grip the back of the chair until the contraction passes. Wiping the sweat from my brow with the hem of my apron, I check the time again. Zac should have been back by now.

I walk the length of the kitchen and the living room once more. The pain seems to subside a little when I walk.

I check the time again. Logically I know it's only been a couple minutes, but it feels as though an hour has gone by. My anxiety over Zac being late, the pain of the contractions, and the hope of seeing Isaac have all distorted my sense of time.

I'm in the living room, making my fifth rotation around the small room, when I hear the kitchen door open. I can't see the door from my position and my heart stops, freezing my feet as well.

"Harley, don't forget to check on the horses!" The sound of Mary's voice brings tears to my eyes. "Angela?"

The door shuts and I hear her set something down on the kitchen table. I don't respond, but instead resume my walking.

"Angela? Are you in there?"

"Yes." Another contraction hits and it takes all my effort to keep the pain from my voice. I hear Mary shuffling around the kitchen and move myself to the other side of the room, keeping out of her sight. I'm hoping she'll leave after she puts the food away.

"I brought you dinner. There should be enough for when Isaac gets home." My heart surges for a few seconds until I remember she's talking about Zac. I had finally gotten used to her calling Zac Isaac, but today it bothers me. "I still don't understand why he had to go to Chicago. He should have pushed it off, with you being so near to term. Harley will check on the horses after he finishes with the chores in the barn. I've told him to check on you before he leaves."

With the last few words, her voice grows closer. Clenching my jaw, I try to bite down the pain. I turn so I'm not facing her.

"Angela? Are you all right?"

"Yes, fine."

There's a hesitation before I feel her hands on my shoulders, turning me to face her. Her eyes sweep over me in a quick inspection. "How close are the contractions?"

"I'm not having contractions. He just kicked—"

"Nonsense. You're in labor." She turns and hurries into the kitchen. She opens the door and I hear her call out a string of instructions to her son. She comes back and takes me by the arm. "Let's get you upstairs. It might be a while yet, but it's hard to say since you're too stubborn to tell me when the contractions started."

I consider responding with a sharp remark, but clamp my mouth shut. I don't want this baby to come yet, but it seems I don't have much of a choice.

I let out another scream. When the peak of the pain passes, I drop back on the pillow. Mary won't tell me how long I've been at this, but it's dark now so I know it's been a few hours.

"Wipe her brow." One of Mary's daughters, I can't remember her name at the moment, complies with the request. "You're doing great, Angela."

"Isaac. Where's Isaac?"

"He's not back yet. You've been doing fine without him so far, and you can keep doing it too."

"No, I need Isaac. The baby can't come until he gets here."

"You don't have a choice, dear. If you don't start pushing with the contractions, it could be very bad for both of you. Your baby is ready to come out, but he needs help." I can't see Mary. She's somewhere at the end of the bed. Despite the soothing voice, I can clearly hear her frustration and disappointment. Just then the door bangs open. Heavy footsteps enter the room and quickly stop.

"Isaac! Get over to Angela, now. She's been asking for you and refuses to deliver this baby without you at her side."

I try to sit up, searching frantically for Isaac. Instead, I find Zac's eyes. He's frozen in shock. Mary yells at him again, this time in Deitsch, and he finally hurries to my side. I look back at the door.

"Isaac? Where's Isaac?"

Zac holds my gaze and slightly shakes his head. I collapse on the pillow in a fit of sobs.

"Isaac is here, dear." I feel the cold wet cloth touch my forehead again. "Isaac, get behind her. You'll have to help her push. Her strength is low."

Mary keeps talking, telling Zac what to do. I'm told to push. The pain is too much—contractions mixed with a broken heart. I can't fight it any more. I have to push. I have to get this baby out.

I push and scream. At some point I think I bite Zac's hand.

At last, the pressure in my abdomen is gone. I hear a cry that for once doesn't belong to me. I want to see him, but Mary's taken him to the side of the room. I lean against Zac's chest, breathing heavy. A few minutes later, Mary returns to the bed.

"Congratulations, you have a healthy baby girl!"

Girl? No, it's supposed to be a boy. "Are you sure?"

"Isaac, what did she say?"

"I think she asked if you were sure. She always thought the baby would be a boy."

"Well, I wouldn't be much of a midwife if I couldn't tell the difference between a boy and a girl. It's a girl." Mary places the wrapped bundle on my chest. "Isaac, help Angela hold her."

Zac, still behind me, wraps his arms around me so they are supporting my own. I look down at her delicate face. Her eyelids flutter open and tiny brown eyes stare at me for a few seconds before closing again.

"What's her name?"

I look over my shoulder and meet Zac's eyes. They're wet with unshed tears. I look back down at the sleeping baby in my arms. I haven't thought of girl names. She was supposed to be another Isaac. Lacking any previous consideration, I give her the only girl name I can.

"Abigail."

Zac reaches into the folded blanket and takes one of her tiny hands into his own. "It's nice to meet you, Abigail."

My heart aches at the tenderness in his voice. It's just how I imagined Isaac would have sounded in this moment.

The tears flowing from my eyes are so heavy my vision blurs. I'm not sure if I'm crying due to the joy of finally holding my baby, or from the pain of not having Isaac. Both emotions are affecting me equally, so I have to assume it's due to both.

2: Can't Let Go

The door opens, pulling me out of the memory. I open my eye and see Goon and Goon Two walk in. Goon remains by the door, and I notice he's holding a gun. I guess they don't want to risk me trying to run again. Although, with my fractured ankle I'm not sure what they think I can do.

Goon Two walks over and crouches down in front of me. He looks me over and smiles.

"I have to say, Angel, seeing you like this does something to me. You're starting to become more my type."

I'm guessing that means he's turned on by women who bare the marks of his fists, but I don't dare try to validate my theory. I look past him and lock my gaze on Goon. I study his form, how he holds his gun in his left hand. I notice he stands with his weight slightly shifted to his right, as if he's favoring his left leg.

My vision blurs as a sudden slap strikes my face.

"Pay attention." Goon Two waits until I lock my gaze with his. "The boss will be here in a couple hours. Last chance for an early decision."

He stares at me, and I stare back. His jaw twitches after a few seconds of my silence. It's obvious that he's used to people sitting in fear under his soulless eyes. The fact that I refuse to react, has him itching to get his hands on me. A smile twitches at the corner of his mouth. He leans in close to my ear, holding my head so I can't pull away.

"It's going to be a lot of fun killing you." He bites my ear, hard, and I somehow suppress the scream pushing its way up my throat. He pulls back with a satisfied smile, stands and walks out the door with Goon in his wake.

I place a shaking hand to my injured ear. My body starts to convulse and I finally let go. The sobs come quietly, but they rack my body with a shuddering force.

How did I end up here? What did I do to deserve this life? Why couldn't I have been satisfied with the new life that Zac tried to offer me? Why couldn't I have loved Abigail enough to let go of Isaac? Would I have been able to let go if she had been a boy—who I believe would have looked more like Isaac than me? Would a boy have been enough to fill the hole in my heart and make me stop looking for Isaac? As if trying to answer my questions, my mind flashes back. I try to fight it.

I couldn't see it before I left. Zac tried to tell me, but I didn't listen. I thought the pain of being without Isaac was far greater than the pain of being taken away from Abigail. I had been convinced that Isaac was alive. That he hadn't shown up the previous times because he was waiting for the safest time to meet up with me again.

I needed to be with him.

My mind fights to take me back again. I'm too weak to resist any longer. I go back to one and a half years after Abigail was born—which turns out to be just a few days ago.

⁂

I watch Abigail play with her blocks, a few feet away from me on the floor. I slowly trace my eyes over her, from her mass of blonde curls to her small socked feet.

Nothing about her reminds me of Isaac.

She's too young to know if she will have any of his personality traits, but physically she's just a miniature version of me.

I search my heart, looking for anything that will bind me to her. Of course I love her, and I want to protect her, but I don't feel the depth of connection that I thought I would. Maybe it's because I've never had a mother of my own. I've watched Mary with her children, and I know I should feel different than I do.

Even Abigail seems to know something isn't right between us. She never comes to me on her own. She will let me hold and comfort her, but it's with a hint of reluctance.

The door opens and a few seconds later Zac enters the room. Abigail instantly jumps up from the floor and runs to him, arms outstretched.

"Da! Up, up!"

My jaw tightens as I watch Zac scoop Abigail up in his arms, placing a kiss on her cheek. He tickles her side, releasing a squeal of laughter. He turns to look at me, his smile fading as his eyes settle on the bag sitting next to me.

"So you're still going?"

I don't respond, except for a slight nod. I know it will only cause an argument if I speak my mind, and we don't like to fight in front of Abigail. He closes his eyes for a moment and then sets Abigail down.

"Go give your ma a kiss good-bye before I take you over to Mary's house." Abigail hesitates, holding on to Zac's leg. He reaches down and pats her gently on her butt. "Go on."

She walks slowly over to me, finger in her mouth. I kneel down on the floor in front of her. A small lump tries to form in my throat, but I swallow it down.

"You be a good girl while I'm gone, okay?" She just chews on her fingers and looks down at the floor. "I'll be back soon. Can I get a hug?" She stands still and lets me wrap my arms around her, but she doesn't hug me back. The tears sting my eyes, but I refuse to let them fall. I pull away and look her over one more time.

There's a part of my heart, fighting against me. It doesn't want me to walk away. It's warning me, telling me that I might never see her again if I go. I try to lock every aspect of her face into my memory. On impulse I reach up and remove my necklace. I hold the tiny wings in my palm for a few seconds before clasping the chain around Abigail's neck. She looks down at it and then back up at me. A smile brightens her face and she throws her arms around my neck. It takes me a couple seconds to break through the shock and hug her back. I press her to my chest. If only I could wake up my love for her through the energy of our hearts beating against each other.

I feel on the edge of losing control over my emotions and gently push her away. "Go now. I'll be back soon."

She hurries back to Zac, showing him the necklace. I don't dare look at him. I know what I'll see in his eyes, and it's more than I can handle at the moment. When the door closes behind them, I finally let go of the hold on my emotions. The sobs hurt and I double over on the floor.

It's different this time. The other two times I went to find Isaac didn't feel this way. I don't understand why it hurts so much.

The voice in my head is telling me not to go—Isaac won't be there anyway. It's been two years since I last saw him. If he were free, then he would have shown up by now. I have to assume the man found him.

No. No, I can't believe that. He just couldn't get to the location. He wanted to make sure that he wasn't being followed. He won't show up until he knows it's completely safe. He might also be trying to set up our new identities, like he did the last time before coming to get me. I have to go. He deserves to know that I'm all right. He deserves to be the one Abigail calls dad.

The door opens again and I quickly wipe my face with the sleeve of my dress. I'm still kneeling on the floor and look up when Zac enters the room. He stops just inside the door.

He no longer looks like Isaac. His facial features are more distinct now with his fuller beard and the shaved area above his lip. The muscles in his arms, chest, and legs are more defined due to the amount of labor he's done on the farm. The differences are so significant that it's hard to believe I once couldn't tell them apart on first glance.

"Don't go."

I let his words replace some of my pain with anger. The last two times I went, I knew he didn't want me to go, but he never said anything. It makes me angry that he's chosen this time to voice his objection. It's harder for me this time, and I don't need the added guilt. "You know I have to go."

"Then let me go with you."

"No, you need to be here to take care of Abigail."

"You're taking an unnecessary risk. You stay and I'll go. Abigail needs you here."

An involuntary laugh escapes. "No, she doesn't. She'd much rather be with you."

"That's only because you're never here!"

"Of course I'm here! Where can I go? The only time I leave is to go find Isaac every six months!"

"That's exactly what I mean! You live your life centered on the meetings with Isaac. In the month prior to the meeting, you're so anxious and nervous you won't talk to anyone. When the time comes, you leave for a few days only to return home alone. Then you spend the next two months isolated in your room, so depressed you can't do anything. Abigail has to sleep in my room because you won't even get out of bed to feed or change her! When you finally snap out of it, you're left with two, maybe three, months before it starts all over again. And even in those 'good' months you're still not fully here. Your mind is still off looking for Isaac. It's no wonder you're a stranger to your own daughter!"

I look away, crossing my arms, knowing that he's right.

"She needs her mom, Angela. You can start to give her that if you stay here."

I turn to face him. "That's where you're wrong. I can't give her what she needs. Not without Isaac. I can't be *me* without Isaac, let alone a mom!"

He walks over to me and places his hands on my shoulders. "Stay here and let me help you."

I shake him off and walk to the other side of the room. "No. I appreciate the offer, but I need to go find Isaac."

"You know he won't be there, right?"

"No, I don't know that. And neither do you."

I hear him let out a sigh of frustration. "Okay, so let's assume for a moment the unlikely possibility that he is there. What then?"

I turn to look at him, feeling the confusion clearly on my face. "What do you think? I bring him back here."

"And then what? You don't expect for us all to live together again, do you? That won't work here."

"I guess we'll leave. Find our own place. I'm sure that's why Isaac hasn't shown up so far—he's been establishing our new identities."

"And what about me?"

His question is soft, yet it still hits me hard in the chest. "Well, I . . . I assumed you would stay here. I suppose you could come with us if you wanted."

He shakes his head. "No, I wouldn't go with you. But what am I supposed to tell my family, and the community that you are now a part of? You joined the church, Angela."

"Only because your grandparents forced me to join! I'm no more Amish than I am your wife. Just tell them I left you, then find a nice young Amish woman to marry for real."

"Most of the Amish women my age are already married. And, having a wife and child that ran off won't exactly make me the top candidate for those who aren't. In the eyes of my community, I'd still be a married man."

Regret pushes at me and it makes me angry. "I never asked you to bring me here, and I certainly didn't ask you to tell everyone we were married! You offered to help Isaac in the first place, so don't go blaming me for ruining your life just because I choose to live with my family!"

He tugs at his beard. "You're right. I'm sorry to imply that it would be your fault. I just . . . I just need you to understand that your actions impact everyone. It's not just you and Isaac any more."

He sits down on the couch, hanging his head. He's silent for a few minutes before he speaks again. "And what happens if you don't come back? What if they find you?"

I clear my throat and sit in the chair across from him. "My answer is the same as it was the last two times I went looking for Isaac. If . . . if something should happen, then I want you to raise Abigail as your own. She already considers you her father."

He blinks and looks away for a few seconds before locking his eyes with mine once more. "Can't you even consider the possibility that you could be happy here, with me? We could be a real family, Angela. I know that I'm not him, and that I never will be, but can't you learn to trust me?"

My heart pounds at his offer. He watches me, waiting for my answer. There is a small part of me that wants to accept—it's just not big enough to turn me away from Isaac.

There's a knock at the door. The sound breaks Zac's gaze and I rise from my chair. "That will be the driver. He'll take me to the bus station and I'll go the same way I did last time, changing into English clothes at one of the stops where I change busses."

I bend to pick up my bag, but Zac reaches out and grabs it first. He hands it to me, but doesn't let go right away. He pulls me into a hug so quickly I don't have time to resist. "Please be careful. My offer remains if you change your mind."

I pull away, managing only a nod, and walk out the door.

I shudder against the chill of the wind, second-guessing my decision to put on a dress. Even though this is my third time here, my anxiety always makes me forget just how much wind comes off the great lake. Jeans would have been warmer, but I'm used to wearing dresses now. And I suppose that there's a part of me that wants to look nice for Isaac. I watch the dark green material float in big waves around my legs. Even though it's not one of my plain Amish dresses, it's long enough to keep me mostly warm.

I glance around once more, but see only hair. I pull the mass of curls off my face and watch the group of people on the other side of the observation deck. They appear to be part of some sort of work gathering. One women turns in my direction and I smile slightly as I look away. Isaac would be proud. I've finally learned the art of trying to act friendly to other people.

My eye traces the horizon of the lake before me. I know from my study of maps that Michigan is somewhere on the other side. However, it's easy to pretend that it goes on forever.

I glance at the inexpensive watch in my hands, purchased from one of the shops at the pier. In fifteen minutes the cruise will start. That gives me five more minutes before I have to invent some excuse to get off the ship. I suppose I could stay for the lunch and cruise, but Zac has always made it clear that I need to get off the ship ten minutes before it undocks if Isaac doesn't show. I don't fully understand the logic, but I comply because I'm usually too upset by the absence of Isaac to remain in public.

I close my eyes and an unwelcome image of Zac holding Abigail pops into my mind. I quickly open my eyes and shake my head, but it's too late. I'm now thinking about Zac's offer of a new life.

Could I be happy with him? Could I really give up Isaac to move forward with a new life?

I don't know how to do it. I wouldn't even have the opportunity for a new life if it weren't for Isaac. How is it fair to leave him behind? I can't let myself believe that the man caught him. It's too painful. That means he's out there, and if he's out there then someday he will come looking for me. Isaac doesn't know about Zac's Amish family, and he would never find us. I can't let him worry and wonder about what happened to me.

But wouldn't Isaac want me to try? Wouldn't he want me to live a happy life, and give our child the best life possible? Wouldn't he want that more than anything else?

The answer is there, but I don't want to hear it. Zac was right, risking my life every six months—and not living in between—is not honoring Isaac's loyalty to me. Or his love.

Every hair feels like it's standing on end. I felt it from the beginning. This trip just felt different than the other two. Somehow I've known all along that it would be the last.

It's time for me to say good-bye.

"I'm sorry, ma'am, I don't mean to interrupt. It's just that we're about to push off and you're not looking very well. Are you all right?"

I jump at the man's voice just behind me. It's one of the waiters. I blink a few times and wipe the tears from my cheeks.

"Um, no, I'm not feeling all that well."

"Can I help you get back to the rest of your party?"

"The person I was meeting couldn't make it. Actually, I think maybe I should skip the cruise."

"Well, I'm sorry to hear that, ma'am. You might want to stop by the ticket office on your way out. Maybe they'll refund your money. Do you need assistance off the ship?"

"No, I'll be fine. Thank you."

"Okay then. Just don't linger—we will be preparing to undock in just a couple minutes."

I nod in appreciation of his assistance and glance at the watch once more. I should have left five minutes ago. I look out over the lake one last time, letting myself remember the day at the ocean with Isaac.

I slip the ring Isaac gave me off my ring finger. I turn it slightly and let the sunlight dance off the small stone. I press the ring to my lips and drop it over the ship's railing.

"Good-bye." The whispered word hurts to say. I take one last deep breath and then turn toward the stairs. I manage one step and then freeze.

Everything vanishes, except him.

I blink a few times, trying to make sure he's really here. His eyes lock with mine and I know it's him. I'm moving before I even remember to breathe again. He's moving toward me and I collapse in his arms when we meet. He lifts me off my feet, his strong arms holding me like a vise. He sets me down and tries to step away, but I cling to his chest. He gives up, and I feel his hands slide to my hair. His lips work their way from the top my head to my ear.

"Ang, what are you doing here? You weren't supposed to be here."

Everything inside me transforms to lead and settles in my legs. My hold on him relaxes and I inch back enough to see his face. He's crying. His eyes are full of pain. His beard has been shaved off, and I can see the scar on his cheek from that painful night so long ago. I see another on his neck just below his right ear that wasn't there before.

"Ang, baby, why did you come? You weren't supposed to be here! I'm so sorry." His voice is only a whisper, but it's frantic. My chest fills with panic and I look around. I spot them just a few feet away behind Isaac—blocking the exit. I look over my shoulder, hoping to find the waiter who I spoke with just a few seconds ago.

Instead I see Watcher.

He slides up behind me and presses something sharp to my side. "It's been a long time, Angel. What do you say we go home now?" He grabs Isaac by the collar with the hand that's not holding a knife to my side. He shoves us a few steps forward before one of the ship's employees appears at the top of the stairs. Watcher leans down to press his mouth to my ear. "Try anything and your boy here will have a very slow and painful death."

"Ah, have you found her then?" The ship employee darts his eyes rapidly from me to Watcher to Isaac and back again. He's short—nearly as short as I am—and speaks with a heavy accent.

"Yes, thank you. However, it appears she's not feeling well. I fear it might be motion sickness. I'm afraid she won't make it through the cruise if it's this bad while we're docked. Unfortunately, we'll have to get off the ship."

"What a shame. Maybe next time?"

"Yes, maybe. Thank you for your help in locating her. We were almost too late."

The staff member beams with pride. "No trouble at all." He pats me on the shoulder before passing by. "Hope you get to feeling better."

Watcher pushes us down the stairs. Isaac's hand finds mine as we walk, and I suddenly notice he's limping.

I don't understand what's happening. Isaac led them to me? They must have tortured him. It's the only explanation—for his betrayal and the physical damage he seems to have experienced over the last two years. They tortured him, repeatedly, until he finally told them how to find me.

My body starts to shake and I trip on a step. Watcher curses behind me, and Isaac quickly sweeps me up into his arms. It creates enough of a stir that we're quickly ushered the rest of the way off the ship. I hear Isaac say something, but he sounds far away. I try to focus, but everything dims to black.

I slowly open my eyes. It's dark and I can tell that I'm in something that's moving. For a moment I think I'm in a trunk and that reminds me of the night under the fireworks with Isaac.

Isaac.

I sit up quickly, knocking my head into something hard, and I hear a muffled grunt in response. I jump at the sound. Hands gently grip my shoulders and pull me close.

"Shh. It's me, but we're not alone." His voice is whispered and close to my ear. He holds me close, running his hand up and down my back. Somehow his lips find mine. His kiss is everything I remember, yet different at the same time. "I'm so sorry. I'll find a way to get you out of here. I—"

There's a sudden jolt to the vehicle and something loud crashes to the floor not far away. Someone lets out a string of curses and then a light flashes on, blinding me. I squint and look away. I can see enough now to determine that we're in some sort of van. Although, it's not like the vans the Amish hire. This one doesn't have any seats and I can't see the driver.

"Ah, you're awake now. Hands off each other."

Not liking the tone of the voice guarding us, I pull back. However, Isaac pulls me back in, holding me tighter. The man with the flashlight—I decide to call him Goon—is crouched before us with surprising speed. He clamps his hand around my neck, choking out all the air. "I said hands off."

"Fine, fine! Just let her go." Isaac scoots away and Goon gives one final squeeze before releasing his grip.

I double over in a coughing fit. When the pain eases away, I lean back against the van wall. The flashlight is still on, but at least it's no longer pointed in my face. A few seconds later I feel Isaac's fingers reaching for mine. He tucks our joined hands under the folds of my dress that hang loosely around my crossed knees. I look over at Goon. His head is leaning against the wall of the van, but every few seconds it falls forward and he jerks it back up. It might actually be funny if this were any other situation. After a few minutes of this, he rubs his face and points the light back in our direction.

"You sure have been a difficult one to catch. I thought your boy here would never give up the information." Goon shifts the beam of light so it lands directly in Isaac's face, and he puts a hand up to block it. "You want to tell her how you caved, or should I?"

"Why can't we just go back to being quiet? And do you mind getting that damn light out of my face?"

"Watch your mouth, boy. You may be the boss' son, but you're no longer on the right side of the operation. We get to treat you just like any other punk-ass kid around here." Goon pauses as he stares at Isaac. Finally he lowers the beam of light again. "I need to stay awake, so we talk. I'll ask again—are you telling her or am I?"

I look at Isaac and watch as he closes his eyes, leaning his head against the van wall.

"Very well then, I'll do the talking. As I said, your boy showed an impressive amount of restraint. I think the old man was almost proud. Considering the situation, though, it fed his anger more than his fatherly pride. We took time with it, of course. Boss didn't want to actually kill him. The months rolled on, each of us trying to top the other with a new method of . . . *motivation*. I thought for sure the little ear surgery I did would have done the trick. Did you know it left him deaf in that ear?"

I look at Isaac in horror, my eyes tracing the length of the scar under his ear. Unfortunately, in my shock I move and our still joined hands come uncovered.

"I said no touching!" Goon stands abruptly, but we separate our hands before he can take a step. He stands, hunched over in the small space, for a few seconds before sitting back down on his box. "Now, where was I? Oh, right, his ear."

Goon proceeds to go into gruesome detail about the so-called surgery. My stomach starts to churn and bile rises to the back of my throat. Goon's light is back in my face.

"Don't you fucking puke in here! I'll make you eat it if you do." I concentrate on breathing in and out, counting numbers to get the image of Isaac being operated on by this hack out of my head.

"If you don't want her to puke, then skip past the details."

"I said watch your mouth. Fine, I'll move along. To everyone's surprise, that couldn't even get him to talk. It was clear he was going to die before giving you up. That's when the boss had us take a little break. Then, about a month ago, the boss found the right motivation. It seems your boy can't stand watching people he loves get hurt." Goon laughs.

I look back at Isaac. There's only one person other than me that he loves. "Your mom?"

Goon laughs again. "You said it too soft for him to hear. Remember, he's deaf in that ear now." Goon taps the flashlight to his own ear, emphasizing his point. "But you're correct. Man, she sure was a fun piece of ass. Maybe the boss will give us a turn at you too before this is over."

Isaac launches himself at Goon so quickly it takes me a few seconds to realize what's happening. Isaac lands a punch square in Goon's face before he's knocked to the floor. Goon is on top of Isaac and knocks him out with a series of solid punches. Goon sits back on his box, wiping his brow.

"As I said, Junior can't tolerate even the thought of something bad happening to one of the two women in his life. At least now I can finish my story without interruption." Goon looks at me and shifts his position. "It's too bad the boss said we can't touch you. I can think of a better way to spend our time while Junior is out cold."

I pull my knees to my chest and scoot as far back as I can. Goon notices my reaction and laughs again.

"Like I said, maybe before this is all over the boss will share you too—a reward for a job well done at bringing you in. Now, where was I? Right, Junior finally squawked after he was forced to watch us take turns on his mother. Of course, he led us astray a few times. Sent us out on some rather wild goose chases. But that's all right—most of us like the hunt just as much as the kill. We were pretty confident that this trip would lead to success since we were able to tweak the process to recognize when Junior was lying. I am surprised though that he didn't try to tip you off somehow. It's pretty clear that the last thing he wants to do is hand you over."

Goon stops talking as the van slows and then comes to a stop. A few seconds later, the back door opens. Watcher looks from Isaac to me to Goon.

"What the hell happened back here?"

"Junior thought he'd get a little fresh with me."

Watcher mumbles something under his breath and climbs in the back of the van. He squats over Isaac and rouses him somehow. Watcher pulls him to a sitting position and climbs back out. "Time to go piss. We won't be stopping again for several hours." He looks at Goon. "Stay with her until I bring Junior back."

Watcher drags Isaac out of the van and shuts the door, leaving me alone with Goon. He's watching me and it makes me uncomfortable. "I really would like to find out what makes you so special. You don't look like much. I can see the appeal for those that like little girls, but other than that . . . it must be good though, for all the effort the boss went through to find you. And all the effort Junior went through to protect you."

Isaac stumbles back in a few minutes later, Watcher right behind him. Isaac doesn't look good, and it takes all my restraint to not go to him. My heart skips a few beats as Watcher pulls out a set of plastic ties and binds Isaac's hands behind his back.

"There, now he shouldn't cause you any more issues."

Goon nods his head in my direction. "Do her too, that way I can ride up front. My ass is killing me, and I need to shut my eyes for a bit."

Watcher looks annoyed, but pulls out another set of ties. "Fine. Take your turn in the woods while I finish up with her."

Goon hops out of the van and Watcher motions me forward. "Come here, Angel. I'll let you relieve yourself before I bind your hands."

"I don't have to go."

"This is the only chance I'm giving you to go before we get to our destination. And once there, I have a feeling you'll be too preoccupied to use the toilet."

"I said I don't have to go."

He shrugs his shoulders. "Suit yourself. Get over here so I can tie your hands." I remain where I am, and I see Watcher's frustration growing. "You don't want to make me come and get you. Cooperate and I'll leave you a little slack." Reluctantly I slide over. He shoves me face down and ties my hands behind my back. "There. Now, you might want to get some sleep. Junior won't be much company for the rest of the trip, but he'll be fine—eventually." He smiles as he climbs out of the van, taking the flashlight with him.

The door closes and I'm surrounded in darkness. Isaac stirs next to me but doesn't speak. I move as close to him as I can, touching my forehead to his.

I don't want to think about all the things Goon told me, but I can't help it. Isaac has given up so much for me. I close my eyes but open them again when I hear Isaac's whispered voice.

"You weren't supposed to be there."

My heart pounds harder. His breathing tells me he's asleep, but I wait to see if he says anything more. Time passes and there is nothing but his steady breathing.

He's right. I wasn't supposed to be there. For one, I should have left the boat five minutes earlier. Isaac and Zac had carefully worked out the timing. Now I understand the emphasis on getting it right— Zac making me promise to get a watch, set it by a certain clock at the pier, and get on and off the boat at very specific times. Had I followed the plan correctly, I would have been off the boat before Isaac led Watcher and his men up to the observation deck.

However, deep down I know he's talking about more than my botched timing. I shouldn't have gone to the meet at all.

I had known, somehow, that this time was going to be different than the others. Looking back, I recognize the feeling—it was dread at having to say good-bye. On the ship, I thought I was finally saying good-bye to Isaac.

Turns out I was saying good-bye to everyone.

I look through the darkness and try to see Isaac's face. It's too dark, so I close my eyes and let my memory take over.

"You're a father. Her name is Abigail." The whispered words are out of my mouth before I even realized I wanted to say them. His breathing tells me he's still asleep. Despite that, I hope he still heard me. Maybe his subconscious will remind him when he's awake.

Then I remember. He's now deaf in this ear.

1: Resolution

The hour warning this time is a series of quick raps on the door, making it sound like some sort of melody.

In one hour the man will be back.

I have one hour left to live.

Or am I already dead, and soon I'll just be the definitive kind of dead to match my emotional death?

I've been shattered—the pieces floating around inside, trying to pull me in various directions. I visualize the pieces, orbiting around my internal black hole. A piece of me wants to cry, but I don't have any tears left. Another wants to fight, but all my strength has been depleted. Another wants to hope for a different outcome, but I'm too hardened to believe with enough conviction. I push past all of these, and the others, searching for the piece that I can cling to.

I finally find it. I don't just visualize it—I feel it. It's pulsing, and glowing, and pulling me in. Warmth spreads through me as my resolve sets its course. Every memory I've thought through over the last twenty-three hours has brought me here. I can see it now. The clarity shows me that over my whole life there have only been three constants.

The man's need to shatter me completely.

Isaac's unyielding love and need to protect me.

My inability to let go.

These three things in combination will never let me, or the people that I love, have a happy life as long as I'm alive.

I've always felt an imbalance in the amount of sacrifices I've made for Isaac compared to what he's done for me. Despite what Isaac had said about my trust being more than he could ever give, I still see the imbalance. If I choose to go back with the man, I know that Isaac will never stop trying to save me.

And I have no doubt that it will eventually kill him.

I can't let that happen.

I also can't risk the man ever finding out about Abigail.

The piece of me that wants to fight surges forward one last time, trying to tell me that Isaac and I could escape again. We could find a way to be a family with Abigail. I shut it down, knowing that the man would never let it happen. If I went back, he would probably just keep me tied up at all times. He'd continue to torture Isaac.

My life has never been my own. I've survived all these years by pretending to be someone I'm not.

I don't even know my real name.

The only moments that ever felt real were those early years in the hole with Isaac.

I've finally been given the chance to make my own choice. As difficult as it is, and as much as I would trade anything to have a different outcome, I know what I have to do.

I have to protect my family.

My mind once again brings up *Wuthering Heights*. One of the main lessons I gained from that book was that love isn't always enough. I see now that I was both right and wrong.

Love isn't enough to keep two people together. Sacrifices have to be made. Battles have to be fought. Trust has to be given.

However, love is all that's needed to make the right choice. My love for Isaac and Abigail is all the strength I need to be able to do what's needed to keep them alive.

I cling to that piece of me. It's all I have left, and I won't let the man take it as he's done with everything else. I clear away all the other pieces and hold tight to the one I've chosen. I then let my mind go where it wants to for the rest of the time I have left.

I go back to the ocean.

I smile as the water rushes over our toes, causing Abigail to laugh.

Isaac picks her up and swings her around.

0: The Decision

The door opens without warning. My head feels heavy and it's hard for me to pull out of the dream. I reluctantly open my eye and see the man staring at me from the doorway.

"Bring her out here." The man turns and walks out.

Goon walks over and pulls me by my hair. He starts to drag me across the room, and I struggle to my feet. When I put pressure on my right ankle, I stumble and fall. Goon mumbles something under his breath and tugs on my hair. Somehow I'm able to keep him from dragging me by my hair, forcing him to grab me under my arms. He takes me out into a wide open space within the warehouse. When he drops me to the floor, I see that Goon Two wasn't joking—he really did put down a tarp.

"Get up, Angel."

I think about refusing, simply because I can't stand the thought of doing anything that the man says. However, I know that if I don't then Goon will just yank on my hair until I do.

I struggle to my knees, deciding to live out my final minutes holding on to as much control as possible. I look around the space. The man stands a few feet in front of me, next to Goon Two. There are a couple other guards holding guns a few feet behind the man. I think I hear at least one person to my left, but my injured eye doesn't allow me to confirm.

The man slowly walks in my direction, stopping at the edge of the tarp. His eyes travel over my face and down my body. "Given your attempted escape earlier, I'm inclined to believe that you've already made your decision. However, I'm going to ask anyway. What's it going to be? Are you ready to come back, or does my cousin here get to kill you?" He nods his head in the direction of Goon Two.

The man stares at me, waiting for an answer. There's a brief crack in my resolve, but I swallow hard and find the remainder of my strength. "I'll never go back with you."

The man's left eye twitches slightly, but that's his only reaction. "You sound certain about that. I believe my cousin gave you a warning—he won't kill you quickly. It will drag out, all night, and I guarantee he will inflict the maximum amount of pain. You really feel that's better than coming back to your old life, with me?"

This time I don't respond. I just stare at him with my one good eye. It's the first time I've ever held his gaze willingly.

He walks slowly to me and stands behind me. He tugs on my hair, pulling my head up to meet his eyes again. "I know you miss me. I could feel it when we were together yesterday. You know I'll take care of you when you come back. All you have to do is say it and we can get back to fun times."

I jerk my head forward. "I said I'll never go back with you."

There is a sudden ringing in my ear and I'm knocked sideways. I swallow hard, trying to clear the pain.

"Get back up." The man's voice sounds muffled and far away. I place my hands under me and push, but fall back down. "Help her up!" I'm pulled back up to my knees by Goon. As soon as he lets go, I start to fall back down. "Stay there and hold her up!" Goon grabs my right arm and holds me upright as I sit on my knees.

I had wanted to hold my head up on my own until the end, but I no longer care how I get there. I just want it to be over.

"Bring them in here." The man's voice is still muffled by the ringing in my ear. Goon's grip on my arm tightens and I glance at him out of the corner of my good eye. He's favoring his left leg again. His gun is tucked into the back of his pants. My mind starts to clear as my eyes focus on the butt of the gun. A thought tries to take hold, but it's gone as soon as I hear his voice.

"I can walk on my own, damn it!"

I snap my head around, searching. Isaac enters the space, two men holding his arms. Behind him, his mom is being led by another man.

My head starts to shake. He's not supposed to be here. The man can't make him watch. It will crush him.

Isaac's eyes finally settle on me and he lunges forward. "Let her go! Ang!" The men holding his arms yank him back and knock him to his knees. They continue to hold his arms and one points a gun to his head. Isaac's hands are behind his back and I assume they are bound. I glance at his mom and she is also on her knees, hands bound behind her back, and a gun pointed at her head. She no longer resembles the woman who came to see me all those years ago. Now she looks beaten, empty, resigned—shattered. She only glances at me for a few seconds and then lowers her head to look at the floor.

Is he going to kill all of us, or just make them watch what happens to me? I start to shake and Goon's grip tightens around my arm.

"Keep him quiet. And if he tries to move then take it out on her." The man points at Isaac's mom before turning to face me. "Now, I'm going to ask you again. Are you ready to come back?"

The ringing in my ear is gone, so I know I've heard him correctly. I don't understand why he keeps asking me to make a choice. I already told him my decision. I look at Isaac, hoping that something in his eyes will give me clarity, but the man steps between us.

"Answer me!"

I open my mouth but no sound comes out. I clear my throat and try again. "I said no."

The man's jaw sets in a hard line. He steps to the side, allowing me to see Isaac again. "Do it."

One of the men holding Isaac's arms—the one not holding the gun to his head—pulls up sharply. Isaac's arm twists and he screams out in pain.

"No!" I lurch forward, but Goon holds me back.

The man steps in front of Isaac again. "We'll keep doing this, over and over, until I get the right answer. Are you ready to come back?"

I feel all the blood drain to my legs. I stare into the man's evil eyes. I should have known all along.

He's never going to let me die. I never had a choice. He gives the illusion of choice, but there is always only one right answer. He won't take me back unless I say I want to—that way he can claim that I chose my life. Yet he won't let me die either, because he wants me. He will keep hurting Isaac until I say yes.

Anger pushes all the blood back through my veins. No. He doesn't get to take this from me. He doesn't get to have this. He doesn't get to win this time. I feel my instinct kicking in one last time, and I don't resist. I know that this time I will get the result I want.

"Move."

The man's surprise is clear on his face. "What did you just say?"

"If you want my answer, then move. I want to see him."

The man's mouth twitches into a disgusting smile as he steps to the side. Isaac's head is hanging down and his body is shaking.

"Isaac." He tries to lift his head, but he drops it back down. "Isaac, please look at me." He tries again. This time he's successful and his eyes lock with mine.

"I—I'm so sorry, Ang. I love you. I don't know how to fix this. I'm sorry."

He's crying so hard I can barely make out his words. It takes everything I have left to keep my tears from turning into uncontrollable sobs. I feel their slow descent down my cheeks, and I close my eyes. For the first time in my life, I pray. I don't know who I'm praying to—I don't believe in the same things as Zac—but I do it anyway. I pray for the right words that will bring an end to all our suffering. When I feel them come to me, I look again at Isaac.

"I love you. I always have and always will. You've done so much for me, but there is one more thing you have to do. You promised you would find her. You have to find Abigail and keep her safe. You promised."

The pain on Isaac's face transforms into confusion. I see his mom's head slowly lift to look at me.

The man is on the side of my injured eye, and I can't see him. But I can hear him.

"What did you say?" He's on me in an instant, hands tight around my neck. "What did you say? Why are you talking about Abigail? She's dead!"

I claw at his hands, desperate to breathe. He's looking at me, but I don't think he actually sees me. I dig my nails deeper into his hands.

"Dad, stop! It's just her doll. We named her Abigail!"

Isaac's words are enough to bring the man out of his trance, and he relaxes his grip on my neck.

It's now or never.

I throw my weight to the right, crashing into Goon's left leg. He lets out a yell and falls to the floor, pulling me down on top of him.

I grab his gun.

I see the other guns point in my direction.

I remember to switch off the safety and aim.

I hear Isaac scream no. Maybe the man screams too.

I pull the trigger.

Epilogue

Six and a half years later . . .

It's crowded today. It seems that the break in the summer heat has brought people here from all over. I'm sitting in my usual spot, watching and waiting. Anxiety washes over me, just as it has on each market day for nearly six months. I know there's a chance she won't be helping today, and my gut knots at the possibility. The days when I don't get to see her are always difficult. Although, I'll have to move on soon since the market season is almost over. I'll have to figure out a way to function without seeing her.

I finally catch a glimpse of her and my heart beats a little faster. I try not to be obvious in my stare, but it's hard to look away.

She looks so much like her mother.

Even though her hair is pinned and tucked under her cap, a few curls escape and dance around her face. When I first started searching, I feared I wouldn't be able to recognize her since the standard Amish clothing tends to mask unique physical traits. But somehow my heart knew it was her as soon as my eyes landed on her.

The sight of her causes vivid memories of Ang to surface and crash into each other inside my mind.

I watch her spin in circles until she falls on the bed, laughing.

I watch her play with a lock of hair as she learns to read.

I feel her jump as the fireworks explode around us.

I feel her heart beat against mine as I hold her close.

I hear her laugh as the ocean waves crash around her toes.

I hear her tell me that she loves me.

I close my eyes for a moment, trying to still my mind. Once the ache subsides, I turn my attention back to Abigail. She smiles, and even though I'm out of earshot I know she's laughing. It's a sound I long to hear.

Someone suddenly sits down in the open space to my left. "I've often wondered if you would show up some day."

I force my eyes away from Abigail and look at Zac. He looks a lot different than the last time I saw him. The look in his eyes makes it clear that he's thinking the same about me. I turn my attention back to Abigail without responding.

"Are you here alone?"

I understand Zac's question and give him a small nod in response. I hear him let out a slow breath before he speaks again.

"I assume it's safe for you to be here? I hate to ask, but I think you understand why I do."

I nod again. I wanted to start searching for Abigail the moment I figured out what Ang was trying to tell me the night she died, but I couldn't until I was sure it was safe. I've thought about this moment over and over again for several years. I've practiced what I would say to the man raising my daughter as his own more times than I can count. Now that the moment is finally here, I've forgotten everything. I simply say the only thing that's in my mind.

"She looks happy."

There's a slight pause before Zac responds. "I'd like to think that she is."

"She looks so much like Ang at that age. She was happy then too. She didn't know there was more to life than me and a doll. It was all she needed, and she was happy."

Abigail suddenly turns and spots us. Somehow her smile gets wider as she hurries toward us. My body tenses. I'm afraid to move, fearful that if I do she'll turn and run back the other way.

She slides up to Zac and speaks to him in the customary Amish language. I don't know it, but I've been hanging around various Amish markets long enough to recognize it. Zac responds and then clears his throat before turning Abigail to face me.

"Abigail, I'd like you to meet a friend of mine. This is Isaac. He once knew your mother too."

She smiles and my heart melts. "She died before I turned two."

I take a deep breath and find my voice. "I know, and I'm sorry that's she's gone. You look a lot like her when she was your age."

Her eyes open wide. "You knew her when she was eight?"

"I did. I knew her for a very long time."

She pulls something out from under her dress. "She gave me this." She holds out the angel wing charm.

My arms feel too heavy to lift, but somehow I do. I hold it between my fingers and feel a tear slide down my cheek.

"She would be happy to know that you still wear it."

She giggles and it's all I can do to keep from pulling her to my chest. Her face becomes serious as she looks at my scar.

"Does that hurt?"

"It hurt when it happened, and it still hurts a little, but not much."

"How'd you get it?"

I'm not prepared for her question. I certainly can't tell her the truth. "I was cut by something sharp."

This seems to satisfy her and she looks away from the scar. "Are you coming by our house for dinner?"

"No, I'm not able to stay."

Sensing my growing struggle, Zac pats Abigail gently on the shoulder. "Why don't you run along and help Mary. I'll be there soon."

"Bye!" She waves and runs off in the direction she came. I watch as she approaches a woman at the booth. Abigail says something to her and the woman who I assume is Mary looks in our direction. She tilts her head to the side as she looks at me. A few seconds pass before she gives me a slight nod and then turns away, leading Abigail by the hand.

"Is that your wife?"

"No, she's my cousin. I'm not married."

I look back at Zac. "Abigail could use a mother."

Zac laughs slightly and tugs at his beard. "Yeah, well, it's complicated. Although . . . there is a new school teacher who's moved here from another community. She's a widow with two small children of her own. She's nice and we get along well enough."

I suddenly understand how much he's sacrificed of his own. "A mother and siblings all at once—sounds perfect."

Zac eyes me carefully. "So you're not here to take her away?"

I turn my attention back to the booth to see if Abigail has returned. She's not there, but I don't look away. "There's nothing I want more than to be with Abigail. But I'm not fit to be a father. And it wouldn't be fair to her. Her whole life you've been her father—I can't take that away from her."

"Thank you."

I don't need to look at him to see the depth of his gratitude. He loves her as his own, and it would have crushed him to let her go. I suppose I owe it to him as well to let her stay.

"I'm the one who should be thanking you. You've sacrificed a lot to protect her and make her happy. It's more than you signed up for."

There's a short pause before Zac responds. "You asked me once why I agreed to help you. Why I gave it all up to be a part of your plan. I didn't have a good answer for you then. All I knew was that I felt compelled to do it. That it was my purpose in this life. Because of my faith, I had to go where I was being called. Now I understand that it was because of Abigail. It was God's plan for me to be there for her—to take care of her."

Something inside me stirs. I wish I had Zac's faith. I'm still finding it hard to believe that any of this was meant to be, but the level of his conviction makes me want to believe it. "You're not going to start quoting scripture to me, are you?"

"I would, if you thought it might help."

"No, I don't think I'm in the right frame of mind to hear it."

Abigail comes back into view and I watch as she helps Mary set quilts out on the table. We watch in silence for a few minutes before Zac speaks again.

"I'm sorry I didn't stop her from going. I tried, but I could have tried harder. I was the only one who went the first two times, just as we planned. By the time the date for the third meeting came around, I thought it was time to let go. I told her I wasn't going. I thought that if I didn't go, she wouldn't either. She had never been anywhere on her own. She didn't do well in public places, surrounded by strangers. I really didn't think she would go. But she did. And she kept going, no matter what I said."

I study his profile. His pain and guilt are clear to see. I think back on those first couple years after she died. I was angry at everyone—including Zac. Especially Zac. He was supposed to keep her safe. Ang never should have been on that ship. If I'm being honest, I'm still somewhat angry at Zac. But now, seeing his pain, I feel that anger fade just a little bit more.

"I don't think there was anything you could have done to stop her. If anyone is to blame, it's me. I should have been stronger."

"Why do you say that?"

"I was the reason she was caught. I should have been able to resist telling him about the meet." As the words leave my mouth I know that they're not complete. I do feel I should have been stronger; however, I also know that ultimately I'm not responsible. It's just hard for me to accept the truth.

"I don't know exactly what happened, and I don't want to know. I decided a long time ago to let go and move forward, and I owe it to Abigail to keep doing that now. However, I do know that you would not have given up the details about the meet willingly. As for being stronger . . . I don't know how you could possibly be any stronger than you already are. You have to be able to see that."

I watch Abigail skip to the adjacent booth to play with another Amish girl. I nod my head in their direction. "That's what Ang should have had. She should have had a life full of laughter and love. I wanted to give her that, but I couldn't."

"But you did. You gave her the chance to experience a kind of love that most people can only read about. That was all she ever needed in her life, and she had it."

I close my eyes and absorb Zac's words. They resonate right to the part of my heart that has been trying to tell me the same thing over the past year. It's still not something I'm ready to accept, and I'm grateful when Zac changes the subject.

"I assume it's all over then, since it's safe for you to be here."

"Yes. He's locked away for good, along with his men. At least those that were still alive at the time of the bust."

"How were you able to do it?"

I give him a funny look and then remember. "Right. You don't have a television. After—" The words catch in my throat and I swallow hard. "After Ang died, I was a mess. Both physically and emotionally. It took some time, but once I recovered enough to be angry I became obsessed with bringing him down. I wanted to kill him, but I knew that if I did then another family member would just take over the business. The whole thing needed to be stopped. I couldn't let Ang die for nothing. I went to the Feds, but I didn't have enough for them to bring him in. By that point I wasn't allowed to be anywhere near the business. I'd been kicked out of the house—out of the family really. I was surprised he let me go, but I think he thought I was too broken to be a threat. Then one day I got a call from Roxy. She was the one he put in charge of the other women when he wasn't around. After everything that happened with Ang, she took a risk and turned against him. We worked together to get the information the Feds needed. It took a few years, but at least there's no chance he'll ever see the outside of a prison. It turned out to be one of the largest human trafficking busts in the US to date—it made the national news."

"Where do you plan to go now?"

"My mom . . . she's not well. She's in a treatment facility and I plan to move near there. At least until she's recovered."

Zac nods. He opens his mouth to speak, but closes it. He sighs and tries again. "I have to ask, how did you find us? Did Angela tell you?"

"No, she never got the chance. Right before—right before she died she said something that I didn't understand. She told me that I'd made a promise to find Abigail, and that I still needed to do it. I thought she was talking about the doll. It was my mom who figured it out. She said that it took a mother to understand that Ang was speaking as a mother protecting her child. It took me a long time to figure out where you were. I didn't attempt to find you until my father was locked away. I couldn't take the risk. My mom remembered your old address, and I looked up your parents. I didn't approach them, knowing they would never give your address to a stranger. Especially one that looks as battered as I do. So I did what I do best and put the puzzle pieces together, which led me to your Amish background. I've visited a lot of Amish communities throughout the Midwest over the last couple years. It was almost six months ago when I was sitting right here and I saw her. I come here often, just to watch. I thought maybe you'd seen me a few times, but you never did. Until now."

Several more minutes pass in silence. Finally, Zac clears his throat. "It's time for me to get back, but there's one more thing I want you to know. I may have sacrificed a lot to raise Abigail, but she's not a burden to me. Quite the opposite in fact. " He pauses and tugs at his beard before standing. "I hadn't planned on bringing Abigail to the market tomorrow, but I will. I'll try to make sure she's here every day until the market closes in a few weeks. After that, you're welcome in my home any time. If you ever feel that Abigail should know the truth, then I'll stand by your decision."

He extends his hand and I take it in mine, giving him a slight nod, and then watch him walk away. He goes over to Abigail and she instantly jumps up from the ground and into his arms. He picks her up and holds her close. Even from this distance, I can see the love in her eyes as she looks at him. He kisses her cheek and then sets her back down. She resumes playing with her friend as Zac walks away.

Yes, this is the life I had wanted Ang to have. However, watching Abigail has made me realize that it wasn't meant to be. I know this because of the joy I see on Abigail's face—it's the same joy that I saw whenever I looked at Ang. She may not have had all that I wanted her to have, but she had what she needed to be happy.

I've been so obsessed since she died over what I've lost and how I failed to give her a different life that I haven't given myself a chance to see what I still have.

I have a life free and clear of my father.

I have comfort knowing he will never be able to hurt Ang again.

I have a mom who is strong enough to recover.

And I have my love for Ang, and her love for me.

If my life has taught me anything, it's that love cannot be taken away. Our love was forbidden and threatened before either of us even knew it existed. Yet it grew and developed into something powerful. Even though she's not physically here, her love remains. I know she died so I could live my life, just as I tried to do for her. She'd want me to move forward, just as I had wanted her to do when I left her with Zac.

My skin pricks at the thought of moving on without her. I don't know how to do it. I've taken my father down and his business along with him. I've found Abigail, just as Ang asked me to do the day she died. I know she will live a happy and safe life with Zac. The only thing left for me now is to take care of my mom and live my life.

The sun breaks through the cloud cover, and in that same moment Abigail turns in my direction. A glint of light sparks from her chest.

I realize it's the sun reflecting off her angel wing charm.

Warmth suddenly spreads through my body, and Zac's words from moments ago resurface. He reminded me that Ang and I shared the kind of love many people will never experience.

Just as Zac will experience the love of a daughter in a way that I never will.

Watching Zac and Abigail has finally given me the clarity I've been searching for since Ang died.

It's love that moves us forward.

Acknowledgements

As with my previous novels, I have to acknowledge my M&M gals: Jaime, Jennifer, Melanie, Melinda, and Phuong. I'm truly blessed to have you in my life. We have shared books, laughs, tears, fears, accomplishments, goals, food, wine, chocolate, and so much more for nearly ten years. Ten years! I'm looking forward celebrating this milestone with you all later this summer.

I also want to thank my amazing beta readers! You continue to provide your thoughts, and are not afraid to tell me about things you think should be changed. It's so great to have all these wonderful people on my team: Kelly Babb, Kari Desnoyers, Eric Fay, Lisa Freers, Robin Gray, Linda Kozlowski, Steve Kozlowski, Holle Psota, Beth Ramsey, and Lara VanValkenburg.

A huge thanks to fellow author, Ron Collins. I appreciate you taking time out of your busy schedule to read my manuscript and provide your suggestions. I know the final product is much better as a result.

My wonderful husband, Jason, and my beautiful daughter, Julia—I love you both so much. Thank you for not only continuing to support my writing, but for also being just as excited about each new book as I am.

While I absolutely love each novel I've written, I connected with *Shattered Angel* in a very special way. Angel and Isaac represent people who had to face unthinkable circumstances. *Shattered Angel* is a work of fiction; however, there are real people who can relate to their story.

I want to acknowledge all those who have suffered at hands of abuse. May you find your inner strength and endure to a better day.

About the Author

Carrie Beckort has a degree in Mechanical Engineering from Purdue University and a MBA from Ball State University. She spent seventeen years in the corporate industry before writing her first novel, *Kingston's Project*. She lives in Indiana with her husband and daughter.

For more information about Carrie Beckort or her books, visit her website or social media sites:

Website: carriebeckort.com
Facebook: facebook.com/carrie.beckort
Follow on Twitter: @carriebeckort

More from Carrie Beckort

Kingston's Project
ISBN 978-0-9912764-0-0

How do you find the strength to embrace a future that's different than the one you planned? For Sarah Mitchell the answer is simple—you don't. For two years, Sarah has shut herself off from most of the world around her. She needs to move on, but doesn't know how to begin. Unexpectedly, Sarah is presented with an opportunity that could change everything. Elijah Kingston, her firm's largest client, wants her to lead a highly confidential assignment. When Sarah learns the shocking nature of Kingston's project, she is torn between Elijah's promise of healing and her fear of falling deeper into despair. Kingston's Project is a poignant story about the effects of grief and the loss of hope. Can Sarah find happiness again, or is the hold from her fear and guilt too strong to break free?

Kingston's Promise
ISBN 978-0-9912764-2-4

"I promise." Two words meant to inspire trust and hope. When kept, a promise can be powerful. When broken, it can shatter just about everything around it. Marcus Kingston spent twenty years searching for the woman he was meant to be with forever. The day he found her, he made a promise. He would spend the rest of his life trying to ease her pain and give her happiness. Her past wouldn't make it easy, but he was determined. He thought the difficult part was getting her to give him a chance. He told her she couldn't predict the future—that she needed to take a leap of faith. What he didn't anticipate was the one unavoidable obstacle to every promise—life. Now, he's the one who needs to take the leap.

Made in the USA
Middletown, DE
04 March 2015